A WEDDI

June is the month of br... and what better way to celebrate than with a charming collection of regency stories, each featuring a June wedding. As roses begin to bloom in the bright sunshine and the scent of brightly colored flowers tickles the nose, laughter and love pave the way for a regency romance.

Bouquets of fresh flowers, gaily dressed guests, a handsome fiancé — the scene is set for a wedding celebration of the first order. So share in the pomp and circumstance of a regency wedding with six of Zebra's bestselling regency writers. And be the guest of honor of Teresa DesJardien, Mona Gedney, Valerie King, Emily Maxwell, Elizabeth Morgan, and Dawn Aldridge Poore as they lead you down the aisle to six summer weddings you'll never forget!

A Memorable Collection of Regency Romances

BY ANTHEA MALCOLM AND VALERIE KING

THE COUNTERFEIT HEART (3425, $3.95/$4.95)
by Anthea Malcolm

Nicola Crawford was hardly surprised when her cousin's betrothed disappeared on some mysterious quest. Anyone engaged to such an unromantic, but handsome man was bound to run off sooner or later. Nicola could never entrust her heart to such a conventional, but so deucedly handsome man. . . .

THE COURTING OF PHILIPPA (2714, $3.95/$4.95)
by Anthea Malcolm

Miss Philippa was a very successful author of romantic novels. Thus she was chagrined to be snubbed by the handsome writer Henry Ashton whose own books she admired. And when she learned he considered love stories completely beneath his notice, she vowed to teach him a thing or two about the subject of love. . . .

THE WIDOW'S GAMBIT (2357, $3.50/$4.50)
by Anthea Malcolm

The eldest of the orphaned Neville sisters needed a chaperone for a London season. So the ever-resourceful Livia added several years to her age, invented a deceased husband, and became the respectable Widow Royce. She was certain she'd never regret abandoning her girlhood until she met dashing Nicholas Warwick. . . .

A DARING WAGER (2558, $3.95/$4.95)
by Valerie King

Ellie Dearborne's penchant for gaming had finally led her to ruin. It seemed like such a lark, wagering her devious cousin George that she would obtain the snuffboxes of three of society's most dashing peers in one month's time. She could easily succeed, too, were it not for that exasperating Lord Ravenworth. . . .

THE WILLFUL WIDOW (3323, $3.95/$4.95)
by Valerie King

The lovely young widow, Mrs. Henrietta Harte, was not all inclined to pursue the sort of romantic folly the persistent King Brandish had in mind. She had to concentrate on marrying off her penniless sisters and managing her spendthrift mama. Surely Mr. Brandish could fit in with her plans somehow . . .

Available wherever paperbacks are sold, or order direct from the Publisher. Send cover price plus 50¢ per copy for mailing and handling to Zebra Books, Dept. 3781, 475 Park Avenue South, New York, N.Y. 10016. Residents of New York and Tennessee must include sales tax. DO NOT SEND CASH. For a free Zebra/ Pinnacle catalog please write to the above address.

A June Wedding

**TERESA DESJARDIEN
MONA GEDNEY
VALERIE KING
EMILY MAXWELL
ELIZABETH MORGAN
DAWN ALDRIDGE POORE**

**ZEBRA BOOKS
KENSINGTON PUBLISHING CORP.**

ZEBRA BOOKS

are published by

Kensington Publishing Corp.
475 Park Avenue South
New York, NY 10016

First printing: June, 1992

Printed in the United States of America

CONTENTS

The Reluctant Bride

by

Teresa DesJardien

"But, Mama, he is positively *stupid!*" Imogene wailed.

"Now, that's not a very nice way to talk," her mama replied crisply.

"But he *is!*"

"Well, even if he is, what has that to say to the matter?"

"Mama!" Imogene cried in horror. "You are telling me I am to marry him! *That's* what it has to say to the matter. I couldn't possibly marry such a witless creature."

"You most certainly could, and consider yourself lucky at it, too. Most young girls would have very little say in how their life goes on, but I daresay you shall have plenty of freedoms, just so long as meals are served on time, and you smile occasionally upon the fellow. These malleable types make the best husbands, you'll see."

" 'Malleable' is quite a different matter than 'stupid'!"

"Imogene Bradshaw! You are allowing yourself to become hysterical. Cease at once! Your father has already agreed, the banns have already been sent to the newspapers, and that's the end of the matter."

"But it just can't *be!*" Imogene wailed again, her fists clenching in a physical manifestation of her exasperation. "I can't believe you didn't even ask me. I can't believe you would think I'd be happy about this!"

"Happy, happy, happy! You modern girls are the silliest creatures. No one expects you to be happy; we merely expect you to accept that the deed is done. A betrothal has been made, and you will be marrying two weeks from today at Saint Martin-in-the-Fields, at seven in the evening, to be exact. It is all arranged."

Imogene sank into the nearest chair, her face buried in her arms on the chair back, an unmistakable flavor of abject misery in her posture. At the pathetic picture she made, her mother allowed her until now repressed softer feelings to surface. "Come now," she cooed, crossing to drape her arm over her daughter's shoulder, as though to buck her up a little. "He's not so bad as all that. Why, Mr. Garrant is much that a girl could want. He's rather fine to look upon, you cannot deny that. He will be the Earl of Norfleet one day, and that not too many days from now, if one but judges by the current Lord Norfleet's unfortunate health. And he has an enormous income — your father made sure of the veracity of that rumor — and he does have genteel manners."

"Manners!" Imogene moaned, in much the way she might have done had she been told he had a third eye.

"And he's a gentle kind of fellow, you know the sort I mean. He'll be clay in your hands. You'll be able to establish your household any way you should care to do so, without interference I feel sure. Mr. Garrant is just the type to want only a quiet drink now and again, a plate of good stuffs, and a fire in the grate to be happy."

"You could say the same of a dog," Imogene's embittered voice floated up from where it was buried in her arms.

"Yes, exactly," Lady Bradshaw said approvingly. "Now you're seeing how it will be!"

Imogene looked up at that, horrified amusement mingling with denial on her fine features. It was entirely too much. Here she had spent most of her life just one step away from being labeled a bluestocking (because, unlike her contemporaries, she preferred a book to a gossip, a geography lesson to a riding session, and a challenging word puzzle to a bit of embroidery), only now to be told she had to marry simply the most hollow-headed man in England. Her parents could not have come up with a more ironic attachment. "Oh, Mama!" she sighed, but her diversion lasted only a moment. "Must I? Is there no other way?"

"No, not really. You . . ." and finally her mother faltered just a little as a thought occurred to her, ". . . you weren't *fond* of someone else, were you?"

"No."

"Well then, there are no obstacles to your future contentment."

"I should so much more prefer to be happy than to be merely content," Imogene said, but she said it to her mother's back, for Mama was already halfway across the room.

"I must run, my dearest. I shall be serving tea to a dozen ladies in not more than thirty minutes, and I haven't checked on Eaton's crumpets. He tends to undercook them, you know. I must watch him every moment. If it were not for his gifted touch with a roasting pan, I should have let him go long ago! I shall announce your engagement to the ladies." This last was a concession, indirectly showing that Mama understood that Imogene was far too upset to make an appearance and engage in polite conversation just at the moment. That is to say: she didn't want Imogene to speak up and deny the whole thing. Under duress, it was not unknown for Imogene to be precipitous, not to mention contrary. Give the girl time to adjust to the idea, that was the way to do it.

Lady Bradshaw went on, even as she passed through the doorway, "Do go through those copies of *La Belle Assemblee*, please, and see if anything catches your eye for a wedding gown. I daresay Madame LeBlanc can contrive most anything you fancy."

Imogene stared after her mama, frowning terribly. Her companion, had she seen her, would have scolded her for making such a face, informing her it was such faces that left a woman's complexion prematurely wrinkled. Imogene might have welcomed the comment, for then at least she could have had the pleasure of putting out her tongue. As it was, she was left alone in her misery, and that rather literally. Mama obviously thought her a silly goose for kicking up a fuss. Papa would simply stare in astonishment if she voiced the thought that she did not care to do what he had dictated would be done, and her two brothers might look up from their plates or their newspapers for all of seven seconds, but that would be the end of their involvement in

11

the matter. She had no one, no sympathetic ear into which to bewail this terrible twist in her formerly pleasant life.

It was not that she did not know she would be expected to marry, and being of the *haute ton,* marry well. She had never been under the illusion that she would "choose" her spouse—it simply wasn't done—but she had always assumed that she would at least be given the courtesy of a review prior to any announcements being made. She had always thought that if she had a particular Romanesque disapproval to offer any particular gent put before her, that her parents would take the matter into consideration. It had never occurred to her that her opinion would be completely unsolicited and utterly beside the matter.

And of all the men they could have chosen, to choose Mr. Eduardo Garrant! If ever there was a sapskull, he was it. Eduardo indeed! His parents had named him aptly, giving a stupid name to a stupid child, she thought with undampered severity. She did not know Mr. Garrant well, but she knew that her handful of five-minute conversations with the man had been enough to convince her he was severely lacking in the area of his brainbox. Furthermore, when his name came up in conversation, there was never a word said to make her believe otherwise. Indeed, everyone seemed to speak a little slower when they spoke with Mr. Garrant, or the lads that made up his cronies. Had it been her imagination, or had she truly sensed that people used smaller words and stayed to a rather simple conversational style with Mr. Garrant?

Now she found herself hoping—rather desperately—that first (not to even *think* about second, third, and fourth) impressions were not always correct. Sometimes a person had a great deal of hidden depth . . .

. . . *And sometimes pigs fly!*, she finished the thought grimly. Well, there was nothing for it; she was just going to have to brave the man's company and see for herself if there was any possibility she had been even a little bit mistaken.

Just as this thought settled heavily on her shoulders, the butler, Wurdon, crossed the threshold to announce

12

that Mr. Garrant had come to call.

"Did he ask for me or for Papa?" Imogene asked, struggling with little success to suppress the sour note in her voice.

"The gentleman said he was calling to speak with my lady," was the answer.

A moment of panic came over Imogene, but she suppressed it with a little more success than she had the sour note. "Send Miss Drisdon to me, then please show Mister Garrant in," she said, referring to her hired companion.

Miss Drisdon made her appearance quickly, giving Imogene to imagine that she had been close at hand. Her first words only confirmed that notion, "Is it true? Are you betrothed?"

So the news had spread to the servants' quarters already!

"Yes," Imogene said shortly.

Miss Drisdon flew to her charge's side, the gray ringlets at her temples flying back as she did so. She seized up Imogene's hands and cried, "Oh, how wonderful! Our little Genie, a June bride! Only imagine it!"

"Must I?" Imogene said under her breath.

"I'm sorry . . . ?"

"I said 'tra-la, it's true'."

Miss Drisdon's brows drew together, for she was well acquainted with the various moods of her charge and had to wonder at the telltale symptoms of resistance, but before she could speak, Wurdon announced Mr. Garrant.

Since her mother's pronouncement, Imogene's mind had been working feverishly on the image of Mr. Garrant. She was somewhat startled, therefore, to be reminded at the sight of him that he was not in fact a rather hideously imbecilic ogre. The jaw that she had begun to believe to be suspiciously slack and studded with fangs was seen to be anything but; his hunched and shuffling manner was shown to be a natural grace as he stepped into the room; and the throaty, croaky voice of the kind that bellows from under bridges was heard instead to be clear and pleasant, as he came and stood before her to say, "Miss

13

Bradshaw? Oh, yes, I see you are."

She stood slowly. She started to offer him her hand, but he made no reciprocative move, so instead she clasped her two hands together before her. "Well!" she heard herself say. For a moment her mind was completely blank, but then in a voice that sounded falsely cheerful, she went on, "We meet again."

"Yes," he said, looking down at her from his superior height of what she guessed to be four inches or better. He turned to glance in the direction of Miss Drisdon.

"This is my companion, Miss Drisdon. Miss Drisdon, Mr. Garrant."

He made a half bow from the waist, but offered no greeting beyond a sudden and quickly faded smile. He turned back to Imogene, simply looking down at her. He did not blink, making his gaze rather unnerving. She felt a blush growing on her cheeks as they stood thus, awkwardly silent.

"Er, um," he said, shifting his position, putting his right hand, which held his driving gloves, on his hip.

"Would you care to sit? May I offer you some tea?" Imogene belatedly thought to say, blushing even more at the knowledge of the omission.

"Er, um," he said again, shifting his position so that now it was the other hand on the other hip.

Imogene threw Miss Drisdon a quick, rather desperate glance, and that lady gave her a signal to sit down. Imogene complied at once, followed by Miss Drisdon, who chose her seat across the room.

Mr. Garrant turned to glance at the companion a second time. "I say, I had not envisioned an audience somehow."

"An audience?" Imogene echoed, all at sea.

"Makes no never mind, I suppose. Er, um, Miss Bradshaw, I have come to request your hand in marriage."

Imogene startled visibly. She ought to have expected that, of course, for though her parents had not seen fit to ask her opinion, there was a correct procedure for these kinds of things. It was only logical, indeed predictable, that

14

he should come and formally ask the lady herself.

Miss Drisdon cleared her throat delicately, letting Imogene know that she had stared up at the man a little too long for politeness.

"I . . . er . . . um." She followed his example of speech for a moment, but then shook off the strange stupor that threatened her state of mind and tried to assemble a sensible answer. Her face shifted a number of times as her lips parted and moved silently, obviously striving to find a response, until finally she blurted out, "Do I have any choice?"

"Miss Genie!" Miss Drisdon dared to rebuke her.

Mr. Garrant only shrugged a little and answered, "I suppose you do."

Imogene stared again, but this time it was with a measure of hope in her gaze. Yes, that's all she need do: tell him "no." What could Papa do? Oh, he'd be upset, but he couldn't *force* her to marry Mr. Garrant. Well, maybe legally he could, since she was under the age of her majority, but he wouldn't in fact. She was fairly sure of that. Maybe.

"You haven't answered the man," Miss Drisdon said, her expression pained. Her charge was not showing very pretty manners; it reflected badly on a companion, these lapses. "He's waiting, Miss Genie. Aren't you going to give him an answer?"

"Yes," Imogene said somewhat crisply to her companion.

"All right then!" Mr. Garrant said, slapping his gloves against his palm. "Good day, Miss Bradshaw. I'll call again soon." He turned on his heel, leaving the two ladies to stare at each other in bewilderment.

"Oh!" Imogene cried with dawning comprehension. She was frozen in place, startled by the realization of Mr. Garrant's misinterpretation of events. When she looked away from her companion's confused frown, she saw that Mr. Garrant was no longer in the room. Belatedly she startled into movement, calling out toward the door of the parlor as she ran to it, "Mister Garrant. I say,

Mister Garrant! I did not mean—"

"Oh!" squealed Miss Drisdon as she, too, comprehended what had just happened. "Oh, I see!"

"Mister Garrant, don't leave! I've got to explain something—"

Wurdon was just turning from the door, closing it behind the departing guest.

"He thought you were answering *him,*" Miss Drisdon said aloud as she trailed her charge out to the vestibule.

Wurdon looked up, startled to see an agitated Miss Bradshaw flying at him.

"Mister Garrant!" she cried shrilly.

"He's stepped out, Miss Genie," Wurdon said with a curious sideways glance at Miss Drisdon, who appeared almost as agitated as her charge.

"Stop that man!" Imogene cried, pointing directly at the closed door.

Wurdon stared at her openly now, glanced at the door, and back at her. "Are we speaking of Mister Garrant, my lady?"

"Yes! Yes, stop him, I say!"

"But, my lady . . ." he sputtered, moving to do as he was bid, but before he could get to the door, Imogene was already there, tugging on the heavy handle herself. She slipped out the door and gave a funny half howl, half growl, for Mr. Garrant was already not only mounted, but was nearly free of the drive.

"Mister Garrant! I must correct your thinking!" Imogene yelled after him through cupped hands, but the rattle of a cheesemaker's cart drowned out her efforts. She spun to Wurdon, pointing down the street, and crying, "Go after him, Wurdon!"

Wurdon stared at her with rounded, offended eyes, for the very thought was beneath his dignity as a butler.

He stuttered, "I couldn't catch him, not even in my younger days, Miss Bradshaw." His astonishment at the request was only deepened as he heard his young mistress utter a curse.

"Oh, it is too absurd!" Imogene said hotly, even going so far as to stamp her foot. She spun to face Miss Drisdon, the startled, comprehending look she saw there turning her fit of temper into something bordering on tears. "Drissy," she wailed, calling her companion, and former nurse, by the pet name that had long since become a nursery standard, "what can I do now?"

Miss Drisdon put a knuckle to her lower lip and pondered the question quite seriously. After a too-long pause she looked up and answered, "Why, nothing."

"Nothing?"

"Nothing. The man believes he was given an answer."

"I can't believe this! I have to marry a fool because he is too much a fool to know I wasn't even talking to him!"

"What is all this commotion?" Lady Bradshaw asked sternly as she came down the stairs.

"Miss Genie has accepted Mister Garrant," Miss Drisdon supplied.

"I did *not!* I mean, I did, but I never meant—"

"Oh, Genie, how wonderful. I knew you would see reason when you'd thought it over for a while. But where is our guest?"

Imogene took a deep breath and let it out slowly, counting silently to ten, at which time she was composed enough to lift her head and make a haughty exit from the front hall.

Her mother began to trail her from the room, presumably thinking Imogene meant to conduct her to where their guest had been hidden away, but Imogene turned just then and confronted her mother, crying, "He's too stupid to know that I don't want him! I just don't see that I shall marry him, that's all. That's it. That's final!"

Lady Bradshaw said nothing, allowing her daughter to flee the room. There was absolutely no purpose in talking to Imogene when she was in such a pet. Time enough to set the girl straight later.

Mr. Eduardo Garrant, the heir apparent of the title and

fortunes of the Earl of Norfleet—who seemed more than a little unlikely to produce a son at the late age of eighty-three—rode toward home at an unusually hasty pace. His mind was agitated, causing him to be a little heavy with his heels.

An acquaintance passed, lifting a hand in greeting. He called out pleasantly, "Halloo! Eddie!"

As their two horses moved past each other, too swiftly to pull up for a bit of conversation, Eduardo turned in his saddle and called back over his shoulder, "Brisby! Dinner?"

"At nine," came Lord Quenton Brisbane's reply, just as he was forced to turn his mount around a bend that was blocked from view by some high shrubberies.

It did not matter that their conversation had been so short. They both knew full well that they would have most likely met tonight anyway without this confirmation, for they always dined, every night, at the same time at their same club.

Eduardo rode on, thoughts of supper later dissolving as he returned to thoughts of the scene just past. Well, he had done it. He had asked the female to marry him. "Imogene," he said aloud, frowning faintly at the sound of her name. It seemed a somewhat overbearing name, of the "Brunhilde" variety, though he had to admit the girl herself had not seemed quite so harsh as the vision her name rendered.

Perhaps she had some ancient Spanish blood in her veins, even as he did? She certainly had a lot of black hair, or very nearly black, at any rate. The twin braids caught up at the nape of her neck suggested her hair, unbraided, might stretch far down her back and might be of some distant Spanish descent. But then again perhaps not, for "Imogene" was a decidedly un-Spanish name. Of course, not all parents were as fond of the names, artifacts, and images of foreign soils as was his own—hence his always oddly sounding un-English name of Eduardo. He himself much preferred "Eddie," though his mother forbade the shortened nickname's usage in her home.

At any rate, he would have to make an inquiry as to this

Imogene's forebears, to see if perhaps they both had the blood of conquistadores to create a commonality between them. He was not at all sure that they had any other single thing in common at all, but then he'd only spoken, maybe, twenty sentences total to the girl, and most of those mere polite nothings. Not much to judge another being by, that was certain. It flashed through his mind that perhaps he should have bestirred himself to chat a bit with the girl before popping the question . . . ah well, as to that, what was done was done.

Contrary to popular opinion, Eddie Garrant was not stupid. He was, in fact, quite bright. There was a small collection of longtime friends that knew this of him, and even though they liked him very well, they were all to a man mildly repulsed to see the large collection of volumes he treasured in his own personal library. No popular print here; no, there were volumes on any number of weighty subjects from anatomy to zoology, all of which were intended to sharpen and enhance the mind. Added to this, he had a fine personal collection of art objects; an extended library of sheet music from all the masters; and two walls in his home were dedicated to extraordinary paintings—some of which weren't at all valuable, but which he admired greatly; and reams and reams of paper upon which were inscribed various written works. Some were his own compositions, including the numerous volumes of the journal he had been keeping faithfully since he was seven years old, some were valuable manuscripts of famous authors, and some were copies he had made of writings that had particularly inspired him. The few friends who ever entered Eddie's beloved and intimate domain took one look at such a ponderous collection of intellectual works and boldly told him what dull stuff it was, which came as no surprise to him at all.

He had been more or less told as much since he had first developed the ability to read at the mere age of four. He had delighted his tutors, and then his professors, with his sharp, absorbent mind, but over the years and throughout

19

his education, his fellows had roundly and uniformly given him the raspberry for his academic excellence. Being a sweet-natured boy, and then a well-built lad, and always wishing to please as he might, he had found a balance by being a good student for his teachers, and a wonderful athlete for his peers. He had a wicked leg—capable of sending a ball consistently and accurately straight for over sixty yards—and a throwing arm that made the other fellows howl with regret whenever they were partnered against him in Dodge-the-Ball. Being consistently one of the taller, well-muscled lads of his class, he had regularly been called upon to save the day for his wrestling team, or to even the score in a game of football, or was placed aftmost in the hull for crewing, as he could row the deepest and strongest while still maintaining the captain's tempo. His teams had won a good many awards for their efforts, greatly enhanced by his own, and so the somewhat shy, bookish lad had managed to gain a satisfactory popularity that stood him well, even to this day.

Eddie, however, was not completely unaware that he was considered not very bright by society in general. His friends were all compatriots from those days at school, and admittedly, as a group they had achieved very little in the way of educational excellence. They drank, they chased pretty girls, they stayed up far too late to please their parents, and most of them were lucky if they could read anything more profound than the large-print titles of a newspaper's front page, never mind the smaller print. That they never cracked open that same newspaper for any purpose other than to note who was racing where and when was a known fact.

Eddie was in with "the fast set," and since he had been so since early on, he was perfectly content among them. He read his books at night, went to lectures as it pleased him, alone, and never mentioned anything to do with Horace, or the Mongols, or J.L. Burckhardt's discovery of the Great Temple of Abu-Simbel, or anything remotely like these mere samples of his intellectual repertoire. He knew his friends were a brainless lot, but that held no sway with him.

In point of fact, his very best friend, Brisby, had a huge heart, an organ much, much bigger than his brain. That was what held sway with Eddie: a good disposition, a gentle bearing, and the ability to laugh and enjoy life.

In female company he found no different set of facts, for the ladies wished only to discuss their hats or gowns or the latest contraption introduced by fashion. He was never such a bore as to insist on forcing his opinions or his findings upon his fellow man; he certainly would not do so to the fairer sex. He knew of fellows, considered stuffy, usually old, who prosed on for hours about one topic, and he knew with what disregard they were held by his mates, not to mention the girls who yawned behind their fans. Those fellows never caught a pretty girl's eye, that he knew. It did not matter to Eddie that the girls wanted banal, mindless chatter; he often felt tongue-tied in their presence anyway. Their minds seemed foreign things to him, and he approached them with a combination of caution and curiosity. Chatter was easy. And besides, if one muttered little nothings, it sometimes led to a pretty girl letting a fellow sneak a kiss or two. They, as a lot, seemed to thrive nicely on airy words, even while allowing a little indiscretion or two, and so his impressions of the fairer sex's sharpness of mind were not enhanced by experience. He did not think about it overmuch, lost in his studies as he was most of the time, and when he did, it only mildly astounded him to see that not a one of them seemed the least bit like his own world-wise mother.

His mother had traveled extensively, sometimes taking her children with her, sometimes not. It had been a stimulating household, full of travels and tales, and wonderful objects to touch and savor and identify. But even in mother's case, a great deal of her time had to be given over to not only what she was going to wear, but what her family was going to wear, and how the house was to look when guests arrived. Eduardo just assumed his mother had a rare hobby — the study of anything besides fashion and gossip — and that he could not expect such a rarity among the ladies

21

of his circles. He had heard some girls called bluestockings, but the one particular girl he knew to be so called (and whom he had bothered himself to attempt a bit of conversation with) had turned out to be only a patron of lurid lending-library romances. She'd had no more idea who Plato was than dear Brisby. When responding to his question about the book she was currently reading, the silly chit had claimed she would dearly love to be carried off by a pirate, just as the book's heroine had been.

"A pirate, Miss Danford? I cannot think you would like the life."

"I'd adore it," she'd said with fluttering eyelashes.

He had stared at her, forbidding himself to ask if she really wished to be a ship's doxy. No, he'd decided at once, if this was a bluestocking, then he would have to foreswear such "educated" company.

With such an attitude, he had settled into a most content bachelorhood. He had made no plans to change this fact . . . but plans began to grow around him nonetheless.

His mother pestered him each time she saw him—which was every day of his life—to marry, claiming he was soon to be the Earl of Norfleet. She would not accept his reply of "And so?", going on to tell him it was an earl's duty to marry and beget yet another earl.

"Just look at Uncle Edward" (for whom he had been named, rather providentially, as it turned out), said his mother. "He never married, and here he is on his deathbed with no son to inherit his title. As pleased as we must be to think of you as the earl, Eduardo, it ought not to have been. A man of such estate ought to have married and begotten heirs. Your Uncle Edward is lucky he has you to carry on the Norfleet title."

"And so I shall, married or no."

"You naughty boy! You do this deliberately to antagonize me! You know I mean that when you are taken from this earth, that you must have a son to inherit the title."

"I needn't 'must.' It's not a requirement that has to be met for me to go on existing, you know."

"Eduardo!" she had snapped, exasperated, ending the conversation with a glare, at least for that day, but the subject had come up any number of times since.

It was not, then, a complete surprise when one day his mother announced that she had found just the girl for him to marry.

He had said no; she had said it was the thing to do.

He had said he was happy; she had assured him he'd be happier once he was married.

He had said he found "girls bothersome"; and his mother had said, "She won't be a girl. She'll be your wife." Eddie had stared at her, puzzling out that cryptic message, when his mother came to the attack again, crying out, "Don't you want your mother to be a grandmother?"

He had assured her his pair of older sisters had already done the pretty in that regard. The concise observation had not improved her demeanor, and it was then that she rapped out that he was an ungrateful boy who meant to live with and beleaguer his parent until the end of her days, and had proceeded to allow a single tear to roll down her cheek.

"Oh, I say!" he had countered helplessly, and had known even then by the tearful glint in her eyes that the matter had become a lost cause. He gave his best for several weeks, but in the end he had agreed to her plans, if only to have some peace. He had no inclination to marry, but it seemed he would do so anyway.

Her parents had been contacted by his parent, tea and cognac had lubricated the negotiations, and that night he had been told Miss Bradshaw's Christian name: Imogene. It had not been a promising name at all, and for an hour he had paced in his room, thinking to repudiate the betrothal. It was only the recollections of his mother's daily attacks that had kept him from doing so.

Imogene. Even now he had to think a moment to recall her features. At least she had not giggled or fainted or cried. That would have been most uncomfortable. He supposed she would do any one or all of those things at certain points in time during their marriage, but at least the proposal had been gotten through rather tidily. That, at least, was to her credit.

A glance at his watch caused him to consider the date; it was only two weeks until the day of this marriage. He must remember to tell his man to start assembling some sort of special ensemble, he supposed with a sigh, to spiff up a bit. A wedding, particularly one's own, would seem to require a little more attention to detail than the usual day about town.

His thoughts of his room and wardrobe at home reminded him that he might not particularly enjoy the catlike grin his mother was sure to show him at the news of the girl's formal acceptance, so he turned his horse and rode to his club a little earlier than usual. He settled among his fellows, reading his newspaper, sipping a brandy while he waited for Brisby and his other mates to make their nightly appearances, and generally did his best to pretend that his life was not about to change.

Imogene stared into her mirror, practicing a smile. The smile — in truth a grimace — faded quickly. It was very difficult to maintain even this sickly imitation. Why did she have to smile, anyway? Surely even Eduardo Garrant was not so very thickheaded that he believed she was happy to be marrying him? Still, there would be other people at the betrothal party today, as her mother had pointed out. "You must look radiant, Imogene. Everyone will be expecting that."

It was absurd, of course. Everyone who knew anything about either she or Mr. Garrant would know they hardly knew each other. They would know everything was neatly arranged regardless of affections, or a lack thereof.

"I suppose there are certain standards to maintain," Imogene mumbled to her reflection. It *would* be rather uncomfortable if she sat and cried while the guests passed her hankies . . . but, still, she wasn't going to grin like a fool all afternoon either. She'd made up her mind. She'd smile only

24

naturally, or at worst when it seemed unavoidable by simple politeness.

"Come along," her mother chirped at her open door. "Mister Garrant is here. You should be at his side to greet the guests."

"I'll be right down, Mama," Imogene said, surprising herself with the meekness of her tone. She supposed she'd given up fighting; one way or another she'd have to get through this day, so it might as well be in a fashion to please somebody. However, as soon as her mother slipped away, Imogene turned back to the mirror long enough to make a series of terrible faces, most of which involved sticking out her tongue and rolling her eyes.

Eddie turned to see his bride-to-be, having done so when her father called out, "Ah, there you are, Genie. Come along, come along! Our first guest's carriage is just arrived.

She was very prettily dressed in a gown of pale sky blue, with a cream-colored overlay of organdy that left bits of blue revealed at the sleeves and hem. Lace to match the organdy trailed from her half sleeves and graced the square neckline of the dress. He noted that just the right amount of neckline was revealed, upon which lay a single strand of ivory pearls. It was a charming ensemble, one that caused him to sigh, not with appreciation but regret. It seemed to confirm that fashion would be foremost in her mind and her discourse. How dull. There was one thing that had caught his ear, however, that he had rather liked. Her father had called her "Genie." It was a much softer sound than "Imogene." If she'd allow it, he thought that perhaps in the privacy of their home he'd call her thusly.

He was not the only observant one of the pair. Imogene noted at once that he wore dark blue—how dull—enlivened only by the lighter blue waistcoat that peeked from beneath his jacket. His cravat was nicely knotted—not showy, but finely done—and his hair was rather short for fashion, but rather striking on him. There was quite some natural wave to his blondish-brown hair, making it look full somehow despite the shortness, and there were naturally formed curls at the nape of his neck and across his forehead. It was perhaps those curls that encouraged him to wear shorter hair. A man could not like a head full of tight curls, even if a hundred females would love to possess the same. Strangely enough, the arrangement worked on him. If Imogene had such hair—instead of her own straight, straight black hair—she'd be ecstatic. As it was, her maid spent nearly twenty minutes each day with a curling rod, striving to give the illusion of curl to her bangs, never bothering with the lengthy rest.

Imogene gave him a second covert looking over, and realized once again, belatedly, that his form and features were pleasant to look upon. She knew herself to be striking—dark hair combined with light skin, and a pair of dark brown eyes that had known a compliment or two—and was surprised to realize anew the fact of his comeliness. Oh, not godlike at all, but really his was a face that combined its elements well. Good forehead, neat brows, straight nose just the right size for his face, a generous mouth, and a solid chin. He was clean-shaven, and his eyes were hazel, or perhaps gray. No, hazel. Well, this was something, she supposed. At least she would not have to sit across from an ugly fellow every morning for the rest of her life.

She stepped up to him, and made a belated, and quite small, curtsy to his bow. "Mister Garrant," she greeted him, no smile about her lips.

"Miss Bradshaw." He did not smile either. In fact, he looked a little pinched, as though his shoes were too tight, or he did not wish to be here either, and there was just a tiny twinkling of communication between their glances that made her think it must be the latter. She did not like him any the better for it—after all he had been fool enough to allow the betrothal to happen, and so was deserving of no pity—but at least she need not pretend to be having a wonderful time, certainly not with him. He was slow enough that he probably would not notice any lapse in her behavior anyway. That was a rather liberating thought, enough so that she turned a glittering eye his way, and whispered rather sarcastically, "Won't this be fun?"

He hesitated, then murmured, "Er . . . um . . . rather."

One tiny corner of her mouth twitched down, and her gaze rolled away from his dismissively. Words failed them both then, and she stood beside him silently, awaiting their guests.

Her legs were aching a bit by the time the last guest had arrived, for she had been holding herself rather still and stiff for nearly an hour. She thought longingly of a chair, but her heart sank as she heard the first stirring of musical instruments, their discordant tunings announcing a dance was about to commence. Would she have to dance with Mr. Garrant? It would be expected, of course, it being the first dance, but if she hurried, right now, she might be able to attach herself to her father for the honor, and after that she could sit out as she wished.

"Er . . . um," Mr. Garrant said at her side, crushing her hopes. "Looks like we'll be dancing, eh? A waltz. Do you dance the waltz?"

"Yes. Do you?" she asked with only some slight hope he did not.

"Quite. One must be able to do so these days."

"One must," she echoed, laying her hand atop his proffered arm. There was that in her face which said it was going to be a rather long night.

He escorted her to the center of the floor, where several couples mingled. The maestro tapped his stick on his music stand, and then the melody began. Mr. Garrant's one hand took up hers, his long fingers eclipsing her smaller hand, and the other moved to cup her waist lightly. It took them a few tentative steps, but then they found the rhythm together, and began the turns of the waltz. The other couples looked on approvingly, and then drifted back several steps, leaving the floor to the betrothed pair. Imogene refrained from groaning in vexation when she saw they had been given the entire floor, and gritted her teeth together, hoping it passed for something resembling a smile.

Mr. Garrant said something under his breath, but she did not catch it.

Eventually other couples drifted on to the dance floor, making the bright pink spots on Imogene's cheeks recede a little. It was hard enough being on display as the bride-to-be, but being the center of all attention while in the groom-to-be's arms was too much.

It was only as the dance was ending that she realized she had said nothing to her partner, and that he had proved himself to be a rather fine dancer. Well, that was to be expected of an empty-headed fellow. He *would* spend hours practicing something as nonessential as a waltz. Ask the man the difference between a Tory and a Whig and he'd look at you blankly, but ask him to show you where to place your foot, and he'd rave on for an hour, no doubt.

For himself, Eddie had two impressions. The first was that he'd never danced with a girl before who did not talk his ear off—a pleasant novelty—and the second was that he did not think Miss Bradshaw liked him very much. There was something in the way she held herself, the stiffness of her mouth, that spoke of disapproval. He wondered why. Had he said or done something offensive? When? If she found him objectionable, why had she agreed to marry him? Ah, the title, of course! More the fool he, to think it might be for any other reason. Well, you could dislike a fellow and still marry him; the proof of that was all about them. Maybe that was just as well; he could go on living life much as he liked it, while she lived hers.

The thought of a future made slightly more rosy caused him to smile down at her. She almost smiled back automatically, and then turned away, bemused. Whatever did the fellow have to grin about?

Imogene was a creature given to many moods, but usually she was a pleasant being, light of heart and full of amusement at life in general. It was not like her to feel sour for long, and she found even now she chafed under the weight of her self-inflicted pouting. It was that which had caused her to almost smile back at Mr. Garrant, surely.

As the dance came to an end, she thought begrudgingly to herself, that, really, she might have enjoyed that dance if it weren't for the fact she was expected to marry the man.

To Imogene's mild surprise, the evening turned out to be quite delightful. Once she was free of her obligation to dance with Mr. Garrant, her mood lightened. She was asked to dance every dance—not a new phenomenon, but still quite complimentary—and she found that conversation with her partners was gay this night. Perhaps they were free with their speech and their compliments because they now considered her beyond approach, but it did not matter, for it was still heady for any young woman to be so fêted and celebrated, and Imogene was no exception to that rule.

When she was saying goodbye to her guests at three in the morning, it was with regret. She could have stayed up until dawn, and happily so, but the pleasant evening must end, as indeed must all things, pleasant or no. The dance card she had dangled from her wrist all evening would go in a box for remembrances, she knew, and then she flushed a little, realizing anew that this *was* her betrothal party. Yes, she would keep the dance card, for even the mixed feelings that came with this thought could not quite dilute the pleasure of the evening.

Mr. Garrant stood at her side, making her aware in a most uncomfortable way that they would be doing so for many years to come. She glanced at him several times from under her lashes, always faintly surprised to see how becoming he was in a quiet way. He was just the right sort for this greeting and sending off of guests. He knew what to say, smiled when he ought, and indeed in all ways proved himself to be socially adept. This would have been fine, if only Imogene could believe that there was more to the man than this. She sighed, and with two more handclasps, their guests were gone.

Mr. Garrant turned to her, and gave her a bow. She responded automatically with a curtsy. "Good night, Miss Bradshaw," he said.

"You must call me Imogene," she said, then wondered why she'd given him the permission. It somehow made their engagement seem more formal, and she could not really like that. Perhaps it was because he had not embarrassed her tonight, at least not so that she knew. There might have been whispers behind fans that amounted to "Poor girl! She's marrying Mister 'Er-Um'," but she had not been aware of them if they had occurred.

He blinked once, twice, and then he cleared his throat, and said, "Er . . . might I be so bold as to call you Genie?"

She blushed a dark red, flustered by the sound of her nickname on his lips. That seemed *far* too personal. "Oh, I . . ." she said faintly, unsure how to deny him the privilege.

"And you must call me Eddie. Please. 'Eduardo' is so peculiar. 'Tis an impossible label, but what's a fellow to do?"

Her chin twitched as though to force her lips to say him nay, but then she found she was nodding. There was nothing for it, short of being rude. "Yes. All right."

Eddie and Genie. Oh dear, it did make them sound like a couple of bumpkins. It almost made her shudder to think that was how they would be perceived.

He looked at the floor, then up at the ceiling, then said, "I suppose we ought to drive about, eh? The wedding's still ten days away, so there's time yet to do the expected. Tomorrow, at four?" he came to the point at last, finally gazing at her.

Suddenly she was very tired, with no strength left to fight the facts this night. Ten days! She knew this, of course, but to hear it aloud made her ears sting. "Yes," she said simply.

He gave her another bow. "Tomorrow, then." He turned and left to pursue his coat and top hat, and then his carriage.

As she walked toward her room, her brother, Raymond, hailed her from the doorway wherein he leaned. "Genie! That was some party, eh?" He was gnawing on a chicken drumstick, balanced in his fingertips above a linen napkin.

"I enjoyed the dancing," she answered with a tired smile.

The smile was partly from remembrance, and partly for her brother's benefit.

"Mister Garrant seemed an acceptable parti. I guess I'll let you marry him," Raymond said.

She said nothing, merely turning to find the stairs up to her room. She was tempted to turn back and demand that he find some reason or way to *keep* her from marrying Mr. Garrant, but pride stopped her tongue. Either way, she would still be marrying, but at least if she kept silent, Raymond would not be able to tease her, or give her curious glances on her wedding day. She would not be able to bear any pity, she was sure of that. That is, if she ever did actually marry Mr. Garrant.

Imogene's day went by at a dizzying speed. She had been captured in her room for over an hour as the dressmaker fitted the folds of her wedding dress about her for the first time. It had not been an idle time, as she had been instructed to "turn," "lift your right arm," "walk to and fro," and so forth. During these exercises, she had been verbally assaulted by her mother, who had the dressmaker's assistants bringing in armloads of wedding finery for her review. They rejected twenty hats and veils before more or less settling on three favorites, one of which they would eventually have to choose. They did the same for gloves, stockings, and shoes. Mama had then brought out the family jewels, and they had argued at some length before it was determined that Grandmama's ivory brooch would serve nicely as her single adornment. Mama had wanted Imogene to grace her gown with the diamond and pearl choker and bracelet, but Imogene thought they clashed with the lace of her dress.

"Impossible! Diamonds never clash!" Mama had scoffed.

"It's too busy, Mama."

Imogene had won that battle, but lost the next. Lady Bradshaw announced that they would now select night clothing. This was not at all to Imogene's liking, conjuring as it did actually having to spend the night with Mr. Garrant, but Mama waved her into silence, and another parade of garments were carried in and out. Imogene put no thought into the choosing, other than to eliminate all those that hinted at vulgarity. Her Mama said nothing at her choices, silently approving her daughter's sense of virtue and appropriateness.

After this trying period, Imogene was not released from this unwanted matrimonial preparation. Now it was time to sit down and decide where all the guests were to be seated for the banquet to follow the wedding.

The invitations had gone out the same day Imogene had learned she was to be married. "Why all this haste?" she cried once in the midst of her mother's many fashion sketchings and highly scribbled-upon pads full of names, a desperate edge to her voice.

"Mister Garrant requested it," her mother explained, as if it were perfectly normal to rush into a wedding this way. Of course that was nonsense, for most of the girls Imogene knew that had married had been betrothed for a year, at least.

"I wish you had spoken to me, Mama. I would have told you that it is unseemly to hurry so."

"Oh, posh," replied Lady Bradshaw. "It will be June by then, don't you see? He's being very thoughtful, allowing you to be a June bride. The stuff of every girl's dreams! Very considerate." At her daughter's steady gaze, she cleared her throat and tried a different approach. "Imogene," she said, with a motherly tilt to her head that showed she was not completely free of maternal leanings. "Don't you see? Mister Garrant is operating on a bit of 'dutch courage,' as the vulgar slang goes. He wants it done and over with before he has time to think about it."

"That's not very promising, is it?" Imogene said, while managing not to cringe at this revelation. "To say nothing of not being very complimentary."

"Oh, Imogene." Her mother laughed. "How you do go

32

on! There's not been a man married yet who wasn't quaking inside, mark my word. It's the nature of the beast."

Imogene's eyes narrowed, but she refrained from pointing out that her mother had fairly painted a picture of Mr. Garrant as a cowering dog. It worried her quite some bit to think that the image was easy to hold, as he seemed about as bright as a puppy as well.

So the morning and afternoon had flown by, until suddenly the chiming of the clock revealed that there was only half an hour until Mr. Garrant came to take her up for their ride in the park. Her mother hustled her off upstairs to change, and then took herself off to become presentable, as she was to be her daughter's chaperone this day. Such was the shortage of time that when Imogene was finally dressed, it was ten minutes past when Mr. Garrant had said he would call. Her mother's appearance at her door provided her with the information that Mr. Garrant was waiting downstairs.

"You look fine. Come along," chided Lady Bradshaw from the doorway as she saw Imogene glance back at her mirror. Mama could not know that it was not to gauge her attractiveness that Imogene looked again, but rather to check and see that the mild dislike she felt was not reflected on her face.

Mr. Garrant was dressed rather somberly today—it seemed to be his habit. Dark brown. It made his hazel eyes seem more brown today, leaning toward topaz. She blinked once at the thought, looked again, and decided that had been just a bit of fancy. They were just eyes, rather plain, one could say. Nothing special. Not riveting like the vibrant blue or dark brown eyes she preferred in her daydreams.

Imogene herself had dressed rather nicely. The impulse had something to do with being seen riding with Mr. Garrant. Perhaps it was to show the world she did not care what they thought of her betrothed . . . or to show that her life was going on despite the plans that swirled around her threatening to marry her to a simpleton . . . maybe? She could not say. She only knew that the small, close-fitting hat she wore highlighted her cheekbones, and that her gown of creamy Brussels lace would be envied by any cognizant female. She deliberately left her rose-colored pelisse unbuttoned that the gown might show, and she slipped on cream-colored gloves to finish the look. Even Mama had given her a second look. It was a surprise to her, then, to see a shadow cross Mr. Garrant's face. She could not think what it might mean.

Eddie made a point of not complimenting Miss Bradshaw; he was dismayed at the thought of the stream of commentary it would provoke. He did not know what else he hoped Miss Bradshaw would have to talk about, but he refused to bring up the subject of fashion himself.

Consequently the outing started on a sour note, and continued that way. There was little conversation between them, and most of that generated by Lady Bradshaw. Twice, when Mr. Garrant was looking the other way, she gave a quick elbow to her daughter, but Imogene could not think of a thing to say beyond a mumbled comment as to the weather. Since the two elbowings meant she mentioned the weather twice, her mother gave up her physical attacks upon her daughter, and instead concentrated on giving Imogene long, speaking glances.

What was she supposed to do? Imogene thought in exasperation. Prattle on like a pea-goose? That was no doubt what Mr. Garrant expected. Perhaps if she gave it a try Mama would cease these facial gyrations that she believed passed for subtlety.

Heaving a silent sigh, Imogene turned to him and said, "I am surprised you are not driving us, Mister Garrant. It is said about town that you are quite the one with the whip."

Now Mama beamed at her, so it was worth the effort. Mr. Garrant, however, merely said, "Er."

She waited for the "um," but it was not forthcoming. She almost shuddered to think of whole, long, suffocating evenings in this gentleman's company engaging in such "conversation," but she suppressed the reflex, turning it into what she thought might be a bright smile.

34

Eddie looked down at the silly grin on Miss Bradshaw's face, and one corner of his mouth drew up in a sickly imitation thereof, as he strove mightily to be polite.

She gazed up at that rather twisted smile, and sat completely still for a moment. There was something in his face that spoke of torture, an expression that so mirrored her own interior feelings that she was as struck to see it on him as she would have been to see its like upon a cow. Was that mere matrimonial terror, as her mother claimed all men to know, or was there just a flicker of cognizance in that suffering visage?

Unable to answer the question, she shook her shoulders in a small shudder, and fled back to the conversation. "Is it true, Mister Garrant?"

"Is what true, Miss Bradshaw?" he asked. Her inane smile had so nonplussed him that he had forgotten her earlier comment.

She sighed aloud this time, an unspoken hope dimming at his thickheadedness, then repeated herself by saying, "Are you a creditable whip?"

"Oh, yes. Rather. Like to drive, I do. Member of the Four-in-Hand Club, and all that. Really like horses," he rambled. Really, he liked her better when she didn't smile. There seemed to be some hint of depth there when she did not give him all those teeth to gaze upon. It was almost as if her smile erased any semblance of an orderly mind. *An orderly mind?* he thought with sudden astonishment. Why had he even thought that? He had no reason to believe Miss Bradshaw was one whit brighter or more forthcoming than her feminine contemporaries, and yet for a moment he had known disappointment that it appeared she was like all the rest, perfectly willing to be ignorantly shallow. Could it be that he had seen something in her manner, her speech, or her gaze that reflected something more substantial? He could not think why he might have thought so for even a moment, and yet now he turned to look upon her with a less sure eye.

Just then, as they stared at each other with uncertainty

and mixed emotions on both their faces, Imogene's name was called. They turned as one, and it was Lady Bradshaw who identified the caller. "Ah, Julietta." To Mr. Garrant she added, "That is to say, my niece, Miss Herron."

A pretty girl with a button nose rode up beside their open carriage, the sea-blue ribbons of her white gown and straw bonnet blowing in the slight breeze. Her hair, the color of ripened corn, was twisted into becoming ringlets that peeked out from beneath the confines of her bonnet, and her blue eyes sparkled with gaiety. Imogene felt some of her confusion melt away at the sight of the girl, for Julietta was her favorite cousin, only one year younger. She was a happy, flighty creature, with perhaps just a streak of naughtiness in her, which—truth be told—was a goodly part of her charm.

"Cousin Genie. Aunty Florina. How nice it is to see you! Do you see, I am here for the season."

"I had heard your mother and father might come to town," Lady Bradshaw said, nodding a greeting.

"Mama said you might be so good as to allow me to tag along on some of your outings. I hope she is right," Julietta said artlessly, and both ladies nodded at once.

"Julietta, how are you?" Imogene asked, smiling now rather more sincerely.

"Very well, thank you. How are you?"

Imogene paused for just a moment, but then she answered, "Well." She half turned toward Eduardo, one hand lifting slightly in his direction. "Julietta, please allow me to introduce you to . . ." she hesitated again, too long for politeness. She tried again, "To my . . ." She almost squirmed, but Imogene was no coward, so she spoke suddenly and rapidly, "My fiancé, Mister Garrant." She had not said those words before. They felt quite foreign on her tongue, yet, too, there was a curious little tingle of pride at the sound of them. Of course, there was an undeniable pleasure to be had from making a socially correct match, even if privately it made one's stomach a little sour.

"Your *fiancé!*" cried Julietta, leaning forward on her

horse's neck, stretching her hand out to her cousin. "Oh, this is so exciting! Oh, I can't bear it; I must dismount and give you all a hug."

Mr. Garrant was not slow on the uptake in this regard, taking his clue as a gentleman should. He had slipped from the carriage and presently reached up to circle his hands around Julietta's waist to lift her down to the ground. There was nothing untoward about it, yet for just a moment Lady Bradshaw scowled and Miss Bradshaw frowned. The moment passed, and soon Julietta's horse was tied to the back of their carriage, and she was settled among them, hugging them as the mood struck her, except for Mr. Garrant, instead whose hand she took up and squeezed rather familiarly.

Oh well, that was to be expected, for he was to be family now, Imogene excused the girl in her own mind.

"Oh, I am so glad I came to town! Mama said something about a wedding, but I'll confess I never heard her say it was to be yours, Genie. It would have been terrible if I should have missed it!" She laughed gaily then, and the others smiled with that infectious laughter. "I am assuming we've been invited, so Mama will know where and when?"

"Of course you've been invited," Lady Bradshaw said, silently thinking she was glad they were staying in town, as then she would not be expected to house Julietta's noisy family.

"Wonderful! But tell me anyway; where and when is it to be?"

"Saint Martin-in-the-Fields, on Saturday next," answered Lady Bradshaw when Imogene looked down at her folded hands.

"So soon! Oh, I am so glad I shan't miss it!" She turned to Eddie then, and said, "Do you know that we have met before?"

He looked blank for a moment, but then he said slowly, "Ah . . . yes, I believe I recall. Was it . . . a hunting party?" he asked.

"Quite!"

His brow cleared then, and he smiled at her. "You are the daring Miss Herron. Of course. Never saw a girl take a jump as well as you."

She laughed again, a tinkling sound. "How kind you are! You cannot have forgotten that my horse cleared the last jump, but *I* did not. I landed on my head!"

"We were all quite pleased that you were not hurt."

Julietta turned to her cousin. "My hat saved me, but its sweet little crown was flattened right down to the brim. It looked rather as though I had stuck a parasol directly on my head when I was done."

Mr. Garrant laughed then, as did they all, even Imogene. As she laughed she turned to look at her fiancé, startled by the sound he made. Somehow she had not thought of him as being capable of responding to humor. He had a very pleasant laugh, low and masculine. It erased from his face the faintly puzzled look he had sported all during this ride, and there was a light behind his eyes which now made them appear almost blue. Such changeable eyes. It seemed that clothing and attitude could be reflected in those eyes . . . blue for mirth or pleasure . . . But, of course he *would* laugh. All these young fribbles who called themselves pinks would like a merry time; as far as rumor had it, it was their main purpose for existing, to amuse themselves. Though, she amended with a little puzzled frown, one could not exactly call Mr. Garrant a "pink," as his fashion was rather subdued. Perhaps he preferred his comfort over fashion, or perhaps he was too slow to realize his valet did not turn him out in much along the lines of "dash."

But there was no denying he ran with the merry crowd, especially when they came to the end of their ride. By that time Imogene had been introduced to some of the most fashionable and/or notorious names in the land. That experience, as when she introduced her cousin to her fiancé, had its pleasures. She had never received so many flattering compliments and felicitations in all her days. It fairly made her head spin, and she had to admit there was nothing counterfeit about her smiles by the time the carriage pulled up to her home.

Mr. Garrant stepped down first, assisting each of the ladies out of the carriage. The driver moved to untie Julietta's horse, handing the reins to the boy who had come running from the stable at the sound of the wheels on the drive. Julietta was the last out, and she seemed inclined to linger. Certainly her hand lingered in Mr. Garrant's, as she gazed up at him and finished telling a tale of another riding mishap in her youth. He smiled at the ending, and then finally released her hand as he stepped back. He bid them all adieu, then turned to Imogene. "Might I have the honor of accompanying you to the opera tomorrow evening?"

Imogene did not hesitate, for she adored the opera, even if she had to go with Mister Garrant. Really, that was not nice at all, for he had been most pleasant today. "I'd be honored," she responded in kind, perhaps a little more nicely than she might have done yesterday, to compensate for her unkind thoughts. Her hands were loosely laced together before her, so that if he made any move to reach for her hand, to hold it for a moment as he had been holding Julietta's, she would be prepared. It still managed to surprise her a little, however, when he did just that, and she actually startled at his touch. His eyes flew to hers, even though he did not release her hand, and for a moment there was a curious tension between them. He made a sketchy motion—not quite a kiss—in the air above her hand, stepped back, made a bow to the company, then leaped up into the carriage once more. He lifted a hand in farewell, and then his driver gave the cluck to the horses.

She found herself lifting that clasped hand in return, rather as though it had a mind of its own. Certainly it felt a little lighter than her other one, so if it wanted to float up into a farewell wave, well then, she would just let it do so.

As the carriage pulled out of sight, the hand fell, and she shook her head briefly, allowing the curious thought of *now, why did I think he might take my hand anyway?* to course one short time through her mind. She dismissed such ruminations at once, however, for Julietta was tugging on her sleeve, pulling her into the house.

Julietta continued to urge her cousin to follow in her wake, moving without hesitation to Imogene's room. As she opened the door to admit them, she gave a gasp of wonder to see all the various wedding items about the room: the white dress hanging, waiting for another fitting; the three veils that still had not been decided upon and all the other paraphernalia of ribbons, lace, silk, and satin. She closed the door at once, leaned against it, and gave a huge sigh, her expression dreamy. "Oh, Genie!" she cried. "You are the luckiest girl alive!"

"Me?" Imogene questioned, one eyebrow raising in amused doubt. She glanced at her finery, not finding it that impressive herself. Oh, the dress was lovely, and the shoes were rather sweet with their multiple pearl buttons up the side—

"He's such a dream!" Julietta breathed, her hands clasping together at her breast.

"He?" Now both eyebrows rose in surprise. Good heavens, her cousin did not envy Imogene the wedding, she envied her the *groom*. How extraordinary!

"Mister Garrant," Julietta supplied the proof.

"Mister Garrant?"

"Of course, you silly!" Julietta laughed. "He's so wonderful. Such a gentleman. And handsome. And rich. And smart. I vow, I'm half in love with him myself," she cried, and then bit her lower lip, a deep blush staining her cheeks.

Imogene stared at her, astonished to see that Julietta might very well be speaking the truth, at least as she saw it. "Really?" she murmured quietly, the muted tone in direct opposition to her astonishment. She was aware her stare was making the girl uncomfortable, but she was unable to respond otherwise for several moments.

"I . . . well, what a silly thing to say," sputtered Julietta with a little toss of her blond curls, throwing in a fabricated laugh. "I merely meant to tell you . . . tell you how fortunate I think you are! I couldn't be more pleased for you. You'll have a lovely life, I vow."

"Thank you," Imogene said, turning away then in a belated attempt to hide her surprise from the other girl—someone thought Mr. Garrant was a wonderful catch!—and then, as an idea formed rapidly in her mind, she remained in that position to hide the dawning grin on her face. Oh, it was too good to be true! Could Julietta really have come along at exactly the right moment?

"You know," Imogene said slowly, smothering her grin ruthlessly as she turned back to her cousin, "Mister Garrant and I do not know each other well. I think . . . well, it might be nice to have someone—a third party—there to help us do that. I was wondering . . . as you know him somewhat, and—you must tell me 'no' if you don't wish to do so—if I might presume upon you to accompany Mister Garrant and me on our outings for the next ten days or so . . . ?"

"Oh," Julietta said, looking as though she would decline out of politeness, knowing her manners, despite a flash of eagerness that lit up her eyes. The internal battle to do what she wanted instead of what was correct, though, was clearly reflected on her features.

"Please," Imogene said, putting a note of pleading into her tone. She knew her cousin well, and felt that Julietta's mischievous streak would work to her advantage. If, as seemed quite evident, Julietta was attracted to Mr. Garrant, Julietta would be willing to see if he was attracted to her, affianced cousin or no affianced cousin. It was her nature.

"I . . . yes. Yes, of course. If it would be helpful to you." Julietta breathed, the internal battle lost and over.

"Oh, extremely so," Imogene said, and then she could not help but smile.

Julietta smiled back, and then the girls were hugging again. Imogene's smile broadened over her shoulder, her eyes sparkling at the thought that there might yet be a wedding . . . but it was not necessarily *she* who was going to be the bride.

* * *

Eddie looked at the blond girl, laughing along with her. She was quite witty, even if it was in a limited kind of way. All the pretty thing knew was town prattle, but at least she had a clever way of retelling the tales. He appreciated that. If he had to spend a great deal of time making silly conversation, it ought to at least be somewhat amusing.

He was well aware that he had been deliberately thrown into the girl's company. He had become aware of that fact on the evening she came unexpectedly along to the opera with him and Genie. He never thought of Genie as "Miss Bradshaw" anymore, and often failed to refer to her as such even in mixed company. He had decided he liked the shortened name much better, and had dismissed the more formal one without further ado. He sensed his use of the nickname often flustered her, despite her permission, and that was in part why he used it. Her blushes intrigued him.

Now she was far across the room, supposedly deeply involved in a picture puzzle, leaving him to hold up the conversation, once again, with Lady Bradshaw and her niece, Miss Herron. They were, after all, in Miss Herron's home, and it behooved him to be polite. He always called her Miss Herron, even though she had hinted he could call her "Julietta."

Miss Herron was rattling on about a new hat—or was it a scarf?—and he had to stand, turning his back to her that she might not see his quick yawn. He tried to surreptitiously flex his muscles a bit, hoping to stimulate himself out of the somnolence that had stolen over him. The trip to the art gallery had been boring—except for when Genie called his attention to a tiny two-inch-square painting, in a frame many times the size of the artwork, that was rather clever and intricate for such a tiny area of work—and the ride in the park had been the same old thing. A fashion parade. Bah. Miss Herron had been popular, or so he thought, though truth to tell he had not been watching her. He had been watching Genie.

He had been observing her since the night at the opera.

She had not only enjoyed the presentation thoroughly — her brown eyes dancing with enthusiasm — but she had also interpreted the lyrics and the actions of the players for her cousin. He had gawked at her, astounded by her utterances, of which clothing was mentioned only as it applied to the advancement of the opera. He listened closely, more and more amazed as he heard that her speech was not only spontaneous but also astute.

Here was a woman who could put her mind to something more intricate than the seating arrangement at her next dinner party. He felt his chest expand with self-praise at his own keen talent of observation, for he was not completely floored by this display of Imogene Bradshaw's wit. He had seen flickers of something deeper in the girl before, yet her erudite discussion of the performance had been a revelation of hither-to unknown depths. His eyes had been opened, the obscuring veil of assumption ripped away, and to his wide-eyed amazement he saw before him a marvelous, unlooked-for creature. He had spent the rest of the evening, over a late supper, ogling the girl, or when he felt he could no longer do so with any semblance of gentlemanly behavior, listening attentively to her words with an averted eye. The comments of the other operagoers whom had joined their box at the first intermission only served to spur her on, their banter growing sparkling, so that others looked on enviously at the laughter and quick repartee that went forward.

To Eddie, Genie might as well have been a violin now, for her every utterance seemed like music. She had a mind! Not only a mind, but a clever, bright, informed, and educated mind. How rare a creature! He knew that females were seldom exposed to, and consequently uncomprehending of, references to mythology, or the troubles in the Indian Empire, or the latest agreement between the French and the Prussians. And even if they heard of these things, he certainly could not think of any woman he knew who could actually *discuss* them with this marvelous give and take method of hers.

He watched in growing fascination as she cleverly advanced the conversation, filling in when a lull threatened in a manner that also served to put her cousin forward to best advantage. She did more than a creditable job of showing off Miss Herron as a desirable companion, at least to judge by the three gentlemen who competed for the honor of bringing Miss Herron her lemonade. Eddie knew quite well that the ploy of "a little jealousy" was being utilized here, and it was working perfectly, though not quite as Genie had hoped. He was grateful for the other bucks that vied to keep the conversation going, that he might sit and merely lap it up.

When asked what she thought of the building of the Strand Bridge, Miss Herron looked blank, but Genie replied that "just the other day dear Julietta was out riding, and commented on how much work has been done on the bridge already." When the subject of the forming of the Royal Yacht Squadron was mentioned, she murmured something in her cousin's ear; only then did the blond girl speak up to say, "Oh, wouldn't a day trip to see the ships on the Thames be pleasant?" When Byron's publication of "Childe Harold's Pilgrimage" became the topic, Genie extracted a promise from Julietta to do a reading from it for them three nights hence, to which all were invited. Eddie listened avidly, but it was not with Miss Herron's charm that he became enraptured. He was fairly sure they shared a comment or two, but later all he could recall of the evening was the marvels that had tripped from Genie Bradshaw's tongue.

When he had at last delivered the ladies to the safety of Genie's home and was alone in his carriage, he had bent his head as though deep in thought. A grin had slowly formed on his face until it stretched from ear to ear, unable to help himself. He knew she meant for him to be attracted to her cousin, but that was all silliness now . . . now that he knew the real Genie. There was no question he would ever care for Miss Herron's prattle, not when a beautiful, clever, quick-minded girl sat beside her. He tapped his shoe on the floor, then the other one, smiled even wider, did a quick little set of dance steps with his feet, reached for his cane to bounce the tip off the squabs opposite, gave a happy humming sound, and finally succumbed to the impulse to give a giant, triumphant shout.

His driver pulled up short, but a rap on the roof of the carriage signaled him to go on. He was surprised, then, when he heard a voice calling his name. He turned and saw that his master had pushed down the carriage window and stuck his head out, his light hair disturbed by the wind that passed the carriage. "Mister Garrant, sir?" the driver asked at the unusual sight.

Eddie grinned, then laughed. He shook his short curls happily and cried, "I'm in a fine mood, Toppin!"

"Not three sheets to the wind, are yer, sir?" asked the driver, fairly sure the fellow was not drunk, but he was acting mighty queer.

"No." Eddie laughed. "Just in a fine, fine mood!"

"As yer say, sir."

Eddie laughed again, then pulled his head inside the carriage, leaving Toppin to turn back to his horses and murmur, "Coo! Must be love then. That's what I thinks, old girls. Come on, then, let's get the lover boy to his home, as that's where he says he wants to go."

Eddie never heard this interchange, but he wouldn't have minded it in the least if he had, for he was well aware that he had been smitten, at long last really and truly attracted to a woman. No, more than attracted; in the course of that one evening, he had felt a growing admiration, which had rapidly given way to some grander emotion, something that had him giddy all through the night.

When his best friend came to call the next morning, he, was still reeling with his new findings, convinced by the long, restless, nearly ecstatic night that he had, indeed, fallen madly in love. He even told Brisby as much over the breakfast table.

Brisby set down his fork to stare at his good friend. "In

45

love, you say? Oh dear."

" 'Oh dear'! Aren't you going to wish me happy?" Eddie cried with a laugh.

"I would, old boy, you know I would. 'Tis just that . . . well, it seems a most awkward time, what with you getting married soon and all," Brisby had explained.

Eddie had stared, and then howled with laughter for a full five minutes, and Brisby had joined him, even though Eddie never explained exactly why they were laughing so uproariously.

Later in the morning, Eddie and Brisby presented themselves at Julietta's town house. After being ushered in, Eddie rushed to the library to join the newfound and highly regarded object of his affections at the picture puzzle, his changeable eyes filling with light as he ruthlessly and without regret abandoned his attempts at polite conversation. However, Imogene, without looking up and with that curious catlike sense that women sometimes have, leaped up, made a hasty excuse, and exited the room. He couldn't very well follow her, though he did wander in the direction of the doorway by which she had exited. He would catch her when she returned, and she would be forced to give him more than a smile and a nod and a murmur or two.

Imogene did not go very far, just across the hall to the parlor opposite. She knew her cousin's town house well enough to make the hasty escape to a room that would probably be deserted, and she had guessed right. She stood there, behind the rapidly closed door, her hand to the heart that bounced uncertainly in her breast. It seemed to her it took a moment to recover her breath, and she could not think why her health seemed so given to these pulses lately. Well . . . perhaps, if she was a little bit truthful, it might have something to do with a certain way a certain gentleman looked at her the last few nights and now today . . . rather as though she were a cream puff and ought to be devoured. It quite embarrassed her, but, too, it caused this hammering of the heart and racing of the blood, and she could not like it.

Well . . . she *did* like it a bit, truth to tell, but it was awkward, even as her efforts to promote Julietta were awkward. Mr. Garrant was all that was pleasant, but he did not seem to be catching on to the fact that he was supposed to be falling in love with her cousin. It was yet another sign that he was not one of God's brightest creatures, for Imogene had been quite forward about it all. Fortunately, Julietta had not minded a bit being championed so consistently and artlessly, proving that she was just the right one for such a gentleman. Julietta did not care at all that Mister Garrant was slow. Imogene only wished *she* could remember what a dullard Mr. Garrant . . . Eddie . . . was when he was gazing down at her, and holding her hand, and asking her for yet another dance. There were times when she quite forgot to dislike him, and, too, those times when his presence made her nearly tingle. Oh, it was all so unsuitable, and quite insupportable!

Eddie stood at the door, resolved to wait out this latest of Genie's disappearing tricks, when a movement caught his eye. "Good day," he said down to the tousled, dark-headed child who crawled down the hall. The begowned infant looked up with somber eyes, evaluated him with the weighty stare of innocence, sat back on her nappies, and stretched up her arms to be carried. Always obedient to a lady's request, he bent and scooped her up. Eddie, who had long since grown used to being considered odd by the few who knew of his educational pursuits, was also aware that he was regarded as a curiously rare kind of male creature: one who actually has a fondness for children. He and the infant had a one minute "conversation," an exchange of gazes and wordless murmurs, and then a nursery maid appeared. "Sir!" she cried, and then explained, "Oh, that little Diana! She is too fast for me these days."

"Mobility is a wonderful thing," Eddie assured the maid. He did not, however, hand over the child, a sudden thought striking him. He had heard the thumps and bumps coming from over their heads, and had rightly deduced there was a

47

full nursery above stairs. It sounded as though the occupants were having so much more fun than the visitors below stairs, especially since Genie had gone into hiding, and surely no one could fault him for giving a little time to the younger Herrons. It seemed a proper enough thing for a guest to do. "Might I visit the nursery?" he asked the maid.

The maid looked at him as though he were half mad to make the request, but she nodded, turning to lead the way.

Imogene stayed in the room for over half an hour, finally slipping out when she was sure Mr. Garrant would not be looking for her, and quite possibly might have left altogether. She had no more than closed the door behind her when a streak of hair, knees, and elbows flew past her. A startled glance revealed this to be one of her cousins: eight-year-old Benjamin.

"I've taken the hill, you monster!" he cried, waving a broomstick in triumph.

"Hills are meant to be taken, but can you hold it?" cried a familiar voice. Imogene turned to look down the hall in the opposite direction, her mouth falling open when she saw Eddie Garrant there, his coat discarded, charging toward her.

She shrank back against the door as he dashed past her, and saw that he was brandishing a toy gun carved from wood. "Genie!" he called genially as he sped past, grinning as he tipped his head in her direction. Benjamin gave a whoop of alarm, "fired" his broomstick rifle once, and turned to run, his little legs pumping along the tiled corridor in haste. Eddie gave a growl, hot in pursuit, and the two disappeared into the kitchens.

"Good heavens," Imogene said faintly. She knew Eddie was slow-minded, but she had not envisioned him reduced to entertaining himself at the level of a child.

Just then another growl erupted from the kitchens, heralding their return, only now it was Benjamin's high-pitched voice doing the growling. Eddie loomed into view, his hair mildly disordered, glancing over his shoulder as he paced his retreat to be just a little in front of his pursuer.

"Genie!" he cried as he approached. " 'Tis lions, Genie. Run for your life!" He grabbed up her hand, yanking her along with him suddenly, just as she got a glimpse of other young cousins streaming from the kitchens behind Benjamin, their fingers held up in the posture of claws. She stumbled but recovered herself quickly, giving an involuntary laugh. Benjamin growled again, the sound imitated by his pursuing siblings, and with a glance at his serious little face, she gave up any struggle to retain a hint of dignity and cried, "Oh, lions! Mister Garrant, do protect me, please!"

He slid to a halt, pushing her behind him as he turned and raised the toy gun. "Bang!" he said, giving the gun a little pretended kickback motion. "Bang! Bang! Bang! I have shot every lion right through the heart."

Benjamin came up short, his hands springing to his chest. "Ahh! Ohh! Ehhh," he moaned, slipping slowly into a pile on the floor, his tongue lolling, his eyes closing. His brother and two sisters following suit, howling terribly until their voices faded away as they lay in a tangled heap of dead lions. Benjamin twitched a few times for effect, then lay still.

"Oh, my hero!" cried Genie, clapping her hands together, partly as her role called for it, and partly to commend the children's performances. Eddie turned to her, made a sign of triumph with a raised arm, and then grinned at her. The grin warmed, turned to a smile, and slid up to fill his eyes, joining some even warmer emotion there. He passed the gun from hand to hand, and finally allowed it to drop to the floor with a small clatter, his now empty hands reaching to slide over the top of hers, moving to stand rather near as he did so.

"It was my pleasure, ma'am," he said, and there was something throaty in the way he said it that made that funny tingling feeling start in her again.

They stood thus, he trying to catch her eye, she studiously avoiding it, when suddenly he lurched into her. Another feline roar resounded, and it was seen Benjamin was dangling from Eddie's waist, his arms firmly clenched around his victim's waistcoat.

"I did not manage to kill the beast!" Eddie cried, and then fell to his knees, aswarm with small bodies, knocked over by the relentless attack. He was quickly mauled, the participants laughing and tumbling in a heap at Imogene's feet.

She looked on, a part of her brain saying how wonderful Eddie would be with his own children. Should Julietta be able to attach his regard, she would be lucky in that particular respect. Really, that was a lot to wish for in a man, if one thought about it, to have a papa for your children who would not only parent them, but also enjoy them. It was certainly something Imogene would like to see in a man she meant to marry.

But . . . she sighed, thinking that Julietta must make great inroads with Mr. Garrant in the next few days, for the wedding was only three days hence. So far there had not been much in the way of sparks there. What was Imogene going to do? If only she had seen some warmer regard between the two, she would not now be having to worry so. As it stood, if nothing positively explosive happened in the next little while, she would find herself . . . what? Would she really go to the altar with Eddie? Or would she simply decline to show up? A few days ago she had known the answer to that, but now she was not so sure. All this fuss, with the wedding plans and clothes and all—could she just turn her shoulder coldly to it? Her father would be furious! Her mother would be humiliated, not to say anything about poor Eddie, left at the altar.

Imogene winced a little at the thought of hurting his feelings, even be they limited ones. *Would* it be so bad to be married to a man of Eddie's character, even if it was a flawed one? He was really a very good sort. She liked him a lot. What were a few brain cells? They had dealt rather well together the last few days, and he did not seem to gamble, drink, smoke, or do anything else to excess. But . . . she pursed her lips, wondering how she could live with a man who had not earned her regard. No, Eddie Garrant would be a perfect husband for Julietta, who saw no flaws in him at all. *She* even thought he was smart.

"I am Murat, and I have deserted Napoleon to join the Allies," Eddie cried, throwing his hands over his head in a sign of surrender.

"Then kneel, and pledge loyalty," Benjamin responded as he scrambled off the top of the well-dressed gentleman, his siblings following suit.

"I do so pledge," Eddie replied, one hand on his heart as he moved to one knee.

"Brave sir!" cried Benjamin, giving him a Frenchman's kiss for each cheek.

Eddie laughed, and saluted. "Now, my general, we must defeat the French at La Rothiere."

"Then Paris?" Benjamin cried.

"No, we must first take Bar-sur-Aube, and also Laon. Then we will be in Paris before we know it!"

Eddie leaped up and the pack bounded away again, he at the lead, leaving Imogene to stare after them. Slowly she stepped forward, following them, her ears ringing. Could that have been Eddie Garrant discussing military affairs? Not only discussing them, but incorporating them into play in a way that children could enjoy it, rationally and with correct detail?

She found them in the nursery, engaged in yet another fracas, the Napoleonic wars apparently abandoned for now.

"Governor," cried Benjamin.

"Governor-General," corrected Eddie.

"Governor-General, it is being reported that we have declared war. Is it true?" Benjamin stood stiffly at attention, awaiting his commander's reply.

"It is. The Gurkha of Nepal shall know we mean business!"

Benjamin's military stance fell aside for a moment as he leaned forward with bright eyes to ask, "May we fight from a fort?"

"Of course!" cried Eddie, leading the way to a pile of

toys, which they swiftly began to combine with furniture and anything else at hand to erect into a barricade. From behind this, they fired dozens of invisible shots, all of which were of perfect aim, at least to judge from the loud and frequent reports thereof. The cities of France? The peoples of Nepal? Was it possible Eddie knew whereof he spoke? Imogene looked on with the visage of someone who'd seen an apparition; amazement mingled with disbelief.

After a while she removed herself silently from the scene—where presently a recreation of Stephenson's steam locomotive was being ridden—and discovered her mother had left. There was a note for her that said she had shopping to do. Who could blame her, abandoned as she and Julietta had been for over an hour?

Julietta was working on the picture puzzle now, seemingly unaware of the commotion above stairs. There was another guest who had joined her: Eddie's good friend, Lord Brisbane. He was sitting rather near Julietta. Imogene knew him socially, and had been given to understand he was a good friend of Eddie's, and would in fact serve as best man. He was frowning over the puzzle, seemingly perplexed by the piece in his hand. He put down the piece, looking relieved, as soon as he saw her enter the room. "Ah, Miss Bradshaw!" he called genially.

Imogene smiled at him uncertainly, for she knew without a doubt that Quenton "Brisby" Brisbane's reputation as a simpleton was well based in fact. She had helped him find his carriage one night, a remarkable thing as his driver had been waving frantically at him from between two other carriages for at least five full minutes without being noted, and Lord Brisbane had been as sober as a judge. He was all that was good and kind, but swift in thought he was not.

Imogene sat down at the opposite side of the table, idly picking up a puzzle piece. She tried it at several places, then gave up the pretense. Instead she looked at her cousin, and said baldly, "I have heard you say that you think Mister Garrant is smart. Why is that?"

"Because he is. Or at least so I assume. Everyone says he hasn't a thing to say for himself, but I've seen his study."

"His study?"

"At his house," Lord Brisbane chimed in, nodding like a small boy who was proud to be included in an adult conversation.

"It's simply stuffed full of things, Genie," Julietta went on, giving Lord Brisbane an approving smile. Her eyes lingered on his not unhandsome face for a moment, but then she turned back to her cousin to explain further. "Books, newspapers, sheaves of paper. It's rather messy, and there's about a hundred things to look at every way you turn. Urns. Paintings. Statues. His housekeeper let it drop that she's not really allowed to clean up in there much. She says he doesn't like his work disturbed."

"His work?"

"He writes. Page after page, that's what she said. And it certainly looked like it. He would have had to clear off a chair if he'd wanted someone to sit down. Every surface with some project or other on it. We didn't stay though. He closed up the door right away, and said it was old, boring stuff."

"Why were you at his home?" Imogene said in a very quiet voice, her thoughts tumbling. She felt as though someone had just turned the world upside down.

Julietta smiled and shook her head. "For a party, of course, silly!"

Lord Brisbane joined her in a chuckle, and Imogene was not so far gone in thought that she missed the shy gazes they exchanged.

"Of course," Imogene murmured. She turned to Lord Brisbane. "And what do you say to my question, my lord?"

"Question?" Brisby echoed, his eyes finally having left Julietta's. One finger flicked at a puzzle piece on the table before him as if it were too near him, with its inherent challenge, for his comfort.

"Do you find Mister Garrant to be intelligent?"

"Oh, my yes!" Lord Brisbane said with several nods of

53

his head. "Scary what all he knows. Makes me shiver to think of it."

"Well then, if you do not mind my asking, how is it that you two are friends?" she asked bluntly.

He took no offense at the question. "Don't mind at all! Talked about it any number of times, we have. Me, so simple; him, so clever and all. We just like each other, you see. Eduardo's not one to stand on pretensions. Never has."

She looked upon Lord Brisbane, upon what instinct told her was a growing notice between he and her cousin, and knew that Julietta was not about to attract Mr. Garrant, not while he romped upstairs and she sat downstairs with Lord Brisbane at her elbow. She could plainly see the old adage was true, that "like runs to like": simple Lord Brisbane was attracted to uncomplicated Julietta, and she . . . yes, admit it, *she,* Imogene Bradshaw, was attracted to Eduardo Garrant. Suddenly that attraction made some sense to her, and she gave a funny hiccuping giggle. "Like runs to like," she mouthed aloud, thinking she could certainly just forget about her plan for Julietta and Eddie, as it obviously had failed. The strange thing was, she was not at all sure how she felt about that.

She rose slowly. She was so busy silently trying out the name "Eduardo"—which had a certain refinement to it that she had never noticed before—that she forgot to say goodbye to the hostess and her guest. She moved up toward the nursery.

She met Eddie in the hallway that led to the stairs. He had pulled off his cravat—no doubt ruined during the playing—and his face was slightly flushed. He smoothed his hair back into place with one hand, and smiled at her as he saw her.

Her heart did a triple somersault, and she stopped dead in her tracks, quite wary of letting him come close to her, for reasons she could not explain. All she knew was that his presence before her was making her heart pound quite uncomfortably. She said rapidly, "I was just coming to see if you could escort me home. Mama has left already."

"Of course," he answered brightly, his eyebrows arching up briefly when she turned and all but ran away down the stairs.

In the carriage, she was quiet. Perhaps that was because Miss Herron was not here, or perhaps it was because they were alone, without benefit of a mama or a chaperone. That would explain why she seemed a little pensive, with no female to lend their ride propriety and no cousin to promote.

Suddenly she asked, "Might we stop for a moment or two at your home, Eddie?"

"Of course," he said. Ah yes, she would want to see where she would be living after the wedding. Sometimes he was not at all sure she would actually arrive at the wedding, nor take a vow beside him, but this was a good sign. He made a practice of trying to catch her hand now and again, for when she lowered her eyes at his touch, he found he was able to hope it was not so much rejection as maidenly uncertainty. Something in the way she allowed him to hold her hand now and again encouraged him that she was going to see the betrothal through. Of course, no sooner would he think that then she'd be standing figuratively and literally behind Miss Herron. It was maddening, and caused flashes of panic to appear as green flecks in his eyes, for he had come to realize he wanted nothing so much as to marry Miss Genie Bradshaw.

This past week has been demmed difficult, for he found that when he was forward, she retreated. When he was solicitous and refrained, she came toward him, but all the while touting her cousin's charms. He gained nothing either way it seemed to him . . . but now she had asked to see his home. Wild hope leaped in his chest, which he carefully hid away, lest it be seen and cause her to change her mind. She seemed in a strange mood, and he had enough knowledge of women to know that one should not aggravate them when they are in strange moods. Especially not ones that you are in hopes of marrying.

She allowed him to take her hand as they stepped down

55

out of the carriage, but this time he was not so gentlemanly as to release it. Instead he pulled her behind him, until she stepped up to his side, then he wrapped her hand over his arm, fairly pinning her to his side. She said nothing, but neither did she pull away. He led her up the steps to the front door, still not releasing her. Was it possible she was trembling just a little? "Are you cold?" he asked as he reached for the handle.

"No," was the answer, given with lowered eyes.

He opened the door, leading her in.

"Your home is beautiful," she said with only one glance of the front hall, for it was tasteful and slightly understated, a reflection of the man, and she instinctively knew that the rest of the house would also be nicely appointed.

"Thank you," he said. "I suppose you would like to see the parlors or the ballroom first —"

She interrupted him, "No. I would like to see your study."

"My study?" he echoed, a quick flush staining his cheeks.

"Please." Now she did look up at him, and there was something deep and compelling about that look.

"Of course," he murmured though it was the last place he wished to show her. He knew his scribblings and his research did not impress the ladies. Of course, Genie was proving herself the exception to the mold, and that was enough to give him the fortitude to lead her down a short corridor, and push open the door to his study. He stepped in before her, at last releasing her hand that he could cross the room to pull back the curtains and let in some light.

The room was just as Julietta had described it: cluttered, filled with artifacts, a room where a great deal of intellectual pursuits took place. "Eddie," she said in a small voice. "This is really your study?"

He nodded, the stain on his cheeks growing a trifle larger.

"And this is really your work?" She touched a finger to a page of script on the desk near the window, the handwrit-

ing neat, a correction neatly initialed with the letters "E.G."
Again he nodded.

"Genie, just so you know . . . that is to say, I won't bore
company with talk of all this." He made a sweeping motion
that encompassed the whole room.

She turned to look at him, her head a little to one side in
a questioning manner, a slight smile beginning to form on
her lips.

He stepped toward her, taking up her hands, at which he
gazed, not meeting her inquiring look. "In fact, Genie . . .
I will understand if you don't wish to marry right away. I
know this has been hasty. When I was asked 'when,' June
seemed the right answer at the time . . . but, the thing of it
is, I wouldn't mind waiting. I know you have not had a lot
of time to adjust to this whole marriage idea." He gave a
short, embarrassed laugh. "I also know you've been trying
to make me aware of Miss Herron's charms—and she certainly has many—but the thing of it is, I don't really wish
to know Miss Herron any better." He lifted his eyes then,
briefly, only to glance down at her hands again where they
were suspended in his own. "But . . . so . . . we can put off
our wedding, if that's what you want. It doesn't have to be
in June. It doesn't even have to be soon. That is . . . the
thing of it is . . . just so long as you promise me that we
will marry one day."

"Why, Eddie," she said softly, for today had been a truly
amazing day, filled with amazing revelations. A warmth
flooded through her, and it had everything to do with the
entreaty in the eyes he raised again to hers.

Her voice, her words seemed warm and inviting. When
his hazel eyes looked into her soft brown ones and saw that
she was looking at him, really looking at him, with something far different from the disapproval he was used to seeing there, his lips parted slightly and he ceased to breathe
for a moment. "Genie?" he said tentatively, his hands tight-
ening over hers.

Now it was her turn to blush, but she did not look away.
"Eddie, I don't care what you wish to discuss with our

guests. Anything. Everything!" A laugh tripped from her mouth; it was an inviting laugh.

He shook his head, "I never want to look like a stupid, foolish boor for you—"

She laughed aloud then. "Oh, Eddie! You'll never seem that way to me, not after today."

"Today?" he echoed, puzzled but smiling along with her laughter.

"Ask me to explain on our first anniversary. Our *June* anniversary."

He blinked, stunned by the words. She would have him, and soon, and with apparent pleasure at the prospect. He pulled her a little closer, and when she did not pull away, indeed leaned into him, her face raised toward his invitingly, his hands slipped from hers to slide around her, pressing her firmly along his length. He lowered his head, his breath mingling with hers, their eyes caressing each other's faces, reading the astonishing news of attraction and approval there. Then he pressed his warm lips to hers, tentatively at first, but when her hands slid up to his shoulders he kissed her more deeply, as he had longed to do for a week past. It didn't matter that they had only recently learned the truth about each other; in that kiss they learned a lot more, knowledge that rocked them both when at last their lips came apart.

"I've been such a fool," she murmured.

"To say you'd marry me?" He felt a moment's panic.

She shook her head emphatically. "To think that I might not."

He hugged her tightly then. "Shall we wed on Saturday after all? Say we shall."

"We shall."

A throat was cleared, and they turned in each other's arms to find Julietta and Lord Brisbane standing there, the latter's eyes large and rounded. "Er . . . um," Lord Brisbane said.

Imogene did not know if Eddie had gotten the habit from Lord Brisbane, or the other way around, but now it made her shake her head and grin to hear the familiar mutterings.

Lord Brisbane rubbed his nose, looked confounded, and finally made a fluttering motion with his hand in her direction. Eddie seemed to understand the cryptic motions, for he smiled at him, and said, "Yes, Brisby, this is the lady I was telling you about."

"Jolly good!" Brisbane approved. "Had me worried for a minute there. I appreciate it that you've made it simple for me to remember who's who and what's what! Very convenient that the one you're in love with is your bride, don't you know."

"I couldn't agree more." Eddie grinned down at Genie, pulling her closer into the circle of his arms.

"Whatever does he mean?" Genie smiled up at him, mildly perplexed, but her eyes were glittering at the acknowledgment he had just made.

"Ask me on our first anniversary. Our *June* anniversary," Eddie echoed, and then he kissed her, uncaring that they had an audience, just as he kissed her three days later, not caring that their obvious infatuation for one another might make them look unfashionably foolish.

A Match For Marigold

by

Mona Gedney

"The very idea of leaving a young girl without a penny to bless herself with!" muttered Sarah into the depths of the trunk she was carefully packing. "I suppose that he never gave a thought to what would become of his only child when he died."

Miss Marigold Morrison, the young woman who was the subject of her diatribe, had been until just two months ago Miss Marigold Morrison of Thurston Hall, daughter of the dashing Sir Vincent Morrison. Now, with the untimely demise of that gentleman in a boating accident in Greece, she found herself literally without a roof over her head. Sir Vincent's estate had been so encumbered with debt that the Hall had had to be sold to settle his affairs and satisfy his creditors. Selling it had been painful for Marigold, but it had also been the final impetus needed for her to decide to try her luck on the London stage.

"Yes, but, Sarah, I don't believe Papa *meant* to die just yet," responded Marigold absently, her mind on their imminent removal to London. "I know that he didn't seem to think of me often, but he was still quite a young man. I'm sure that he thought he would have time to provide for me properly."

An eloquent sniff from Sarah indicated her opinion of the late Sir Vincent's honorable intentions. "Your mother would turn over in her grave if she knew that you were being turned out of your home without a feather to fly with."

Marigold smiled as she looked at the silver-framed picture of her mother lying on the coverlet, waiting to be wrapped in tissue and packed away in the trunk. "It isn't quite that bad, Sarah. I do have a little of

Mama's money left, so I'm not entirely penniless."

Sarah, snapping a drawer shut smartly, forbore to mention the fact that the late Sir Vincent, after squandering all of his own inheritance, had run carelessly through most of his wife's money as well. Only the part specifically left in trust for Marigold had been left intact. If he had devoted any thought at all to his only child, left motherless at the age of eight, it had not been apparent in his actions. Beyond providing Marigold with a suitable governess and sending her a present now and then from his travels, he had troubled himself not at all about her. Miss Ismene Turner, the governess, had left her last year, Sir Vincent having decided that Marigold had no more need of her services. It had worked out quite neatly, for Miss Turner's annual wage just covered one of his smaller but more pressing debts, and an elderly uncle of Miss Turner's had chosen to pass to his heavenly reward and to leave his earthly goods to her. Sir Vincent had naturally not concerned himself about Miss Turner's situation, but the news of her inheritance had soothed Marigold's conscience. Marigold had been sorry to lose her, for she was very fond of Miss Turner, but she had not been inconsolable for she had still had Sarah to turn to. Sarah had been her mother's maid from the time they were both girls of sixteen, and she had stayed on after Lady Camilla's death, devoting herself to Marigold.

"Come now, Sarah," Marigold said cheerfully. "We are quite poor, but not penniless. That is the way things are at the present moment."

"Well, that may be the way things are, Miss Marigold, but it *oughtn't* to be the way things are! And that's all that I have to say!" Sarah paused in her efforts to close the lid of the trunk, pushing back a wisp of graying hair that had escaped from her cap. Plump and pink-cheeked, she had protected and fussed over Marigold all of her life and had never forgiven Sir Vincent for choosing to spend his life away from his child.

Marigold smiled to herself and drew a chair close to their work. She knew from years of experience that Sarah's words indicated the beginning of a speech rather than the end of one. As she waited for Sarah to continue, she began to hum softly, patting one small slippered foot in time.

"And what's more," resumed Sarah, having straightened her cap and apron to her satisfaction, "if I had my say in the matter, you would not for a single moment be thinking of going to London. You, a gently brought up young woman, talking about going on the stage! Why, I don't know how I would ever explain this to poor Lady Camilla!"

"Mama would understand," responded Marigold firmly. "I really have no choice, Sarah. You know that the money that I have will not keep me very long. Even if I take up permanent residence with Ismene in London as she has very kindly asked me to, I should have to pay my share of the household expenses."

"Yes, Miss Marigold, but to think about going on the stage—"

"Is to throw my good name away with both hands," her graceless charge finished smoothly, having heard this speech many times before. "But I am to be a singer, Sarah dearest, not an actress. And you *know* that I can sing and make people stop what they are doing and listen to me!"

She stood up quickly and leaped lightly upon her chair, striking a pose with a hand on each hip, and began a lively rendition of "Jack the Jolly Tar." From the moment she had been old enough to walk, Marigold had climbed on top of anything that would serve as a stage and sung her heart out, and invariably she had drawn an admiring crowd. Her mother and Sarah had learned early to keep a careful eye on her in public places; otherwise, they had been likely to find themselves the center of attention while she gave an impromptu concert. Indeed, she was likely to be the focus of all eyes whether she sang or not, for her warm loveliness had drawn others like moths to a candle flame, her feathery gold curls framing a dimpled, merry face and roguish brown eyes.

Her beauty still turned heads, as it had when she was a child. Small, but elegantly formed, her figure was graceful, and no local lady was more adept on the dance floor. Sarah reflected grimly that if Sir Vincent Morrison had provided even an adequate portion for his daughter, she could have had her pick of any young man in the country, for she was not only lovely, but sunny in disposition as well. And when she sang — well, everyone within earshot stopped what they were doing to listen to her. They smiled, or laughed, or cried, all as her voice commanded.

Despite her disapproval now of Marigold's hoydenish behavior and equally hoydenish choice of song, Sarah could not help smiling and tapping her foot in time as she listened to the amorous adventures of Jack, that jolly tar. When the song was over and Marigold hopped off the chair in a flurry of lavender skirts and black velvet slippers, Sarah quickly assumed a disapproving frown.

"Ned Miller should never have taught you so many of those sailors' songs, Miss Marigold. It's not proper for a young lady to be singing such things. And at the top of your voice, too."

Taking Sarah's worn, capable hands in both of her own, Marigold pulled her to her feet and turned her briskly around the room as she hummed a lively little tune. "Sarah, you fraud," she chuckled. "You love Ned's songs as much as I do. And I've seen you dance with him, so don't play the prim and proper lady with me."

Sarah straightened her cap and smiled reluctantly as

Marigold released her hands at the end of the dance. "And so I may have, Miss Marigold, but neither Ned nor I are ladies with a reputation to consider—a reputation that you seem to care nothing about."

Marigold sighed and patted the stack of sheet music on the little table next to her. "Of course, I care about my reputation, Sarah, but it must be a pretty poor thing if singing a sailor's song can sully it."

She sat down and began to thumb through the music. "And I *must* sing, Sarah. You know that. It's of no use to tell me I mustn't. And I must make my way in the world. I am not suited to be a governess, for although I read a little French and play the pianoforte, I have none of the other skills someone like Ismene has."

She grabbed Sarah's hands and smiled into her worried eyes. "And besides, Sarah, can you imagine anything more outrageous than me as a governess?"

"You needn't become a governess, child. You know very well that you could marry young Will Grantham any time you say the word," returned Sarah.

"Indeed I could not!" replied Marigold sharply. "I've not the slightest intention of marrying Will Grantham and settling down to a dull life of horses and children. I wouldn't be happy nor would I make poor Will happy. His father and mother would forever be casting it up to him—and to me—that he had married a penniless girl. So, no, Sarah. I won't consider Will Grantham or any of the others you are about to name," she added, forestalling any further suggestions.

And so it was that a few weeks later Marigold, accompanied by the reluctant Sarah, set forth for London to seek her fortune. Marigold planned to make her residence with the faithful Miss Ismene Turner, and there to set about the business of becoming a singer and earning her bread and butter. Sarah, still heartily disapproving of the scheme, insisted nonetheless upon accompanying her. Dragonlike, she announced darkly that she would accompany Marigold wherever she went in London. She also insisted that they spend the money to make their journey by post rather than by the common stage for she knew what was due a lady even if Marigold did not. Marigold gave way to her, grateful to have her company, but insisted that Sarah accompany her as companion rather than maid.

The second evening of their journey found them at the White Hart, a pleasant country inn that catered to the carriage trade. Sarah, having settled Marigold comfortably in her quarters, went downstairs to order a snug little supper to be served in the privacy of their room. Marigold had protested, wishing to dine downstairs and observe their fellow travelers, but, upon seeing that Sarah was firmly set against it, had submitted meekly, reserving her energy for more important battles.

Instead, she had opened her casement to the sharp night air of early spring, hoping to have a glimpse of some late arriving travelers. To her disappointment she saw that her window overlooked a quiet garden, but she settled herself comfortably, staring up at the stars and dreaming dreams of a great musical triumph in London. She had been lost in thought for several minutes when she heard the low murmur of voices from the darkness below.

"Full of juice, the old lady is. Shouldn't miss a chance like this, me lad. She's only got one other Friday-faced old maid with her."

There was a snort from his companion. "Simple enough for you to say, Riley. You're not the one as will lose your place if something goes amiss."

"Nothin'll go wrong. I'll use the ladder and come in by the window. You've done your job a-pointin' out her room. It'll be plain as a pikestaff that it weren't somebody what lives in the inn that nabbled the goods. Don't be such a pudding-heart, man."

Amid muttered protests at this term, the voices faded

from her hearing as the two men made their way around the corner of the building. Marigold leaned out as far as she could, straining to catch a glimpse of them in the shadows, but she could see nothing. Turning quickly, she opened her door and ran lightly down the stairs in search of Sarah.

That good lady was scandalized to see her charge come hurrying into the common taproom, threading her way through a host of interested gentlemen. Before she could begin to scold, however, Marigold was pouring forth her story in a low voice and asking Sarah if she knew of an elderly lady traveling alone with her maid. Together they sought the landlord and Marigold again recounted her story. The landlord, a thin, harried man, looked as though he would like to doubt the possibility of a servant of his being party to a robbery, but, upon being questioned sharply by the redoubtable Sarah, was forced to admit that there was such a lady staying at the inn.

"But every precaution will be taken, miss," he assured her. "There is no need to trouble Lady Ariadne with such a matter."

Marigold stared at him open-mouthed. "Do you mean that you do not intend to tell her of this?" she demanded.

The landlord looked uncomfortable, thinking of the unfavorable reaction his news was likely to draw from one of his more faithful, but irascible, customers. Lady Ariadne Stone stopped at the White Hart frequently on her way to London, for that hostelry was a comfortable halfway point between the city and Valwood, her country estate. She was fond of her comforts and regrettably quick, the landlord felt, to point out any shortcomings in the service.

"Lady Ariadne Stone has a somewhat uncertain temper. Such news as this would undoubtedly keep her from sleeping well tonight," he informed them.

"You must mean that you don't wish to tell her because she would be angry," said Marigold briskly. "Well, it can't be helped, for she must be informed of this. Tell me, landlord, in which room I may find her, and I will tell her myself."

Relieved to at least be spared of breaking the news himself, the landlord hastened to inform her that they would find Lady Ariadne in the Blue Room at the top of the stairs, and please to tell her that every precaution was being taken to ensure her safety and the apprehension of the would-be thieves.

When Marigold, closely accompanied by Sarah, knocked upon the door of the Blue Room, it was opened by a tall, angular woman, gray with regard to hair, complexion, and dress. Before she could open her mouth, a sharp voice from within the room demanded, "Well, Spence, don't just stand there, woman! Who is it?"

"I'm sure that I don't know, my lady, not having had time to ask the young woman," responded the gray lady dryly, glancing over her shoulder at the invisible speaker.

Then, turning back to Marigold, she said, "May I say who is calling, miss?"

"Tell her ladyship that Miss Marigold Morrison, daughter of the late Sir Vincent Morrison, wishes to speak with her," said Sarah briskly, taking charge of the situation.

The gray lady regarded Sarah with some surprise, and Marigold felt compelled to add, "And this is my traveling companion, Miss Sarah Appleby."

"Sir Vincent Morrison, is it?" called the voice from within. "Went and got himself killed, didn't he? Not but what it's to be expected if you go gadding all over the world! Well, Spence, what are you waiting for? Bring the girl in so I can see her!"

Spence stood back, opening the door wide enough for

the two of them to enter, then shut it briskly behind them. Next to a blazing fire sat an elderly woman as gray and angular as Spence, but with an infinitely more commanding presence. Jewels sparkled on her hands and at her throat as she studied Marigold keenly through gold-rimmed spectacles perched on a thin, hawklike nose.

"So you're Sir Vincent's girl, are you? He was a charming man—a ne'er-do-well, of course—but a charming one."

Marigold regarded her with a mixture of amusement and indignation. "What you say may be very true, ma'am, but I don't believe it's quite the thing to be saying so to his daughter."

Spence looked at her in amazement and appeared to brace herself for a storm for Lady Ariadne was not accustomed to having people speak to her in such a fashion. Instead, Lady Ariadne uttered a sharp bark of laughter.

"Good for you, my girl! Give as good as you get. Come in and sit down. Spence, what are you waiting for? Bring us some tea!"

While Spence hurried about to take care of the refreshments Marigold and Sarah seated themselves, and Marigold found herself being carefully scrutinized again. "Your mama was Camilla Greystokes, wasn't she?"

Marigold nodded and Lady Ariadne sighed. "You have something of her look about your eyes and mouth. She was a lovely child—wasted on a man like Vincent Morrison though."

Sarah regarded Lady Ariadne with a more kindly eye, being of the same opinion herself, but Marigold coughed gently and the old lady laughed. "Trying to call me to order, are you, my girl? Well, perhaps you are in the right of it. I'll say no more about your father."

71

She sat deep in thought for a moment, and the others waited politely for her to take up the conversation again. Spence served their tea, and over the rim of her teacup Lady Ariadne studied Marigold again.

"Very kind of you to come and make yourself known to me, Miss Morrison, but how came you to do so? I'm sure your parents never spoke of me."

Marigold shook her head. "No, that isn't what brought me here, Lady Ariadne. I'm afraid that I overheard a plan to rob you tonight."

Spence gave a small shriek, but Lady Ariadne's dark eyes only glittered more brightly. "A plan to rob me, you say?"

Marigold nodded and proceeded to recount the events of the evening. When she told Lady Ariadne that the landlord had been less than willing to tell her of the plot, that lady chuckled.

"He knew I'd give him the rough side of my tongue, that's what, and he was anxious that you bear the brunt of my bad temper." She sat for a moment, thinking deeply. "I'm very grateful to you, my dear, both for telling that dratted landlord and then for telling me. He'd never have had the backbone to do so himself."

She turned to Spence. "Spence, go to the stable and tell John Ballard that I need him right away and that he is to bring Cox with him, too. The landlord may make whatever arrangements he wishes. I'll trust my own people to see after me."

Spence hurried to do her bidding and Marigold and Sarah stood to take their leave. Lady Ariadne, however, settled herself more comfortably in her chair and said, "Now, Miss Marigold Morrison, sit down and tell me about yourself. How came you here and where are you going?"

And so, in an unselfconscious, natural way, Marigold did just that, with Lady Ariadne listening closely. Her manner did her no harm in the old lady's eyes, for the artificial airs and graces of young society misses bored her. Marigold told her story simply, with no hint of self-pity in word or tone. When she had finished she sat quietly, studying Lady Ariadne in quite the same manner that that lady was studying her.

"And so you think you can sing, do you?" she asked abruptly.

Marigold simply nodded in reply.

"Let's hear you then!" commanded Lady Ariadne. "Don't need a pianoforte to be able to sing, do you?"

In reply, Marigold lifted her voice in a merry tune, her dimples deepening as she watched Lady Ariadne's expression. Sarah lifted her eyes heavenward. Of all the melodies she might have chosen, the child had to pick "There's Whiskey in the Jar," an Irish song about a gentleman of the roads who robs the English landlords. Marigold showed what Sarah could only regard as a regrettable tendency to put herself into the song heart and soul, swaggering about the room as she sang, "I rattled me pistols and I drew me saber."

It did not appear that either her choice of song or her manner had done her any disservice in Lady Ariadne's eyes, however, for once the initial shock had worn away, the old lady was patting her hand against the arm of her chair and humming the refrain with Marigold. When the last "whack fal the daddy-o" had died away, she smiled at the girl and nodded her head once, sharply.

"You'll do, my girl," she said enigmatically. "There's nothing missish about you."

"I take it that you mean that as a compliment, Lady Ariadne, so I'll thank you. There are some who I could name that feel I should be a bit more missish than I am." Here Marigold arched her eyebrow in Sarah's direction.

"Don't listen to 'em. London's swarming with girls like that, but you're something quite out of the ordi-

73

nary—and you are quite right—you *can* sing. Your voice would charm a bee out of a honey pot."

Lady Ariadne sank into a brown study, and Marigold and Sarah, uncertain as to whether or not she had fallen asleep, waited for Spence's return before standing up to leave.

Before they reached the door, the old lady raised her head and spoke suddenly. "I would like to thank you again for your warning, Miss Morrison. And I must see you again before you leave tomorrow morning. Will you come to my room for breakfast?"

Marigold assured her that they would like to check on her before leaving and, looking back before closing the door softly behind them, saw the old lady sitting with her chin resting on her hands, staring into the fire. Marigold thought that Lady Ariadne had sunk into a gentle doze. She would have been greatly surprised to know that the old lady's mind was working rapidly and still more surprised to hear her final words to Spence before going to bed.

"She may be just what I'm looking for, Spence." She nodded her head emphatically, tied the ribbons of her nightcap under her chin, and plumped her pillow. "Just what I'm looking for."

The night passed without incident—or at least without any incident that disturbed the slumbers of Lady Ariadne and Spence. John Ballard and Cox, assisted by the landlord and two of the stableboys, captured Riley, an itinerant peddler, in the very act of hoisting a ladder to Lady Ariadne's window. Despite his protests he was taken firmly in hand and turned over to the local magistrate. He promptly identified his partner in crime, one of the cook's assistants, who was also brought before the magistrate. The ladder was put away and everyone except the vigilant John Ballard adjourned to their beds. Ballard allowed that they had caught the thieves, but announced that he, for one, would not rest easily

74

until they had made it through the entire night without further incident. So Lady Ariadne slept on, well protected.

At breakfast the next morning, Lady Ariadne took Marigold entirely by surprise.

"You must come home to Valwood with me," announced Lady Ariadne abruptly. "You and Appleby both."

Marigold looked at her in astonishment. "But we are going to London, Lady Ariadne. It is very kind of you to invite us, but—"

"Kind, fiddlesticks!" retorted that lady. "You saved my jewels and my money and, for all I know, my life as well. It's no more than right that you come to me for a few weeks. Particularly when you have no family of your own now."

"But, Lady Ariadne," said Marigold patiently, "I'm going to London to become a singer. I explained that to you last night."

"Not the thing for a gently bred young girl," said Lady Ariadne firmly. "Not the kind of life for you at all."

"And so I have told her, my lady, time and time again." Sarah, recognizing an ally, rushed into the fray.

"But it's what I *want* to do and what I need to do as well. And Miss Turner is expecting us."

"We'll send a message to your Miss Turner that you'll be along in a few weeks. In the meantime you could spend some time with me at Valwood, and," she hurried on, before Marigold could begin to protest again, "I can invite a few of my London friends who are knowledgeable about music down to meet you. That would help you, would it not, my girl?"

Marigold stared at her, and then nodded slowly. "Indeed it would, Lady Ariadne. That would be very kind of you, for of course I know no one in London, except Ismene Turner. It would be very helpful to know some

75

people connected with the music world there."

"Consider it done then. Pack your things and John Ballard will be to your room in two shakes to pick them up."

And, true to her word, within the hour they were all on their way to Valwood, Marigold somewhat bemused by this sudden change of plan, and Sarah clearly elated by it.

In Havisham's of London, an exclusive dining club for gentlemen, Mr. Charles Lawford sat back comfortably in his chair after an elegant repast and prepared to enjoy an hour or so of good conversation with Lord Easterley, one of his oldest and dearest friends. Later that evening they would adjourn to the theater and later still to a delightful supper with two very charming ladies. All was as it should be in Mr. Lawford's carefully ordered and very satisfying world.

"Will you be attending Lady Jersey's ball tomorrow evening, Dev?" inquired Mr. Lawford lazily, holding his glass of claret to the light and admiring the richness of its color. "I shall have to order a waistcoat of this shade," he murmured to himself. "It really is quite striking."

His friend was watching him with an air of affectionate amusement. "I would say that you should order one in that shade, Charles. It would become you. And within two days half of the young bucks in London will be wild to have that very same color and that very same cut. You will make your tailor another fortune."

Lawford shrugged gently. "Forbes is a good man, Dev. He deserves it." He continued to regard the color of the wine thoughtfully. "It isn't a shade that everyone should wear, however. Someone like Crawford, for instance," and here he indicated with a nod a tall, beefy man at another table, "would look better in bottle green. His complexion is already the color of claret. To add a waistcoat of the same would be too much of a good thing."

Lawford held up his quizzing glass and scrutinized his companion carefully. "You could wear claret, Dev. Or bottle green or primrose for that matter. I have often envied you that dark hair and coloring. You must always appear to advantage in any color."

"You flatter me, Charles," returned Lord Easterley gravely, although his eyes were bright with amusement. "Since your taste is held to be impeccable, I can only feel honored."

Lawford inclined his head slightly, acknowledging the justice of his thanks. His fair good looks and finely chiseled profile could mislead the unwary. More than one young gentleman new to London, having made a disparaging comment about Lawford's manner, had been shocked by his whipcord strength and the quickness of his responses. Lord Easterley, however, knew his man and prized him. Lawford was no milksop but a man of many parts, quick-witted, agile, cynical, and amusing.

"I repeat, Dev, shall you be going to Lady Jersey's tomorrow evening?"

Lord Easterley nodded. "Which lady will you honor with your attention, Charles?"

"The lovely Davington, I believe," said Lawford thoughtfully. "I should like to draw attention to her, and so I think I shall make one of her train."

"You will surely place the seal upon her success then, Charles. She has been cast into the shade by Miss Lyle's arrival in London, but attracting your regard must surely be a feather in her cap."

"Your confidence in me is touching, Dev."

"But not misplaced. There is no man in London with your power to command the respect of the ton. Only Brummell has come close to equaling you."

"But I, Dev, shall not have to leave the country under a cloud."

Lord Easterley chuckled. "Hardly," he agreed. Charles Lawford was a man of considerable fortune, unlike the unfortunate Beau Brummell. Like Brummell, however, he could make or break the reputation and popularity of any newcomer to the ton, and his presence at any gathering assured the hostess of an instant success. His taste was considered faultless, his manners distinguished, his wit delightful.

There was a sudden bustle at the door, and Mr. Lawford held his glass to his eye, frowning as he saw his valet bearing down upon him.

"What is it, Netherington?" he inquired.

Netherington, almost as elegant a figure as his master, bowed. "I beg your pardon for intruding upon you, sir, but I knew that you would wish to receive this letter immediately, and I did not wish to entrust it to a footman."

Here he handed a large cream-colored envelope to his master. "Cox, Lady Ariadne's man, brought it personally and indicated that it was most urgent, or I should not have interrupted your evening."

Lawford slit open the envelope, still frowning. Lady Ariadne Stone was his aunt, and although they disagreed about almost everything, they were nonetheless very fond of one another. He scanned the missive quickly while Lord Easterley discreetly studied the paintings on the opposite wall.

"Did Cox tell you what this was all about, Netherington?" inquired Lawford sharply, folding the sheet of heavy paper and placing it within its envelope.

Netherington shook his head regretfully. "I did my best, sir, but he insisted that he knew nothing of the matter."

"And that I do not believe. Cox always knows everything about my aunt's affairs." He shook his head and sighed. "But if he is not supposed to talk of it, he won't. So I suppose that I must post down to Valwood immediately."

"Tonight?" exclaimed Lord Easterley indignantly. "Do you mean to say that we must cancel our plans for theater and supper?"

Lawford nodded regretfully but firmly. "I'm afraid so, Dev. She writes that she has a serious emergency on her hands and that only I can help her with it. So, you see, I have no choice. I must go."

"I suppose so, Charles. But what the devil does she think you can do to help her? She has her own man of business, a very competent one, and someone to oversee the estate, doesn't she?"

Charles nodded. "But she doesn't state the nature of the emergency, Dev, so I have no idea what I may be encountering."

Turning to his valet he said briskly, "I shall plan to stay at Valwood two or three days, Netherington, and you, of course, shall accompany me. Have Hatcher prepare the carriage for us."

When Bowles showed him into Lady Ariadne's drawing room late the following evening, he was surprised to find her chatting cozily with a very lovely young woman quite as though nothing was amiss. Not unreasonably after his hurried trip, he felt a decided irritation of spirit to see his aunt in a situation that indicated no distress of spirit. Advancing toward the ladies, he prepared to deliver a razor-sharp setdown to his aunt for having inconvenienced him for no apparent reason.

Anticipating his purpose, however, Lady Ariadne said pleasantly, "Why, Charles, how good of you to come so quickly. I would like to make known to you Miss Marigold Morrison. Marigold, this is my nephew, Mr. Charles Lawford, of whom I have been telling you."

Balked of his prey, Lawford stopped to bow over the hand of the young lady whose loveliness had already

79

struck him. Indeed, so enchanting was the face she raised to him as they were introduced that he felt oddly short of breath. Like any halfling, he told himself irritably, rather than a gentleman accustomed to the company of the most celebrated beauties of the ton. He noted with mounting annoyance that his aunt was aware of his reaction, so he raised his quizzing-glass to his eye and regarded her frostily.

"From the tone of your letter, Aunt Ariadne, I scarcely expected to find you calmly taking tea in the drawing room when I arrived. I thought at the very least some of the local villagers would be storming the battlements of Valwood or that I would find you at death's door. Perhaps I misread your note?"

"Don't be so cross, Charles. It's not becoming. And take away that ridiculous glass from your eye and stop looking as though you'd like to give me a heavy setdown for you can't do it."

She turned to Marigold, who had been watching this exchange with interest. "Don't judge him by this, my girl," she said briskly. "And don't be put off by any of his languishing, dandified posturing either. He is a man worth his salt and he came straightaway because he thought I was in the briars."

Marigold, glancing at Lawford, saw that amusement had struggled with outrage and disbelief and had overcome them. His mobile, intelligent face still retained its grim expression, but his lips were twitching and his blue eyes were bright with laughter. Letting his glass fall and dangle from the black ribbon that held it, he seated himself next to her, crossing his legs gracefully. Not even a hurried trip could cause him to look less than immaculate: his biscuit-colored pantaloons were uncreased, his top boots shone in the firelight, his cravat was snowy and folded artistically, his blond hair was carefully arranged in the fashionable windblown look. Marigold, regarding him with a mixture of amazement and amusement, reflected that he could have stepped from the pages of one of her fashion magazines. She noted, however, that although his pose was a languid one, his expression was alert. She had no doubt that this was a man of quick perception.

"You are impossible, aunt. I rush down from town in a neck-or-nothing fashion to rescue you from some unknown peril, and I find you calmly sipping tea and cutting my character to shreds."

"Much better, Charles," said Lady Ariadne approvingly. "You are much more taking without that toplofty manner."

Charles inclined his head graciously. "Your opinion, aunt, must ever be of the greatest consequence to me."

"He doesn't mean that, of course," remarked Lady Ariadne to Marigold. "That's why Charles and I have always gotten on well. We neither of us give a groat for what anyone else thinks of us."

"How attractive you make us sound to Miss Morrison, aunt. Two care-for-nobodies. She must be wondering what ill fortune brought her to us."

Lawford turned his attention to Marigold, wondering indeed what *had* brought her to his aunt. Lady Ariadne had a host of female relations who were eager to spend their time with their very wealthy relative, but she would not allow them at Valwood, saying that she found them all annoying. "Wouldn't want my company if I were a penniless old woman!" she had snapped when he had inquired once why she did not invite at least one of them to keep her company. "Wouldn't have the time of day for me then, and I know it, so they can save themselves the trouble of writing me pretty notes and sending little kickshaws and inquiring after my health and naming their children after me! They won't get a shilling now or when I'm gone!"

The young lady before him bore little resemblance to any of Lady Ariadne's grasping relatives. They were all inclined to be dowdy and rather plain, but Miss Marigold Morrison was what the young bucks in town would describe as a diamond of the first water. Her silk gown was simply but elegantly cut and of precisely the same shade of claret that he had been admiring the evening before. No poor relation this. His suspicions were aroused though, for he wondered what circumstances could place a young woman like this in company with Lady Ariadne. She might not look like the greedy relations, but she might share their interest in his aunt.

"Miss Morrison is Sir Vincent Morrison's daughter, Charles," said Lady Ariadne.

He looked at her in surprise. "Then I must offer you my condolences upon your loss, Miss Morrison. I had the pleasure of meeting your father and dining with him once in Venice. He was an excellent companion."

"So I understand, Mr. Lawford." He glanced at her questioningly and she continued, "I did not know him well, you see. He was home very little even when my mother was alive, and since her death ten years ago he had been back to Thurston Hall only three times."

She spoke lightly for her father's defection had long since ceased to trouble her. Had it not been for the change his death had made in her own worldly circumstances, his loss would have touched her no more than that of a chance acquaintance. Thus the face she turned to Lawford was bright-eyed and merry, rather than the sorrowful one he expected to see in such a situation.

He felt himself drawn by her liveliness and freshness, as well as her beauty, but he resisted the feeling. Lawford was no hypocrite, but he was vaguely troubled that her manner should be so cheerful only three months after her father's death, no matter how distant their relationship. He noted also that she was not dressed in the deep mourning that society dictated.

"Miss Morrison is doing me the favor of spending a

few weeks at Valwood," explained Lady Ariadne. "She has already brightened this place amazingly."

Mr. Lawford looked surprised, as well he might since Lady Ariadne had never before indicated that she felt Valwood needed brightening. He cocked a questioning eyebrow at her.

"Having a fit of the dismals, aunt? I had no idea that you were or I would have posted down here immediately."

Lady Ariadne, revolted by this mawkish picture of herself, denied it with spirit. "Naturally I have not been moping about, Charles. I am not so poor-spirited that I need you posting down here to hold my hand because I feel blue-deviled. I told you that I needed you here, Charles, and that nobody else but you would be able to help me. And that is absolutely true!"

"My apologies, aunt. How may I help you?"

There was a slight pause during which Lady Ariadne studied her nephew closely. "I was very fond of your mother, Charles. She and your father—and you, of course—are the only relatives I have ever had the least use for."

He looked at her in amusement. "I am touched by your tribute, naturally. But what has that to say to anything? You must have had a reason to send for me other that to tell me that you are fond of me."

Lady Ariadne nodded abruptly. "Of course I did, Charles. If I weren't so fond of you, I wouldn't trouble myself about you and I wouldn't have told you to come."

As he waited for her to make her meaning clear, his eyes strayed back to Marigold. She, too, was watching Lady Ariadne, a small furrow of perplexity lining her brow. Suddenly she arose, smoothing the skirts of her claret gown.

"If you'll excuse me, Lady Ariadne, I'll allow the two of you to speak in privacy. I beg your pardon for not having realized sooner that my presence was not needed."

Lady Ariadne shook her head sharply and raised a be-ringed hand to stop her. "No, Marigold, this concerns you as well."

Marigold's puzzled expression deepened and Lawford's eyebrows lifted almost to his hairline.

"But, Lady Ariadne, how could your affairs and those of your nephew concern me? I am virtually a stranger to you and . . ." Here she paused and glanced at Lawford, then continued, "to your family."

Lawford looked at her approvingly. "I must admit, aunt, that I was thinking much the same thing as Miss Morrison, although I would have hesitated to say so in her presence."

"Well, it does concern her, and it concerns you, too, Charles. I didn't know Marigold until we met a few days ago, but I had met her parents, Sir Vincent and Lady Camilla, whose mother, Isabella, Duchess of Clarington, was a dear friend of my childhood. So you see, I know about Marigold. She is of good family. And it is a thousand pities, child," she said to Marigold, "that the title should have passed to another branch of your family."

Her nephew looked at her quizzically. "I grant you that Miss Morrison comes from an excellent family. I have no reason to doubt that at all." Nor any reason to wish to doubt it, he added silently, wondering what his aunt was about. She had always been a remarkably keen-witted woman, but it appeared that her mind must now be slipping. Her next words confirmed his worst suspicions.

"I think, Charles, that you should marry Miss Morrison."

If she had announced that she was about to take a trip across the Sahara on the back of a camel, her listeners could not have been more shocked.

"I *cannot* have heard you aright," responded Lawford in disbelief. "What are you talking about, aunt?"

Marigold stood stock-still, her hands clasped tightly together. Her eyes had not left Lady Ariadne's face.

"Lady Ariadne, I thought I had explained quite clearly that I do not mean to marry. If I had planned to do so, I would have married Will Grantham and had done with it."

"You see, aunt," said Lawford dryly, not particularly pleased by her reaction, "your suggestion meets with no approval from either of the parties most concerned. And I confess that I cannot imagine what possessed you to think for a moment that I would be willing to marry now and at your command, and to marry a lady of your choice rather than my own."

"I have seen, Charles, that you have made no effort to choose a bride and to settle down. For ten years you have had your choice of eligible girls, but no one has taken your fancy. You have been catered to and your every whim satisfied for too long. You have been spoiled and no simpering miss with die-away airs will do for you. You need a quite extraordinary wife, someone intelligent and charming, with a will to match your own. When I met Marigold, I knew that I had found her."

"I am certain that Miss Morrison is all that you say she is," replied her ungrateful nephew in a tone that indicated he was certain of no such thing, "but choosing a bride, should I ever decide to do so, is a matter I would prefer to attend to myself."

His tone was not lost upon Marigold, who spoke as soon as he paused for breath. "And I most definitely do not wish to be the bride of Mister Lawford or anyone else," and here her scornful gaze raked over him, "no matter how exquisite the gentleman might be. You know that I have my plans, Lady Ariadne."

"But, child, there is no assurance that you will be successful, and even if you are that is not the life for you, not the life your mother would have wanted for you. Marrying a man like Charles would make you secure for the rest of your life."

"You overwhelm me, aunt, by attributing to me at

least the attraction of wealth."

"Well, of course, Marigold can see that you are a fine figure of a man, even if you *are,* as she said, quite precious in your tastes. And he is charming," she added, turning to Marigold, "although I grant that you can't tell it just now. He is reasonably good-tempered, considering that he has always been spoiled outrageously."

Lawford bowed briefly to his aunt, but directed his attention to Marigold. "May I inquire, Miss Morrison, as to the nature of the plans that you mentioned?"

"I am a singer, Mister Lawford, and I shall sing in London."

"For great audiences and important people, I am sure," said Lawford, his voice tinged with irony.

"Of course," she assured him proudly, her head high. "Would you like to hear me sing?"

Without giving him a chance to reply she seated herself briskly at the pianoforte, and Lady Ariadne settled herself, wondering what the girl would sing. Lawford made himself comfortable, prepared to hear the same sort of insipid performance given by countless pretty misses in countless London drawing rooms each season.

That was not, however, what he heard. Instead, the words of Ben Jonson's "Drink to Me Only with Thine Eyes" flowed over him like liquid gold. Even though the words and melody were familiar, and Lady Ariadne's drawing room certainly was, Lawford had the oddest sensation that he was being swept away from Valwood and everything he had ever known before. His attention was focused entirely on the slender figure at the pianoforte. Despite his determination to evince only a detached, casual interest, he found himself drawn to her side.

When he glanced at Lady Ariadne, he saw that she was watching him closely and that his reaction must be obvious, for she was smiling. Despite his aunt's pleased surveillance, Lawford remained at Marigold's side. There was no music to be turned for she was playing from memory, so she was free to meet his eyes as she sang. Before the last notes of her first song had died away, she had swung into a second tune, a lively, bouncing invitation to "Take Me to the Fair." Her dark eyes sparkled with laughter and, for the few enchanting moments that she sang, he felt that there was nothing on earth that he would rather do than join her at that fair and buy Gypsy ribbons to bind up her honey-colored hair.

"Well, sir, what do you think?" Marigold asked, folding her hands demurely in her lap. "Am I a singer?"

For Lawford the spell had broken when she ceased to sing. He felt like a man who has unwittingly almost fallen from a precipice and now looks down into the chasm that had almost claimed him. Instinctively, he became as aloof and remote as possible. There was no need for her to know that he found her voice more captivating—and more dangerous—than any he had ever heard.

"It was a pleasing little performance," he remarked carelessly. "Quite passable for someone from the provinces." Even as he said it, he knew that his words were unforgivably patronizing and boorish, but that would be all to the good if it kept her from the preposterous notion of going on the stage—and if it prevented her from realizing her effect upon him.

Marigold's cheeks were stained with the same wine red of her gown, and her voice quivered slightly when she spoke, but it was with anger, not with shame. "I suppose that I should be distressed by the opinion of a fine London gentleman."

Here she paused and studied him quite deliberately, from the tips of his burnished top boots to the crown of his artfully arranged locks. "However," she continued, "if the gentleman's judgment is no better than his manners, I have little to trouble me."

There was a sharp crack of laughter from Lady Ariadne as Marigold rose from the pianoforte and brushed by Lawford. She paused to say good night to her hostess, then walked majestically from the room without a backward glance at its other occupant.

"Aunt Ariadne, whatever possessed you to do such a corkbrained thing as this?" Lawford demanded wrathfully, descending upon her.

Unperturbed, Lady Ariadne surveyed him in much the same manner as Marigold had. "Called you to book quite nicely, didn't she, Charles? You put on your coldest care-for-nobody air and it didn't do. She is quite your match. I thought she would be."

His normally serene expression grew darker. "I want you to answer me directly, aunt. I have never asked you to find me a wife. How came you to do this?"

She stopped chuckling and looked at him seriously. "You're the only relative I have left that I care a button for, Charles. I don't like to see the frippery fellow you have become."

Charles swept her a deep bow. "Thank you for your kind opinion, aunt," he said dryly.

"Don't try to humbug me with your fine gentleman's airs, Charles, for you'll catch cold at it, just as you did with Marigold. I know your airs are a pose, and they used to amuse me. But now you have used them so long and grown so accustomed to having others toady to you for your good opinion that you have forgotten that you assumed them to play a game. You're not playing anymore, Charles. You have become the affected, dandified fop that you used to mock."

Stung to the quick by what he considered the injustice of her remark, he swept her an even deeper bow. "Your opinion must ever be of the greatest consequence to me, ma'am. I sometimes forget how large your fortune is."

She made an impatient gesture. "I know that you don't care about my money, Charles, because you have no need of it. That's one of the things I like about you; you don't care if I leave you a shilling."

He stood before the fire with his back to her as she continued. "But I do think you care about my opinion, Charles. I'm an old woman, and I want to see you properly settled before I die. If you continue as you are, you'll have no one who cares for you as you really are—except perhaps for Easterley. You will have played your part as the dandy so long that *you* won't even remember who you are."

He turned and eyed her coolly through his glass. "I assure you, aunt, that I know quite well who I am. And if I choose to marry, there are a host of amenable young women who would be eager to become Mrs. Charles Lawford."

"Addlepated fashionplates, all of them!" snapped his aunt. "Not an ounce of spirit or intelligence among them! Why, you require more in a horse than you do in a wife!"

"That is so," he assured her, with an affability nicely calculated to infuriate. "For, you see, I must entrust my life to my horse. The same may not be said of a wife."

This was too much for Lady Ariadne. "I see that I misjudged you after all, Charles. You are as impossible as those young dandies that toddle about the town, making a great show of their finery. Marigold Morrison deserves someone better than a Bond Street Lounger."

Lawford bowed to her once again, but she did not see it, having already reached the door. It could not be said that someone of Lady Ariadne's age and dignity flounced from the room, but it was a very near thing. Lawford was left to think over this very remarkable evening in solitude.

He sat long in the drawing room, and not until the fire burned down to ashes did he take himself to his bedchamber. A most extraordinary voice and personality, the little Marigold—but far too aggressive to live with comfortably, even if he had been inclined to allow his aunt to order his life. And of course it was out of the question for her to sing professionally. Not only was it unsuitable for a woman of her breeding, but it was also unlikely that she would have the fortitude to survive in such a milieu. A pity, he thought, that such a face and such a voice would be wasted on some country squire, but undoubtedly it would be so. He knew that Sir Vincent's affairs would have left her few choices.

"We return to London immediately after breakfast tomorrow," he announced to the interested Netherington, who had been patiently awaiting the arrival of his master upstairs before retiring. "It was nothing but a bag of moonshine that brought us down here."

Netherington was obliged to be content with that, and if he noted that his master hummed a few bars of "Take Me to the Fair," an unprecedented occurrence for a man who never sang anything, he kept the matter to himself not even sharing this interesting event with Cox.

Marigold, on the other hand, shared all of her thoughts about the evening with Sarah Appleby.

"He held up his nose after I sang, Sarah, and told me in the most condescending manner imaginable that I had given 'a pleasing little performance. Quite passable for someone from the provinces.'" She imitated his voice perfectly for mimicry was another of her gifts, a dangerous one since she had a wicked talent for detecting the idiosyncrasies of those about her.

"He may be a fine gentleman, but if his manners are a sample of what I may expect, I do not look forward to meeting more of them!"

Sarah recognized her opportunity and seized it. "Doubtless he is much like them," she said, shaking her head dolefully. "Spence told me that he is all the crack in London. Perhaps we should go home again, dearie. London's not the place for us."

"But we can't, Sarah. There is no home for us any longer. The Hall belongs to Sir Chester Fullerton now."

Marigold suddenly sat bolt upright, her back as stiff

as a ramrod. "Don't sniffle, Sarah. Mr. Charles Lawford be hanged! I don't know why he took me in such dislike, but he did. He *did* like my singing; I saw it in his eyes. But when I stopped he suddenly pokered up. No matter what he says we're going to London, and I *am* going to sing and I shall be wildly successful and make our fortune!"

Lady Ariadne had breakfast in her chamber the next morning, having no desire to set eyes upon her recalcitrant nephew. Marigold, however, thinking that he had already shaken the dust of Valwood from his feet, had the misfortune to encounter him in the dining room.

"Miss Morrison! What a charming surprise," he said in dulcet tones, carefully holding up his glass to examine her.

She inclined her head to him in a brief nod. "I am certain that it must be, Mister Lawford. After all, it cannot be often that a grand gentleman meets a country miss with a pleasing little voice."

"Ah, that grates, does it?" he inquired gently.

"I have always found poor judgment annoying, sir, and when coupled with poor manners, it does indeed grate."

"A gently bred young woman should not be thinking of a life such as you are striving for. I should think, Miss Morrison, that you would listen to the advice of my aunt upon that subject."

"Just as you listen to her advice, Mister Lawford?" inquired Marigold sweetly.

"There is no comparison between the situations. I am a man experienced in the ways of the world, Miss Morrison. I need no one to guide my steps through life, unlike an innocent such as yourself."

"You are quite wrong about me, Mister Lawford."

He arched his eyebrows questioningly. "Indeed? In what way?"

"I may be unworldly, and, as you phrase it, 'an innocent,' but that does not mean that I must abide by someone else's decisions for my life."

"You cannot imagine what you will encounter in such a life in London. You overestimate your abilities."

"And you underestimate them, sir, just as you underestimate my imagination." Marigold paused at the door to look over her shoulder at him. "I shall send you an invitation to my first concert."

"And I shall be there with bells on, Miss Morrison," he called after her retreating figure.

Lady Ariadne did not descend to the drawing room that day until Spence had assured her that she had actually seen Charles pulling away from Valwood. She had expected relative peace after the departure of her nephew, so she was disturbed to find Marigold in a decidedly militant frame of mind.

"Child, you cannot expect to go to London and make a career for yourself. It is absolutely unheard of for a young woman of breeding to do such a thing."

"Lady Ariadne, when you invited me to Valwood, you led me to believe that you would help me. I would not otherwise have come with you."

Lady Ariadne sat for a long moment, her eyes hooded in thought. "Charles said that he would come to your first concert if you sent him an invitation, did he?" she asked abruptly.

Marigold nodded. "With bells on," she responded thinly.

The old lady laughed. "Well, we will have to get him some bells, my girl. And if I help you with your singing, will you do something for me in return?"

Marigold nodded again. "Anything you ask, Lady Ariadne."

"You will be staying with me, and my credit, I think, will carry you far with the ton. I will also introduce you to a number of eligible young men—and some, perhaps, who are not so young, but eligible nonetheless."

"Why?" asked Marigold bluntly.

"Because it will do you no harm as a performer to have admirers among the members of the ton—and because one of them might make you change your mind about marriage."

Marigold chuckled. "That won't happen, Lady Ariadne, but I shall be happy to broaden my circle of acquaintances."

"Tell your Sarah Appleby that we are going to London, Marigold. We will leave tomorrow."

Lady Ariadne was as good as her word. They left the next morning for London, having sent Cox ahead to alert the staff of the London town house of their arrival.

"You will, my girl, be the talk of the ton before I have done with you. We will take you to Madame D'Arconte for your wardrobe. No one will be able to hold a candle to you."

"If she wore her old blue muslin there would still be no young lady who could shine her down," retorted the faithful Sarah, who was feeling uneasily that things were moving at too rapid a pace.

Lady Ariadne surveyed her charge critically. "I believe you are in the right of it, Sarah. Even without the stylish dressing, I don't know of anyone to equal Marigold."

"But I can't allow you to do all of this for me," protested Marigold. "There was no money to spare for clothing after my father's death, so I certainly cannot afford a new wardrobe, nor can I allow you to buy one for me."

"Nonsense, child. Had it not been for you, I would have lost my jewels and perhaps been murdered in my bed. I *wish* to do this. It is a pleasure to outfit a beauty like you."

She studied Marigold critically. "Such a blessing that you could not go into full mourning," she murmured, half to herself. "And there's no need to do so now, the relationship being what it was. Madame D'Arconte will be delighted and you will be grand advertising for her handiwork. She will practically make you a present of the clothing."

Marigold, growing restive under the weight of so much praise, interjected, "I am most grateful to you for doing this, but what of my singing, Lady Ariadne? When will I be able to begin searching for a position?"

"One thing at a time, Marigold. First we will let you charm everyone with your personality and with a few impromptu songs such as young ladies sing at their mamas' request. Then, when you have them eating from your hand, you will give your first concert."

With that Marigold was obliged to be satisfied, and she whiled away the hours of the trip by picturing to herself the chagrined expression of Mr. Lawford when he received an invitation to her first concert. He would, of course, be overcome by her talent and humbly beg her pardon for his lack of judgment. She would receive his praises carelessly, of course, like one long accustomed to such compliments and a trifle bored by them.

Untroubled by any awareness of her plans for his comeuppance, Lawford had returned posthaste to London determined to put behind him the unpleasantness of Valwood and to resume his customary round of pleasures. The whole episode had overset him, however, and he could not seem to put the memory of Marigold completely from his mind. His uneasy awareness that his role in the whole unsavory business had been a less than chivalrous one troubled him, too, but he had reasoned with himself that he had actually done Miss Morrison a kindness. Had he praised her singing, she might have been encouraged to view her shatterbrained notion of a career as a possibility. Although he had explained it to himself, he felt that once he could explain the matter clearly to a good friend, he could lay it to rest.

It was several days, however, before he could meet again with Lord Easterley at the Havisham Club and give him an account of that extraordinary experience. Finally, however, that evening arrived, and Lawford prepared to regale his companion with the story. Marigold's remarks about his lack of manners still rankled and he looked forward to hearing Easterley sympathize with him for the outrageous tampering of his aunt. When he came to the part about Lady Ariadne's suggestion of a marriage partner, Lord Easterley interrupted him.

"Do you mean Miss Marigold Morrison, Sir Vincent's daughter?" he asked in disbelief. "Why, you fortunate rascal! If Lady Ariadne had to take a bee in her bonnet about getting you leg-shackled for life, she couldn't have selected a more fetching partner. Miss Morrison is the most striking beauty I have seen in many a season."

Lawford stared at him "So you know her?" he asked irritably. "If you do, you must realize that her disposition is a little uneven and that she harbors some most unsuitable ambitions."

Easterley looked at him curiously. "What ambitions does she have? Don't tell me that she wishes to set up some society for the preservation of something-or-other that no one cares about except for a few old ladies."

Lawford shook his head. "Nothing of that nature," he responded.

"Thank heavens for that." Easterley sighed, relaxing again. "She seemed too charming and sensible a young woman to do something like that."

"Charming and sensible?" inquired Lawford in a shocked tone. "Dev, are we speaking of Miss Marigold Morrison still?"

"Well, of course we are," replied his companion, eyeing him with some concern. "Are you feeling quite the thing, Charles? You seem to be in pretty queer stirrups."

"Did you know that she plans to be a singer? To actually go on the stage?"

Easterley looked mildly shocked, but rallied quickly. "I haven't heard her sing yet, just met her yesterday, in point of fact. But I suppose even if she couldn't sing, the audiences would come just to sit and look at her."

"Well, don't tell her that, Dev, whatever you do, for she'll very likely sing at you and then part your hair for you if you don't think that she is as great a singer as Sarah Siddons was an actress! And then she will insult you to your face and stalk from the room as though you are at fault for being a sensible human being."

His friend stared at him in fascination. "She *has* put you into the deuce of a pucker hasn't she, old boy? Is that what happened to you?"

"Precisely! And since she seems to have more hair than wit, she is probably telling this tale, complete with the story of my refusing to marry her and insulting her voice to anyone who will listen."

"I shouldn't think so," demurred Easterley. "At least I have heard nothing of it. She didn't mention you at all when I called."

A most unwelcome realization came to Lawford as he listened to his friend. "Do you mean, Dev, that she is in London now? That you have seen her recently?"

"Just this very afternoon," said Easterley complacently. "Met her last night at the theater and did myself the honor of calling upon her today. A lovely creature!"

"Where did you call upon her, Dev?" demanded Lawford, sitting bolt upright.

"Why at Lady Ariadne's, of course, Charles. Where did you think she would be? You just told me yourself that she was at Valwood with your aunt."

"But they said nothing to me about coming to town! And my aunt always sends round a servant to notify me when she is in residence."

Easterley shrugged. "Why shouldn't they make a bolt to the village if they wish to, Charles? It does get tedious in the country. Besides, it doesn't sound to me as if you did anything but brangle with them while you were down there. Probably decided it was as well not to let you know they were here."

He looked very hard at Lawford. "This flying up into the boughs isn't like you, Charles. You never trouble yourself about what anyone says to you or thinks of you. I can see why you crossed swords with Lady Ariadne for being so high-handed, but the devil take me if I can understand why you're being so maggoty about Miss Morrison. Why, she was as much a victim as you were. She didn't set her cap for you like some of these young misses in the Marriage Mart. Didn't want to step into parson's mousetrap with you, did she?"

"No, she did not," replied Lawford shortly. "She made her feelings on the subject quite clear."

Lord Easterley studied his friend's face a moment and then grinned broadly. "Not exactly needle-witted, am I, Charles? That is the thorn, of course. You are on your high ropes because she wasn't interested in you, aren't you, dear boy?" He threw back his head and laughed in what Lawford considered a remarkably ill-bred fashion.

"Naturally not, Dev," he retorted. "I don't know what put such a bacon-brained notion into your head. I certainly do not desire some country wench as my wife. I do not, in point of fact, desire a wife of any sort."

"Ah, but that's not what I said, Charles. I said that you are in a pelter because she don't want you, not because you don't want her. Therein lies the critical difference. You have never before been turned down, have you, my boy?"

"No, I have not, Dev, and I *still* have not been refused because I have never asked anyone to marry me!"

"Begging the question, aren't you, Charles?" he asked, watching Lawford with a wickedly gleeful expression. "She refused you just as plainly as though you had offered for her and it flicked you on the raw, didn't it? You're accustomed to being the one who walks away, not the one who is left standing. Miss Morrison delivered you quite a facer, did she not?"

"You forget, Dev, that Miss Morrison is the guest of

my elderly aunt, and that anything she does here must reflect on Lady Ariadne. Therefore, Miss Morrison *must* be a concern of mine. I have no confidence in her ability to act discreetly nor in my aunt's ability to control her."

"Pokering up, aren't you, Dev, and trying to divert me to another part of the problem? Very well, I can see that you're on your high ropes. I will say no more of your disappointed hopes. And if you weren't so high in the instep, Charles, you wouldn't imagine that Miss Morrison could or would damage your aunt's credit. You are fighting windmills simply because Miss Morrison wounded your vanity."

Lawford found himself growing quite angry with Lord Easterley, another unprecedented occurrence, for he never exerted himself enough to lose his temper with anyone save his aunt, and Easterley was of all his friends the most genial. He had expected to be able to confide his problems in Dev, to have Dev commiserate with him, and then to forget the whole episode and go on. Instead, the whole matter had mushroomed and he was more distressed now than he had been before dinner. His friend's Parthian shot before departing that evening did not help matters either.

"You'd best watch that I don't steal a march on you, Charles. I've never been in the petticoat line like you are, but Miss Marigold Morrison has almost persuaded me to change my mind."

Netherington observed that evening that his master alternated between humming snatches of "Drink to Me Only with Thine Eyes" and "Take Me to the Fair" and pacing up and down the length of his bedchamber, a practice that made it difficult for him to help Lawford disrobe. When Netherington had finally achieved his goal and been dismissed, he paused at the door and looked back to see his master staring into the fire, his hands behind his back, still humming. Netherington shook his head and softly closed the door. He had never seen his

98

master like this, not in twelve years of service, and it troubled him. That it was a problem with a woman Netherington doubted not at all.

The next morning Lawford was one of his aunt's first callers. He was not, however, the first. When he entered the drawing room, he found Lady Ariadne and Miss Morrison seated with Lord Easterley and a young gentleman who was introduced to him as Percey Stokes, son of Sir Pericles Stokes of Wolvingham Manor.

Lady Ariadne greeted him coolly, as one might a very distant acquaintance whose presence is not particularly welcome. "Do sit down, Charles, if you must."

With this greeting and a frosty nod from Miss Morrison, he was obliged to be content. Young Stokes was inclined to view him as an interloper and only Lord Easterley smiled upon him, but it was a wicked, knowing smile, and Lawford was left to reflect bitterly upon the fact that he had unwittingly nursed a viper in his bosom all of these years.

"Did you notice the lovely shade of claret of Miss Morrison's gown, Charles?" inquired Lord Easterley innocently. "I believe it is just the shade that you had considered for a waistcoat. I recall that you remarked it is not a shade that everyone can wear, but it becomes Miss Morrison, does it not?"

Silently cursing the companion of his youth, Lawford nodded shortly. "It becomes her."

Easterley turned to Marigold. "You must believe me, Miss Morrison, when I protest that Charles is normally a man with a honeyed tongue, who would say that the color of the gown makes your hair more golden and your skin more glowing, that the claret wine of the gown is more heady than the claret sipped from a glass."

He smiled deeply at Marigold. "Charles would say it more gracefully, of course . . . but that is the type of thing that he would normally say to you."

"I prefer to hear such words from you, Lord Easterley," replied Marigold, without so much as a glance at Lawford. "They would not sound natural coming from such a man as Mr. Lawford."

Lawford, notable for his aplomb in all circumstances, flushed lightly. His discomfiture was not lost upon the traitorous Easterley, who was enjoying himself immensely.

"Come now, Miss Morrison, Charles is really a very good sort. I believe that you both merely misunderstood one another. Perhaps if you began again . . ."

"I believe that it is doubtful that my nephew would conduct himself any better on this occasion," commented Lady Ariadne acidly. "At any rate, he will not find out just now, for Miss Morrison has an engagement that she must keep. The carriage will be round to pick her up in just a few minutes, so I fear, gentlemen, that you must make the rest of your visit with me."

Marigold rose and gracefully excused herself. Young Stokes departed immediately, but Lord Easterley, having better manners as well as a desire to speak with Lawford, remained. He was not astonished to see his friend turn upon him wrathfully.

"Dev, what in thunder do you think you're about?" demanded Lawford.

"Forgive me, Charles," replied Easterley, chuckling. "It is just that I have never seen you at *point non plus* before."

"Yes, this is quite a setdown for a popinjay like Charles," Lady Ariadne agreed thoughtfully, quite as though Lawford were not sitting in the room with them. "Perhaps it will be beneficial."

"How could this rigmarole be beneficial to me?" exploded Lawford wrathfully. "My character is being pulled to shreds and I am being held up to ridicule by my closest relative and my closest friend! And for what reason? Because a young woman whom they have known for less than a month has taken me in dislike! Well, I wash my hands of the problems Miss Morrison brings with her. I wish that you all may be very happy together!"

And so saying, in a voice that cast some doubt upon the sincerity of his wish, he strode from the drawing room and the house.

Lady Ariadne smiled at him. "Quite delightful, isn't it?" she inquired pleasantly. "Do what you can to fan the fires, Devlin. It is all in his own best interests."

"If I did not think so, my lady, I would not be pursuing Miss Morrison so attentively. She seems to me quite an excellent choice for Charles."

Lady Ariadne nodded in satisfaction. "My thought precisely, Devlin. We will do our best."

Marigold's opinion on this interesting subject was quite otherwise, however. She had at first glance thought Mr. Lawford quite a striking figure, and she had had the decided impression that he had been drawn to her as well. She had noted with pleasure his quick humor and the laughter in his eyes, but once Lady Ariadne had sprung her little surprise, all of that had disappeared in a puff of smoke, and Marigold was no longer certain that her first impression had indeed been accurate. It was more likely that his haughtiness had been in evidence the whole time, and she had simply been too taken by his pleasing personal appearance to note it properly. None of this mattered, of course, for it was quite clear that they would have no dealings with one another, each of them having taken the other in extreme dislike.

She was pleased, however, with the attentiveness of Lord Easterley, and equally pleased to see how it grated upon Mr. Lawford. She had been surprised to see him in Lady Ariadne's drawing room, knowing as she did that his aunt had given him a stiff reprimand. It seemed unlike him to come and expose himself to a possible rebuff simply for the sake of paying his respects. She smiled to herself as she remembered the brief but appreciative glance he had thrown her way when he first entered the

101

room. He might not care for her, but there was a certain satisfaction in knowing that he was keenly aware of her presence in a room.

The carriage bowled up to the front of Madame D'Arconte's establishment and, attended by Spence and the faithful Sarah, she went inside for the fitting of the new gowns that Lady Ariadne had ordered for her. It had been as that worldly old lady had foreseen it would be. Madame D'Arconte had been delighted with Lady Ariadne's patronage and with the striking young beauty she was to outfit. Madame considered herself an *artiste,* but seldom did she have a subject worthy of her genius. With the inspiration of Marigold's exquisite beauty, her creative powers rose to new heights. Or so she informed Marigold during the fitting.

And, indeed, the three dresses that Marigold took away with her at the end of that time gave ample testimony to Madame D'Arconte's assertions. One of them, a ball gown that Marigold would wear that very night, was a confection of golden silk, trimmed at the hem with a deep triple edging of golden fringe. Madame assured her that the gown would reflect the candlelight of the ballroom and make Marigold a radiant vision of delight, the fringe of her skirt shimmering gently with each graceful step. Marigold hoped that this was so, not for the sake of vanity alone, but because she wished to be a striking figure that others would notice. Not for a moment had she forgotten her reason for coming to London. She was aware that Lady Ariadne was hoping to find her a husband, but Marigold regarded this entire social venture as a prelude to her musical career. When she had ordered her gowns, she had done so with an audience in mind.

When she made her entrance at Lady Gayden's ball that evening, the effect was all that she and Madame D'Arconte had hoped for. Gentlemen by the dozen lined up to plead for the honor of a dance. Lord Easterley had the pleasure of leading her out first, but he was rapidly succeeded by a host of gentlemen who had been charmed by the new beauty among them. Mr. Charles Lawford, although present at the ball, did not make one of their number. When Easterley joined his friend after relinquishing Marigold's hand to young Lord Pembroke, Lawford remarked irritably, "Making a pretty cake of yourself, aren't you, Dev?"

"I wish to be as much like you as possible, Charles," he retorted, "although I fear that I can never aspire to be as great a gudgeon as you seem to be."

"How can you accuse me of such a thing?" Lawford demanded. "I have acted like a sensible human being and all that I have gotten for my pains is a scolding from my aunt and the cut direct from you. I never thought that you would serve me such a backhanded turn, Dev!"

"Come now, Charles! I have done no more than pay my respects to Miss Morrison, who is, I might add, a vision of delight. I can't think how you came to subject a gently bred lady to such Turkish treatment at Valwood."

Lawford blinked at the unexpected attack. "I did no such thing," he protested. "What has she been telling you?"

"That you were odiously patronizing when she sang, saying that she had a pleasant little voice for someone from the provinces."

"Well, she does!" snapped Charles. "What was I supposed to do? Go down on my knees and tell her that I have never heard such a melodious voice? That she could have kings throwing their crowns at her feet?"

"If her voice matches her face, she could do precisely that," returned his friend frankly. "But even if her voice is not quite the thing, how came you to say such an unhandsome thing to the lady?"

"She has no business thinking of going on the stage, and my aunt has no business trying to arrange a marriage for me!" said Lawford shortly.

"Charles, you put me to the blush. We have known one another since we were in short coats and I have never known you to be so lacking in address. To think that you of all people could have cut so poor a figure! You have treated Miss Morrison very shabbily and I don't wonder at her distaste for you."

"I assure you that her distaste for me could never equal the revulsion I feel when I think of her!"

"Coming it too strong, Charles," returned his friend.

Easterley paused before speaking again and watched Marigold floating about the room in the arms of Lord Pembroke as the orchestra played a lilting waltz. "What a lovely creature she is!" he said, almost involuntarily. The candlelight had done all that Madame D'Arconte had promised, and the eyes of more than Lord Easterley rested upon that enchanting golden figure.

Easterley turned to eye his friend quizzically. "But I forget myself, Charles. You, after all, feel only revulsion for Miss Morrison."

Lawford glared at him silently, unable to think of an adequately scathing retort.

"And I think, Charles, that I must hear Miss Morrison sing myself. You have aroused my curiosity to a fever-pitch. I am certain that there is a small salon where a few of us could gather and ask her to favor us with a song."

Lawford watched Easterley make his way across the floor to where Marigold was standing with Lord Pembroke and Lady Ariadne. He stopped to speak with them for a few moments, gesturing toward one of the doors to the ballroom. Marigold nodded and smiled, then placed her hand on Lord Easterley's arm and allowed him to lead her from the room, followed closely by Lady Ariadne and Lord Pembroke and a small gaggle of admiring gentlemen. Lawford told himself crossly that Easterley would now realize what he had been talking about, but lurking in the back of his mind was the memory of the spell she had cast when he first heard her at Valwood. Doubtless it had been her face that had mesmerized him upon that occasion and not her voice. However, almost without being aware of what he was doing, he, too, made his way across the ballroom and out the door.

By the time he found the salon where they had gathered, Marigold was seated at a pianoforte, singing a plaintive melody whose refrain seemed to consist of a plea to "search for your true love" and to love her "above silver and gold." Glancing at the faces of the gentlemen listening, Lawford thought sourly that they all appeared to have found their true love. How very inconvenient for them that there was only one Miss Morrison, he reflected wryly. He seated himself unobtrusively on a blue velvet sofa just inside the door and studied the scene before him, attempting to view it objectively.

Marigold's eye alighted upon him just as the last strains of her song died away. Her dimples suddenly came into play and she began again the melody "Take Me to the Fair" that had almost been his undoing at Valwood. He felt himself succumbing as she sang, struggle against it though he would. Light and lilting, the simple song managed to capture all of the green and gold glory of the spring, all of the longing for unknown joys that belong to youth at lilac time. For the moment he gave himself up to it, meeting her eyes across the room whether he willed it so or not. Only when the last note had faded away could he take his eyes away from her and break the spell.

"Enchantress!" he murmured in a low voice, shaking his head gently as though to clear it.

"Yes, she is indeed, isn't she, Charles? I wasn't sure that you had observed it," said Lady Ariadne, who had moved to his side unnoticed during the song. "It can be very hard to appreciate enchantment through a quizzing glass," she added dryly.

"Aunt Ariadne, it is most improper to have Miss

Morrison singing privately for this group of gentlemen," returned Charles, tiring of a defensive battle and deciding to launch an offensive of his own. "I am astonished that you would countenance such behavior."

"What a humbug you are, Charles," said Lady Ariadne ungraciously. "I am her chaperone, am I not? Am I not here? Am I not the person best suited to determine what is suitable behavior for my charge?"

"Apparently not!" retorted Lawford. "Are you trying to put her on the stage right here and now?"

"Of course not, Charles, you ninny. If you weren't being so bacon-brained, you would notice that the gentlemen in this room are very interested in Marigold and some will undoubtedly wish to pay their addresses to her. I mean to find her a suitable husband before she does anything outrageous like going on the stage."

Lawford stared at her blankly. It had not occurred to him that his aunt might take it upon herself to do such a thing. It had outraged him to think that Marigold might become a professional singer, but he found that it outraged him still more to think that she might become the wife of one of these gentlemen. As he glanced up, he caught Easterley's eye across the room. Lord Easterley was standing next to Marigold, and, upon taking note of his friend, leaned down and whispered in the lady's ear. She looked up with sparkling eyes, and they laughed cozily together, obviously unmindful of Lawford.

From the corner of her eye, however, Marigold saw Lawford stand and leave the room abruptly, and somehow his leaving took some of the glitter from the evening. She sang one more song before Lady Ariadne announced that they must be getting back to the ball, and Marigold gratefully rejoined the others in the ballroom. Her singing had been successful, she knew, for the gentlemen remained clustered about her. She noted that Mr. Lawford was waltzing with Miss Davington, a brunette in a charming blue gown, and wondered at the small pang the sight caused her. He was a graceful dancer, of course, and quite the most dashing figure on the dance floor. It was a thousand pities that such a man should be so arrogant.

It was with some surprise that she found him by her side later in the evening. "I believe, Miss Morrison, that we are engaged for this dance," he said coolly, and whisked her away before either she or the gentleman who was about to lead her out could protest.

"You are very high-handed, Mister Lawford," she commented in an acid tone.

"It was virtually impossible to come close to you, Miss Morrison, without dancing with you. You seem to be surrounded by admirers tonight."

"How gracious of you to indicate that tonight must be an exception," Marigold commented dryly. "It may come as a surprise to you, but there have been other evenings when I have been surrounded by admirers."

"Forgive me," Lawford replied stiffly, looking down at her through narrowed eyes. "I did not mean to offend your vanity."

"And there you go again," said Marigold impatiently. "Why must your rudeness suddenly become my vanity? Why must I be at fault? I have heard from countless people since I have been in London that you are the most notable arbiter of fashion since Beau Brummell, and that may well be true, but you are also the most rag-mannered man I have ever met."

"Thank you," he replied coldly, his lips set in a thin white line.

"It was my pleasure," Marigold returned, smiling sweetly. "And now tell me, sir, why you thought it necessary to speak with me. Other than to put me in my place, of course."

His arm tightened around her waist. "Because you are now my aunt's responsibility, I feel it my duty to warn you that such behavior as you have exhibited tonight could do you inestimable damage here in London."

She stared at him in disbelief. "I cannot credit what you are saying, Mister Lawford. How could singing for a group of guests, particularly when I am chaperoned by Lady Ariadne, do me any harm? I think that you exaggerate the situation."

"Not at all, Miss Morrison. I saw the faces of the gentlemen in that room. You have attracted far too much attention to yourself, and done so in the most forward manner possible. This can do you—"

He was obliged to break off here, for Miss Morrison interrupted, laughing. "I see what it is now. You are jealous!"

"Jealous?" echoed Lawford angrily. "How dare you presume to say such a thing?"

"Yes, that must be it!" she continued triumphantly. "Lady Ariadne told me that you had always been her favorite and her heir, but that you and she had a falling-out. Now that I am with Lady Ariadne, you are jealous of the attention that she bestows upon me! I assure you, sir, that I am not attempting to take your place."

Although relieved by her explanation, for he had feared she thought him jealous of Easterley and the others, he was nonetheless annoyed that she thought him so childish as to be jealous of his aunt's favors or so greedy as to be thinking of her will.

"Not at all," he responded smoothly. "You quite mistake the matter, I assure you. I am merely trying to act in my aunt's best interests—and in your own, I might add."

"And just how, Mister Lawford, are you acting in my best interests?"

"Obviously, Miss Morrison, it will be a far simpler matter for my aunt to find a husband for you if you are not one of the scandalous *on-dits* of the ton."

"And why, pray tell, would I be considered scandalous?" she inquired angrily.

"You know perfectly well that singing in a public place

would scandalize society and that very few men of good family would wish to fly in the face of convention and offer for your hand. They would indeed believe that they could offer you *carte blanche* instead."

Marigold's cheeks again took on the color of claret, as they had the first night that they had met and he had angered her. He had no time, nor indeed any inclination, to admire its effect on her appearance, for she returned angrily, "You take too much upon yourself, sir. You are neither my father nor my brother nor my friend. My affairs are none of your concern." Then she turned abruptly and walked away, ignoring his short, stiff bow.

"You seem to have lost your magic touch with the ladies, Charles," said Lord Easterley jovially. "Miss Morrison seems quite immune to your charm."

Lawford had not seen his friend and was less than pleased to realize that he had overheard their conversation. "What are you doing lurking about in the shadows, Dev?"

Easterley looked hurt. "Lurking in the shadows? I was merely coming over to join you when I suddenly realized from the tone of your conversation that my presence was not required."

"She is quite a little harridan," commented Charles, looking across the floor to where Marigold had joined a bevy of her admirers.

"That is not the word that comes to my mind," responded Lord Easterley, also staring thoughtfully across the floor at Marigold. "Indeed, Charles, I almost believe that it may be time for me to step into parson's mousetrap myself." Without waiting for a reply and ignoring his friend's startled glance, Easterley made his way through the throng to Marigold's side.

Lawford stared after him in disbelief. Dev, the eternal bachelor, had surely been bewitched. Never before had Lawford heard him indicate any serious interest in a lady, despite his family's fevered attempts to marry him off to a suitable lady so that he would settle down and produce an heir. He had a sudden unpleasant thought. What if Dev should actually marry the chit! There would be no more happy times for the two of them, for Miss Morrison had made her distaste for him quite obvious, and Dev looked to be well on his way to being top-over-tail in love with her. He would doubtless dance to her tune.

"Well, you won't do it, Miss Morrison," he said to himself grimly. "Dev has been my friend all of my days and no one is going to snatch him away and make him live under the cat's paw, as he undoubtedly would with a witch like you." And then, remembering her desire to go on the stage, he smiled. That would be her undoing with Dev's family. They would never allow him to marry someone they considered ineligible. And, catching Dev's eye across the crowd, he smiled again, enjoying his friend's puzzled glance.

The next morning found Lawford once again in his aunt's drawing room, his arrival having been preceded by that of a dainty bouquet of marsh marigolds, a tribute to Miss Morrison that was no mean achievement. It had required special effort on the part of the shop keeper to find these, for marigolds were scarcely the flower most in demand. Indeed, he had attempted to convince Lawford that no lady would wish for them, and tried to press roses upon him instead. Finally, he had been obliged to send a boy scurrying to his mother's garden to produce these.

"Well, Charles, so there you are!" said his aunt sharply as he entered the room.

"As you so aptly noted, aunt, here I am," he returned affably, disregarding her tone and bowing pleasantly to Miss Morrison. "And, I might add, I am most pleased to be here."

"Don't do the pretty with me, Charles! It won't wash. What are you about now, sir?"

He turned an innocent gaze upon her. "What do you

110

mean, aunt? I have come to pay my respects to you and to the loveliest lady at the ball last night." And again he inclined his head in the direction of Miss Morrison, this time letting his glance linger.

She smiled at him hesitantly, not wishing to be rude, particularly in the face of his offering of marigolds, but she was suspicious nonetheless. "It was very kind of you to remember me, Mister Lawford," she said, indicating the marigolds in a blue vase beside her. "And your choice of flower was very gallant."

"Their glowing gold pales beside your own golden beauty, Miss Morrison," he replied smoothly, taking one small hand in both his own.

There was an unladylike snort from Lady Ariadne, who was watching him sharply, and a light, silvery laugh from Marigold. "That sounds like something you rehearsed for many another lady, Mister Lawford. Remember that Lord Easterley has warned me about you."

He looked wounded. "But of course I rehearsed it, Miss Morrison—but for you alone. I assure you that never before have I sent marigolds to a lady. I know how many admirers you are gathering about you, Miss Morrison. I could not hope to compete with their eloquence unless I did practice."

She laughed again, carefully disengaging her hand. "From what I have heard of you, Mister Lawford, you have no need to practice. I believe that I have heard you described as the most accomplished flirt in London."

He looked at her in mock dismay and inwardly cursed Easterley's careless tongue. "Surely they were thinking of someone else, Miss Morrison. I swear to you that I had never set eyes on true beauty until last night."

"Now you sound more like the Charles Lawford that I have always known," said Lord Easterley from the doorway. "This, Miss Morrison, is the man that I have been telling you about."

"He certainly seems a stranger to me, Lord Easterley,"

she replied. "He is most unlike the gentleman I met at Valwood."

"You must forgive me," said Lawford contritely. "I don't know how I came to be such a sapskull. Please say that we may begin again."

She looked at him doubtfully. He seemed sincere enough, but so different was he from the man that she had met that she could scarcely credit her own observations. Glancing up, she caught Lord Easterley's eye.

"Yes, Miss Morrison." He laughed, amused by her confusion. "It is indeed the same gentleman. But now he is himself again."

"Then I may say that I am now most pleased to meet you," said Marigold prettily, extending one small hand to him. Although I do wonder at the change, she added silently to herself, regarding him carefully.

"And I am most grateful that you have given me another chance, dear lady," said Lawford, bowing over that hand and kissing it lightly. "And now, if you will excuse me, I have urgent business that I must see to before the day grows older. With your permission, I shall do myself the honor of calling again, Miss Morrison."

"Of course," she replied graciously. "We shall look forward to it."

On his way to the door, his aunt caught him and pulled him down next to her. "Don't think that you can flummery me, my boy," she murmured. "What deep game are you playing now?"

"Really, Aunt Ariadne, you wrong me. Truly you do," he insisted, ignoring her attempts to have him pay attention to her warning.

"Hrumph!" was the only reply.

The rest of Lawford's day was extremely busy. He called at a small but elegant theater called The Rose and had a prolonged conference with its owner and manager. Business had been good, but that gentleman found himself quite unable to refuse the amount Lawford offered him for the rental of the whole theater for a single night. Although he privately considered it most unusual for a young lady of quality to be making her singing debut in a public theater, he was aware that the ways of the ton were unusual, and he solemnly promised his benefactor that the young lady would be able to rehearse prior to her performance and that all of the paid attendants would be in place in order for the evening to proceed smoothly.

Pleased with his arrangements, Lawford left The Rose, imagining with satisfaction the excitement with which Marigold would greet the announcement of his gift. She would doubtless be speechless with gratitude.

As it happened, his vision was only partially correct. Marigold was certainly speechless when he told her the next day of his plans for her, but gratitude was not the cause for her silence, a fact that she proceeded to make painfully clear to him.

"You did what, Mister Lawford?" she inquired, when she could regain her breath.

"Yes, do say that again, Charles," chimed in Lord Easterley, holding up his glass to survey his friend carefully. "I think I could not have heard you clearly."

Lawford looked as though he did not particularly care whether or not Lord Easterley had heard anything, but he directed his attention to Marigold instead, repeating his words. "I know how much you have longed to sing on stage, Miss Morrison, and I have made arrangements for you to sing at The Rose next Saturday evening."

"Have you really, Charles?" asked Easterley admiringly. "However did you arrange it? Has the manager heard Miss Morrison sing? That would certainly explain the whole matter," he said in an aside to Marigold. "Anyone hearing your voice would know that you have a gift that should be shared."

Marigold colored under his attentive gaze and Lawford could cheerfully have strangled his dear friend. "*Has* he

113

heard Miss Morrison, Charles?" persisted Easterley.

"No," admitted Lawford reluctantly. "He is looking forward to doing so, however."

"Then why has he asked me to sing?" asked Marigold, puzzled.

Lawford stirred uneasily in his chair, well aware that all three of them were studying him. Lady Ariadne had not as yet said a word, a most unusual state of affairs which left him vaguely uncomfortable. He was beginning to feel like a mouse in the midst of several watchful cats.

"I told him how appealing your voice is," returned Lawford, feeling that this much at least was true.

"And because you said I have an appealing voice — although a provincial one, of course — he has invited me to sing on Saturday night?" inquired Marigold, her disbelief obvious. "And what will he do if you are wrong and his audience gets up and walks out during my performance, requesting that their money be returned?"

"That would never happen," said Lawford, persevering bravely.

"But what would he do if it did?" persisted Marigold. "I can understand his taking a risk on his own judgment after hearing me sing, but why should he listen to you?"

"Yes, Charles," said Easterley, taking up the chase, "do tell us why. I am fascinated. I had never realized that you have the ear of theater owners and managers. You have opened up a whole aspect of yourself that I had never before known existed."

Lady Ariadne spoke sharply. "Guaranteed him the price of the audience, didn't you, Charles?"

Lawford looked uncomfortable and hesitated just a moment too long before replying. "Why would you think I would do such a thing, Aunt Ariadne?" he parried, feeling instinctively that a truthful reply would be his undoing, no matter how benevolent his intentions.

"Just the sort of thing you would think of. You're accustomed to having your own way and money will usually buy it for you."

Marigold turned large, accusing eyes on him. "You *paid* him to allow me to sing?" she demanded. "I suppose that you think no one would pay to hear me of their own volition."

"No, that is not the problem at all, Miss Morrison," he protested, but his words fell on deaf ears.

"I suppose that you did this hoping that I would be an abysmal failure," she said, standing abruptly. "Although why you should have troubled yourself with the matter at all, I cannot see."

"No, I did not at all think that you would be a failure; there was no insult intended!" Lawford persisted. "I am sure that you will be a great success."

She turned at the door and stared at him. "If you believe that, then I truly cannot think why you did this, Mister Lawford. I do see, though, that I was wrong to come to Lady Ariadne. Sarah and I should have gone to Ismene Turner as I had planned, and I should have undertaken my own arrangements."

"No, child!" protested Lady Ariadne. "Coming with me to London was the only practical thing to do. We can still work things out."

Marigold went back to her side and knelt down beside the old lady, placing her bright young cheek next to Lady Ariadne's wrinkled one. "You must not think that I am ungrateful, Lady Ariadne. You have been all that is kind, but I see that I cannot stay here and let things drift as they have been doing. I thank you for your kindness to me and for the gowns you have bought me. I will indeed repay you for them."

"Nonsense, Marigold! We will—" But she was speaking to the empty air, for Marigold had left the drawing room, closing the door softly after her.

Lady Ariadne turned on Lawford in a fury. "She will leave me now, and I have no right to keep her here!

What possessed you to do such a thing, Charles Lawford?"

"Now, aunt, surely you can see that my intentions were—"

But she would not allow him to finish. "That your intentions were all for the good?" she snapped. "I know very well they were no such thing! What *did* you have in mind, Charles? You know very well that the child would have been a success. So why did you set her up to do the very thing that you said she must not do?"

He flushed, but did not reply.

Easterley also regarded him grimly, but did not address him directly. Instead, he turned to Lady Ariadne and bowed. "If you will excuse me, ma'am, I will see if I may be of service to Miss Morrison."

Lady Ariadne watched him leave the room, approval in her eyes. "I like to see a gentleman *act* the part of a gentleman." She turned her gaze upon Lawford, who stirred uncomfortably under her scrutiny. "I had always adjudged you a gentleman, Charles. I have never seen you be deliberately unkind to a young lady before. What *did* you hope to accomplish by hiring that theater for her?"

"I have told you, aunt—" he began.

"What you have told me is folderol! I can't think why you wished to put her upon the stage, knowing she would do well. It wasn't to make her happy, for you don't like her above half. The only other thing it would accomplish would be to provide gossip for the ton and damage her reputation so that I would have trouble marrying her off . . ."

She paused and stared at him a moment, smiling coldly. "That's it, isn't it, Charles? Of course, it is," she went on, not giving him a chance to reply. "This could very well ruin her, and then she will be marrying no one, including Easterley."

"I think I have listened to quite enough of your foolishness, aunt," Lawford announced, rising to take his departure. "I will call on you when you are a little more reasonable."

The old lady stared at the door as he closed it. "A little more reasonable!" she said aloud, slapping the table beside her. "Ha! You'll think I'm reasonable when I have done with you, my boy. You'll not cut up my peace and ruin my plans in this fashion!"

It was late in the afternoon when Marigold and Sarah drew up before Miss Ismene Turner's humble residence. Lady Ariadne had insisted upon having John Ballard escort them, and Cox had gone round personally earlier in the afternoon, bearing a note to Miss Turner to see if they might begin their stay with her. Marigold had won the affections of the staff, and he had been unwilling to entrust her message to a mere footman.

Miss Turner, a thin, anxious-looking spinster, fluttered down the steps to greet them, quite overcome by the elegance of their equipage and of Marigold herself.

"Why, you look quite French, Marigold dear. And that bonnet does so become you." She looked admiringly at the chip bonnet with its smartly curled plumes. "Forgive my abominable manners. Do come in, both of you, and we will be comfortable and you can tell me all about what you have been doing."

When Marigold disclosed her plans for her singing career during tea, Miss Turner very nearly overset her cup onto the cat reclining on the footstool beside her.

"The stage? Oh, I shouldn't think that would answer at all, Marigold dear," she demurred, dabbing ineffectually at the tea stain on her skirt with a wisp of handkerchief.

"It's of no use at all to try to dissuade me, Ismene. My mind is quite made up," replied Marigold. "But you may stand my dear friend and help me, you and Sarah."

"Well, of course I want to do anything I can to help you, Marigold. So sad about your poor father."

A snort from Sarah threw Miss Turner, who was keenly

aware of Sarah's opinion of that gentleman, into greater confusion. "What I mean, Marigold dear, is that it is so sad that your poor father . . . that your father's death left you in such unfortunate circumstances. And naturally I wish to help you."

"Of course, you do, Ismene," agreed Marigold, smiling. "You have always been my good friend, and I do so appreciate your having us here to stay with you."

"Well, I'm delighted to have you. Of course, it is not what you have been accustomed to at Thurston Hall or with Lady Ariadne. I do hope that you won't be dreadfully uncomfortable." And her kind, spare face looked worried.

"We will love it," Marigold assured her. "And tomorrow morning we will begin to set my plan in motion."

At the mention of her plan, Miss Turner's face grew even more worried, and she darted a furtive glance toward Sarah Appleby, who shook her head in resignation.

"We will have to do as she wishes, I am afraid. I have tried to convince her this is not the thing to do, but she simply has her mind set upon it."

Marigold laughed. "So you see, Ismene. If Sarah has given up struggling against it, you know there is nothing more to do."

Recognizing the force of her argument from years of association with the two of them, Miss Turner put up no more resistance, but accompanied them docilely the next day on a round of visits to theaters Marigold knew of that employed singers. They carefully avoided The Rose, however. By the time several hours had passed, all three of them were tired and discouraged. Together they returned to Miss Turner's for refreshment and rest.

As their hired hack set them down in front of Miss Turner's, Marigold heard her name being called. The three of them looked up, and there they saw Lord Easterley, waving anxiously from his curricle. Leaving his reins in the charge of a blissful neighbor boy, he hurried over to the ladies and was duly presented to Miss Turner.

"I was quite afraid I had missed you, Miss Morrison," he smiled, bowing over her hand. "And I had come to extend an invitation."

"An invitation?" inquired Marigold, her eyebrows arched. "Don't you recall, Lord Easterley, that you and I are no longer part of the same social circle?"

"I cannot accept that as true, Miss Morrison," he protested. "And at any rate my invitation is of a different sort."

"Indeed? And what sort of an invitation is it?" she inquired, smiling. Marigold looked kindly upon Lord Easterley, who always treated her with respect. Quite a rare commodity among gentlemen, she had reflected acidly.

"I would like to invite the three of you to be my guests at Vauxhall Gardens tonight," he announced. "The weather is fine and we should take advantage of such a moment as this."

"Vauxhall!" echoed Miss Turner nervously. "I hadn't thought . . . that is . . . do you think, Marigold dear . . . that it would be quite . . ."

"There will be singers there, will there not, Lord Easterley, and an orchestra?" Marigold inquired.

He nodded. "There most certainly will be."

"Then we would be delighted to accept," she informed him, and he arranged to call for them at eight that evening.

Miss Turner spent the intervening time fluttering and worrying. "Vauxhall!" she murmured to Sarah for the two hundredth time. "Vauxhall for a young girl like Marigold. I can't think that it is the thing to do . . . yet Lord Easterley seems like such a gentleman."

"He is," returned Sarah calmly. She was not particularly pleased about their destination either, but she had complete faith in Lord Easterley's discretion. "He will look after Marigold, and we will be there, too."

Miss Turner allowed herself to be soothed. "I suppose

it might be quite unexceptionable," she admitted. "After all, you are correct. Marigold will have two chaperones, so it isn't as though she will be going to such a very fast place alone."

"Not at all," Sarah assured her. "We will be with them all of the time. Marigold will be quite all right."

As it happened, Sarah was only partially correct. Marigold was quite all right that evening, but Sarah and Miss Turner were not with her all of the time. Lord Easterley had reserved a box for them, where they partook of a delightful supper of the burnt wine and wafer-thin ham for which Vauxhall was famous, Marigold being confined to lemonade to accompany her supper. Lights sparkled everywhere and the ladies were as busy inspecting the passersby as were the passersby inspecting them. Fortunately, Lord Easterley had selected a more secluded box, so they were not as exposed to inquisitive eyes as they might otherwise have been.

After supper, Lord Easterley proposed a promenade along one of the delightful walks for which the garden was famed, informing the ladies that there was a most interesting statue of Mr. Handel to be viewed along one of them. Marigold accompanied him eagerly, with Sarah and Miss Turner following closely behind them. Unfortunately, at one point where their walk joined several others, they were swept along in a throng of merrymakers, including a somewhat rowdy party of Oxonians, down for a lark. When these young sprigs of fashion had moved noisily on their way, Sarah and Miss Turner could no longer see their companions. They began to walk briskly in the direction Sarah was quite sure they had taken, but a fifteen-minute walk did not bring them into sight.

In desperation, the two ladies turned to one another, but before either of them could speak, they heard a familiar voice.

"It is Marigold," whispered Sarah unnecessarily, for

Miss Turner could not mistake the voice for anyone else's. "She's doing it again, Ismene, just as she did when she was a child."

As quickly as they could, the ladies followed the sound of her voice and made their way to the center of the garden and through the crowd standing before the temple of music where the orchestra was playing.

"Oh, *Marigold!*" breathed Sarah softly, as she looked up and saw her mistress standing beside the musicians. The tune she was singing was a lively one and a few of the couples were dancing, but the majority stood and stared at the lovely face above them. When she had finished, the applause was thunderous and the orchestra leader invited her to sing again.

Her next number was a haunting melody about a young girl who loses her true love to "the wild, wild sea" and who, in desperation, finally gives herself to that same sea. No one danced now, and all of the faces turned upward to the pure young voice that sang so plaintively of a deep and innocent love that few of them would ever know, but which, for the moment of the song, was theirs. When Marigold finished this song, there was silence for a few moments and then an even more tumultuous ovation than her first.

Sarah had, by this time, caught sight of Lord Easterley, and she and Miss Turner bore down upon him.

"Oh, sir, how could you let her do this?" asked Miss Turner in a voice made breathless by their hurry. "How could you let her sing before all of these people?"

Sarah was more practical. "Never mind blaming Lord Easterley, Ismene. You know what she is. He could no more have stopped her than he could have stopped a force of nature. Think of all the times she has done this to us."

She glanced around her for a moment, then smiled a little ruefully. "Of course, we were just in the village then, not in Vauxhall Gardens before half of London."

Lord Easterley did not think it necessary to tell them that he and Lady Ariadne had discussed the matter and had planned for precisely this event. Since Marigold would not allow Lady Ariadne to help her any longer, she and Easterley had decided that she should have her opportunity to sing and they would put Lawford to the test. A word from them to Mr. Wardell, the gentleman in charge of the gardens, would have been enough to ensure Marigold's invitation to sing. As it happened, however, their trouble was quite unnecessary. As Mr. Wardell later told them, when he heard her humming the tune that Lord Easterley had enticed her to sing, it did not matter a whit that they had offered him something for his time and trouble. Simply hearing her sing was reward enough, and he would accept nothing from them. Vauxhall had just opened for the summer months and having a fresh young talent like Marigold's would be a certain attraction for the crowds.

Marigold came down from the platform, making her way through the admiring crowd, her cheeks glowing. "He has asked me to sing!" she announced proudly. "I am to begin tomorrow night, and I shall sing five times a week."

"Congratulations, Miss Morrison!" exclaimed Easterley. "I knew that you could do it! By Jove, if you didn't make all of these gabsters stop their talking and joking and listen to you."

Marigold turned to Sarah and Miss Turner, who were staring at her with wide eyes. "Well, aren't you going to say anything to me?"

"Oh, yes, Marigold dear," faltered Miss Turner. "I am so pleased . . . if you are, of course . . . but it seems so . . . so public."

Marigold laughed. "Well, of course, it is public. How else will I be heard if not in public?"

Turning to Sarah, she said, "Will you not say anything to me, Sarah? I know that you don't approve, but aren't you the tiniest bit happy for me?"

Sarah suddenly hugged her mistress hard. "I don't know what I'd say to Lady Camilla," she said, wiping her eyes.

Marigold went home that night a very happy young lady, and before she went to bed, she sat down at Miss Turner's desk and wrote an invitation to Mr. Charles Lawford to attend the Vauxhall Gardens concert the very next evening . . . with bells on.

Lord Easterley very kindly insisted upon escorting them all to the gardens again the next evening, so Sarah and Miss Turner breathed a little more easily. Nonetheless, they stayed as close as possible to Marigold.

Mr. Wardell had requested that she begin tonight with "The Wild, Wild Sea" and, as she had the night before, she wove a spell that drew her listeners to her. As she looked out at the sea of faces she found at last the one for which she had been searching. Charles Lawford stood at the fringe of the crowd, his fair hair shining in the lamplight. Like the others, he stood transfixed until she breathed the last note. While the audience stood calling for more, she slipped away from the lights—and from Sarah and Miss Turner—and made her way toward him. The conductor promised the audience that Miss Morrison would sing for them again in half an hour, and they were forced to be content with that.

"And so, Mister Lawford, was mine a passable performance for a girl from the provinces?"

Taken by surprise, he smiled involuntarily. "You will cast that up to me forever, will you not, Miss Morrison?"

She nodded. "Why did you say such a thing to me, Mister Lawford, if you did not mean it?"

He smiled again, ruefully this time. "I shall have to admit to childishness, I fear."

"What do you mean?"

Taking her arm, he guided her away from the crowd, down one of the less traveled walks. "It is quite simple. I

123

was afraid, Miss Morrison."

She stopped in the middle of the gravel path and stared up at him, her eyebrows drawn together in a puzzled glance. "Afraid? Why should you have been afraid? What had you to fear?"

Gently he smoothed the crease between her brows, then tenderly tilted her chin and looked into her eyes.

"Myself," he replied simply, and in one quick motion he had drawn her tightly to him and pressed his lips against hers. The other sounds of the gardens grew muffled, for Marigold could hear only the pounding of her heart. When his lips finally released hers, he still held her firmly in his embrace and she laid her cheek against his jacket, untroubled by the fact that he had drawn her gently off the path into the darkness of the trees.

"I had a dream," he whispered into her curls. "Do you know what I dreamed of?"

She shook her head silently, not looking up.

"I dreamt of a field of golden kingcups, marsh marigolds they call them. I told an old woman who sells flowers on the street corner about it, and she said that the dream was a good omen, that if you dreamt of marigolds, it meant that you would have riches, success, and a happy marriage."

There was a pause and Marigold stood perfectly still as he kissed the curls that fringed her cheek. "Do you believe in dreams, Marigold?" he whispered.

Before she could reply, the stillness was shattered abruptly. "Miss Marigold Morrison!" said Sarah sharply. "Whatever has come over you, miss? Come here immediately, if you please!"

Marigold felt Lawford's hand on her arm, detaining her, but she moved away from him quickly and stood beside Sarah, overcome by the enormity of her offense. A gentleman did not take liberties with a gently bred woman, of that she was quite aware, nor was the young lady to allow them. But undoubtedly Mr. Lawford had felt that she no longer fell into the category. Marigold stared at the toes of the blue leather slippers that peeped from beneath the hem of her skirt as though they might be able to explain to her why she had allowed this to happen.

Sarah stood on the gravel pathway, accompanied by a horrified Miss Turner and a grim-faced Lord Easterley. Marigold took her place beside them, not meeting their eyes

"Charles! Have you taken leave of your senses, man? You forget that Miss Morrison is a lady and that you are compromising her good name!"

Sarah and Miss Turner had taken her between them and were leading her silently away from the two men, but Marigold could hear their conversation clearly.

"I forget nothing!" replied Lawford coldly, cursing himself inwardly for the fool's course he had taken. He had meant to hear Marigold sing and to leave without seeing her. Her sudden appearance at his side had taken him completely by surprise and he had allowed himself to give way to his emotions. "And I have done Miss Morrison's name no harm!"

"No harm?" returned Easterley angrily. "Treating her as though she were some little barque of frailty is doing her no harm? Would you treat Miss Davington in such a manner?"

"I might point out to you that Miss Davington does not sing at Vauxhall nor does she attend such places unchaperoned. You seem to be taking this very much to heart, Devlin. Does this make you think twice about making Miss Morrison Lady Easterley?" inquired Lawford in a distant, patronizing tone. He placed his quizzing glass to his eye. "Surely your mother and your sisters would not approve such an alliance, Devlin."

Marigold was able to hear no more as Sarah hurried her toward her dressing room, and for that she was grateful. He had done all of this—made love to her—not because he wished to, but because she seemed available and because he wished to point out to his friend the dangers of offering for her.

"Dash it all, Charles, if you weren't my friend, I'd call you out for this! I've never known you to be guilty of such vile behavior!"

"You refine too much upon it," drawled Lawford in his most annoying tone. "Miss Morrison will recover quickly and I see that your affection for her continues undiminished despite my actions. I'm sure I wish you very happy, Devlin." And so saying, he took himself away, leaving his friend to stare after him.

Later that evening Lawford wrote a stiff note of apology to Marigold, to be posted the next day. "Quite as cold and impersonal an apology," Marigold told herself upon reading it, "as if he had trod upon the train of my gown and torn it." A brief note from Charles to his aunt, dashed off later that same evening and carried round by a footman, notified her that he had business at his country home that demanded his immediate presence and that he was uncertain as to when he would be in town again.

"Drat the boy!" exclaimed Lady Ariadne, as she discussed this new and annoying development with Lord Easterley the next morning. The two had become allies in their determined efforts to marry Lawford to Marigold. "How someone usually so needle-witted could be such a muttonhead in this affair escapes me!"

"He thinks that I am going to offer for Miss Morrison," said Easterley ruefully. "I daresay that he has taken himself away so that he won't have to see it."

"But he thought that having her sing would cause you to cry off," protested Lady Ariadne. "He knows that your mother and sisters would frown on such an alliance."

"I know. But I believe he thinks that I am too smitten to let that stand in my way."

"And what of Marigold? What can you tell about her feelings?"

He shrugged. "I think she has been drawn to him from the first, just as Charles was to her—but I cannot be certain."

"I believe that I am," remarked the old lady grimly. "I think the girl likes him well enough if he were man enough to do something about it. If he will not stir himself in this matter, I will! He thinks he has taken himself away to safety, but I will see to it that he has not! He is going to be forced to face his feelings and make a decision instead of running away."

Lord Easterley looked at her admiringly and somewhat fearfully. He had come to recognize that Lady Ariadne was a force to be reckoned with and he almost felt a moment of compassion for his friend. He had no doubt that the old lady would see to the matter.

Singing at Vauxhall filled Marigold with the deep pleasure that singing had always given her. Seeing others held in thrall by her voice gave her a heady feeling of power, but since the emotion of the song always held her in its grip as well, the sense of power did not turn her head as it might have. Instead, she and the audience became one in the joy or sadness of the ballad.

She had never been lonely as long as she had someone to sing to, but she found to her dismay that this was no longer true. Suddenly, in the midst of a song, she would find herself searching the faces in the audience, and then an unfamiliar emptiness would come over her. Marigold chose not to face the matter directly, but she was aware that Lawford was at the root of the problem. He came no more to hear her sing, and when she sang "Take Me to the Fair," she found no more joy in the ballad, and told the orchestra leader that she did not care to sing it again, despite the demands of the crowd.

Sarah and Miss Turner watched her carefully, and one of them was always with her. They allowed no more opportunities for stealing away alone, not noting that the reason for doing so was no longer present. It would be too much to say that she grew listless, but the two ladies noted that her eye was not quite as bright nor her manner as joyful as it had been. Troubled, they took counsel with one another, but were unable to help her.

When John Ballard arrived at their door one evening, the ladies welcomed him profusely, hoping that a letter from Lady Ariadne would brighten Marigold's mood. Unfortunately, it did nothing of the sort.

"But this is terrible, John!" she cried, lifting her eyes from the hastily scribbled note. "Spence says here that Lady Ariadne is dying! Whatever has happened?"

Ballard's usually jovial expression was wooden. "I'm sure that I can't say, Miss Marigold, but the doctor was with her when I left, shaking his head and looking grim. Spence could scarcely pen that letter."

"I will come at once, John. Let me change and pack a valise." She turned to Sarah and Miss Turner. "Spence says that she is asking for me, and I must go, of course. Ismene, will you send a note to let them know I cannot sing just now?"

Miss Turner nodded and hurried away to take care of the matter while Sarah set about packing their things. Together, the ladies made the journey to Valwood with John Ballard, sadly recalling the many kindnesses of Lady Ariadne.

Lawford's summons to his aunt's side was received with understandable suspicion on his part, but a glance at the shakiness of Spence's handwriting and at the grim face of the footman who bore the message convinced him of its seriousness, and he too quickly made his way to his aunt's side at Valwood.

When Marigold and Sarah arrived, they were told that the doctor was attending her and then that he had given her a draught to make her rest. They were shown to their rooms and, after changing from their travel costume, retired to the drawing room to await their summons. The evening wore away and when Marigold noted that Sarah was drowsing, insisted that she retire. An hour or two later Spence appeared at the doorway, smelling salts and handkerchief to her face, and indicated somewhat incoherently that Marigold might be able to see Lady Ariadne soon.

It was very late that night when Lawford arrived. He stopped abruptly as he strode into the drawing room and saw Marigold dozing before the fire. She heard the sound, and her eyes flew open immediately.

"May I see her now, Spence?" she asked, standing and turning toward the door. When she saw who it was, the color flew to her cheeks, but she maintained her composure and held out her hand to him. "I am so very sorry about your aunt, Mister Lawford. I know how close you are."

Caught completely off his guard by the unexpected sight of her, he replied coldly, "We were close, Miss Morrison, before she met you. Seeing you here first should not surprise me. I should have realized that she would, of course, send for you. Doubtless you have expectations concerning her estate."

Her eyes flew to his face and she drew back as though he had slapped her. Saying nothing, she turned her back upon him and faced the fire, her shoulders stiff.

He watched her in remorse, knowing even as he spoke the injustice of his words. Cursing himself for a clumsy fool, he said stiffly, "Forgive me, Miss Morrison. I spoke too hastily."

When she did not respond or turn toward him, he took a step closer. "Will you not look at me, Miss Morrison, so that you may see that I mean what I say?"

Marigold turned toward him slowly and his heart rose again as it had when he first glimpsed her upon entering the room. Her eyes were bright with unshed tears, but she held her head proudly. "How came you to say such a thing to me, Mister Lawford? What have I done to deserve such an unkindness from you?"

"Nothing at all, Miss Morrison . . . nothing at all, I assure you. It is my own bad temper that caused it. Forgive me." And he extended his hand toward her.

She took it hesitantly and looked up at him. "I had never heard it said that you have a hasty temper, Mister Lawford."

"Usually I do not, Miss Morrison. I seem to lose it only with my aunt . . . and with you."

Marigold withdrew her hand and said gently, "I think that it must be because of the sadness of the moment, sir. I am afraid that Lady Ariadne is not going on too well. Spence said that we will be called as soon as she awakens again."

They took their seats before the fire and sat silently watching its flames for some minutes, disturbed only by Bowles, who came in quietly to offer them some refreshment.

Finally, glancing at her grave face, Lawford inquired casually, "And how do you go on at Vauxhall, Miss Morrison?"

Her cheeks darkened and she glanced at him resentfully. "That is quite an unkind remark, sir. Is it meant to remind me of my embarrassment there?"

"Not at all, Miss Morrison. I was sincere in my apology; I regret any distress I may have occasioned you by my ungentlemanly conduct. I merely wondered if you are enjoying the life there as you thought you would."

"I do very well, thank you, sir," she answered briefly, her chin tilted up a little defiantly.

He noted the lifted chin and smiled a little. "I am quite certain of that. I am sure that you are beloved. It could not be otherwise."

She looked at him in surprise, but said nothing. As they sat looking at one another, Marigold found herself wishing that she had needlework with her, or any occupation to which she could give her attention and gracefully escape his gaze.

"And is Lord Easterley well?" he inquired. "And does he come to hear you sing?"

She nodded. "He has been all that is most kind and gracious."

"All that I have not been," he commented bitterly. "When, pray, am I to wish you happy?"

Marigold stared at him blankly, and he laughed, a little bleakly. "Forgive me," he said. "I did not mean to steal a march on Devlin. I had thought he meant to offer for you immediately."

"Offer for me?" exclaimed Marigold. "Why would Lord Easterley wish to offer for me, pray tell?"

"Why, because he is top-over-tail in love with you, of course!" returned Lawford impatiently. "Any fool could see that."

"He does not mean to offer for me, Mister Lawford," Marigold replied firmly. "He is a most excellent friend, and he has even confided in me that he is giving serious thought to offering for Miss Lyle and settling down."

"Miss Lyle!" said Lawford, in disbelief.

"Yes," said Marigold pleasantly, "he thinks that they would suit one another quite well, and he said that there would be little pleasure in jauntering about alone now that you are about to marry."

This was too much for Lawford, and he stood abruptly and stared down at Marigold. "And who am I about to marry?" he demanded.

Marigold faltered a bit here. "Well, Lord Easterley did not mention the lady's name, but I had thought . . ."

"What had you thought, Miss Morrison?"

"I had thought that perhaps it was to be Miss Davington, for I had seen that you were quite attentive to her."

"Miss Davington!" And to her amazement, he began to laugh.

"Are you quite all right, Mister Lawford?" she asked anxiously, thinking that perhaps the strain had been too much for him. "Have I said something that I ought not?"

He took both her hands and pulled her to her feet. "Trust Devlin to cause me trouble even when he is not here to do so in person!"

"What do you mean, Mister Lawford?" she asked fearfully, thinking that he had quite possibly run mad.

"What I mean, Miss Morrison . . . Marigold, is that Devlin has been making a May game of me, and that I have never been so happy to be made a fool of!" Pulling her close to him, he said softly, "And I take back my apology for making love to you in the gardens, my dear. My only apology is that I allowed myself to be interrupted."

"And you think that because I sing at Vauxhall I am now fair sport for any gentleman?" she demanded, trying to pull herself from his embrace.

"Not for any gentleman," he corrected her gently, maintaining a firm arm around her, "for *this* gentleman only, if you will consent to becoming my wife."

"Your wife?" she gasped incredulously. "Your wife, a girl that has sung in Vauxhall Gardens?"

"My wife," he returned, "will be Marigold Lawford, a young lady with a most enchanting voice. Our guests will beg to hear you sing 'Take Me to the Fair.' "

Believing him now, she allowed herself the luxury of surrendering to his embrace, and for a moment she was aware of nothing in the world but him. Then, however, a noise brought them back to the world. It was Spence, clearing her throat uncertainly as she attempted to attract their attention.

"Yes, Spence?" said Lawford. "May we see my aunt now?"

Spence, her face scarlet, nodded wordlessly, pressed her handkerchief to her eyes, and fled. Together, they

132

made their way to Lady Ariadne's room. Only two candles lighted the room, and they could dimly see her propped against her pillows.

"Charles?" she whispered in a weak, wavering voice.

"Yes, aunt, I am here," he said firmly, coming to her side and taking her hand in his. "And Marigold is here as well."

"Marigold, is it?" she asked, her eyelids flickering.

He smiled. "How are you feeling?" he asked gently.

"I'll do," she replied briefly. "What of you, Charles?" Her voice faded so quickly that Lawford had to bend very close to catch her next words. "What will happen to you now?"

He pressed her hand. "I will be well, aunt." He leaned close to her again and raised his voice a little. "Marigold and I are to be married, aunt. I want you to know that. Marigold and I are to be wed."

Lady Ariadne's eyes flew open. "Married?" she whispered. "When?"

He looked at Marigold. "As soon as we can get a special license, aunt," Lawford replied, and Marigold nodded in agreement, patting the old lady's hand.

To their dismay, Lady Ariadne sat straight up in bed and threw off the covers. "Spence, did you hear that?" she demanded.

Thinking that she was working herself into a dangerous frenzy, Lawford tried to take her arm, but she shook him off impatiently.

"Spence, bring me my dressing gown and open the window and get some air into this room! And ring Bowles and tell him to bring me some decent food and a bottle of champagne to toast the bride-to-be!"

Without pausing to take a breath, she turned on her nephew and Marigold, both of whom were staring open mouthed at the transformation. "Do you realize, Charles, how much trouble you have put us to? A dratted inconvenience you have been. I've been locked up in this room for a week, and poor Spence, who hasn't an ounce of acting ability, has had to go about looking sad-eyed, pretending that I am about to die."

"Do you mean to tell me, Aunt Ariadne, that this has all been a sham? That you planned this whole thing to bring the two of us down here?" demanded Lawford indignantly, ignoring his bride-to-be, who had given way to laughter.

Lady Ariadne jerked off her nightcap and glared at her nephew indignantly. "Don't get on your high horse with me, Charles Lawford! If you had been sensible and listened to me, you would have offered for Marigold when I told you to and saved us all this trouble! Why, I've very nearly starved to death on chicken broth. I would have wasted away entirely if Spence hadn't sneaked in an occasional roll. You've very nearly been the death of all of us, including Easterley."

He stared at her in disbelief, then began to chuckle. "Devlin just thinks that he has seen trouble at this point. I shall show him real trouble when we return to London."

"Never mind Devlin, my boy," retorted Lady Ariadne. "Keep your mind on your own affairs. There stands your bride. Kiss her!"

Lawford bowed to her. "We have frequently disagreed, aunt, but upon this occasion I can do your bidding with pleasure." And he drew Marigold into his arms, unmindful of their admiring audience, and pressed his lips to hers. Marigold's loneliness of the past days vanished in a moment, and in the safe circle of his arms, she listened to him murmur gently, "A dream of marigolds . . ."

Spence wiped her eyes in earnest this time, and even Lady Ariadne was observed to blink suspiciously. "A June wedding, Spence! Exactly what I had hoped for!"

Spence nodded her agreement tearfully into her handkerchief, but the subjects of their conversation were blissfully unaware of their presence. Marigold was humming lightly and Lawford, catching the melody, smiled and cupped his hand beneath her chin.

"Yes, my dear," he said gently, quite as though she had spoken. "This time I shall indeed take you to the fair. I have been wishing to do so since I first heard you sing."

He guided Marigold toward the door, ignoring his aunt's indignant demand to know what had kept him from giving way to that wish at an earlier and more convenient time. Just as the door closed behind the happy couple, Spence and Lady Ariadne heard something that caused them to stare at one another in amazement.

"Well, I wouldn't credit it before this, but Charles's man Netherington was quite right," said Lady Ariadne. "Charles *is* singing."

Spence nodded in wide-eyed agreement. "And Mister Lawford has *never* been musical."

Through the open window they heard the sound of his deep voice joining in Marigold's silver song. "Nor is he musical yet," commented his aunt, listening critically.

Then her face relaxed into a rare smile. "But Marigold will have him believing that he is." She chuckled. "She will very likely have him singing at Vauxhall before the summer has ended. Charles has gone to the fair indeed."

June Masquerade

by

Valerie King

"Come, come," said Tom's father, "at your time of
   life,
  There's no longer excuse for thus playing the
   rake—
It is time you should think, boy, of taking
   a wife."
  "Why, so it is, Father—whose wife shall
   I take?"

*Rothley will take a mistress before wedding bells have
pealed from St. James's. Poor Miss Wilde!*

Venetia Wilde, sitting in Miss Hargrove's drawing
room among a dozen giggling young ladies, watched as
one of her tears plopped into the cup of tea she was
sipping. A pain as tangible as the bitter taste of the tea
had attached itself fully to her heart and was wrecking
havoc with her usually tranquil and easy spirits. Her recent betrothal to the notorious earl of Rothley had
transformed not into the fulfillment of her girlish daydreams as she had dared hope it would, but rather into
an acute disappointment which as yet no exertion upon
her part had availed the least effect. Rothley was
wholly, completely, and utterly bored with her and they
had not been engaged much above a month.

The tear, now swimming in the amber brew, had been
shed this morning because of a certain painful memory
that had been possessing her mind ever since its origi-
nation on the previous night at Almack's. She had had
the most wretched misfortune to overhear a devastating
conversation between Lady Jersey and Mrs. Chastleton.

"Rothley will take a mistress before wedding bells

have pealed from St. James's!" Sally Jersey had cried. "Poor Miss Wilde!"

Mrs. Chastleton unfurled her fan and shielded her gossiping lips with the whole of it. Clucking her tongue and shaking her head she queried, "Did no one warn her of his lordship's propensities? I have been told she entered willingly into the engagement."

"I blame her mother for this piece of folly—an encroaching mushroom if ever one had been born and bred." Only then had either lady noticed Venetia's close proximity.

"Oh! Oh, dear! I am sorry, Miss Wilde," Lady Jersey had mended. "Were you privy to my entire discourse with Mrs. Chastleton? I regret none of it, if you were! My poor, poor child! You should not have been permitted to even entertain the notion of becoming Rothley's wife. He is a rakehell of no mean order. And do not think you will reform him! There is not a female among us who could!"

Reform Rothley! How could anyone think such an absurdity. She had no wish to *reform* him, not one whit. She only wished—but what she wished was an utter impossibility when the earl would scarcely speak three words to her during the course of an evening's entertainment!

Venetia sat staring at her cup of tea. She had brought her struggling emotions to heel, her tears set aside as she began directing her attention to the excited chatter of the young women around her. The bevy of young damsels, some clustered about her knees, the rest disposed on a comfortable assortment of sofas and chairs, all glowed with a nuptial fever peculiar to the month of June. The elegant blue and gold chamber was alive with the flurry and flutter of issues of *La Belle Assemblee,* and with heated discussions of various kinds of lace and whether or not a veil—such as Josephine Bonaparte had worn for her wedding—ought to form part of the bridal ensemble. Most of her friends had become engaged during the Season's lively courtship dances—fêtes, balls, routs, Almack's, the opera, the ballet. Her dearest friend, Isabelle Hargrove, had even won her future husband's heart at Astley's Amphitheatre, of all places!

But with every exclamation of delight and excitement erupting from one or another of her friends, Venetia felt her spirits sink lower. Her cherished dreams of adventure as the earl of Rothley's wife now gave all the appearance of turning to dust before even the marriage vows were spoken. Her hopes that wedding his lordship would fulfill the deepest longings of her heart were as cold ashes in what was once a fierce bonfire in her soul. As she gazed about at the happy countenances of her friends, she realized there would have been a time when she would have entered into such a discussion of bridal fripperies with every joyous fiber of her being.

Not today.

Not after having endured Lord Rothley's stiff civilities and bored, restless demeanor whenever they were in company together.

Venetia had never been so disheartened, so disillusioned in her entire nineteen years. She had come to believe her betrothal to the earl had been a terrible mistake, one she intended to terminate the next time she met with his lordship. It would of course result in a terrible scandal, and she would be banished to her home in Oxfordshire for an entire year, possibly more, but she was convinced only misery—instead of love—could come of a union with a man who treated her as though she were a statue rather than a woman.

Her gaze drifted to the windows overlooking the street and she could just barely hear the rattle of carriages as the mobile *beau monde* hustled about Mayfair

141

during an afternoon of "at homes" and "morning" visits. Forgotten and fading into the fringes of her hearing was the jubilant chatter of the betrothed within the receiving room and in its stead, the world outside caught Venetia's full attention. She set her teacup aside and pressed her hands tightly together, as a familiar drumming of her heart began a steady rushing sound in her ears.

She rose from her seat, oblivious to the curious glances of several of her friends, and crossed the room to the windows. With a slight movement of her hand, she pushed back the thin muslin drape which obscured her view of the street, and watched the traffic pass by. Several men were abroad walking the length of the flagway with canes tucked beneath their arms and stylish beaver hats settled jauntily atop their heads. Two pretty young ladies, who Venetia recognized as the somewhat hoydenish Misses Long, emerged from a town house across the street, clambered into a waiting town coach, and leaned improperly out the windows espying something or other at the top of the street.

Venetia glanced in the direction of their joint gaze and noticed that a group of men on horseback had begun making a bold, aggressive progress down the street as though they intended to dominate everyone and everything in their path. When they caught sight of the Misses Long, their collective interest was at once sharpened.

They seemed to be a riotous bunch, descending upon the ladies with whoops and cries, teasing and flirting with the young women outrageously, causing other carriages to draw up, answering the unkind epithets of the drivers of those carriages with boisterous, rowdy words, and in general raining chaos and turmoil down upon the entire street! Much to the delight of the Misses Long, Venetia noted.

One voice, in particular, rose above the others, cursing the driver of a foppish high-perch phaeton, and with a start, Venetia realized Rothley, himself, was the possessor of that wicked voice. Her attention was immediately and intensely riveted to the tops of the high-crowned beaver hats on the street below.

Leaning forward and nearly pressing her nose against the windowpane, she searched carefully the markings of each horse, until she recognized Rothley's shining black gelding. How her heart turned completely upside down at the mere sight of him. Powerful sensations of love, worship, adoration flooded her heart causing a peculiar weakness to invade her knees.

"Oh, my love," she whispered into the pane. "Why can't you taunt me as you do these pretty, lively ladies? Do I displease you so very much?"

The tear, which had earlier flowed into her teacup and had sent a shrill warning to her heart, was now joined by a dozen others which filled her eyes to brimming. She had only one consolation in her love for Rothley, no one, not even the earl himself, knew of her consuming *tendre* for him. Isabelle suspected, but even she was not to be privy to the heighth and breadth of her love for the rakish earl.

Rothley began pirouetting his horse about in a circle next to the carriage in which the young women were situated, raising his hat aloft and giving a shout. He had never done as much for her. Never!

"What was that?" she heard Isabelle call out from behind her.

Venetia did not know what to say and so remained silent hoping that her friend would not attempt to discover the origin of the reckless cry.

Unfortunately, at that moment the other bloods, taking Rothley's lead, responded in like manner. Each guided their respective mounts about in circles or raced

143

them between the now jammed vehicles along the street. All the while, the wild gentlemen raised their voices like soldiers in full charge, and amid their revelry the delighted squeals of the ladies could be heard.

Again Isabelle demanded to be told what was going forward and Venetia could hear the interest of the remaining ladies become equally marked. The rustling of skirts, the murmurs of curiosity, the rising from chairs and sofas, all bespoke a shift in attention. The noise in the street below mounted ominously.

Isabelle cried out, "Venetia! Whatever is happening? Is there a riot brewing? Oh, I hope our windows will not be shattered. The bread riots in the city last week caused such damage — my heart is near to bursting! Only tell me what is transpiring! Tell me at once!"

Venetia could not tear her gaze from the scene below. Her fingers were clenched tightly about the muslin drape, her eyes still clogged with tears as she felt her friends press around her. "It is only Rothley," Venetia responded at last. She strove for a note of composure and disinterest as a terrible sense of despair overtook her.

She felt Isabelle's arm encircle her waist. "You mustn't repine," she whispered. "Once he is married to you I'm certain he'll behave just as he ought."

"That is what I fear most," Venetia murmured. Isabelle appeared as though she did not understand her, her brow wrinkled and questioning.

Venetia would have tried to explain, but at that moment, Miss Chastleton, a plump, girlish young lady, cried out, "Why it is Rothley! And he is flirting with the Misses Long! If my Stephen ever did such a thing, I vow I would box his ears! Poor Venetia. Lady Jersey was saying to Mama only last night — ow!" After a sharp intake of breath, Miss Chastleton leaned forward, caught Venetia's eye and said, "Oh, my dear Venetia, I

144

do beg your pardon! I meant no harm—oh, I say, I am sorry!"

Venetia took in a deep breath and was preparing to don her most cheerful smile and pretend she was unaffected by any of it, when another friend exclaimed, "Do but look! The Misses Long are directing the gentlemen to look up at our window!"

Venetia tried to pull away, knowing full well Rothley would recognize her at such an insignificant distance—and would not for a moment relish the idea of his bride *spying* on him—but the minute it was made known to the young ladies that several gentlemen were likely to ogle them, the press behind Venetia increased as all the ladies vied for better positions. She was prevented, therefore, from moving even an inch!

A second later, Rothley, his eyes stormy with exasperation, his brows drawn together in a deep frown, looked up at her, directly into her eyes. His expression was condemning and it was impossible to mistake his displeasure for anything other than what it was. Rothley was clearly regretting their engagement as much as she was!

She felt a hot blush cover her cheeks. She felt foolish, ill-used, and deeply mortified, not less so when he smiled sardonically at her and from astride his horse, slung his hat across his chest in a mockingly affectionate manner and bowed to her. If only the window had been open and she had had a sharp rock in her hand, she would have gladly thrown it with what her brother always called a dead accuracy, and smote his handsome, jeering face. But the window wasn't open, she hadn't a stone curled about her fingers and more to the point, she would give no one present the satisfaction of seeing her unhappiness. Therefore, she merely inclined her head to him and waved.

Not surprisingly, he seemed to decide the moment

had come to retreat and within seconds, the hot-blooded bucks which formed his entourage, raced off down the street, their shouts shocking every decent drawing room along the prestigious row of some of Mayfair's finest town houses.

Also not surprisingly, Venetia's plight soon became the sole object of every female present. Consolation in every form flowed over her like hot lava from a volcano. If only her friends would desist with their expressions of pity!

Poor Venetia!

Poor, poor Venetia! To have been ransomed to such a dreadful rakehell as the earl of Rothley!

She returned to her chair by the fire, her tears long since put carefully away, her visage masked in cool smiles, and her countenance composed. She was able to convince her friends after a few minutes of laughing denial that she was not in the least perturbed by Rothley's raffish misconduct. "Ours is to be a marriage of convenience only. Rothley may do as he pleases. I am to be his wife not his gaoler."

If her calm words and mechanical description of her wedding arrangements convinced most of her acquaintance she was resigned to her fate, Isabelle was not fooled.

Later, having settled herself cozily upon the foot of Venetia's bed, Isabelle confronted her. "You can make as many fine speeches as you wish but I know your heart is breaking! You've been in love with Rothley for years. And to be treated with such callous disdain—! My darling Venetia, it was nearly more than I could bear! That arrogant, horrid, odious smile as he looked up at you—!"

Venetia stood in front of her dressing table of gleaming mahogany and listened to her friend's commiseration, her heart feeling strangely aloof. She fingered

146

absently the black silk ribbons of a half mask dangling from the top of the looking glass. "I shan't pretend otherwise with you," she responded quietly.

"My poor darling," Isabelle whispered.

At that Venetia turned around quite abruptly and, leaning against the dressing table, cried, "If I hear *poor Venetia* one more time today, I vow I shall scream with vexation! I entered into this engagement with a clear understanding of what was expected of me—"

"—but you had such hopes!" Isabelle interjected. "Such extraordinary hopes that he would change!"

Now the tears, which Venetia had wished could be put away for eternity, showed themselves again, stinging her eyes. But this time they were an angry display. "No—no—no!" she exclaimed adamantly. "Not *change!* Not by half! I have loved Rothley because he is absurdly heedless of the opinion of society, because he dares to flaunt the strictures of a narrow-thinking set of people who don't give a fig for who he is or what he believes, because he is—oh, never mind!"

"No, Venetia, pray go on! I didn't know—"

"—how can I explain it to you, or to myself. I was raised with such restraints upon every aspect of my conduct that when I first met Rothley I fell in love with his absolutely untrammeled mind and behavior. Yes, he is reckless, but not more so than I believe I am at heart!"

"You don't mean that!" Isabelle responded, greatly shocked, her hand pressed to her bosom, her large blue eyes bulging from her head. "Do you mean you would wish to take as many lovers as he has taken—*bits of muslin?*"

"Oh, hush! I don't mean that precisely. I once read a verse by Alexander Pope, which went, *Men, some to bus'ness, some to pleasure take; But ev'ry woman is at heart a rake.* That is me! A—a rake! And the first, *to*

147

business, to pleasure, that is Rothley. I know most of my acquaintance believe he is useless but I know things about him that no one else does. Do you know he has been to Coke of Norfolk's to examine his methods of husbandry? And as for me, oh, Isabelle, how very much I long to travel, to see the world! I would adore to live five years on a sailing vessel—"

"—oh, Venetia, not a sailing vessel. Do but think of—of scurvy and of the terrible creatures which infest the flour—"

"—five, nay ten years on a sailing vessel," Venetia returned strenuously. "Through violent storms where we would emerge on the other side of the world to visit hot, humid lands where people scarcely cover themselves—oh, you see how wicked I really am!" She moved away from the dressing table and threw herself carelessly into a burgundy-and-gold-striped chair by the window. Leaning her head against the back of the chair, Venetia closed her eyes and sighed. "It hardly matters anymore, however. I beg you will say nothing to Mama, or to anyone else, for that mátter, but I intend to end my engagement to Rothley as soon as I am able. Tonight, I think, at the Chastleton ball."

An uncharacteristic silence reigned upon the bed.

When it had lasted for a full two minutes, Venetia raised her head and opened her eyes. She saw that Isabelle had been struck dumb by her announcement. Her mouth was unhandsomely agape, her expression shocked. "End your engagement?" she queried at last. "But you cannot! And whyever would you wish to forfeit being a countess? Besides, Rothley would never permit it! He is relying upon your fortune to restore his lands, his home!"

Venetia shrugged. "I don't give a fig for the title and as for Rothley, he is a man of honor, even if his reputation is sadly lacking. He will let me go, make no mistake, and that without recrimination or hostility. I know that much of him, at least, though I do wish it were entirely due to his chivalric nature rather than the truly lowering knowledge that he finds me tedious and wretchedly dull! He will be glad to be rid of me!"

"Well," Isabelle said with finality. "If you mean to break with Rothley, you won't be able to do so tonight. Now that I comprehend your sentiments I do not hesitate to tell you he will not be in attendance this evening."

"What do you mean? He—he has already promised!"

Isabelle grimaced. "He will proclaim a serious illness, no doubt. You will be informed by means of one of his footmen bringing round a note, bearing the grievous tidings—though I don't see how he means to explain such an illness when we all saw him in such excellent health this afternoon! But I know the truth as do a score of others! He means to attend the masquerade at Vauxhall tonight. I had it from young Mister Chastleton, who you know has recently been admitted to Watier's where he chanced to overhear some of Rothley's set teasing him about enjoying one last adventure before he becomes leg-shackled to the *ice maiden!* Now that I think on it, Venetia, I'm glad he is not to be your husband! He would break your heart!"

This last part, Venetia ignored. "The ice maiden?" she queried, stunned. "The *ice maiden?* Do not tell me I am known by such an unhandsome appellation?"

"Well, you must admit, your extremely decorous behavior and elegance—all of which I'm sure must someday please a more fastidious creature than Rothley—your carefully arranged braids and close bonnets, the way you always say what is expected of you and never cross your mama! The way you keep your eyes cast down in her presence! It is no wonder—oh, dear, now I see that I have distressed you sorely!"

149

Venetia was on her feet at these innocent recriminations of Isabelle's. She began pacing the chamber, wringing her hands first then pressing the same to her face. "You see, it is not entirely Rothley's fault! Mama would have me dress as though I were a schoolroom chit of thirteen—I have never once shown my bosom in society! And worse! I don't know how it is, but whenever I am in Rothley's presence, oh, Bella, I feel so much that I can say so little! Not that I alone am to blame. He has been stiff, too, but perhaps he was merely taking my lead, oh, I don't know, I don't know! It is all so useless! Well, never mind. If I cannot end our engagement tonight, then tomorrow will serve as well. Oh, Isabelle, I feel as though I have ended before I have even begun! It isn't fair!"

"Rothley's a beast," was all Isabelle could think to say.

"He is the only man I shall ever love," was Venetia's mournful reply.

Venetia sent Isabelle away only a few minutes later, begging off from an excursion to Hyde Park, proclaiming she was fast developing the headache. She returned to her dressing table, sitting down and again fondling the ribbons of the half mask. At first she felt angry that Rothley thought so little of her that he must sneak off to Vauxhall when he had promised to escort her to the Chastleton ball, but then she smiled. If only she could steal away to Vauxhall for the evening, just one evening of madness, perhaps flirting with a hundred gentlemen at once, and none the wiser that she was Venetia Wilde, heiress, *ice maiden,* betrothed of Rothley!

She sat bolt upright suddenly, a brilliant thought streaming into her head and exploding with all the flash and spark of a huge display of fireworks.

She could even flirt with Rothley himself, if she were

careful and clever enough!

With that, she decided the headache, she had professed earlier, would develop into gargantuan proportions forbidding her to even consider attending the Chastleton Ball.

And with that, she penned a missive to her betrothed informing him he was released from the horrendous duty of doing the pretty tonight, but would he be so kind as to wait upon her tomorrow morning at eleven o'clock when she was certain she would be fully recovered.

Lord Rothley, seated in a vile-smelling hackney, leaned heavily against his boon companion, Mr. Barrett. He was half foxed already from the evening's amusements and gave every indication of intending to succumb to the joys and perils of Bacchus before the night was through. The party, whose general purpose was to grieve the end of the earl's bachelorhood, was composed of three of his dearest friends — each a member of the Four-in-Hand Club.

The evening had begun at Barrett's rooms on Half Moon Street where the gentlemen had enjoyed an enormous repast including two excellent boiled cods with fried soles arranged around them and covered in oyster sauce, lark pasties, a fine swan roasted with currant jelly sauce, rump of beef *à la Mantua,* fillet of turbot, and sweetbread Provençal accompanied by a dozen side dishes and a constant outpouring of claret. Madeira adorned a display of desserts consisting of apricot cakes, chocolate soufflé, and grape pudding. Afterward, the party removed to Watier's where two hours of gaming had been enhanced by several bottles of port shared among the athletic, riotous gentleman who were joined by several of their acquaintance.

151

Even now, as Rothley lifted heavy lids to survey the exterior of Vauxhall Gardens, his mind was cloudy and uncertain. "Are we at the opera?" he queried of Mr. Barrett.

"The devil take it, are we?" his companion responded with a hiccough. "I'll have the hackney's head, damme if I won't—Oh!" He gave Rothley a shove, pushing him upright. "Open your eyes, man, we're at Vauxhall! At least, looks like the cursed gardens! Whyever did you wish to come here? Can't abide listening to the deuced orchestra, screeching away on those *violets!*"

"Violins!" Rothley corrected his friend, staring hard out the window and blinking several times to clear his gaze. "Dash-it-all! It is Vauxhall! But I don't see Holland or Tyers!"

Upon this observation, the door suddenly flew open and the large, hamlike hands of George Holland reached in to grab Rothley by the lapels and pull him forcibly from the carriage. He would have protested under ordinary circumstances but of the moment, the effects of so much wine had robbed his knees of their ability to work and of his well-shaped, athletic legs to support him. "Hallo, George," he said warmly, slinging an affectionate arm about the bulky form of his friend as Mr. Holland set him firmly on his feet. "Thought we'd lost you. Appreciate your assistance."

"Don't mention it!" George replied, the deep tenor of his voice slurring over his words slightly. "Anything for a friend. 'Specially one soon to be leg-shackled to"— here he paused and rolled his eyes dramatically—"to the *ice maiden!*"

The gentlemen all regarded one another with mournful expressions. As one, they repeated morosely, "the *ice maiden.*" Whenever Venetia's nickname had arisen during the course of the evening, they solemnly intoned the unfortunate name. The ceremony, such as it was, seemed likely to be repeated throughout the masquerade as well.

Upon this last recital, however, Lord Rothley wasn't so completely in his altitudes that he was incapable of experiencing a familiar sinking sensation at the mere mention of his betrothed. He felt as though a perpetual gloom had been cast over his head since becoming engaged to Venetia Wilde. Was ever a more imperfect wife created for a rogue of his stamp? She was in every respect an ice maiden; cold, wordless, soundless. She reminded him of the statuary in the British Museum! He had once looked at her auburn braids carefully to discover whether cobwebs and dust had collected among her careful, dull, unfashionable tresses! How surprised he was to discover none had! How she had blushed at his scrutiny!

As the small party ambled and swayed toward the busy entrance to the dark, enchanting plantation, the earl thought with irony that the only thing he truly loved about his soon-to-be wife, was her name. For as long as he could remember, several years in fact, whenever she would be recommended to him as a suitable heiress to restore his estates, he had been enchanted with her name — Venetia Wilde!

Venetia Wilde!

He had not thought he had permitted silly, schoolboy fantasies to possess him when he offered for her. He had believed he was a rational enough creature to separate his profound appreciation for her name with what manner of female such a delicately and closely nurtured young lady would undoubtedly prove to be. Still, he had been unprepared to meet a female as cool and as insipid as his betrothed.

She had not two words to say for herself.

She dressed with a propriety he found repulsive.

She stared at him with a mixture of fear and some

153

other sentiment he could not comprehend.

And she was apparently as resigned to her fate as he was, which only led him to believe she had entered into the bargain because she wanted a handle to her name—why else would she have agreed to wed a man of his sordid reputation?

He shuddered slightly. Theirs was not, nor would be in a sennight's time when they spoke their vows, a propitious beginning. The devil-take-it, why had he agreed to offer for her? Why had he not been more careful in his choice of a bride? Why had he not at least conversed with her before laying his proposals before her father?

Why?

He laughed aloud, which caused all his friends to cast concerned, questioning glances toward him.

Why, indeed?

Because his creditors would no longer wait and had threatened to force him to sell the Hall.

There was another reason, too, one which had gotten buried beneath the ice maiden's cold demeanor—she was deucedly pretty, even beautiful when she could be charmed into a smile. A feat which he had never yet been able to achieve.

"The *ice maiden*," he murmured with a heavy sigh.

"*The ice maiden*," his kind supporters echoed gravely around him.

"Oh, Miss!" Venetia's abigail cried. "They're all badly foxed and not even sporting dominoes or masks! Are you sure you ought to enter the gardens anyway? Do you be wishful that I should attend you?"

Venetia had been waiting for more than an hour in a closed town coach, the blinds pulled down save for a narrow aperture through which she was able to observe every arriving conveyance. "No, you mustn't come with me. I can't risk anyone recognizing you and therefore me. And yes, I must go. I must!"

She heard a melancholy sigh pass her maid's lips. "Aye, that you must." Mary had been aware of Venetia's heart from the first, many years ago, when her mistress had first laid eyes upon the handsome peer. There was very little which escaped her knowing eye and her tender, sympathetic heart. "But I think his lordship a proper beast for not even taking the trouble to disguise his identity! Every backstairs in Mayfair will be humming with gossip about his adventures at Vauxhall, particularly if he takes up with a—a certain ladybird, as you might say!"

Venetia glanced at her abigail, and saw the teasing light in her eye. Mary was nearly forty years of age, rawboned in her features, yet warm in her affections. She also possessed a somewhat wry sense of humor which she had just directed at Venetia's costume. A delicate gossamer of featherlike shapes, attached to a muslin gown, gave Venetia the appearance of a very beautiful, elegant, intriguing bird. In addition, her auburn hair was completely covered with a close, white hood decorated in real feathers. "A ladybird," Venetia repeated, smiling wickedly as she tied the strings of her white mask about her head. "How perfect!"

She turned back to glance at her betrothed and watched him pass through the entrance into the gardens, still hanging upon Mr. Holland's shoulder for support. When Rothley and his three fellow supporters had stumbled from the two hackneys, she could have laughed for the worry she had been so unnecessarily sustaining. When she had first arrived at the gardens, she had been anxious. Now, she could be at ease. Especially since her presence at Vauxhall would serve to prepare her for any malicious reports which would be circulating among the *haut ton* on the following morning. Even though Mary was quite right in criticizing his lordship for having been so indiscreet as to have left off wearing a mask, in fact she was grateful, since she would have little difficulty in discovering his whereabouts once she entered the gardens.

As Venetia alighted from the coach, she realized, much to her delight, that for the first time since she had come to London she was feeling pleasure such as she had imagined as a young schoolroom miss. Real pleasure, for she was embarking on her first of what she promised herself would be, many adventures.

"Monsieur! Monsieur! You must help me!" a frantic, yet distinctly feminine voice called out, quite near Rothley. He was standing next to the supper boxes, awaiting Bartlett's return with the location of their box, when he first heard the distressed voice. The moment he turned toward the source of the frenzied supplication—and greatly to his surprise!—a feathered female cast herself upon his chest, tugging upon his coat sleeves and further imploring his aid. *"S'il vous plait,* please, you must help me! Z'gentlemen, they follow me and try to hurt me! There you see! There they are! Such brutes! So unkind to a stranger in your country." She tilted her face up toward him, the gentle curve of her lithe, feathered costume, both intriguing and supplicating.

Rothley, still suffering acutely the effects of too much wine, gently pushed the charming creature away just far enough to look at her. She was wearing a striking ensemble which resembled a glorious white bird. Her headdress covered her hair entirely and was a mass of snowy white feathers, several of which formed a delicate, weaving crown that seemed intent upon brushing and torturing just the tip of his nose whenever she turned her head.

"Madame," he began, only to draw in his breath and exhale a hearty sneeze. "I do beg your pardon! It's your curst feathers, that is—I am sorry, your downy, er hat, has made me sneeze!"

The woman seemed amused as she apologized. "I am so very sorry, monsieur. But you will help me, won't you?" She leaned enticingly toward him and lightly placed her small hands, which were covered in lacy, ruffled gloves, upon his chest.

He tried to see behind her mask, to determine the color of her eyes, but the lighting was dim, even though the gardens were illuminated by a thousand lamps. "Help you?" he queried, confused. "Ah, yes! Scoundrels attacking you, is it? I'm 'fraid the gardens draw the riffraff from every corner of London!" He glanced about him, not so much for confirmation of the rogues' whereabouts, since he was by now convinced they would have vanished into the shrubberies rather than disturb the evening's revelries with a skirmish, but to see if he might catch sight of the lady's accompanying maid or companion.

The young woman also glanced left and right, apparently quite overset by the pursuit of her *admirers,* and the feathers once again wrecked havoc with his nose. "You are right!" she cried. "They are gone! I have you to thank, monsieur! How kind you are to take pity on me!"

Holding back a sneeze as he again looked down into her face, he queried, "Are you truly alone and unprotected, madame?"

"Oui, monsieur! It is true," she responded, her voice catching on a sob. "It was so very foolish of me, but I have not been in your country more than a month, perhaps a little more, but I so wanted some amusement! I can see now it was wrong of me, but I could not help myself! Do you ever feel like zat, like you wish for your life to be full of excitement and — and adventures?"

Rothley looked down at the creature he was almost holding in his arms, a feeling very much like wonder pervading his senses. He caught the faint scent of attar of roses and thought it was familiar but could not place it. "Yes, very frequently," he murmured, his hands resting lightly upon the woman's arms. Who was she? She did not seem like the usual bit of muslin who might accost him in such circumstances. For one thing she was French, but it was more than that. The excellent quality of her costume bespoke wealth of some sort, and she smelled so sweetly fresh!

He was completely charmed, he realized with a start. Her lips, the only visible part of her, were invitingly curved, and her smile was simply delicious, her teeth even, glistening, and pearlescently white, promising beauty behind her mask. He wondered if Barrett had found this exquisite creature and arranged for her to join them on this, his last escapade before his dreaded nuptials.

Bartlett, however, arrived at that moment with information about the supper box he had hired, and denied having ever met the woman before, as did both Holland and Tyers in turn. The latter adding in a low, appreciative voice, "And should I ever have come upon such an angel, I certainly would not have cast her your direction! You must take me for a buffle-headed clunch, what Rothley, to have given up such a fancy piece as this! Why even Tyers opera-dancer hasn't such a delightful figure nor such a well-turned ankle!"

The earl, who had taken great pains to secure one of the woman's lace-covered arms tightly about his own, knew a slight twinge of conscience as he posed a question to his friends. "What say you then? Shall we offer

158

protection to Miss, er, to Madamoiselle—?"

They all leaned their heads expectantly toward the young lady awaiting the revelation of her name.

She seemed enchanted by their joint attention, going so far as to slip her arm from about Rothley's, to unfurl a large, feathered fan which dangled from her wrist, and to drop a deep curtsy. Only then did she make her name known to her admirers. "Madame," she began with emphasis indicating she was either married or widowed. "Madame Maret, but you kind gentlemen must call me—Babette."

Rothley heard himself and his three friends all sigh at the sound of her pretty French voice as she said sweetly, *Babette*. She was a dream he had once had, a vision so exquisite, as to be unreal, an apparition embodying his ideal. He took in the rest of her costume, which was composed of a hundred beautiful, delicate spangled gauze pieces, shaped into feathers and tiered from beneath her bosom to trail behind her. Similar feathery pieces shaped the sleeves of her gown and the bodice was of white velvet, cut very low, revealing a tantalizing bosom. Pearls encircled a graceful neck setting off elegant sloping shoulders. The headdress of feathers trailed down her back and an embroidered half mask, stitched with seed pearls, was molded to features he could see were Grecian in line. Still he could neither determine the color of her hair nor the color of her eyes. She was the best of adventures, a complete mystery.

He was utterly entranced, his conscience, which for the barest second had warned him to consider his betrothed's sentiments should she learn of his scandalous conduct by attending the masquerade at Vauxhall, obliterated by his desire to make Babette, the most beautiful ladybird he could ever have imagined, his own.

* * *

Two hours later, Venetia sat at table with the four outrageous bucks, and was so deeply satisfied with her success, that contentment eased through her heart the way a bath of warm water could relax every overwrought nerve of her body.

She had learned more about Rothley in two hours, and about his friends, than she had been able to glean from her betrothed in a month consisting of a hundred hours of labored conversation. She knew for instance that they were radicals in their political beliefs, denouncing rotten boroughs and insisting vehemently on reform if England was to prosper in its pursuit of liberty. She knew Rothley loved his estates and desired desperately to restore them to their original glory, that he had instigated many of Mr. Coke's farming methods in hopes of improving his rent rolls. She knew Bartlett had been rusticated from Oxford for having unloosed screeching peacocks into the dean's chambers and that Tyers was greatly addicted to cock-fighting. And Holland! For all his love of boxing, he was an aspiring poet. She was enchanted by them all and when one anecdote would end, she would beg to hear another. Not surprisingly, such genuine, enthusiastic interest in their respective pursuits, earned her their full attention and devotion for the entire evening.

And how delightful was the dancing! When it was learned she enjoyed the science, she was kept on the tips of her white satin slippers—the very one's she had intended to wear for her wedding!—hours on end. She had always known Rothley was a fine dancer, but her reticent spirit when held within his arms had made her enjoyment of his abilities an impossibility.

Waltzing in his arms as Babette, she was able for the first time to revel in his skill and in his company. It was clear to her as well, that he was taking an equal degree of pleasure in her. As the evening progressed, as

160

the champagne flowed, as the musicians' fingers wearied upon the strings, Venetia's heart glowed with happiness, never more so than when she was held in Rothley's arms.

During the final waltz before the nightly display of fireworks, she whirled about the floor, amid a riotous collection of masked adventurers, Rothley's arm held tightly, scandalously about her waist. Her heart pounded in her breast as he looked into her eyes. His expression was fierce and commanding. What was he thinking? she wondered.

When the waltz was over, he drew her away from the supper boxes, and into the darkened pathways amid the plantation trees and shrubs. He did not speak, but once they were hid from the scrutiny of other masqueraders, he did not hesitate to draw her forcibly into his arms, and place a full, hard kiss upon her oh, so willing lips.

Rothley had kissed her once before, a rather cold peck upon her lips which had left her feeling horridly dissatisfied. Now, held brutally within the circle of his arms, Venetia had no cause for disrelish. If anything, she was overwhelmed by the experience of being properly assaulted by the man she loved. She felt dizzy and breathless as she slipped her arm about his neck and returned his kiss in full.

Overhead, she heard the sounds of fireworks exploding and thought with an inward smile she had not expected to actually hear fireworks when kissed by Rothley. But there they were! And how very appropriate such a raucous display seemed to celebrate an event which for Venetia meant the fulfillment of her every womanly hope.

After a moment, his lips grew sweeter, more tender, a delicate whisper. His tongue traced her lips, touched the tips of her teeth, and a faint moan escaped her throat. She was utterly captivated by his touch, by his near-

161

ness. She wanted the night to swallow them both up, to transport them to a place of quiet and safety where they could be alone, untrammeled by the expectations of society.

And then, all seemed to erupt about them at once.

A group of giggling, costumed females swept over and around them, tearing them apart, as a cluster of bucks followed quickly behind. Venetia was carried away with them for several feet and realizing the moment was an excellent one in which to depart, she waved gaily to Rothley, shook her head when he took a step to follow, and called out to him, "Zee opera house on Friday. It is to be another masquerade! Ten o'clock!"

In the dimness of the shrubs, she watched him nod, after which she turned and ran to her waiting carriage outside the gardens.

When Venetia had originally requested Rothley to wait upon her at eleven o'clock, he had responded, by use of his cold pen, that he would be happy to oblige her, stating with icy civility that her happiness was his sole object as her future husband.

She held the note now, staring down at it, a smile teasing the edges of her lips. She intended to give Rothley a severe shock today and had every hope of charming her stiff, reluctant bridegroom out of his betrothal sullens.

First, she had dressed recklessly for the occasion. How to charm a rake? she had asked herself. Modesty and propriety must go, even though she knew she was calling down upon her head a heap of maternal coals in relegating her maidenish gowns to the back of her wardrobe. Her mother's no doubt stunned disapproval would be vigorous, but she didn't care. Her heart, her

162

life, her future happiness had been staked upon the effects in the next few minutes of her simple scheme which she hoped would blast Rothley's indifference to—to the nether regions!

She stood before a tall, gilt-framed looking glass in the corner of her bedchamber and surveyed her appearance. She was dressed in a round gown of the finest French cambric whose very prominent advantage was the extreme cut of the neckline. She had no doubt whatsoever Rothley would find it charming. She had let her auburn hair, which was quite long, flow in loose curls about her shoulders and down her back. She knew instinctively her coiffure would please him. And she had even applied a faint glow of rouge to her cheeks and just a touch to her lips. Perhaps such artifice might at first startle him, yet she was convinced he needed to be jolted a little, if for no other purpose than to open his eyes a trifle to the truth of her hidden heart and secret, fanciful desires.

She nodded briskly to herself as she took one final perusal of her appearance in the mirror. She could do nothing more than this, she thought. Her heart swelled with hope as she lifted the curt missive to her lips, still held tightly in her hand, and kissed it once. "Rothley," she murmured into the stiff paper, her fingers trembling. "If you do not love me a little today, you never will!"

Mary scratched three times upon the door and entered with a brilliant light in her eye. "His lordship is arrived, miss, with four midnight black horses harnessed to his curricle. You will cut a dash, make no mistake!"

Venetia took in a deep breath and found her nerves were close to shattering. Weaving once upon unsteady legs, she put aside the rattling palpitations of her heart, and set her feet firmly toward the door and toward her

163

future. "That I will if he agrees to my scheme," she responded. "But first I must face the dragon!"

When her mama caught sight of her costume and the wild appearance of her hair, the severe frown between her parental brows, the martial light of her cold blue eyes and the flaring of her nostrils indicated that a violent storm was about to break upon the drawing room. Since Venetia had waited purposely to quit her bedchamber the moment Rothley had arrived, she was fairly certain, however, that she could hold the impending storm at bay until he crossed the threshold.

"What a lovely June day," Venetia began easily, ignoring the thundercloud resting heavily upon her mother's face. "I hope Rothley has brought his curricle. I daresay a drive to Bond Street would be most agreeable."

Mrs. Wilde, rising stiffly from the rose damask sofa upon which she had been regally seated, again flared her nostrils and opened her mouth with the evident intention of giving her errant child a severe scolding.

But before she could do more than bark her daughter's name, the butler announced the arrival of his lordship, much to Venetia's intense relief.

One bridge crossed.

How weak her knees felt. Now if only she could cross the second without mishap she would be safe!

Turning toward her betrothed, Venetia ignored her mother's whispered outrage and braced herself to confront Rothley. She let her mind flood with all the memories of the evening before—how wondrous it had been to waltz with her beloved, how warm was his discourse with her and with his boon-companions as they chatted hours on end, how intimate was the kiss he had placed on her lips. She could feel a warm heat rise to her cheeks, a veritable cloud of butterflies flying about her stomach as her heart swelled with love for the man before her.

Taking another breath, she began her attack.

"Rothley!" she cried, moving toward him brightly and extending her hand to him. She had never been so bold before and he seemed quite taken aback. "I am ever so grateful you sent round a note expressing a desire to place yourself at my service. I am in a dreadful quandary, you see. I don't know how it has come about—though I suspect there was some grievous error at the, the modiste—but not one garment of my bride clothes has yet arrived! I was hoping you might accompany me and use your influence to prevail upon the shop's owner, a certain *Madame Colette Duval,* to see that my clothes are prepared in good order! Madame Duval is a dear woman, though rather ancient, I fear, which must account for the unfortunate oversight in the preparation of my gowns and other furbelows."

"Venetia!" that sorely tried woman exclaimed hotly. "Why are you burdening Rothley with matters which must be of complete indifference to him! My lord, if you must know—"

Venetia whirled on her and said, "—yes, I know it is an imposition on his lordship, but who better to oversee how I am begowned than my betrothed, since it is his admiration that I seek above *all* others."

Mrs. Wilde seemed aghast and for the barest second was unable to speak. But only the barest second! "I don't know what to say to you, Venetia," Mrs. Wilde said sternly. "You are behaving quite irregularly! Are you feeling well?" She turned to her future son-in-law, and with a weak, anxious smile, continued, "Lord Rothley, you must pardon my daughter! I fear, unbeknownst to myself, she has developed a—a brain fever, or some other malady! I am so sorry! You must think her quite addled! I assure you, I have seen carefully to her education, to the shaping of her manners—"

"—Mama, enough!" Venetia countered quietly.

"Rothley knows all too well you have done your duty by me." A fearful silence weighted the room following this terrible pronouncement and for perhaps the first time in her life, Venetia had effectually silenced her good parent.

Turning toward her betrothed, she drew very close to him and possessed herself of his hand. "I am not at all unwell, my lord," she said serenely. "So I ask of you, will you oblige me in this one thing?" She could not keep from smiling a trifle, a wicked glimmer entering her eye as she added, "After all, in your missive you said my happiness was now your sole object."

Rothley opened his mouth as if to speak, but words did not issue forth. He narrowed his eyes at her, as though trying to make her out. Finally, he smiled, ever so slightly, and gave all the appearance of comprehending the fact she was teasing him. An answering gleam stole into his rakishly blue eyes and a spark of life replaced the habitually bored expression which had frequently marred his countenance while in her presence. "It isn't done, you know," he whispered enticingly. "A gentleman does not accompany a lady—even his future bride—to her dressmaker's."

"I beg you will indulge me then," Venetia added with another pressure to his fingers as she presented him with her most dazzling smile. His gaze dropped to take in the even rows of her teeth, a faint look of awareness coming into his eyes, then vanishing. His gaze dropped lower, to the scandalous cut of her gown, and he returned the pressure of her fingers. When his eyes shifted back to her face, he no longer wore the expression as one who had been bowled over by a mail coach but instead sported a look of genuine interest, the first since his having offered for her.

Venetia knew then that some small victory, in her campaign to conquer his heart, had been won.

Lifting her fingers to his lips, and placing a gentle salute thereon, he said, "I should be happy to squire you to your modiste and to offer what advice I can, however pitiful it might prove to be, regarding the suitability and style of your bride clothes. That is, if your mama hasn't the least objection." Here he turned to bow to Venetia's afflicted parent.

Since Mrs. Wilde was frightened of both Rothley's rank and the satirical eye with which he was wont to dispose of encroaching mushrooms, she merely shook her head and murmured that whatever pleased his lordship, pleased her. The only comment she offered was, "I shall see that your abigail brings down your pelisse and bonnet, my dear."

Venetia further excoriated her parent's nerves by saying, "No, Mama. Not today. The sun is shining so brightly that I have a sudden and quite inexplicable desire to feel its warmth upon my face." She turned toward her betrothed, and stated, "No bonnet, no pelisse, unless you order it so, my lord."

Rothley seemed stunned. For a lady to go about unadorned by either garment, however warm the June day—and wearing such a ravishing gown at that—was considered a dreadful breach of conduct. "Are you certain you wish for it?" he queried with a challenging spark in his eye.

Venetia regarded him squarely, her spirits soaring. "Yes," she responded. "Today, at least. And tomorrow you may escort me to Hyde Park, if you like, though I daresay I shall no doubt need to cover my head in shame! It wouldn't do to go about setting up the tabbies' backs more than once, I think." She paused, letting her words settle into his mind, then queried, "Or would you consider it a terrible bore to attend me to Hyde?"

"I would be pleased, nay enchanted to do so,"

Rothley returned gallantly, a devilish smile lighting his recklessly handsome face. "As I told you in my missive, your happiness, your pleasure, is my sole object."

At that Venetia could not restrain a giggle. Slipping her arm through his, she guided him gently away from her mama and toward the doors leading to the landing. "What nonsense you speak! As though you ever consider anything but your own pleasure! But pray don't think I'm censuring you, my lord. As it happens, I have admired you for a long time because you do just as you please! I hope to learn by your example!"

As they marched through the portals of the drawing room, she heard her mother behind her moaning and gasping about not being able to find her vinaigrette and how had it come about she had raised such a shockingly ill-mannered, hoydenish daughter?

Late Thursday night, three days following the excursion to Madame Duval's, Rothley stared down at the enchanting creature in his arms as he waltzed Venetia about the floor. They were moving easily to the strains of a competent orchestra in Mrs. Tyer's ballroom, and chatting comfortably as though they had been friends for years. He was simply unable to credit his eyes, his ears, his senses! So much had transpired in the past few days, so altered were Venetia's manners toward him—delightfully so!—that he did not recognize the female now leaning enchantingly into him and teasing him about the enormous quantity of gowns he had ordered for her to take to Paris with them on their honeymoon.

"And several are so outrageous in style, my lord, however will you be able to take me about in public!" she whispered.

He would have answered her but his thoughts were too overwhelmed by the miracle before him. Instead, he merely smiled, pulling her closer to him, and enjoyed the look of pleasure this small action on his part gave her.

Venetia had bewitched him, he realized, but how? When?

He reviewed all that had transpired recently in an effort to determine what had caused such a distinct alteration in her temperament, yet nothing came forward in his mind to explain the remarkable transformation which had somehow magically occurred. He knew instinctively that Venetia was not playing off airs with him, pretending to be what she was not. Rather, she was revealing herself to him. But why now?

He could account for her earlier reticence quite easily since he had come to understand, through her carefully chosen words as well as his own observation, that she had lived an oppressive life under the guidance of her strict, ungenerous mother, whose sole ambition in life had been to see her daughter wed to a man of exalted station.

The family fortune had been made in trade, and Mrs. Wilde was not well received among the ton. She and her daughter had been granted vouchers to Almack's, that select assemblage of high sticklers, only because he had begged Sally Jersey to plead for Venetia with the patronesses who strictly governed the august assemblies. Lady Jersey had not failed him and had even gone so far as to say, only the night before, that though in general she was persuaded a woman could have little effect upon her husband, she was now thoroughly convinced Venetia Wilde would be the making of him.

He wondered. She in no way exhibited the smallest desire to change him. She delighted in his recklessness and heedless disregard for the opinions of others. The oddest thing was, though, that from the day she had driven out with him in the curricle, wearing a quite scandalous gown, given the nature of the excursion, and her hair improperly loose about her shoulders, he had been filled with the strongest and most surprising desire to prevent a reoccurrence in the future—to wit, to protect her. They had been sighted by several members of the ton, and the gossip about her attire had quickly filtered down to even the stupidest of gabblemongers, one gentleman of whom informed him at White's, in a rather slurred speech, that his bride-to-be was a notorious creature without the least regard for decorum! He had quite naturally planted the unfortunate gentleman a facer and called him out, but the coward had wisely left London later that night rather than risk his life facing the finest shot in England. Since then, Rothley had politely requested Venetia to wear her bonnets and pelisses and not to dampen her muslin again as she had tonight!

She was proving somewhat incorrigible and he was enjoying every moment of it! No longer could any of his friends refer to her as the *ice maiden!* But whatever had caused her to melt? He shook his head. He could not for the life of him account for it!

It was therefore with a sense of bewilderment that he undertook to protect Venetia's reputation. She even teased him about how unfair it was that she could not kick up a lark now and then while he—! Well, he had begun to wonder just how much she knew of his former life and even about his adventure at Vauxhall.

It was commonly known he had attended the masquerade since he had foolishly, because of the state of his inebriation, left off wearing a mask. He was in little doubt she had learned of his indiscretion. Theirs was a small society and little was left unnoticed and therefore undiscussed.

To her credit, though, she had not once even hinted

she knew of his having attended the masquerade, nonetheless having spent the evening dancing with a beautiful ladybird.

This last thought seemed ill timed, however. The wayward strains of his mind had been so taken up in examining the recent miracle which had transformed his insipid engagement into a fast-blooming affair, that he only now heard the question he was certain Venetia had repeated at least twice. "Do you mean to squire me to Lady Jersey's ball tomorrow night? Mama wished to know whether or not we should invite you to dine with us beforehand."

Rothley was completely overset. The question, innocent enough, and made with affection gleaming from Venetia's eyes, was one which must perforce cause him to lie—at least if he was to keep his assignation with his ladybird!

Clearing his throat he said, "I'm sorry, Venetia, I won't be able to escort you. A—a prior engagement precedes your claim. I am sorry." He then paused for a moment, looking into beautiful, bewitching blue eyes and added, "Though I think if it were in my power, I should attempt to break it. But alas, it is not possible!"

If he expected a rebuke, he was fair and far off the mark. Venetia regarded him slyly, teasingly, and said, "I hope then you have a remarkable adventure and that on Saturday you might regale me of all the details. I have come to depend upon you as a window to the real world upon which I can only gaze—and occasionally place a trembling foot of my own."

"I wish you could come with me," he said, surprised he had spoken the words. What did he mean by them? He wasn't even sure he knew.

Of one thing he had daily become more convinced, however, that he must relinquish his fascination for Babette and send her gently about her business.

171

Venetia was late for only one reason, she had not considered how difficult it was, or how much time was required for a man to tie his neck cloth! She was attempting the *trone d'amour,* and scattered about her stockinged feet was a beautiful drift of wrinkled, white neck cloths. She tugged, pulled, wrested with the white linen, lifting the fabric, tucking in errant folds of the cloth, until she cried out in sheer frustration. Mary told her instantly to hush else her mama would come rushing into her bedchamber with the intention of discovering if Venetia's supposed headache had resulted in a fit of the ague as she suspected it would.

Venetia rolled her eyes. "It won't matter one whit if she does if I do not leave within a few minutes! Rothley will have very soon forgotten all about his assignation with Babette."

"Do let me give it a try, then!" Mary returned, an anxious frown between her brows as she stepped close to Venetia, forced her chin into the air, and began working nimbly with the unyielding linen.

Greatly to Venetia's dismay, since she had struggled valiantly to achieve an acceptable arrangement, Mary succeeded in tying a remarkable *trone d'amour* within a scant three minutes. She cast a scathing look upon the beaming, bony visage of her abigail and told her to "stubble it" when Mary dared to open her mouth to speak!

Venetia turned her attention fully to the completion of her outrageous toilette. She tied a red silk half mask over her face and settled a black beaver hat atop a short black wig which she was wearing to disguise her incriminating auburn hair.

Once she had donned her black cape, pulling it close about her black coat and black pantaloons to hide her girlish figure, she vowed she did not recognize herself. "He will not know me," she stated, surprised.

Mary agreed, turning her, however, abruptly by the shoulders and pointing her toward the door. "But as you was saying, miss, he'll not wait much longer for you. So, off with you then!"

Stealthily, Venetia made her way down the servants' stairs and toward the mews where she strode casually into the streets. After only a few minutes of walking she was able to hire a hackney to take her to the opera house. If the driver looked hard at her when she gave him the direction, she ignored him and jumped lightly into the vehicle, confident she appeared like a young man. The entire duration of the journey, she smiled. How her heart soared with excitement at the very idea of not only being with Rothley again in the guise of his French ladybird, but of embarking upon another adventure.

When at last she arrived at the opera house, she saw Rothley at once and felt a familiar rush of affection at the sight of his tall, athletic figure. He was dressed elegantly in similar attire as her own, though in lieu of a cape he sported a black silk domino. And suddenly, just as she was sitting forward and preparing to quit the hackney, it occurred to her, with all the force of a truth not yet realized or considered, that he was being unfaithful to her, to Venetia, in meeting with Babette at the opera house!

Her spirits took such a quick, fierce plunge that she fell back into the interior of the musty carriage, her heart pounding mightily in her breast. In her female stupidity, she had thought only of being with him and of having adventures. "Oh, dear," she murmured into the darkness and dankness of the coach. "Whyever did I not foresee such a quandary as this?"

Yet, what had she expected of Rothley? Not to keep

the assignation? Impossible. However much he might delight in shocking the ton with his rakish conduct, he was unerringly faithful in his obligations. Because he did not know where Babette resided, he most certainly could not have either corresponded with her or have paid a call upon her with the purpose of excusing himself from their forthcoming tryst. It would follow then he could have every intention of doing so this evening and all would be neatly settled between them. Or she could turn back at this eleventh hour and return to Upper Brook Street with none the wiser!

The hackney driver spoke sharply to her, was she wishful of going somewhere else?

She must decide what to do. But what should she do? If she ordered the driver to return her to her mother's home, Rothley would never see Babette again, and her current difficulties would be effectually ended.

But that wouldn't serve! If Rothley meant to be unfaithful to her, then she wished to know, she wished to know now. Her heart felt as though it was being pulled apart. Life was ever so much more complicated than she had supposed it would be. In all her hopeful fantasies about the future with the man she loved, she had never once considered the possibility that she would be unable to live with his infidelities.

Now she understood the truth, particularly since she had tasted the sweetness of his kisses, had enjoyed his attentiveness, his interest in her welfare! She could not be satisfied with anything less than his complete love and devotion.

With these last fitful ruminations, her decision was made, but how anxious she felt! Rothley and fidelity seemed an incongruous combination, indeed!

She paid her fare and ignored her betrothed for the present, moving to stand near the entrance where she could watch him. She set aside her weighted concerns and began to look about her and to enjoy the freedom which only men were generally permitted. She had long since known that women like Caroline Lamb—who had once had a violent affair with Lord Byron—would go about London dressed as young gentlemen, and though she had always believed it was for the adventure of it, she now saw the experience in a new light. What devilishly wonderful liberty it was to merely stand by the entrance to the opera house and to have scarcely a single person present pay the least heed to her. She even leaned against the wall, crossing one ankle negligently over the other, and crammed her hands into her pockets. She realized she was, to all intents and purposes, invisible. What joy!

She could even watch with a certain mischievous detachment as Rothley finally gave up his post at the edge of the flagways and moved inside the foyer among a crush of costumed and dominoed guests.

Venetia followed behind at a distance of a scant few feet. Rothley, who was above the average height, scanned and rescanned every female around him. Venetia moved closer and closer, watching him all the while, finally coming to stand next to him. She whistled faintly a tune popular of the day, and rocked on her heels. Rothley glanced at her and though he wore a mask she could see he was clearly annoyed by her presence.

She remained where she was, rocking on her heels, and every now and again looked up at him and smiled. When she had been doing this for about two minutes, Rothley's hand suddenly encircled her arm roughly, as he whispered in an angry voice, "Take yourself off, you young whelp! What do you mean by your smiles? And why the devil do you still wear your hat!"

Venetia was startled into a cry by the firm grip on her arm, but quickly recovered her surprise with a trill of laughter. "Monsieur," she began. "Why do you speak with such anger. I thought you knew it was I—*ici!*—here, standing beside you!"

"Babette," he cried, turning to face her fully and grabbing her other arm. A beatific smile suffused his face, lighting his blue eyes with a warm, affectionate gleam. Venetia knew both exhilaration and intense disappointment. His smile was so full of—of love!

A stream of masqueraders poured by them and Venetia could not help but point out that it might seem very odd in him to be holding her in such a familiar way. "After all, I am dressed as you are—like a man!"

Rothley released her at once and cleared his throat. "Indeed, yes," he responded.

"Are you surprised?" she said, smiling wickedly and leaning into him slightly. "I wanted you to be! I wanted you to fall over in a faint!"

"Well, I almost did, you little baggage. Now take off your hat first, then come with me. I must speak with you."

"Will you ogle z'ladies as you did at Vauxhall? I shall join you of course and zen you shall learn what a woman thinks of the females you choose to admire!"

"Enough," he whispered, a pleading note in his voice. "And pray stop teasing me so delightfully. You only make matters impossible."

Venetia fell silent immediately, not because she felt obliged to obey his command to cease her taunting manners but because she felt his speech could only mean he intended to break with Babette? Oh, if only he would!

Rothley was in a state of acute indecision. He had had only one purpose in coming to the opera house masquerade tonight—to wish Babette every happiness and to bid her a firm farewell. However, the moment he had realized she had dressed herself so shockingly as a man, his former interest in her had been doubled, nay trebled! Everything about her bright, playful temperament spoke earnestly to that part of him which demanded that his life be larger than the narrow confines of the circles in which he moved.

Yet, as he walked beside her, heading toward the box he had hired for the evening, he could not help but think of Venetia and all that she had come to mean to him over the course of the past four, incredulously wondrous days.

But why should he be denied Babette's company, even for this one evening?

For as long as he could remember, as the eldest son of the house, as heir to a peerage and a vast estate however ramshackle its current financial status, he had known his mind, intensely, fully, down to the most minuscule aspect of any matter, however trivial.

Tonight, however, though he had come to the opera house with the strict purpose of relinquishing Babette to other, er, hopeful gentlemen, the moment he had realized it was her standing beside him, whistling a most aggravating melody, his former rather piercing interest in her awoke and threatened to sweep his decision away.

Four nights earlier, at the masquerade at Vauxhall, when Babette had so thoroughly captured his fancy, he had come to an awareness of how impossible it was for him to marry Venetia. When he had first offered for her, it was with the understanding theirs would be a marriage of convenience only. He was prepared, or so he thought, to accept such an insipid arrangement. But as day followed day, and he steadily went about fulfilling his social obligations to Venetia, doing the pretty as it were, the boredom with which he performed these services so paralyzed him he knew at last, if it were possible—particularly after having spent a delightful evening with Babette at Vauxhall—he must beg Venetia to cast him off.

But the next day, when he had arrived at her town house prepared to suggest they part company, he had suffered a severe shock. Not only had she courageously stood up to her dragonish mama, but she had been begowned so enticingly—even seductively for such a modest hour of the day—with her curls loose about her shoulders, his opinion of her had undergone a rapid change. Her manners, almost overnight, had become devilishly flirtatious and gone was every vestige of his recurrent boredom and in its stead a peculiar hope which had taken root in his heart.

Several times during the subsequent days and evenings in Venetia's lively company, he had caught a glimpse of what the future with her could be. He had little doubt she would be a warm, generous wife, hopefully providing him with a vast number of children shrilling their squeals through the dead halls of his house. He had never before imagined such domestic, country felicity before, but now that Venetia had prompted such visions, he was amazingly reluctant to relinquish either her or the dreams she had inspired.

Yet here was Babette, dressed as a young man on the town, trilling her giggles, prepared to share an adventure with him and he found himself as fully drawn to her as he was to Venetia. At the same time, he divined Venetia would not be accepting of his mistresses. Yet how was he to turn away the creature now striding beside him, her hands shoved casually into her pockets, her lips puckered into a whistle and emitting the wretchedest of noises. What a coil!

When he drew her into the private chamber behind the box he had rented, he closed the door and without the least query as to her preferences, drew her into a firm embrace and silenced her whistling lips with a hard kiss.

Rothley watched his betrothed pour out a cup of tea for him. He could see that her fingers trembled slightly in the task and that her cheeks were uncommonly pale. His conscience smote him, thoroughly and deeply. He knew a sentiment he had not expected to feel—he felt like a dog in the manger. Guilt riddled his mind. Should he confess his crime to her, that he had spent an evening with a woman he desired above all things to make his mistress, whose charming manners and love of adventure, whose professions of modesty, all sent every wicked thought flooding his mind? Should he tell her? What a sapskull he would be if he did!

Yet as he gazed upon his betrothed, who again wore her hair clinging to her shoulders and to the long slope of her neck, a very similar desire invaded his heart and he thought for a moment he must be going mad. Never had two women so possessed his mind, his heart, his desires and both within the space of a scant few days!

He wondered, and even felt panicky at the thought, whether Venetia had learned of his escapade at the opera house of the night before. Her countenance, if he was reading it correctly, bespoke such a knowledge, since he could see something was distressing her mightily. But upon consideration, it seemed unlikely that she could have learned of his adventure. If anyone had seen him at all, it would have been in the company of a young man.

Oh, lord! Perhaps that was worse yet!

Decidedly, he was going mad!

They were seated in Mr. Wilde's library partaking of tea and apricot cakes. He was stationed directly across from Venetia, leaning forward on a settee of gold and white stripes, staring hard at her. She kept her eyes cast down, and therefore he could not discern precisely what emotion kept her fingers trembling and her cheeks pallid.

"You are so quiet this morning, Venetia," he began in almost a whisper. "What are your thoughts? May I know them? Have I—have I displeased you?"

There, he gave her an opening in which she could bite his head off if it pleased her to do so.

Instead, she lifted her face and met his gaze squarely, appearing surprised by his query. "Displeased *me?*" she asked, shaking her head. "No, I think that would be utterly impossible. It is I who must somehow have displeased you."

He was so taken aback, that he set his cup down on his saucer with a clatter and spilt his tea on his buff breeches.

She quickly handed him a linen towel, biting back a smile as she did so. Her amused expression threw him into further confusion. He could not make her out! After he had dabbed at his breeches for a moment, he began again, "Whatever do you mean that you must have somehow displeased me! I don't understand."

"But it must be true," she cried, rising impulsively from her chair, and coming around the small table which separated them to sit beside him. She then placed her small hand within his and said, "You've never kissed me, Rothley, not even once! I have been beset with the notion for the past several days that perhaps you have been wishing you had not offered for me. Tell me most truthfully, do I displease you? Is that why you are so reticent and shy with me?"

Rothley had never been so nonplussed in all his existence. "Reticent?" he queried, a form of shock having taken possession of his faculties as well as his limbs.

"Yes," she responded, somewhat sadly, though he

180

thought he could detect a hint of a twinkle in her eye. "You see, I have something of a confession to make to you."

"A confession?" he queried, former feelings of madness again tumbling over his mind. How was it possible she had a confession to make to him when he was the one who was thoroughly caught up in wrongdoing!

"Yes. You see, when I learned you had approached Papa about the possibility of the union of your title and lands with my fortune—" She paused, a faint blush marring her cheeks. "Do I offend you in speaking thusly about our marriage arrangements?"

He was not in the least offended by her forthrightness and said so. At the same time his sense of distaste for having entered into an engagement with any woman because of his need of her fortune, rose up within him and he answered equally as frankly, "I had made numerous efforts to repair my estates without having to resort to such means as our betrothal afford. I wish you to know, I had wanted to choose my bride without consideration of her prospects."

This speech, he realized, placed unspoken conjectures directly between them and he regretted his words knowing that Venetia could interpret his speech to mean that he would not otherwise have offered for her. She nodded once only, comprehending his thoughts, but to his surprise, she did not seem at all overset by it.

Instead, her eyes took on a decidedly warm glow as she watched him. "Ours is a difficult situation, isn't it?" she offered, giving his hand a gentle squeeze. "At any rate, when Papa told me of your interest in me, I did not hesitate to express my most ardent desire to become your wife. Only I fear that hitherto you might have misunderstood my motives."

"You do not mean to tell me you fell violently in love with me," he said lightly, unwilling to believe it

181

could be true, yet hoping in some boyish way it was.

She smiled affectionately at him. "No, silly," she responded, kicking off her slippers, snuggling into the sofa and leaning her head sweetly upon his shoulder. Her hand was still held clasped in his and impulsively he lifted it to his lips and kissed her fingers, then turned her hand over and tenderly placed a kiss on her soft palm.

He heard her sigh with satisfaction. He shifted slightly to better see her, and felt a wave of emotion wash through him. Her auburn hair flowed across his blue coat and onto the gold and white stripes of the settee, her clear blue eyes danced with pleasure and an amusement which escaped him. Why hadn't he kissed her? He couldn't remember. Yet, as he watched her, no woman had ever given him such a warm invitation as this. And tomorrow she would become his wife.

He was thoroughly captivated by her and still possessing himself of her hand, leaned down to place his lips for the first time upon hers. Forgotten was Babette. All his thoughts, desires, hopes were for Venetia. How tender were the lips which responded so sweetly to his, how pleasant the feel of her fingertips upon his skin, as she caressed his face.

After a moment, he pulled back from her and looked deeply into her eyes. "So why was it then that you agreed to marry me?" he queried, wondering what on earth her answer would be.

"Because I wanted your life," she whispered, strange tears burning brightly in her eyes, lighting her soul, and captivating him more fully than ever. "I wanted to experience a little of the freedom I have always known you so fully enjoy. It may seem a little thing to you, but you've no idea how closeted my existence has been. I have been sheltered from every harshness of our society and all I can think about now is wanting to see and hear and feel the dreadful things I have been warned about. I don't mean matters of vice, but Mama would not even permit me to visit our neighboring manufacturing towns in the north because there have been so many unfortunate Luddite attacks. The poor were a mystery to me, until coming to London and actually seeing the misery in which so many exist. And when a troop of heroic soldiers returned from the Peninsula and marched through our village, I was forced to remain at home and practice my fugues, airs, dances and—and French knots!

"I saw you once when I was sixteen, I think. You had been traveling from the north with, oh, it might have been Bartlett and Tyers, I'm not sure, though I am positive Holland was with you—he has the largest hands of any man I've ever seen! You had stopped at the Rose and Crown in our village and by mere chance I saw you laughing and drinking great tankards of ale with your friends. Do you remember what happened next that day, after you left the inn?"

He shook his head. He had only the vaguest recollection of it.

"You found a man beating his servant with his whip—do you recall it now?"

"Oh, yes, of course! Hertfordshire, wasn't it?"

"That's right. I shall never forget that you intervened and hit the man very hard, 'gave him a leveler,' is how I think Holland phrased it. I wanted to marry you from that day. I won't call it love, though! Admiration, most definitely, but perhaps what I feel is merely an acute selfishness that I wished to be aligned with someone who embodies virtues I value and don't possess even in the smallest degree. I hope you won't think I am being too absurd. If I am, you must remember my experience of the world is horridly small."

He was overwhelmed by the expressions of her heart.

He had never believed his existence had had any great value until this moment. "That you would extol my character as having even one virtue is an astonishment to me! Mine is the selfish life. I have seen to nothing but my own pleasure, my own vain pursuits." He would have liked to have added he vowed to do better, but he thought it a far more sensible thing to remain silent and to prove out such a vow by his actions instead.

"You are too hard on yourself, Rothley. I know better! I have seen you with your friends, for one thing. Why, only two days ago I saw you give a very large sum to Tyers in which to settle a debt—and you with so little to call your own! I know you have an interest in reform and were you not speaking recently about the plight of chimney sweeps?

"No, my lord. Your actions, however mightily you keep them from general knowledge, speak of a character any man or woman of sense would admire!"

"Oh, my darling Venetia," he whispered, gathering her up in his arms. "I am so glad you are to become my wife!" Without waiting for an invitation, he kissed her full upon the lips.

Mrs. Wilde opened the door to the library and saw her daughter scandalously caught up in the embrace of the rakish Lord Rothley and would have intervened, had not a tight grip on her arm and a subsequent jerk backward, prevented her from doing so. Mr. Wilde whirled his wife about, placing himself between her strenuous protests and the library, and closed the door quietly upon the happy couple. "Your duties as her mother are now complete, Sophy, and I will not permit you to disturb our daughter further. I have let you have free rein with her until now. You have kept her wrapped up in linens long enough, and if she finds a little pleasure in her betrothed, I would like to think that at long last I can have some influence upon her life as well!"

Since it seemed to Mr. Wilde, his spouse intended to have her way regardless of his speech or his removal of her from the library, he subsequently pulled her forcibly down the hallway, up the stairs, and locked her in the drawing room.

Late that night, Rothley opened a delicately perfumed billet, upon which was a style of scribbling he did not recognize. He sniffed at the fragrance and wondered where he had smelled it before — it was very faint, but familiar, a delicate whiff of roses!

Babette?

Venetia?

He could not remember.

The message was brief.

> *My dear lord Rothley, I have a confession to make. You know me as Babette, a Frenchwoman, but I am no such thing, only a lady who has loved you for a very long time. We travel in the same circles and I want you to know, though I realize this will be a great shock to you, I will be attending your nuptials tomorrow.*
>
> *If you wish me to make myself known to you, please wear a white rosebud on your lapel. If you wish never to see me again, do not wear it.*
>
> *The time we spent together meant a great deal to me, more than you will ever know. If this is adieu, I have no regrets.*
>
> > *Affectionately,*
> > *Babette*

On the following morning, Lord Rothley paced his

bedchamber a dozen times, the billet he had received the night before from Babette pinched between bloodless fingers. Every memory of her had attended the perfumed missive and though he now realized he was deeply in love with Venetia, Babette's voice, manners, her playfulness and boldness haunted him as none, save Venetia's, ever had. He found himself in a quandary, a desperate, painful, anxious dilemma such as he had never faced in his entire existence.

He wanted both women. He wanted both women, badly!

And he had always had what he wanted, from the time he was a babe in leading strings.

He wasn't a child anymore, but to deny himself Babette! Impossible!

He couldn't. He simply could not!

And with that, he pinned a white rosebud to the lapel of his collar. In time, Venetia would understand. In time.

Venetia was sick with apprehension. Had she been wise to force an issue on the day of her wedding? She glanced out the window of her bedchamber. The June morning was brilliant with sunshine, a good omen surely! Yet if Rothley wore a white rosebud on his lapel, she would leave him at the altar before her vows would seal her to him forever.

Was she being wise? She didn't know. She did not have the vast experience of the world which others had. All night she had tossed upon her bed, becoming tangled in the bedclothes, waking from fitful, unrecognizable nightmares, wishing the dawn would arrive, dreading the moment it did. She could not speak with her mother. Her mother would never understand and would never forgive her if she jilted Rothley on the day

186

of a wedding which would be attended by a grand number of the *beau monde*. On the other hand, she strongly suspected that her father, who had already entered her bedchamber this morning, kissed her tenderly upon each cheek, and wished her every happiness, would stand by her.

Mary fussed at her auburn tresses, lacing them with strings of seed pearls and white rosebuds. Her gown was white satin covered with yards of Brussels lace. Pearls encircled her neck. The fragrance of perfume—her favorite attar of roses—swirled invisibly into the air from behind each ear.

Today would either be the happiest of her life, or the worst. Rothley would determine all.

Lord Rothley could not keep from touching the traitorous white rosebud as he watched Venetia slowly walk down the aisle upon the arm of her papa. For the past several minutes, before her satin slippers had begun their dainty progression toward him, he had scanned and rescanned the assembled guests trying to determine which of the women present was his enchanting Babette. More than two hundred august personages were seated in all their finery upon the elegant pews of St. James's Church, yet not one could he believe was his Babette! Not one!

Ode to Joy sounded delicately from a string quartet at the back of the church, the gentle strains lifting to the vaulted ceiling. Not comprehending precisely why, his attention was suddenly riveted fully to Venetia, and for the moment, his anxiety regarding Babette's identity was forgotten.

Venetia appeared as an angel in her wedding costume, her beautiful gown of white satin covered with patterned lace and appearing as a heavenly cloud over her lithe figure. The sleeves of her gown fit closely about her arms traveling to her fingers in a striking lace point. He recalled the sweetness of her fingertips upon his face of yesterday and remembered her speech to him, of how she had longed for his life all these years. Surprising tears pricked his eyelids. How much he loved her, yes truly loved her!

Her complexion, though heightened slightly by the exigencies of so public a ceremony, was as smooth as a rich, delicate cream, contrasting beautifully with her auburn curls which were threaded with small, soft pearls and—oh, lord!—white rosebuds!

Even at the top of the long aisle, Venetia had been able to see that Rothley wore the unhappy rosebud upon his lapel. She should have informed her papa, then and there, before she began her trek toward the altar, that she could not marry Rothley. But something— hope, perhaps—ordered her to silence, and forced her slippered feet to walk slowly down the aisle.

Her mind was in a state of intense turmoil. She could not possibly marry a man who would so betray her, yet she could not keep from moving! She marched forward as though borne along by the strength of Fate entirely apart from her intentions or wishes, her gaze fixed to the curious space located a few inches in front of each foot, her throat constricted with tears.

She had hoped—oh, how she had hoped—that yesterday's *tête-à-tête* with her beloved would have reached Rothley's heart. How wrong she had been! The rosebud was proof of that!

When she was but a few feet away from him, she looked up to ensure she had indeed seen the white rose on his lapel. There it was, a fragrant traitor upon a dove gray coat. She would look at him once, challenging him with a knowing stare, then turn on her heel and quit the church. She knew she would cause a terrible scandal, but she didn't care! She must do what was right for herself. She lifted her gaze, intent upon her purpose, only to suffer a severe shock. When she met Rothley's gaze, instead of seeing inconstancy and doubt, she saw that his eyes were brimming with tears as he watched her.

Tears! Rothley! Impossible! But what did it mean?

As though mesmerized by the sight of the earl so overset, she relinquished her father's arm and moved forward to take Rothley's.

The earl of Rothley knew he had arrived at a tremendously significant crossroad in his life, yet he was still uncertain as to why it was so. After all, once the vows were spoken, only an act of Parliament could render a divorce and separate him from Venetia. He could not, therefore, explain the sensation to himself. All he was doing, in its barest sense, was marrying a fortune to repair his estates. But Venetia had, over the past sennight, placed layer upon layer of flesh and blood upon the stark bones of their contractual agreement, and a living thing had emerged.

A marriage.

He could not have been more astonished than had he been bowled over by a mail coach and six, stuffed and draped with passengers, to boot!

When he finally blinked back his tears, and covered the small hand, trembling upon his arm, tightly with his own, he found himself looking into a pair of troubled, questioning blue eyes. What did she want of him?

He thought of Babette.

And of Venetia.

Suddenly, he knew precisely what to do and also that

189

Babette would understand his actions as well.

"I beg your pardon," he began, preventing the old reverend from beginning the ceremony and startling him into blinking rapidly.

"Yes, my lord?" the gentleman whispered. "Have I erred somehow?"

"No," Rothley said, also whispering. "But I have just remembered something I should have done yesterday—of utmost importance—and with your permission, I mean to do it now."

"Cannot it wait, Rothley? This is quite unheard of!"

"I am sorry. But it will only require a moment and—and my bride's attention."

"As you wish."

Venetia felt her heart grow cold with fear at Rothley's words and her knees began trembling. When he released her hand and her arm, she felt certain she would fall in a faint at his feet. But before her senses would so fail her, she watched with fascination as he unpinned the rosebud from his lapel, and with fastidious care, lifted her lace-clad arm and repinned the rose at her wrist. Whatever did he mean by it? Had he suddenly become aware of her identity?

"Venetia," he began quietly, words which resounded to the elegant rafters of the stone church, and traveled to the ears of every stunningly quiet guest present. "I entered into our engagement with only the most worldly of motives, however acceptable they were within the proscribed dictums of our society. But I present this rose to you as a symbol of my love for you, my earnest desire to please you in all things, and my earnest intention of holding you in the highest regard, above all others, throughout my lifetime. Had I had even a particle of sense, I would have said as much to you yesterday."

Venetia looked at the rosebud upon her wrist and without realizing she had done so, lifted it to touch her cheek. Her own eyes had become so full of tears, she could not see him. She then unpinned the rose, and though he initially resisted her action, she placed it upon his lapel, her fingers trembling all the while. In the accent she had cultivated as Babette, she spoke softly, so that only he could hear. "Monsieur," she began, a tear trickling down her cheek. "You have made me the happiest of women, and I return zis to you, as a token of my love and faith in your goodness."

Rothley, who had at first panicked at the thought that the terrible rosebud should again reside upon his person, heard the familiar French accent, and froze. He could tell Venetia—or was it Babette?—was struggling with her emotions. So many thoughts and memories of Venetia, masquerading as Babette, flew through his mind, so many astonishing images—of a strange, be-feathered bird at Vauxhall laughing among his friends, of a young man rocking on his heels and whistling at the opera house, of the eager way she had permitted him to kiss her—that he could only stare, utterly amazed, at the woman before him. At the same time, he knew Venetia was Babette! All made sense to him now and he understood finally why Venetia had changed so dramatically the day following the masquerade at Vauxhall.

Venetia—Babette.

"Rothley," she said, her accent fading as she touched his cheek with her fingertips. "Do you forgive my deception?"

"Do I forgive your deception! But I could have ruined all! Venetia, you would have left me at the altar had I not extended the rose to you, wouldn't you?"

"Yes, but you didn't fail me!"

"You played havoc with our happiness!"

"There would not have been any real happiness."

"You are too wise for your years."

"I lied to you before, Rothley! You see, the truth is, I have loved you forever! Since the day I saw you at the Rose and Crown!"

"My darling!"

"Rothley!"

If ever a ceremony had been designed to both delight and shock an assemblage of London's *haut ton,* it was this one. Scarcely a word, however incomprehensible the joint meaning was to everyone present—save Mr. Tyers, Mr. Bartlett, and Mr. Holland—escaped anyone. Hushed queries were bantered from one person to the next, a growing rush of disbelief and confusion rolling through the guests.

But when the earl of Rothley, a bachelor who had spurned matrimony as an institution designed to punish all of mankind, actually took his bride-to-be in a crushing embrace, before the ceremony was complete, it was presumed a miracle had happened and his lordship had somehow found an unsuspecting bliss in his youthful June bride.

Sally Jersey, who cried throughout the remainder of the ceremony, which the reverend conducted with his cheeks a ruddy color, exclaimed afterward that it was just what she would have expected of Rothley at his own wedding. "For such a rake, you know, must perforce attack his bride before even the vows are spoken else he would surely lose his fine reputation. And that you know would never do for then he must suffer the most tedious and provoking remarks a wedding usually would occasion. No one can afterward claim he will have been *manacled* to his heiress, not after such a display! Ah, Rothley! Had I only been a few years younger!"

The honeymoon lasted for over a year and was conducted in Europe exclusively. If Mrs. Wilde missed her daughter terribly, such news was worsened by the dreadful tidings that upon several occasions, Lord Rothley had been sighted in the company of a very young man sporting black hair and a mustache. Since there was nothing in Venetia's letters to her mama which conveyed anything but an extraordinary happiness, Mr. Wilde begged his wife not to put too much stock in the gossip of those who had no interest but in causing her pain.

"Venetia will explain all when she returns, my dear!"

Which she did, not one sennight later, by riding up to her parents' house, astride a brown horse, dressed in buckskin breeches, a blue coat, a fawn-colored waistcoat, a natty beaver hat, a black wig and black mustache, accompanied of course by Rothley himself.

She was neat as a pin, her father remarked dryly, a state which she explained was due to Rothley's having taught her at long last how to tie a decent *trone d'amour!* Mrs. Wilde did not comment upon her daughter's neck cloth, since she was still being revived by Mr. Wilde through the use of her vinaigrette!

The Wedding of the Season

by

Emily Maxwell

"I simply cannot believe it!" Euphronia Farington threw down the letter she had been reading and glared at it in disgust. "To think that . . . that mutton-faced henwit is to be wed in the fall!"

"Indeed?" Cecelia glanced at her stepdaughter, a look of mild curiosity in her brown eyes. Euphronia usually reserved the epithet, henwit, for her widowed stepmother, and Cecelia had to admit to some interest in who, besides herself, had earned Euphronia's wrath. "Do I know this mutton-faced henwit?"

"It is Caroline Adams." Euphronia's lips curled around the name. "We attended Miss Wilton's Academy together. Of course she is only to marry that foppish Lord Wrongley who always smells of dogs, but still! To think of it! Caroline Adams will be Lady Wrongley while I am still unwed and a mere Honorable."

"Oh, dear." Cecelia considered the various shades of silk in her embroidery box, selected a lovely shade of Marie Louise blue, and threaded her needle. "How distressing."

"Distressing? Distressing! It is worse than anything, and I shall not stand for it. I simply cannot allow Caroline Adams—did you see her at the concert yesterday? She was dressed worse than yesterday's roast besides having the face of a sheep! To think that she—! No, I cannot—!" Euphronia rose from the gilt-wood settee and took a quick turn about the room, deliberately stepping on the letter which she had thrown to the needlepoint rug, hoping perhaps that one of the silk dragons would devour it.

Cecelia, who had been taking minute stitches in her embroidery during Euphronia's tirade, spoke into the silence. "Perhaps that is why Lord Rightly—"

"Wrongley, Cecelia."

"Well, of course, that is your opinion. But who is to say but that Caroline Adams is not the perfect match? It seems to me that a man who smells of dogs, would quite naturally be attracted to a woman who looks like a sheep. I must say, I cannot understand why you are agitating yourself about it."

"Because," Euphronia swished to the settee and sat down, "because I should have been the first to marry! It is all Mama's fault, of course, for being so selfish as to die during my come-out. Mourning does not become me."

"It must have been a very difficult time for you." Cecelia did her best to sound sympathetic.

"Difficult? I was not even permitted to dance! I shall never forgive her. Never. Why, do you realize that soon I shall be the only one from Miss Wilton's Academy still left on the shelf? I begin to feel like . . . like . . ."

"A jar of fruit?" Cecelia pursed her lips as she executed a careful chain stitch around the edge of a blue cornflower. She was embroidering a sketch she had made of the garden near her home in Somerset, a garden she had not seen except for a brief visit, since her marriage to Lord Farington some two years ago when she was seventeen. "Our cook at the vicarage put up jars of peaches, I remember. They were quite delicious."

Euphronia took a deep breath. "I am trying to discuss a very serious matter, Cecelia. I am not interested in jars of peaches."

"You would be if you ever tasted them." Cecelia snipped off the end of a thread and looked at her embroidery with a satisfied smile. "Perhaps we could go down to Somerset for a visit? I know Mama would be glad to have you and I have not seen her since she came up with Papa for Lord Farington's funeral."

Euphronia tapped one silk-shod foot on the letter.

"You must do as you please, of course. Though I would hope you would not be so selfish as to leave until after the wedding."

"But I hardly know . . . I do not think we have met more than once . . . that is, I do not think Caroline Adams would care whether I attended her wedding or not. Besides, did you not say she is to be wed in the fall? I have no intention of staying with dear Mama more than a fortnight."

"I do not speak of Caroline's wedding." Euphronia dismissed her friend with a wave of the hand. "I speak of my own wedding in June." She rose to her feet and walked to a small inlaid writing desk. Settling the skirts of her jaconet muslin morning dress, she reached into a drawer for pen and paper.

Cecelia, in the act of threading her needle with a most fetching silk of Aurora pink, stopped, frowned at the cornflower she had just finished and said, "This June? You are to wed this June?"

"Yes, of course, this June." Euphronia dipped the pen in the inkstand and began writing.

"Was I aware of this?" Cecelia asked. She was known to have a most appalling memory, but still, to forget that one's stepdaughter was to marry . . .

Euphronia looked up from the list she was making. "You are now," she said reasonably. "And truly, you cannot expect that I shall allow Caroline Adams to marry before me. I am beautiful, intelligent, personable, and rich. Caroline Adams is a henwit with no more than a competence and the face of . . ."

"A mutton chop." Cecelia put down her needle. "But Euphronia . . ."

"Oh, I know some will say it is immodest of me to tout my own virtues, but it is nothing but the truth."

Cecelia, looking at Euphronia's vivid blue eyes and glossy, dark brown curls with something akin to envy, could not dispute this. In fact, her own brown eyes and blond hair had always seemed to her but a pale shadow of her stepdaughter's beauty.

As to Euphronia's fortune . . . at his death from apoplexy sixteen months previous, Lord Farington had been one of the richest men in England. Aside from a few bequests to the servants, and a small jointure bequeathed to his young bride, the remainder of Lord Farington's considerable estate had been left to his only child, Euphronia. Cecelia, two years younger and wed but a brief six months, had been considered no more than a pretty birdwit by her husband, quite incapable of looking after either herself or the Farington fortune.

"We have a full three weeks to plan," Euphronia continued calmly, dipping her pen into the cut-glass inkstand set into the desk. "I shall make a list so that you do not forget anything."

Cecelia's silver needle case dropped from suddenly nerveless fingers. "So that I do not—Euphronia surely you do not mean that you expect me to plan your wedding?" It was a terrifying thought since it was well known that no one could satisfy Euphronia's exacting standards but Euphronia herself.

"Not plan." Euphronia waved away the suggestion with a careless swipe of her pen. "I shall merely need your assistance to attend to a few trifles is all. I shall be busy with fittings for the wedding dress and my trousseau, you know. I cannot be expected to do everything."

"Exactly what trifles did you have in mind?" Cecelia asked carefully.

"You must contact Mister Bennet about the license and have him draw up a marrriage contract for my approval."

Cecelia nodded. Mr. Bennet was the Farington family lawyer and would know just how things should be done. There should be no problem with that trifle.

"Then there will be the decorations at Saint George's, of course, and the bridesmaids . . . I think I shall have twelve. Make a list for me to choose from, but be sure

Caroline Adams is one of them. Then there are the favors to be selected and the cards to be sent out, and the wedding breakfast to be discussed with Cook. I shall want a large cake. At the Overhill's wedding, I remember the cake was two tiers with flowers made of icing. Mine will be three tiers with flowers and birds of icing and my monogram in gold and pearls." Euphronia carefully ticked off items on her list, while Cecelia's brown eyes grew wide with horror.

"But Euphronia . . ."

"I thought we might have the children from that charity school Papa supported . . . what was the name of it?"

"Farington School."

"Oh. Yes. Well, they shall line up outside Saint George's and sing something suitable when I step from the carriage. I imagine fifty or so should do."

"They will need new uniforms, Euphronia," Cecelia said, taking a quick grasp on her dwindling courage.

Euphronia frowned across at her stepmother. "New uniforms? Really, Cecelia, you can't have considered. There will be enough expenses without such foolishness. Papa was right. You would outspend the constable within a fortnight."

Cecelia blushed, needing no reminder of her late husband's unflattering opinion of her. The eldest of eight daughters, she had had little choice but to accept Lord Farington's offer, knowing that the bridal settlement, though small, would do much to ease the financial burden on her family. For his part, Lord Farington called his bride a pretty piece of fluff and made no secret of the fact that he had married only to produce a male heir. When she failed to conceive, he blamed Cecelia, saying that it was a pity she was not a horse, so that he might have had his money back.

"Besides, were they not given new clothes for Papa's funeral?"

"Mourning clothes," Cecelia pointed out, swallowing

201

her chagrin. "You would not want rows of little crows lining up outside the church."

"Hmmmmm." Euphronia brushed the quill of her pen across her chin as she considered the matter.

"The boys should have new suits and wear white favors. The girls must have white dresses and wear little straw hats. They can carry baskets of flowers and strew them on the pavement outside the church. It would be quite lovely."

"Yes . . ." Euphronia nodded. "They shall be dressed to match the decorations. See to it, Cecelia."

Cecelia bent her head as if to examine the ivory thread-waxer in her sewing box, concealing a small smile of satisfaction. She was quite sure that with a bit of careful shopping she could manage to provide new uniforms for all the children and not just the fifty or so who took part in the ceremony.

"And shall you be going away afterward?" she asked, thinking happily of a long summer entirely free of Euphronia.

"The Continent. Paris, I think. It will be nice to see the new fashions."

"You must stay at least a month or two," Cecelia said brightly. "Though I suppose your husband may have something to say about that." She threaded her needle and sighed. With Euphronia married, she might be able to retire to the dower house in peace.

"Husband?" Euphronia asked, looking up from the list she was making of her trousseau.

"Yes." Cecelia nodded. "Do you know, you have not told me the name of the man who has made you an offer."

"Well, really." Euphronia made a moue of disgust and quickly made a note at the bottom of her list. "I knew there was something I was forgetting."

"But . . ." Cecelia put down the porcelain thimble she had just picked up. "But surely you don't mean there is no groom. How can you plan a wedding when no one has—"

"I told you that I could not be expected to attend to everything!" Euphronia interrupted sharply. "You simply shall have to deal with this, Cecelia. It is the least you can do."

The least I can do since Lord Farington's will left me beholden to you for the very bread I eat, Cecelia thought darkly. She was in an untenable position. To quarrel with her stepdaughter would only make things worse. Yet . . . "I can hardly choose a husband for you, Euphronia."

Euphronia shrugged. "You make too much of it. I shall make a list of what I require. You need only find someone who matches."

"But even if I do, there is no saying the man would consent."

Euphronia raised her eyebrows. "Don't be such a ninnyhammer. Of course he will. You need only offer him enough money. Papa taught me that."

Cecelia said not a word but carefully replaced the thimble and thread in her workbasket, and closed the lid. Folding her canvas, and placing it beside the workbasket on the occasional table, she rose to her feet. She was quite aware that Euphronia was referring to Cecelia's own marriage to Lord Farington. It was not the first time Euphronia had made such barbed remarks. Cecelia's only recourse then and now, was silence and swift departure before she gave vent to the words that rose like bile in her throat.

"Aren't you forgetting something?"

Cecelia turned, one hand on the door to the sitting room.

"Your list." Euphronia waved the piece of paper in the air. "I intend this to be the wedding of the Season. So do make sure everything is to my satisfaction, Cecelia. Particularly the groom."

Robert Berryham, Fifth Earl of Stervigton, known as Lord Fox to both friends and enemies because of his unfortunate red hair, sat contentedly in his study at Stervigton House in the fashionable Mayfair section of London. He was reading a copy of *Sense and Sensibility* given to him by a friend and enjoying the peace and quiet of an undisturbed afternoon.

He turned a page, smiled over one of the author's witty comments on fashionable society, and sipped some wine. It was not often that Lord Stervigton had the luxury of such solitude. Rich, titled, and, despite the red hair, quite handsome, Lord Stervigton had somehow managed to reach the age of four and thirty without falling into the parson's trap. Inevitably his single state became like the scent before the hounds of marriage, and Lord Stervigton found himself spending much of his time foiling the wiley strategems of a virtual army of matchmaking mamas intent on hanging his pelt upon their daughters' wall. Often, as Lord Stervigton remarked to his friends, he felt much more like the harried rabbit than the fox.

That morning alone, there had been two minor carriage accidents involving young ladies outside his door, and one fit of the vapors. Yesterday no less than five females of marriageable age had begged shelter from the rain, and one brazen young woman had even demanded that an umbrella wound be seen to by the earl himself. Fortunately, Burrough, Lord Stervigton's butler and Mrs. Tarrinton, his housekeeper, had been able to deal with the onslaught. Even the umbrella wound had managed to recover when it was suggested that a doctor be called.

Sometimes, when Lord Stervigton was in a mood to be amused rather than irritated by the siege of females outside his gates, he would pretend to be a poor relation of the earl's, finding a certain cynical enjoyment in becoming invisible to the assembled female multitude who had no time for a man of little fortune.

Today, he found himself longing once again to be invisible. It was a beautiful spring day, and while he was quite enjoying *Sense and Sensibility*, he also would have enjoyed a quick stroll in Hyde Park. Were it not for his duties in the House of Lords, which Lord Stervigton took quite seriously, he thought he might have skipped the London Season altogether and stayed on his estates in Dorset. At least then he could have enjoyed a walk in his woods or a long gallop through the parkland without worrying about some female being pushed beneath his horses' hooves by a calculating mama.

A shaft of sunlight crossed the page of his book, tantalizing him with its warmth and hint of summer. With quick decision, Lord Stervigton put down the book and rose to his feet, crossing the Aubusson carpet to one of the long windows which looked out on the square. It was unbearable to be cooped up on such a day. He peered carefully around the curtain, there seemed to be no young ladies lurking about the bushes. In three long strides he crossed to the hall.

"My hat and walking stick!" he demanded, heading for the stairs.

Cecelia, whose perusal of Euphronia's requirements for a groom had resulted in a rather bad headache, had also decided to go out. She had no idea how to go about buying a groom for her stepdaughter. And not just any groom. Euphronia had been quite specific. The gentleman must be titled, a duke was preferred but an earl would be acceptable; handsome, dark hair, blue eyes, over six feet and fashionable; and with a fortune at least equal to Euphronia's own.

"I abhor fortune hunters," Euphronia had said with a meaningful glance at Cecelia.

"But it seems to me that if you are intent on buying a husband, Euphronia . . ." Cecelia had tried to protest.

"Rich, handsome, and titled," Euphronia had reiterated firmly, pointing to her list. "As soon as you have taken care of these few other matters concerning my nuptials you may begin looking for the groom. I am sure it will not be at all difficult. Any man would consider himself fortunate to have me for a bride."

Cecelia had sighed, but remained silent. Experience had taught her the futility of arguing with Euphronia. So changing into a walking dress of pink muslin and donning a pair of new half boots, Cecelia had set out, list in hand and worried frown upon her brow. "For it is not as if I can go into one of the shops on Bond Street, hand over Euphronia's list, and expect to pick up a groom made to order by the end of the week," she murmured.

"Beggin' your pardon, ma'am?"

"Nothing, Carter, nothing," Cecelia spoke to the maid who accompanied her. "I was merely wondering if Grafton House will be able to supply what I need or if we must go elsewhere."

The young maid nodded happily, the thought of going into the great London shops quite exciting to someone who had just come up from the country a fortnight ago. "It's wonderful about the weddin' an all," she said. "Everyone in the hall's talkin' about it."

"I can imagine." Cecelia knew the servants were looking forward to the wedding celebration as a break in an otherwise dull life of hard work and drudgery. And, though Euphronia had not thought to include it on her list, Cecelia would see to it that there were white favors for the servants, some guineas distributed in honor of the occasion, and a celebratory meal in the servants' dining hall as well. Cecelia mentally added the items to her list which that day also included a stop at the Burlington Arcade where she hoped to find a certain shade of green embroidery silk which she desperately needed to complete a bit of shrubbery.

"Greens are so difficult," she confessed to the shopkeeper a few hours later. "But I do think . . . the Forrester . . . no, the Apple green. Definitely the Apple green."

The shopkeeper smiled. "Perhaps madam should take both? It is hardly an extravagance at these prices and whichever green you do not use now can be saved for something else."

"Well . . ." Cecelia was tempted. Both greens would doubtless be useful, she was embroidering a garden, after all. Still, she felt it beholden on her to be thrifty seeing as how she had very little money of her own, and though she detested being thought a nip-farthing, there it was. "The Apple green," she said firmly and laid her coins on the counter.

Lord Stervigton put on his high-crowned beaver, thus covering his notorious red hair, and signaled to Burrough to check outside for marriageable females, before deciding it was safe to venture forth. "A lovely day," he commented to the butler as he stepped outside and pulled on his gloves. "I shall probably stop at White's and grab a bite of supper at the Clarendon."

"Very good, my lord," Burrough said, watching as Lord Stervigton stepped briskly forth in the direction of the park.

It was not so very many moments later that Cecelia, walking past Lord Stervigton's town house, began having second thoughts about the green silk. Frowning, she fumbled about with her reticule, deciding that she would just look at the silk once more and this time, truly, truly make up her mind about it. What with the fumbling and her new half boots, which were the right size and not too small no matter that they had begun to pinch quite abominably, Cecelia did not notice the crack in the pavement until her ankle suddenly twisted beneath her and with a cry of pain she fell quite heavily to the ground.

Carter, who had been chosen from several applicants

for the position of lady's maid because of her calm disposition, immediately became hysterical. Throwing the parcels she had been carrying into the air, she screamed for help, declaring, "She's been kilt! Sure as anythin' she's been kilt!"

Lord Stervigton, hearing the screams, steeled himself to walk calmly along. It is all a trick, he told himself. It is just some female determined to get my attention. If I go to help it will prove to be some senseless chit who thinks screams and a pretended faint will win my heart. But I shall prove her wrong.

A small crowd had begun to gather about Cecelia's prostrate form. She was not unconscious, though this was a state for which she was beginning to devoutly wish, but her ankle hurt quite abominably and she was unable even to examine it to determine the extent of her injuries in so public a place.

Carter continued to scream. Seeing that her mistress was sitting up and obviously not dead as yet, Carter had changed her hysterical declaration to "Mortal injured! Sure as anythin' she's mortal!"

Since Cecelia could not be heard above Carter's screaming and could not get to her feet without assistance, they seemed to be at an impasse. Cecelia was just considering crawling between the legs of the interested onlookers, who were paying no attention to her in any case, and begging someone in a nearby house to send for a carriage and doctor when there was a loud *thwack* and sudden silence.

Lord Stervigton had been able to stand it no longer. Combined with his innate curiosity, which would have led to the demise of several cats, was the very real concern that someone might be hurt and in need of help while he selfishly went his way.

"Hysterics are no way to help anyone!" he remonstrated now, giving Carter a shake for good measure.

Recognizing a member of the quality when she saw

one, the maid gulped, sniffed, and began to cry, putting one hand to the cheek Lord Stervigton had slapped.

"A watering pot!" Lord Stervigton said in disgust. "Here, come along. I shall have the housekeeper fetch a cup of strong tea." He ushered Carter toward the steps to his house.

"Me parcels!" Carter whined. "It's as good as my position to lose 'em."

"Yes, yes." Lord Stervigton urged Carter impatiently toward the door. "One of the footmen shall fetch them."

The crowd, sensing that the excitement was over, began to disperse, leaving Cecelia still sitting in the middle of the walk, bonnet askew, flounce torn, and ankle wickedly throbbing.

"Excuse me," she said in a tremulous voice. "But do you suppose you might help me as well? I believe I have twisted my ankle."

"In a moment, child." Lord Stervigton turned, a reassuring smile on his face.

A pair of large brown eyes, surrounded by wisps of golden curls, stared back at him. What he had thought to be a child was quite the contrary. Lord Stervigton stifled a groan. A female. Of marriageable age, no less. Duped again. "I shall send Burrough out to fetch you," he said coldly.

"How kind," Cecelia replied between teeth gritted with pain. "But I am sure could I but presume upon you to call a hackney, I could crawl to it without further inconvenience to you or your household." The stabbing pain lent sharpness to her usual placid nature.

"Don't be impertinent." Lord Stervigton marched over to Cecelia's recumbent form. "And feed me no more lies about an injury. You are hardly the first to think of such a scheme. Nor will you succeed—"

"Ohh!" A sharp groan escaped Cecelia's lips as with a jerk, Lord Stervigton hauled her to her feet. "I am so sorry," she apologized as her senses swam, "but I truly believe I am going to . . ."

"Faint." Lord Stervigton finished her sentence and looked down at the slight form resting in his arms with a sneer upon his lips. He was tempted to abandon her on the pavement, but innate courtesy kept him from doing so. The last time such a thing had happened, the conniving female had declared her ankle was broken and it would be impossible to move her for at least a month. Her recovery period was amazingly shortened when Lord Stervigton left for the country soon afterward.

Seeing her mistress's apparently lifeless form in Lord Stervigton's arms, Carter was once again overcome with histrionics. "Kilt!" she screamed in a piercing soprano. "Dead kilt, she is!"

Lord Stervigton, his arms occupied with Cecelia, stamped one booted foot upon Carter's toe.

"Oh! Oh, why'd you want to go and do that? Oh, that hurts!"

"Ply the knocker, you ridiculous female, before I do far worse," he instructed, wondering how he could ever have forsaken *Sense and Sensibility* for this madness. "And if I hear you scream one more time I shall strangle you. Is that clear?"

The murderous gleam in Lord Stervigton's eyes made it more than clear to Carter, who immediately shrieked again and bounded down the street, leaving her mistress to her fate.

"One down, one to go," Lord Stervigton muttered under his breath, before kicking at the door with one booted foot and calling for Burrough.

"My lord!" Burrough opened the door, a look of astonishment on his face.

"If you value your life, say nothing," Lord Stervigton instructed as he marched inside. "No." He turned to confront his butler. "Say instead why you did not do something when that infernal caterwauling commenced outside. Surely you heard the commotion?"

Burrough looked at him blankly. "Of course, my lord. But your instructions are never to open the door when females are involved. And quite obviously, my lord . . ." His voice trailed off as he looked at the form drooping over Lord Stervigton's arms.

"Yes. Well . . ." Lord Stervigton glanced down at the woman in his arms as well, before turning abruptly and walking into the parlor. "Fetch Mrs. Tarrinton to me at once, and bring some brandy. Two glasses, Burrough. I imagine I shall be in need of something to restore my nerves as well."

Cecelia coughed and turned her head away as Mrs. Tarrinton held the vinaigrette beneath her nose. "She's coming round, my lord."

Lord Stervigton put down the glass of brandy he had been sipping and stepped over to the couch on which he had laid Cecelia some few minutes earlier. "Good. Are you sure it isn't necessary to send someone to fetch the doctor, Mrs. Tarrinton?"

The housekeeper nodded. "With six brothers, I've done enough tending to sprains and broken bones to know what I'm about, my lord. Get some brandy down the young miss and she should be all right. Won't be walking on that ankle for a good bit, of course."

"Yes." Lord Stervigton glanced down at the ankle now resting on a pillow. Mrs. Tarrinton had declared it to be a bad sprain, but not broken. "I imagine I shall be dining at home this evening after all."

Mrs. Tarrinton gathered up the cloths and linens she had used in bandaging Cecelia's ankle, a thoughtful frown upon her face. "You know, I doubt she did this apurpose, my lord. Too painful. Not the sort of thing anyone would do deliberate like."

"Perhaps not." Lord Stervigton looked doubtful. "But when the stakes are high enough, there's no knowing what someone might be willing to gamble."

"I don't believe in gambling myself," Cecelia said, sitting up suddenly and wincing at the sharp pain that shot through her ankle. "And it's very rude of you to stare at a lady's ankle like that when she's unconscious, my lord," she continued censoriously.

"I beg your pardon," Lord Stervigton was surprised into apologizing. Few women other than his redoubtable mother, had ever chided him like that. "But if you don't want me to stare at your ankle, you shouldn't have twisted it upon my doorstep."

Cecelia blinked. "What an ill-tempered man!" she said, the throbbing in her ankle quite sweeping away her natural reticence. "And unkind, too. It is not my fault that your pavement is in need of repair, nor that there are so many shades of green these days that it is impossible to know what one is about. You would not be so critical had you to choose between the Apple and the Forrester."

"Now I am being asked to choose between the fruit or the tree?" Lord Stervigton asked. "Did she hit her head as well, Mrs. Tarrinton?"

"I imagine it's the pain talking, my lord. I'm afraid we had to cut off your half boot, miss. There was no getting it off otherwise."

"Oh, no." Cecelia gulped and sniffed, doing her best not to cry. "They were new," she explained. "And not too small, truly. I am not so vain."

"I'm sure not, miss."

A glass of brandy was thrust into Cecelia's hand. "Here, drink this," Lord Stervigton said. "I've had enough hysterical females for one day."

"I am not a hysterical female!" Cecelia said firmly, feeling as if she would like to hit the quite obnoxious man who stood so calmly staring down at her when her ankle felt positively aflame.

"Of course you're not." Mrs. Tarrinton took the liberty of patting Cecelia's hand. "Now you just drink that up like Lord Stervigton says, and I'll fetch some laudanum. That'll have you feeling better in a trice."

"Laudanum, Mrs. Tarrinton?" Lord Stervigton raised his eyebrows. "Won't that put her to sleep? Shouldn't Miss . . . ah, whatever, wait until she's home to dose herself?"

Mrs. Tarrinton frowned. "Really, my lord. Anyone with half an eye can see the young miss is sufferin' and not to be moved until she's more comfortable. Now I'll fetch the laudanum and you may bundle her into a carriage later if you wish."

"I wish," Lord Stervigton said, watching as his housekeeper bustled out the door, her back ramrod straight in disapproval. "And I don't see why I am the one made to seem at fault."

"Lady Farington," Cecelia said.

"I beg your pardon?"

"I am not Miss whatever, I am Lady Farington." Cecelia sipped at her glass of brandy.

"Ah?" Lord Stervigton's face brightened. He sat down in the brocade chair opposite. "Married are you?"

Cecelia glanced at the contents of the brandy glass suspiciously. "What is this?" she asked, visions of white slavers dancing through her head, which had also begun to ache quite abominably.

"Brandy. Drink up. So you have a husband waiting at home, do you?"

"It tastes awful."

"The more you drink the better it tastes and the better you'll feel." Lord Stervigton was beginning to feel quite benevolent toward his uninvited guest.

Cecelia tilted the glass and took a large swallow, coughing when it seemed that her throat had caught fire, and thus moving her ankle which caused a fresh shaft of pain to stab through her body. "Oh!" Tears welled in her large brown eyes and began to trickle down her cheeks. "Oh, it hurts!"

"There, there." Lord Stervigton jumped to his feet and patted her awkwardly on the head as if she were a spaniel, wondering feverishly where Mrs. Tarrinton could possibly have gotten to.

"I'm sorry," Cecelia wailed, wiping at her cheeks with gloved hands. "I don't mean to be a . . . a watering pot"—she stopped to hiccup—"but it really does hurt."

"Yes, yes, of course." Lord Stervigton thrust his handkerchief at her. He was a man of much experience in avoiding women but very little in dealing with them. He watched anxiously while Cecelia mopped her cheeks, sighing with relief when it seemed that she had gained control of herself again.

"Feeling better?" he asked, seating himself on the chair opposite again. "Perhaps I should send a note round to your home? I imagine your husband will be wondering where you are."

"Dead." Cecelia dropped the word like a small bomb.

"Dead?" Lord Stervigton looked startled. "But you look so much better. And you've stopped crying."

"My husband is dead." Cecelia frowned across at Lord Stervigton.

"Oh? Oh." His experience with young widows was even worse than with matchmaking mamas. Lord Stervigton got to his feet and edged nervously around the back of his chair. Since she was wearing pink muslin, she was obviously not a recent widow, and despite her seeming youth might be growing desperate. Where was Mrs. Tarrinton?

Cecelia leaned back against the pillows and sipped at her brandy again. He was quite right. The more you drank the better it tasted. "The only one at home is Euphronia and I would rather she did not know about my accident."

"Of course." Lord Stervigton nodded while his mind darted about like a rabbit in a cage. "You are probably anxious to remarry and provide a father

214

for your child?" he probed.

"Euphronia is twenty-one and planning her wedding in June. I, however, shall never remarry," Cecelia stated flatly. "I intend to retire to the dower house and devote myself to my embroidery."

Lord Stervigton relaxed visibly. "A worthy cause," he agreed.

Cecelia finished her brandy and squinted up at him consideringly as she suddenly was reminded of Euphronia's list. He was tall, seemingly wealthy, and had not the servants called him Lord Something-or-other? "It's a pity about the red hair, though," she observed.

"So my mother always said." Lord Stervigton nodded. "May I pour you another glass of brandy?"

"Please." Cecelia held out her glass, narrowly observing her host as he crossed to the sideboard. Tall, rich, titled, and, despite the red hair, attractive. "There is always boot black," she noted as he returned with her glass.

"I beg your pardon?"

"I am not a person of roudaboutation," Cecelia said, taking a large swallow of brandy and deciding to get down to business at once. "But first I must have my list. Is my reticule anywhere about, do you suppose?" She blinked and smiled up at the man standing before her.

Drunk as a skunk, Lord Stervigton guessed. But at least she wasn't crying anymore. "I shall inquire of the footman. I believe someone was sent out to pick up the packages after your maid became hysterical."

"Dear Carter." Cecelia nodded. "Always so calm and circumspect."

"Quite." Lord Stervigton went to the bell cord. Lady Farington, he mused. She must be the widow of John Merriweather, Viscount Farington who died some two years or so ago. Lord Stervigton had been sightly acquainted with the man and while he did not keep up with town gossip, he did remember hearing that Lord Farington had snatched the cradle when he remarried,

215

his wife being younger than his daughter.

Well, whether Lady Farington was telling the truth about never wanting to marry or not, she could certainly not be hanging about for a rich husband. The viscount must certainly have left her with a handsome jointure. "I take it you are staying at Farington House near Grosvenor Square?" he inquired. It would be best to know where to direct the carriage. His guest looked as if she were three sheets to the wind already and would soon be incapable of telling her name much less or direction.

"Yes." Cecelia smiled. Such a nice man. Quite perfect for Euphronia. There were always wigs, after all.

"Your reticule, Lady Farington."

"Oh, thank you." She took the purse from Lord Stervigton and opened it, frowning down at the small package containing her embroidery silk. "You know"—she leaned forward—"I simply must ask. I hope you do not mind, being a stranger and all. But I feel I simply must know."

"Yes?" he asked cautiously.

"Would the Forrester green have been better?" She took the embroidery silk from the package and held it up. "I am doing a bit of shrubbery, you know. And I had thought the Apple, but . . ."

Lord Stervigton, who was a bit of an amateur painter himself, did not seem a bit put out by the question. He well knew how difficult it could be to get just the right shade needed for a painting; besides, he had been prepared for a question regarding his income or sleeping habits, and found the question of embroidery silk wonderfully innocuous.

"I should think . . ." He took the silk from Cecelia and observed it through his quizzing glass. "I should think you would need both," he declared. "The darker Forrester for the shading, the Apple for the bits touched by sunlight."

"That is what the shopkeeper said," Cecelia confessed.

"But I am afraid . . . things are so expensive these days."

Lord Stervigton smiled. She was joking, of course. The widow of Lord Stervigton had to be rolling in hay.

Cecelia tilted her head to one side, studying his smile. It was slightly crooked and totally disarming, changing the whole aspect of a face that was otherwise a bit autocratic and forbidding. Stuffing the embroidery silk back into her reticule, she pulled out Euphronia's list. "Here we are. Now let me see . . . blue eyes . . ." she looked up at Lord Stervigton and nodded. "Tall . . . how tall are you, Lord, ah . . . ?"

"Why do you ask?"

"It's on Euphronia's list." Cecelia finished her brandy and waved the paper at him. "Titled, handsome, dark hair, blue eyes, tall, fashionable, and rich. I should think you would do quite nicely, if you don't mind wearing a wig whenever you are around Euphronia."

Lord Stervigton smiled. "Do you mind if I look at that?" he asked, snatching the list from her hand. His eyes bulged as he read, the smile Cecelia so admired, disappearing completely. "But this is monstrous!"

"No, no. I think you must have misread it. I am quite sure Euphronia wrote handsome, did she not?"

"You led me to believe Miss Farington was about to be married." Lord Stervigton glared at her.

"This June," Cecelia agreed. "All she needs is a groom. How lucky I chanced to fall outside your door, Lord Stervigton." Cecelia laid her head back on the sofa pillows. It seemed to be swimming a bit.

"A viper! I have been harboring a viper in my house!"

"I certainly hope not," Cecelia murmured, closing her eyes. "I've never met one, of course, but I have always thought they sounded most unpleasant."

Mrs. Tarrinton bustled into the room, carrying a small bottle of laudanum and a spoon. "Sorry to take so long, my lord. But we had to send to the chemist. We used up our last bottle on those three screechin' females in the carriage accident, and then there was that young lady what was hurt by the umbrella." She stopped beside the sofa where Cecelia had begun to snore softly. "Oh, well. Our young miss is feelin' better then?"

"She is not *our* young miss," Lord Stervigton said testily. "She is Lady Farington. And she is not only feeling better, she is completely foxed." He removed the brandy glass from Cecelia's limp hand. "Tell Burrough to fetch a carriage. We shall stuff her into it and direct the driver to take her home."

"But, my lord! Surely, you can't be thinking of just abandoning poor Lady Farington like that. It wouldn't be proper."

"No, I suppose you're right. Tell Burrough to send one of the footmen along as well." He turned to leave the room. "I shall be in my study."

"Lord Stervigton." Cecelia smiled and murmured his name in her sleep, nestling further into the pillows.

"Lady Farington seems quite taken with you," Mrs. Tarrinton observed.

"They are all quite taken with me," Lord Stervigton said sourly as he walked to the doorway, "or rather with my fortune. If I were poor and without a title they would scurry away fast enough." He stalked down the hall to his study, snatched *Sense and Sensibility* from the side table and sat down in his favorite armchair. "Ridiculous female," he muttered. "If she were not so foxed I should give her the trimming down she deserves." He opened his book. "And I don't believe for a moment that her twisted ankle was accidental. It was all part of some cunning plan on her part."

Lord Stervigton read three sentences and then looked up, a horrible thought having just occurred to him. Lady Farington would go home and tell everyone that she had found the perfect man for her stepdaughter. He had met Euphronia Farington at her come-out. Pushing female. Brassy as they came. If once she got it into her headbox that he was the man for her, he would have no peace at all. Next thing he knew he would be reading the notice of his betrothal in the paper. That was exactly what had happened to poor Bernie Nortram, who had then felt honor bound to marry the woman and had been regretting it ever since. Closing his book with a snap, Lord Stervigton jumped to his feet.

"Burrough!" He opened the study door and bellowed down the hall.

"Yes, my lord?" The butler appeared, anticipating as usual that he would be needed.

"Cancel the carriage, Burrough. I could not be so cruel as to send Lady Farington home when she is still senseless with pain."

"No, my lord."

"Inform me as soon as she awakes." He closed the study door and stared unseeingly across the room at a small tapestry depicting a particularly bloody hunting scene. Lord Stervigton shuddered. His sympathy had always been with the fox. He knew what it felt like to be hunted.

Cecelia woke with a vile taste in her mouth and put out her hand, groping for the glass of water always kept on the table beside her bed. Encountering neither the glass nor the table, she opened her eyes, frowned, and suddenly realized she was lying on a strange sofa in a strange room with a strange man sitting nearby.

"Aggggh!" She gave a little screech, sat up and groaned as both her head and ankle began a painful throbbing.

"Ah, you're awake." Lord Stervigton marked his place in the book he had been reading and smiled his charmingly crooked smile at her. "Mrs. Tarrinton left one of her powders for you to take. Would you like it now?" He mixed something in a glass of water and held it out to her. "I'm afraid your head is my fault. I gave you more

219

brandy than you're probably used to, but you were in quite a bit of pain from your ankle you know."

"I still am," Cecelia said, looking suspiciously at the glass he had handed her.

"It's only a headache powder. Really."

Cecelia hesitated, but her head was pounding quite ferociously and besides, she was beginning to remember what had happened. "Lord Stervigton," she said triumphantly, handing back the glass. "I twisted my ankle outside your house."

"Oh, no, you have it quite wrong," Lord Stervigton said. "This is not my house and I am not Lord Stervigton. It must have been the brandy that confused you."

"But I thought, that is, I am sure . . ."

Lord Stervigton sat down in the brocade armchair and smiled, shaking his head at her. "I'm afraid you have it quite wrong, my dear. I am Mister Foxley. A poor relation of Lord Stervigton's. A very poor relation. Haven't five pence to my name, in fact. Why the very clothes I wear I have borrowed from the earl. Such a generous man."

"Then you are a close relation to Lord Stervigton? You look much alike. Almost as if you were twins, in fact."

Lord Stervigton gave her a look of exasperation. "You have not been attending," he scolded. "You have never met Lord Stervigton. Lord Stervigton is in the country writing the definitive biography of General Volering."

"General Volering?"

Lord Stervigton nodded.

"I daresay I should have heard of him?"

"No. If he were someone you should have heard of, his definitive biography would already have been written."

"I see." It made perfect sense, in an odd sort of way. "And you are Mister Foxley."

Lord Stervigton smiled approvingly at her. "Yes. Mister Foxley. A poor relation, but not a close one. There is no chance that I shall inherit. I am poor. I shall always remain poor. I have red hair. And I am shorter than I look."

"Oh?"

"Miss Farington would not think me suitable at all. Not at all. It's a pity, but there it is." He spread his hands and sighed. "Not that I would ever look so high, in any case. A woman like Euphronia Farington deserves a man who is rich, titled, tall, and with dark hair. Obviously, I am none of these things. But I shall keep a lookout. Now that I know Miss Farington's requirements. If someone suitable comes to mind, I shall send him round to call at once."

"How good of you." Cecelia smiled, her brown eyes sparkling. "You know, from what Euphronia said, I was afraid I would find society filled with toplofty sorts, quite high in the instep in fact. But you have been so kind. Taking me in, caring for my injuries, advising me on the color of my embroidery thread . . ." Cecelia sighed. "I am so glad Euphronia was wrong."

Lord Stervigton frowned, quite unable to decide if the woman before him was the genuine article or a cunning female intent on duping him into letting down his guard. "Yes, well, you know, I have been wondering if perhaps a cousin of Lord Stervigton's might not suit Miss Farington."

"Indeed?" Cecelia looked up hopefully. "I must admit it would be a load off my mind to find someone suitable."

"He has just come up to town, in fact. His name is Etherington, Lord Marlborough Etherington."

"I do not believe I know . . ."

"Good. That is, do you not? You will like him I am sure. He has blue eyes, black hair, and is considered to be quite handsome."

"Oh?" Cecelia clasped her hands in delight. "He sounds quite perfect."

Lord Stervigton nodded. "Shall I bring him around to call tomorrow?"

"Oh, yes. That would be so kind. You are too good, Mister Foxley. To go to so much trouble for someone you have just met."

"Yes, well, here is Burrough to tell us the carriage is ready. Now you mustn't attempt to hobble to the door, Lady Farington. I shall carry you as I carry my poor widowed mother who is an invalid. Did I tell you about her? And my five sisters, all dependent upon me since my father died."

"Oh, you poor man." Cecelia's heart, always open to the misfortunes of others, was touched.

"Poor, indeed. No woman will ever want to marry such as I. But I do not envy Etherington his good fortune. Here, put your arm around my neck, don't be embarrassed."

Lord Stervigton smiled at her, making Cecelia feel rather warm and a bit faint again. Such a nice man. So kind, so thoughtful. Such a charming smile. She looked up at the firm line of his chin, felt the strength of the muscled arms that lifted and carried her. A pity he was poor and without a title. Otherwise he would be perfect for . . . almost any woman.

"I do not care who has promised to call," Euphronia said at breakfast the next day, putting down her coffee cup with a decided click. "I must go for my first fitting tomorrow. Madam Regnier is so exclusive she will not even come to the house. Is it not wonderful? She is French, of course. I would trust no one else to make my bridal clothes."

"But, Euphronia," Cecelia objected. "Surely you would want to meet Lord—"

"Cecelia, you will have to handle this yourself. I have told you that I cannot be bothered with these trifles.

Even you should be able to tell if this lord is suitable or not."

"Very well." Cecelia bit her lip and did her best not to alllow Euphronia to discompose her. She knew her step-daughter regarded her as a complete blockhead. But I am not, Cecelia thought. If Euphronia does not wish to meet this Lord Etherington, I shall do as she suggests and judge his suitability myself.

Leaving the breakfast room, Cecelia limped into the front parlor and settled herself on the gilt-wood settee, her sore ankle propped up on a stool. She would concentrate on her embroidery while she awaited Mr. Foxley's promised call. Taking the new green silk from her work-basket, Cecelia smiled, removed a needle from its silver case, and set to work. There was nothing quite so sooth-ing as the sound of needle and thread being drawn through fabric. She had almost finished filling in the yew hedge with a meticulous satin stitch when the butler came in to announce the visitors.

Mr. Foxley entered first, wearing a beautifully cut coat of blue superfine with pale yellow waistcoat. Doubtless borrowed from his cousin, Lord Stervigton, Cecelia found herself thinking. He bent over her hand in greeting and then stepped aside to introduce his companion, Marl-borough Etherington.

Cecelia had to admit that Lord Etherington was hand-some enough to win any female's heart with his dark hair, blue eyes, and patrician countenance. And though she might prefer Mr. Foxley, Cecelia had no doubt that Euphronia would consider Lord Etherington all that was suitable. It was rather a shame though that someone like Mr. Foxley could not catch Euphronia's fancy. An heiress was just what he needed to provide for his poor invalid mother and five sisters.

The butler brought refreshments, sherry for the gentle-men, lemonade for Cecelia. "For I have quite sworn off spirits, such a head as I had yesterday."

"And how is your injury?" Lord Stervigton inquired politely.

Cecelia replied that it was much better. Lord Etherington looked concerned. "But how comes it about that one so fair has been injured? What cruel fate has allowed such beauty to be marred?"

"I beg your pardon?" Cecelia's large brown eyes opened in amazement. Had the man become foxed on one sip of sherry?

"And yet, how can one say that beauty has been marred, when I see such perfection of face and form before me?"

Cecelia was tempted to wrest the glass from Lord Etherington's hand, but contented herself with saying, "Indeed?"

"I was saddened to hear of Lord Farington's death," Lord Etherington continued looking doleful, "and yet, I must admit, though it shames me to do so, that I also thought, at last, perhaps I have a chance of gaining the fair one's favor."

"But Euphronia is a brunette," Cecelia said, looking to Mr. Foxley for some explanation of his companion's odd behavior. Mr. Foxley, however, seemed intent on removing a thread from his benefactor's jacket and did not meet her eye. Cecelia frowned. Perhaps Lord Etherington was just a bit eccentric? One of those odd relatives that people kept locked in attics unless they were the heir?

The odd relative moved to sit beside her on the giltwood settee. "Ah, but I do not speak of Miss Farington," Lord Etherington said in soft, mellifluous tones, "I speak of you, fair one."

"Me?" Cecelia frowned in puzzlement. "Why should you want to curry favor with me? I have no influence over Euphronia. It is but for me to give her a list of suitable names. She will do the choosing herself."

Lord Etherington's smile faltered. "The choosing?"

"Why, yes. Did not Mister Foxley tell you? Euphronia

224

is to be married in June. All the arrangements are underway. There is but the groom to be chosen, and I quite assure you, Euphronia will have the final word on that. As she does on most things."

Lord Etherington edged closer to Cecelia. "I have met Miss Farington. And it is you I would choose, fair one."

"Well, I'm sure that is most flattering, Lord Etherington. But I'm afraid I am not interested in being chosen. I have no wish to remarry, as I told Mr. Foxley."

"Who?"

"Mister Foxley," that gentleman said with rather too much emphasis.

"Ah, yes." Lord Etherington nodded. "Mister Foxley."

Obviously the poor man didn't get about much, Cecelia thought. And no wonder, he was completely unhinged. Couldn't even remember the name of his companion.

"But truly, Lady Farington. Though you may now say you do not wish to marry, I can only hope that I may persuade you to change your mind."

Lord Stervigton rose abruptly to his feet. "Well, time we were going. Don't wish to outstay our welcome." He glanced meaningfully at his cousin. Lord Stervigton was not used to playing gooseberry, and he found it a role to which he was poorly suited. It was quite obvious Etherington was making Lady Farington uncomfortable with his heavy-handed flirtation and, truth to tell, he was making Lord Stervigton uncomfortable as well.

Besides, he had brought Etherington to draw Miss Farington's fire, not to cotton up to Lady Farington, who despite her widowed status, was still in leading strings when it came to men like Etherington.

"I am so sorry Euphronia could not be here to meet you." Cecelia extended her gloved hand.

"Indeed?" Lord Etherington looked deep into her brown eyes. "I am not." He smiled, the smile that had broken any number of hearts, and took the liberty of kissing the tips of her fingers.

"Etherington," Lord Stervigton warned through clenched teeth. Why had he ever thought it would be amusing to introduce Marlborough to Lady Farington? He must have been all about in his head. Not that it wouldn't serve Etherington right if his name were placed first on Euphronia Farington's hunting list. Lord Stervigton bowed most correctly over Cecelia's hand and smiled, doing his best to make up for his cousin's shockingly forward behavior.

"Really, Etherington," he said as the door of Farington House closed behind them. "I had thought you an accomplished flirt. Your reputation is certainly at odds with your behavior."

"Jealous?" Lord Etherington asked, smiling complacently.

"Certainly not. I was merely afraid Lady Farington would collapse under the weight of all those heavy-handed compliments. And do keep in mind that the object is to secure Euphronia Farington's favor, not her stepmother's."

"Nonsense. I met Euphronia Farington at her come-out same as you did. A more grasping, selfish, conceited—"

"Rich," Lord Stervigton interjected. "Don't forget that she is rich. And that you, dear boy, have quite outrun the constable."

"Oh, I never forget that. The cents-per-cent won't let me. Thing is, it seems to me the widow would have been left handsomely provided for and has not the shrewish tongue of the daughter."

"She is a babe in arms," Lord Stervigton said.

"You did not think so before," Lord Etherington pointed out. "And you had best watch out before you find yourself leg-harnessed by a pair of brown eyes."

"Don't be ridiculous!"

"Not I," Lord Etherington said, his own eyes dancing.

"Now I am afraid I must leave you my dear ah . . . Foxley, was it? But I do thank you for the tip. Rich widows are become as scarce as hen's teeth these days."

A worried frown drawing his brows together, Lord Stervigton watched his cousin stroll down the street. He had certainly set the cat among the pigeons now. It had not occurred to him that the charming widow would catch his cousin's eye. And that would not do, that would not do at all.

Cecelia, for her part, felt rather flattered by Lord Etherington's compliments, even though the man was clearly unhinged. Her husband had been more apt to find fault, and had never bothered courting her at all. After meeting Cecelia at the house of mutual friends, Lord Farington had called upon her father at the vicarage and that had been that. There had been no question of Cecelia's refusing him. Not with seven sisters still at home.

And why not admit it? Cecelia asked herself now, shifting her foot to a more comfortable location on the brocade stool. It had been appealing to think she had attracted the attention of a rich and titled gentleman, no matter that he was old enough to be her father. Then, too, there had been the allure of new clothes, and the thought of seeing the Metropolis with all the excitements she had heretofore only read about.

Cecelia sighed. She had not once thought about what it would be like to be the wife of such a man as John Merriweather, Viscount Farington. It had all seemed like a fairy tale to a girl scarce out of the schoolroom. It was only after marriage that reality had set in. Cecelia shuddered, a cold chill creeping over her though the day was unseasonably warm. Truth to tell, she had not liked her husband overmuch. Nor the stepdaughter who had done her best to make things difficult.

Resolutely pushing such thoughts away, Cecelia reached for her embroidery. Mr. Foxley was right. She would need both shades of green. As soon as her ankle no longer pained her, she would go to the shops again. Cecelia smiled. What a nice man, Mr. Foxley was. If only there were a way she could persuade Euphronia to consider someone like him.

"I must have a matched pair," Euphronia announced, walking into the parlor and tossing her reticule onto the occasional table. "It came to me while I was discussing my bridal clothes with Madam Regnier. A matched pair will be perfect, and I know Caroline Adams will not have thought of such a thing."

Cecelia carefully finished the last stitch on a bit of branching shrubbery before replying. "But is that not a bit of an extravagance? A matched pair just for the wedding? You never drive yourself in London."

"What is that to the purpose? And since I pay the bills, it is hardly an extravagance, if I wish it. Besides, they shall make themselves useful about the house later."

"But . . ." Cecelia frowned down at her needle case. "Are we talking about a matched pair of horses, Euphronia?"

"Horses? Don't be such a ninny, Cecelia. What would I want with more horses in London? I am talking about a matched pair of footmen for the wedding. They shall be dressed in identical blue livery with my initials embroidered on the front. One shall have an H, the other an F. That will put Caroline Adams's nose out of joint. Now, both must be blond, of good appearance, and tall. I shall want them to ride on the outside of the coach and assist me to alight when we get to the church. The girls from Farington School shall wear hair ribbons to match the livery. See to it, Cecelia."

Cecelia nodded while Euphronia sank down on the settee and rang for refreshments. "Do you have a list of suitable husbands for me yet? I thought we might go shopping at Almack's later. It is known as the Marriage

Mart, after all, and there should be any number of men present who meet my requirements."

"Well, Lord Etherington did come to call this morning."

"Lord Etherington?" Euphronia laughed and gave Cecelia a look of pity. "Don't be such a goose. Everyone knows Lord Etherington is a fortune hunter and has been on the lookout for a rich wife for ages."

"But he is handsome and titled, and has blue eyes," Cecelia protested.

Euphronia pursed her lips in a moue of disapproval. "I would not even consider Marlborough Etherington," she said flatly. "Continue."

"Actually, the only other name on my list is Mister Foxley."

"Mister Foxley? I have never heard of the man. Is he suitable?"

"Well, he does not have a title of course. And he is not precisely rich. And he does have red hair. But he is all that is kind, Euphronia," Cecelia continued in a rush as Euphronia's eyebrows lowered ominously. "I am sure he would make a very good husband. He is a relation of Lord Stervigton's."

"Ah." Euphronia nodded. "Lord Stervigton. An excellent suggestion. Though he is considered a confirmed bachelor by some, and a misogynist by others, to bring him up to scratch would certainly be a feather in my cap."

"But, Euphronia, we speak of husbands, not bonnets. You would be married to this man, do not forget. You must think whether you would want to meet him at the breakfast table every morning for the rest of your life."

"Oh, pooh! You speak like a provincial. I do not expect to hang on my husband's sleeve. And certainly you rarely breakfasted with poor Papa."

Cecelia rubbed one finger across the bit of satin stitch she had just finished. What Euphronia said was no more than the truth. Lord Farington had never been at his best in the morning, and after the first week of marriage, Cecelia had done her best to avoid him.

"Besides, I think Lord Stervigton would make an excellent husband. I wonder if it would be possible to meet him at Almack's?"

"I understand he is in the country writing the definitive biography of General Volering."

"Of who?"

"No one we should have heard of," Cecelia hastened to reassure her. "But Lord Stervigton is not in town in any case."

"Hmmmmm. A pity." Euphronia frowned, tapping her fingers thoughtfully upon the arm of the settee until Blackwell arrived a few minutes later with refreshments.

"I hope Cook included some of those macaroons I like." Euphronia cast a critical eye over the tray. "Do pour me a glass of wine, Blackwell. And while you are at it, see about acquiring a pair of matched footmen for me. I have asked Lady Farington to do so but I doubt she is capable of the task."

Cecelia ignored Euphronia's barb and reached for a tea cake. In truth, she was become so used to her stepdaughter's cutting remarks, she no longer felt their sting.

"The footmen must be blond and tall," Euphronia continued. "A simple matter. Tomorrow should be soon enough. They will need to be fitted for special livery." Euphronia put down her wineglass. "And you know, I have just had the most wonderful notion. I shall have two sets of livery made. After the ceremony the footmen shall change into jackets with my new initials embroidered on the front."

"You shall need to know the name of your husband-to-be," Cecelia pointed out.

"Of course. Of course. That is why we must go to Almack's."

Cecelia lifted her foot a little off the stool. "I'm afraid

I cannot dance, as yet, Euphronia."

"That hardly signifies," Euphronia replied impatiently. "You are needed only as chaperone. But what a pity Lord Stervigton is not in town." She selected a macaroon and munched thoughtfully. "Still . . . did we not receive an invitation to the Fortescu ball?"

Since Euphronia insisted on going through the invitations herself, picking and choosing what they should attend, Cecelia did not reply.

"I am almost sure we did," Euphronia continued. "And Lord Stervigton is sure to attend, for the two families have been acquainted for years. Yes. Lord Stervigton will do very nicely. I shall have the initials CS embroidered on the second set of livery."

"Do you not think that a bit premature?" Cecelia ventured to ask.

"Not if the livery is to be finished in time," Euphronia said with a look of exasperation. "Well, I am glad that is settled. And no thanks to you, Cecelia. I swear you cannot manage the simplest of things."

Despite this, Cecelia did manage to locate the invitation to the Fortescu's ball and send an acceptance, and when Blackwell consulted her the next morning about hiring his nephew as one of the two matching footmen, she gave her quick approval.

"As long as he is blond and tall and matches, I doubt Miss Farington will object," Cecelia said, taking her place at the breakfast table.

"That was my feeling, milady. And truly, John has not had an easy time of it. He was dismissed from his last post without reference, you see, through no fault of his own."

"Good heavens." Being dismissed without a reference was no small thing. "Whatever happened?"

"It were the young ladies," Blackwell confided, pouring

Cecelia's morning chocolate. "John is that good looking, you see. The lady of the house said as how he was tempting her daughters and all. But a man can't help how he looks, now can he?"

"Indeed not," Cecelia agreed, thinking of Mr. Foxley. He had not been as strikingly handsome as Lord Etherington but there had been something remarkably attractive about his smile . . .

"I'll tell John it's all right then, shall I?"

Cecelia nodded. "But, Blackwell, I wouldn't mention anything about his past history to Miss Farington." Their eyes met, both understanding that the less Miss Farington knew, the less she could object to. Cecelia sighed, sipping her chocolate as the butler departed.

It was a pity about Mr. Foxley. Cecelia was sure he would make an exemplary husband. His only fault seemed to be a too low opinion of himself, as when he said no woman would want to marry him because his fortune was small and he must support his invalid mother and five sisters. He did not realize that a discerning woman must count his care for his family in his favor. And a great fortune was no guarantee of great happiness.

Which brought to mind another fault of Mr. Foxley's. He was too trusting. Had he not introduced Lord Etherington to her as a possible candidate for Euphronia's hand? Surely he would not have done so had he known Lord Stervigton's cousin was a fortune hunter. No. Mr. Foxley was too guileless, too . . . too caring to deliberately play one such a trick. Unless, of course, he meant it as a good turn?

Cecelia signaled to a footman that she had finished and rose from the breakfast table. Was it possible that Mr. Foxley meant only to help Lord Etherington by introducing him to Euphronia? She was in need of a bridegroom, he was in need of funds. It did seem the perfect match. And was this not Cecelia's own thought when she had named Mr. Foxley to Euphronia?

Strolling into the small withdrawing room, Cecelia walked thoughtfully over to the writing table by the window. There were any number of things to be accomplished before Euphronia's wedding. Speculation was not one of them. Cecelia pulled a piece of hot-pressed paper from a drawer and did her best to put Mr. Foxley and his possible motives from her mind.

A note requesting an interview that afternoon with Miss Pratt, the headmistress of the Farington School was soon being sent round by a footman, and the rest of the morning given to a consultation with the temperamental French chef Euphronia had hired for the Season. Though Monsieur Raphael held English food in disdain, he was an excellent cook, his small brown eyes lighting with excitement when informed there was a wedding breakfast to be planned.

The centerpiece of the meal would be the cake, he declared: three tiers with spun sugar flowers and birds. "And a trellis work of pearls around the tiers," he declared. "I, Raphael, shall see to it."

There would also be boxed wedding cake to be distributed as favors for the guests. "I am not exactly sure of the number of people to be invited, Raphael," Cecelia confessed. "I have begun a list, however, and as soon as Miss Farington approves, I shall let you know."

"It is of no problem, madam. I make over three hundred to be given out last year when Mademoiselle Courtenay was married. For me, it is nothing."

Cecelia smiled. Euphronia had paid a fortune to woo Raphael away from the Courtenays, but Cecelia was beginning to think it well worth it. "All this, and that wonderful sauce last night." Cecelia sighed, her brown eyes wide with admiration. "You are indeed an artiste, Raphael."

Raphael nodded, taking it as his due, and descended once more to the kitchens where he ruled supreme.

Later that afternoon, Cecelia drank a cup of tea with

Miss Pratt and discussed the dress of the children who would take part in the wedding ceremony. "White for the girls with blue hair ribbons to match the new livery Miss Farington means to have made up. I think if we are careful, there should be enough to manage something for the older children as well."

Miss Pratt, whose face wore a permanent look of frowning worry, beamed across at her guest. "How good you are, Lady Farington. It was a blessing for us all when our late benefactor married you."

"Yes, well." Cecelia blushed. It was so easy when one had money. The crooked was made straight with barely the lift of a finger. "I thought, also, that some of the older girls might help with addressing invitations to the breakfast. I could pay them something, not much, but a little for pocket money." Surely, if she practiced the strictest economy, she could manage that, Cecelia decided as she prepared to leave. It would not be so very much, after all.

Stepping outside, Cecelia hesitated for a moment, savoring the warm spring breeze which brought with it the faint scent of flowers. It was a beautiful day, and she fairly ached to be out walking in one of the parks or looking in the windows of the many shops. The wind blew the feather on her bonnet down to tickle her chin, and she smiled faintly before allowing the footman to assist her into the carriage. Her ankle was still weak and would begin to throb if she tried to do too much. There would be other walks on other days, she supposed, looking wistfully at the shop windows as they drove past.

In the small village where Cecelia had spent most of her life, there had been only one linen draper and that with the most meager of selections. Once a year, Papa had treated them to an expedition to Cranton, the nearest town of any size. But Cranton was nothing compared to London with its streets and streets of shops, and at night—!

Cecelia closed her eyes, remembering her first view of London after dark. Pall Mall, Westminster Bridge, the dazzling display of illumination from the many gaslit lamps. She had gaped like a schoolgirl at the fairy-tale brilliance, causing Lord Farington to admonish her to stop acting like a provincial and more like the lady she was supposed to be. Cecelia sighed and opened her eyes. It had sometimes seemed as if everything she did irritated her husband. She wondered, as she had wondered many times before, why he had offered for her in the first place.

The carriage turned a corner, and Cecelia found herself once more looking at the imposing facade of Lord Stervigton's town house. Was Mr. Foxley at home? she wondered. She had seen him at a concert the other evening, though he had not seen her for the crush. Had he enjoyed the music? Cecelia had thought it most excellent though Euphronia had declared the evening insipid, the harpist mediocre.

I wonder if it would be possible for me to learn the harp, Cecelia mused, remembering the grace and beauty of both the music and the instrument. True, she was not particularly musical but— "Oh, dear!"

A young, fashionably dressed woman suddenly slipped and fell on the very steps of Stervigton House. Cecelia immediately pulled the cord signaling the carriage to stop and in a moment was being assisted from the still swaying carriage by one of the footmen.

"See if Mister Foxley is at home," she directed. "He will know what to do. This pavement is treacherous, and should be reported to the authorities. I only hope the poor woman has not seriously injured herself."

"What do you think you're doing?" the poor woman demanded, as Cecelia sank to her knees and began patting her hand. "Go away!"

"You have hit your head," Cecelia said reassuringly. "But never mind, everything will be all right. Do you not have a maid with you?"

"Of course not! That would ruin everything. Now do go away, Mama will be furious if you interfere." The young woman straightened her bonnet, groaned loudly, and lay back once again.

Clearly, all about in her head, Cecelia thought. Fortunately, the footman managed to rouse someone from Stervigton House. "Oh, Burrough." Cecelia limped up the steps as the butler opened the door. "Something quite dreadful has happened. Is Mister Foxley at home?"

"Mister Foxley?" The butler raised his brows. "I am not at all sure, milady, but I shall inquire. If you will just . . ." he hesitated. He could certainly not ask Lady Farington to wait outside on the steps, yet he had a strong feeling Lord Stervigton would not be happy to have the retinue on his steps admitted.

"Please . . ." the woman on the steps groaned piteously.

Cecelia raised large brown eyes to Burrough and stepped forward. "Whether Mister Foxley is at home or not, I know he would want to help this poor woman. You must allow my footman to carry her inside. Once we have ascertained the extent of her injuries, I will take her home in my carriage."

"*Your* carriage? Now wait just a minute here." The injured woman sat up and glared at them. "Is Lord Stervigton at home or not?"

"Lord Stervigton is in the country writing the definitive biography of General Volering," Cecelia said.

"Who?"

"No one you should have heard of," a deep voice replied.

"Mister Foxley." Cecelia smiled. "I am so glad to see you. Now everything will be all right."

"Indeed?" He leveled his quizzing glass at the young woman sprawled on his steps. "And who might this be, pray?"

The woman frowned and lifted her chin. "More to the point, who are you?"

"Why, Mister Foxley, of course," Lord Stervigton replied, eyebrows raised.

She returned his look with one of suspicion. "Are you sure you aren't Lord Stervigton?"

"Do I look like Lord Stervigton?" he asked. "Other than my hair, I mean."

"Mama said—"

"A superficial resemblance only," he admitted quickly. "And not of the pocketbook variety. Now I suggest that you be on your way. You are wasting your time here."

Cecelia's brown eyes opened wide. She could not believe Mr. Foxley was being so callous. "But can't you see that the poor thing has hurt herself?" she protested.

"Oh, stuff it!" the poor thing said, getting nimbly to her feet and dusting off her muslin gown. "I told Mama we should have gone to Lord Billingsley's. But no, try Lord Stervigton, she said, he's much the bigger catch." Still grumbling, the young woman retied her bonnet and stalked off down the street.

"Well, really!" Cecelia watched the woman's departure with an indignant frown. "I'm afraid I must apologize, Mister Foxley."

"No need," Lord Stervigton replied. "It's a bit tiresome, but no harm done. Would you care to come inside for some refreshment, Lady Farington? I promise not to ply you with brandy this time."

Cecelia knew she should say no for she hardly had the excuse of a twisted ankle this time. Still, it was not so very improper and surely there could be no harm if she stayed but a little while. "I would enjoy that," she admitted with a smile.

Burrough brought tea and cakes to the library. "My favorite room," Lord Stervigton remarked. "I hope you don't mind?"

Cecelia shook her head. "There is something about a

room full of books . . . it is almost as if you were surrounded by old friends, is it not?"

Lord Stervigton smiled. "You enjoy reading then?"

"Mama is a great reader, and that has always been my family's main entertainment and extravagance: books sent from one of the London booksellers. I suppose it must seem silly to you who are used to more sophisticated amusements, but we were always quite overset with excitement when the books finally arrived. My sister, Penelope, once had the hiccups for three days afterward." Cecelia smiled fondly in remembrance.

"Where are you from then, Lady Farington?" Lord Stervigton asked, offering her the plate of cakes. "And how came you to meet Lord Farington?"

"Crampton Green, near Somerset." Cecelia looked thoughtfully at the iced cake she had chosen. "The village has two shops, the church where Papa is vicar, and Mrs. Middleburg, who runs a small inn and bake shop with the most delicious cinnamon buns anyone has ever tasted. Mama tried to get her receipt once, but Mrs. Middleburg would not part with it."

"Have you brothers or only sisters?" Lord Stervigton asked, his eyes intent on Cecelia's bent head and the small smile that played about her mouth.

"Sisters only. Seven of them. I am the eldest by two years and then there is Mary, Caroline, Penelope, Prudence, Jane, Emily, and Eleanor the baby. I . . ." She looked up, her eyes suspiciously moist. "I missed them dreadfully after I married. Maybe, that is, I hope once Euphronia is wed, I can go back for a visit. I wanted to return before, after Lord Farington died, but Euphronia thought it improper and insisted I remain on the estate."

Lord Stervigton sipped his tea and leaned back on the brocade settee. "So . . . and how came you to meet Lord Farington?" he prompted once again.

"There was a dinner party at the manor house. Sir Reginald was kind enough to invite me along with Mama and Papa. Lord Farington was some kind of distant relation and was staying for the night. I had no idea of his interest, indeed, he was so much older that I don't think it ever occurred to me that he might be . . . but the next day he called upon Papa."

"Love at first sight?"

Cecelia shook her head. "I don't think so. In fact, I have no idea why he should have decided to make me an offer."

Lord Stervigton studied the perfect oval of her face, the blond hair that curled artlessly about her ears, the large brown eyes that looked so guilelessly back at him. "Have you not?"

"No. For Mary, you know, is much the prettier."

"And what of you?"

"Me?" Cecelia looked up from the tea she had been sipping, a startled expression on her face.

"Was it love at first sight for you?" Lord Stervigton probed.

"Oh, no," Cecelia exclaimed quickly, and then realizing how this must sound, added, "but Lord Farington was all that was kind. At least, he was at first. And it all seemed like one of the fairy stories Mama used to read to us."

"In other words"—Lord Stervigton rose to his feet, his voice harsh—"you married Lord Farington for his fortune and his title."

"Well, of course," Cecelia admitted artlessly. "For I had barely exchanged two words with him before the wedding. But I thought I could grow to love him, and truly, with seven sisters, there was no choice."

"Your parents forced you?"

"No. But I knew how hard it would be for them to marry off seven daughters with no dowries to speak of. Papa is a younger son, you see, and Mama has very little money of her own. It would have been selfish beyond words for me to refuse Lord Farington, though the marriage settlement was not large."

239

"Still, you have your fortune now, do you not?" Lord Stervigton asked, placing his cup on a mahogany sideboard. "The money without the man, must surely be preferred."

Cecelia swallowed the bite of tea cake she had just taken, hoping she would not choke, so dry her throat had suddenly become. Perhaps she was misreading Mr. Foxley's intent, but he seemed almost to be attacking her.

"I do not pretend to distress at Lord Farington's death. As it turned out, we were not well suited. He should have married someone of more years or at least more sophistication. I did not fit into his world which was something he could neither understand nor forgive. And Euphronia made no attempt to hide her dislike of me. Still, I did my best to please my husband. The fact that I did not, cannot be laid fully at my door." She spoke as if she would convince herself, as well as the man who stood looking down at her.

"As for fortune," Cecelia rose to her feet and picked up her reticule from the table, "my jointure is quite small, barely enough to enable me to buy embroidery silk. Euphronia inherited almost everything. A fact you will doubtless want to share with Lord Etherington. Women are not the only ones to marry for money, you know."

Back ramrod straight, Cecelia headed for the parlor door. "Oh!" A small gasp of pain escaped her, as halfway there her ankle suddenly gave way.

"Are you all right?" Lord Stervigton quickly came to her aid as she stood leaning against the brocade settee.

"I will be fine directly I am out of this house," she replied, the pain and indignity of her position making her waspish.

Lord Stervigton took her arm and assisted her to the settee. "I have offended you. I am sorry. I should not have spoken as I did. It is just that—"

"That you think me the same as that young woman who fell outside Stervigton House," Cecelia interrupted

240

indignantly. "Well, I am not. And, in any case, I did not agree to partake of refreshment because I thought you had a fortune. I know you have not, and I am doing what I can to remedy the situation."

"Indeed? And what might that be, Lady Farington?"

Cecelia smiled. "I have suggested Euphronia add your name to her list of possible husbands," she said, quite pleased with herself.

Lord Stervigton stiffened, looking as if he had suddenly been poleaxed. "What! You what?"

"I have suggested that Euphronia consider you as a bridegroom," Cecelia reiterated. Such a modest man. It had never occurred to him, apparently, that a great heiress could become interested in him. "I am afraid at the moment she tends to favor your cousin, Lord Stervigton, but I shall continue to speak your praises to her, for I truly believe an heiress is exactly what you need."

"An heiress is not what I need!" Lord Stervigton replied emphatically. "And certainly not Miss Farington. Were I to become leg-shackled to her, one of us would murder the other within a fortnight."

"Oh." Cecelia considered this. "In that case, you must insist on a large marriage settlement. For whether you are hung for strangling Euphronia or she succeeds in shooting you, your invalid mother and sisters would still benefit."

Lord Stervigton stared at her for a moment, before breaking into an appreciative grin. "I do not say you are a flea-wit, Lady Farington, but your logic terrifies me. I am sorry, I refuse to marry so my family may inherit. Selfish of me, I know."

"Yes," Cecelia agreed, a small dimple appearing in one cheek. "But then, men often are."

"Minx." Lord Stervigton smiled down at her. "And what of women?" he asked, seating himself beside her on the settee. "Are they not just as selfish? Though you say you would not remarry, you would change your mind quickly enough were someone such as Lord Stervigton to offer for you. And that, without feeling a jot of affection or even liking for him."

Cecelia looked down at her gloved hands, fingers primly laced together and shook her head. "No. For you see, I have decided I value my freedom far more than whatever a man's fortune might provide for my sisters. I shall not remarry."

"No?" Lord Stervigton moved imperceptibly closer, his arm along the back of the settee, as he looked into the face now upturned to his. "Not even to a man of no fortune, but growing affection?"

It was fortunate that Cecelia's sudden shyness caused her to look away just then, or she would have seen the dawning horror that crept slowly over Lord Stervigton's face. He said nothing but quickly turned, burying his head in his hands.

The silence between them lengthened as they sat side by side on the brocade settee, the one flustered and slightly embarrassed, the other horrified by what had happened to him.

"Are you . . . are you quite all right?" Cecelia asked, turning at last and seeing his apparent pain.

"No." Lord Stervigton shook his head. "And I am afraid I may never be all right again." Lowering his hands he turned to look at her, wincing at the sight of brown eyes large with concern, not for his fortune, or his title, but for him, a man supposedly of little money and great responsibility. Piqued, repiqued, and capoted. He sighed.

"I must be going." Cecelia waited, hoping he would ask her to stay, but he rose with alacrity.

"Yes, I'm afraid you've stayed too long as it is," he replied rather brusquely, pulling her to her feet and ignoring her small moan of pain. Supporting her as far as the open library door, he immediately relinquished her to one of the waiting footmen.

"See Lady Farington to her carriage, James," he instructed, and without another glance, strode back into the library and shut the door.

Cecelia blinked. Mr. Foxley's behavior bordered on rudeness, and she could not imagine what she had done to deserve it.

"Never you mind, Lady Farington." Burrough dismissed the footman and escorted Cecelia down the steps to her waiting carriage. "He's not himself at the moment, is all. But he'll recover and see that things are better this way."

Cecelia nodded, not really comprehending. Nor did she understand the wide grin which split the butler's usually sober face as he closed the carriage door. Was everyone glad to see her leave?

Euphronia chose an evening dress of white lace worn over a white satin slip to wear to the Fortescu ball. "It will be an insipid affair," she declared to Cecelia as they set out. "No matter that they are well connected and half the ton will be there. I do not know why I agreed to attend."

"But what of Lord Stervigton? I thought you wished to attend so you might see if he is suitable or whether some other initials must be embroidered on the new livery?"

"No, no. I have already decided that he will not do." Euphronia dismissed the earl with a wave of her hand.

A sudden pang of fear shot through Cecelia. "Does that mean . . . do you consider Mister Foxley then?"

"Who?"

Cecelia let out her breath on a sigh. For all she had told Mr. Foxley he needed an heiress, she had found herself quite unable to discuss him with Euphronia. "He is the cousin of Lord Stervigton's I mentioned once before," she explained now. "Short, poor, with no title and a large family to support."

"He sounds quite impossible," Euphronia snapped.

"You must have more hair than wit to even think I would consider him. I swear I would as lief stay home."

Since this was something Euphronia rarely did, and indeed, instead of looking bored, she seemed suddenly more animated that usual, Cecelia could only stare. They were helped into the carriage by John, the new footman who was nephew to Blackwell. Euphronia, who usually insisted on stepping into the carriage first, held back and allowed Cecelia to precede her. "For you are my stepmama," she declared with a little giggle.

Cecelia frowned, wondering at this new amiability and when Euphronia stumbled on the steps of the carriage, almost falling into the footman's arms, Cecelia was seriously alarmed. "Is something wrong?" she asked, as the door was shut and the carriage given the office to start.

"Wrong?" Euphronia widened her eyes. "Whatever could be wrong? I am feeling perfectly splendid." She smiled and looked dreamily out the window.

One would almost think she had been taking nips from the brandy bottle, Cecelia thought, subsiding into her corner of the carriage and eyeing her stepdaughter thoughtfully. Euphronia had been alternating between giggles and wistful sighs for days now, quite unlike her usual snappish and difficult self. Cecelia tried to remember when she had first noticed this change and could only think it was sometime after Euphronia had gone for the second fitting of her wedding dress, taking along the new footmen to be measured for their special livery.

The carriage hit a large rut in the road, bouncing its two occupants from side to side and causing Cecelia's headdress to slip slightly askew. She straightened it and looked across at Euphronia. Her face, in the light cast by the carriage lanterns, seemed as remote and dreamy as before.

Cecelia shook her head. Normally Euphronia would have been hammering on the roof of the carriage, castigating the coachman for his driving. Something was definitely wrong. I shall suggest that she see the doctor tomorrow, Cecelia decided.

The Fortescu mansion was ablaze with lights. Obviously, Maribel Fortescu would have nothing to complain about when remembering her come-out. It was a sad crush even on the stairs up to the main rooms. Cecelia gazed about quite happily. She was still enough of a country miss to enjoy this sort of thing, and besides, she had hopes that if Lord Stervigton attended, so might his cousin, Mr. Foxley. Despite his odd behavior at their last meeting, Cecelia found herself looking forward to speaking with him again.

"We should never have come," Euphronia complained fretfully, her good humor seeming to vanish with the carriage. "No matter that the Fortescus are one of the oldest families. Someone has trod on my foot and I'm sure the flounce of my gown has been torn. And my head is beginning to ache."

"You must think of it as a shopping expedition," Cecelia said, looking about her with excitement.

"Have you taken leave of your senses?" Euphronia stopped to frown down at her. "A shopping expedition? How ridiculous."

"But that is what you said Almack's was to be, and this is surely the same sort of thing. If you have quite decided against Lord Stervigton, you must concentrate on looking about for some other suitable gentleman, Euphronia."

Euphronia looked away. "That is no longer necessary. I have already decided on an eligible parti."

Cecelia, who had been peering around people trying unobtrusively to determine how much longer it would be before they could greet their hostess, was sure that she could not have heard correctly. "I beg your pardon, Euphronia?"

"I said, I had already determined on a husband." It was uttered in a firm voice, as if Cecelia might make some objection.

They moved up a stair. "May I ask the fortunate gentleman's name?"

"No, but you shall find out soon enough."

Cecelia wondered briefly why Euphronia was being so secretive about her groom-to-be, but since even if she had an objection Euphronia would not listen to it, Cecelia merely shrugged, glad to have one less thing she need worry about.

"Actually, he is someone you know slightly," Euphronia volunteered as they neared their hostess. "He is tall, and quite handsome and in every way suitable."

Cecelia looked up at her stepdaughter, who was smiling dreamily again. She had never heard Euphronia go into raptures over anything or anyone before. It showed a new, almost likable side, Cecelia thought.

They reached their hostess at last. Cecelia thought Maribel Fortescue looked quite young and charming in her simple dress of white net decorated with the same pink satin rosebuds as made up her headdress. Though Cecelia was probably only a year or two older herself, she felt as if a vast chasm of experience separated them, and could only hope that the charming Miss Fortescue would have an easier time of things than she had had.

The heady scent of flowers filled the ballroom on the upper floor. Lilies, Cecelia thought, breathing deeply and closing her eyes for a moment. They reminded her of the wild ones that grew along the creek by her home. Every year she had picked a huge bouquet for her mother that scented the house for days.

"For heaven's sake, stop making a spectacle of yourself! You aren't going to faint or something are you?"

"What?" Cecelia blinked and opened her eyes. Euphronia was frowning down at her as if she were a troublesome and stupid child.

"I was just enjoying the scent of the flowers," Cecelia explained.

Euphronia looked around. "Oh. Those. I detest lilies.

Roses would be much more *au fait.*"

Cecelia nodded automatically. She had found that life was much easier when one simply agreed with Euphronia. Besides, these bouquets were not the wild lilies of her remembrance, but huge hothouse affairs, gleaming white and almost unreal in their towering arrangements.

"Let us go and sit down somewhere," Euphronia ordered. "Since we are here, we might as well try to enjoy ourselves, if that is possible." She led the way to a group of chairs set at one end of the magnificent ballroom with its glittering chandeliers. "The music is making my head ache," Euphronia complained again as she sat down. "Really, I would as lief be elsewhere."

"If you truly wish to leave, Euphronia, I am sure we may do so," Cecelia said, trying to quell her own disappointment that there would then be no opportunity to encounter Mr. Foxley. "I am sure no one would wonder at it if you are feeling ill."

"I am not feeling ill, only moped to death," Euphronia retorted peevishly. "Oh, look. It is Lord Etherington. He is doubtless come to look over Maribel Fortescu. Rumor has it that her dowry is vast. Well, fortune hunter or not, Lord Etherington is prodigiously handsome and a wonderful gossip. I shall dance with him." Quite forgetting her supposed ennui, Euphronia sprang to her feet and headed in the direction of the unsuspecting gentleman.

Whatever Lord Etherington's original intention, he soon found himself leading Euphronia to the set that was forming. Cecelia watched them for a few moments, wishing that she might dance herself, though her ankle was not yet fully recovered. Then, through the weaving figures of the dancers, she suddenly saw Mr. Foxley.

He was greeting someone at the edge of the dance floor, smiling at their remark, his tall form and red hair a beacon that drew Cecelia's eyes. She tried not to stare. Their last meeting had not been the happiest, and yet there was something about Mr. Foxley that Cecelia could

247

not ignore. He looked up. Cecelia quickly lowered her eyes and examined the tips of her satin evening slippers with minute attention.

"Lady Farington."

"Oh. Mister Foxley. I did not realize you were here," Cecelia said.

"Really? And yet I was aware of your presence from the moment I entered the ballroom."

Cecelia swallowed. "Indeed?"

"Indeed. Does your injury permit you to dance as yet?"

Cecelia shook her head. "Not really."

"A pity."

"Yes. Well." Cecelia searched a mind that seemed suddenly wiped clean of every thought. "I see that Lord Etherington is here," she remarked at last. "He dances with Miss Farington."

"I should like to call upon you tomorrow afternoon." The words were stiffly said, as if rehearsed many times. "Will you be at home to receive me?"

Cecelia's heart raced, her thoughts darted madly about. Was Mr. Foxley merely asking if she would be at home? Or was he asking if she would be at home to him? What did he mean? What did she want him to mean? What should she say? She must say something.

"I . . . uhm . . . have made no plans for tomorrow afternoon." How disagreeably stiff and ungracious that sounded. Cecelia stared across the dance floor. Should she say something else? Tell him that, indeed, she welcomed his call? But do I? she asked herself, blushing and feeling totally flustered by the conflicting emotions that seemed to be running relay races from her heart to her brain.

The set ended. Lord Etherington and Euphronia, talking and laughing animatedly, returned to where Cecelia was sitting with Mr. Foxley. Euphronia seemed to sparkle. Certainly she was no longer bored.

"Such a goose," Euphronia said loudly as they ap-

248

proached. "Lord Etherington has just been telling me what a henwit you have been, Cecelia. Lord Stervigton, you must forgive my stepmama. I am afraid she still has a bit of country hay in her hair. Though you would think after two years, she might have combed it out." Euphronia smirked.

Cecelia turned to the man who sat like a stone beside her. "Lord Stervigton?"

"Lady Farington, may I escort you into the next room where Lady Fortescu has set out refreshments? I understand the lobster puffs are not to be missed."

"To think that you actually fooled her into believing you were Mister Foxley!" Euphronia crowed. "How droll."

"Miss Farington has been telling me how things sit with you," Lord Etherington said, giving Cecelia a malicious glance. "To think that Lord Farington left you with a mere competence. Tsk, tsk."

"Papa always said Cecelia was a fleawit and obviously he was right."

"Miss Farington," Lord Stervigton interrupted, giving Euphronia a look of acute dislike. "I am trying to behave like a gentleman. I suggest you might try, if it is not totally beyond your capabilities, to behave like a lady."

"Well, really!" Euphronia drew herself up haughtily, while Cecelia did her best to sink into the ground.

"No call to get nasty now, Stervigton. It's an amusing story, surely worth repeating." Lord Etherington looked around at the small crowd that had gathered to eavesdrop and smiled.

"On the contrary." Lord Stervigton's voice was edged with steel. "It is a private matter between Lady Farington and myself." His eyes were hard and challenging, leaving no doubt that whoever chose to dine out on the story would regret it.

Cecelia could not believe this was happening to her. It seemed as if everyone was looking at her, looking and laughing at what a goose she had been.

"Come." Lord Stervigton held out his arm, and when Cecelia merely looked at him, took her hand instead and led her from the room.

Cecelia held her head high, her only thought to get out of the room with some shred of dignity still intact.

"Sit down."

Cecelia sat, and when a few moments later a glass was thrust into her hand, she drank from it without question.

"Are you all right?"

"Yes. Thank you."

"Can I get you anything else?"

Cecelia raised her eyes, meeting Lord Stervigton's blue ones for the first time since Euphronia and Lord Etherington had returned from the dance floor. "No," she said, handing him the glass and rising to her feet. "I have never been fond of lobster puffs."

Limping only slightly, Cecelia turned and headed for the door of the small saloon into which Lord Stervigton had brought her. She would ask one of the footmen to fetch her wrap and call for the carriage. Perhaps she was being cowardly, perhaps she should stay and return to the ballroom, face them all. But I am not going to, Cecelia thought. For the first time in my life I am going to do what I want and hang the consequences.

"I shall see you home."

Cecelia swallowed, very near to tears. "That will not be necessary," she said.

"I disagree," Lord Stervigton replied in a voice that would brook no denial. "It is of the absolute necessity."

"Why? Have you some other lie you wish to foist upon me for the amusement of your friends?"

"I will have one of the footmen fetch your wrap. We shall discuss this in the carriage."

"There is . . ." Cecelia stopped and took a breath to steady her nerves, to keep the tears at bay. "There is nothing to discuss, Lord Stervigton. You have had your

250

fun, played out your game—"

Lord Stervigton, ignoring Cecelia's words, stepped around her and opened the door. "Stay here," he ordered. "I shall have my carriage brought around."

Cecelia blinked as he closed the door in her face, and then gave vent to her feelings by giving the door a quick kick.

"Ouch! My ankle!" Cecelia hopped to a chair, tears coursing down her cheeks.

Lord Stervigton opened the door again and peered around, looking with interest at the slim ankle Cecelia had raised her flounce to reveal. "I begin to think Miss Farington is right and you are a fleawit," he said. "Albeit, an attractive one."

"Oh!" Cecelia quickly dropped her skirt.

"Now do be good and try not to injure yourself. I shall be back in a moment."

Cecelia made no reply. Indeed, she could think of nothing to say. She had made a complete gudgeon of herself, and Lord Stervigton now thought her no better than a fleawit. Not that it mattered. He had shamefully duped her. "And I—I shall never believe another word he says," she told the room at large in a quavery voice. "He . . . they . . . there were probably bets placed at White's to see how much he could get me to believe." Cecelia rubbed her ankle, which thankfully seemed not to be swelling, and did her best to kindle her anger against Lord Stervigton. He was nothing but a dissembler who preyed upon unsuspecting females.

Cecelia sniffed and wiped at an errant tear with gloved fingers. Just because a man had blue eyes and a . . . a crooked smile, he thought he could do as he pleased with a woman's heart. Well, she had been burned once and would now stay far away from the fire.

It was a difficult thing to do, however. Lord Stervigton returned, wrapped her in her cloak and ignoring her protests, carried her down the back stairs and out to his waiting carriage.

"This is much better," he said, settling himself comfortably beside her. "We are private, there is no possibility of interruption."

"It is most improper."

"Yes," he agreed. "Is your injury still paining you?"

Truthfully, from the time Lord Stervigton had lifted her in his arms, she had ceased to be aware of any throbbing except that in the vicinity of her heart. Still, it would not do to admit that to him. "Yes," she prevaricated. "Thanks to you."

"I am sorry to have put the door in the way of your foot," he apologized. "But obviously you need someone to look after you. Will you do me the honor of becoming my wife, Lady Farington?"

"No."

"What do you mean, no?" he demanded. "Women have been strewing themselves in my path ever since I came of age. I have been the most sought after matrimonial prize for these ten years and more."

"And shall continue to be as far as I am concerned," Cecelia replied. "I said I had no wish to remarry, Lord Stervigton. Knowing you has only reinforced my resolution. And I do not need someone to take care of me."

"You expect me to go down on my knees." He nodded to himself in the darkness. "Women have the most nonsensical notions. I shall do so when I call upon you tomorrow to discuss the matter. Does that satisfy you?"

"I may be a fleawit, Lord Stervigton," Cecelia said with a certain relish. "But even I can comprehend a simple yes or no. I do not wish to marry."

"Nonsense. Of course you do. Every woman does. I've had proof enough of that. Your reluctance stems from your marriage to Farington, that's all."

"That and your duplicity."

"My dear lady Farington." He turned and took her hand. "I apologize for misleading you, though you must

252

admit that I had cause. And in any case," he continued, giving her no chance to object, "surely you must see that there is a vast difference between your first husband and myself."

"It is too dark to see anything," she replied waspishly.

"It is not too dark to feel," he countered.

As, indeed it was not. The protests that rose to Cecelia's lips floated away to sink and drown in the dark pool of sensations aroused by Lord Stervigton's mouth and hands. She raised her head for a moment, gasping for air. The darkness veiling them in shadowy night made the world outside the carriage seem distant and unreal; there was only the here and now. Lord Stervigton's duplicity was forgotten. Cecelia no longer cared about protests or proprieties. Was this love? She leaned forward, lips parted, to find out.

Lord Stervigton brought her back to earth with a thud. "If you will give me the direction of your man of business, I shall see that a contract is drawn up tomorrow. If, as you say, your jointure is small, I foresee no problems." He set Cecelia back on her side of the carriage, and rearranged the folds of his cravat. "I shall call upon you to discuss arrangements."

Cecelia blinked, unable at first to comprehend his words, her mind still floating in the dark passion his touch had aroused. Then slowly, the warm glow which had filled her began to dissipate and she shuddered at the cold and bitter memories which seemed suddenly to fill the carriage.

I foresee no problems. My man of business shall draw up a contract. I shall call upon you. Had not Cecelia heard much those same words two years ago, two long, unhappy years ago, when Lord Farington had offered for her? I am free now, she thought. Why fetter myself with a husband again? A husband who will soon become embittered and find fault with everything I do or say. Cecelia drew herself up stiffly, unpleasant memories strengthening her resolve. "I think not," she said.

"But why do you refuse me? I have made you an honorable offer, and that is more than I have done for any other woman." Lord Stervigton sounded both angry and confused.

Cecelia glanced at him, at the hard, unyielding profile outlined by the carriage lanterns. The man who had so charmed her with his smile and wit seemed to have disappeared. Mr. Foxley was no more. His place had been taken by a stranger, an arrogant aristocrat much like Lord Farington had been. "If you wish to marry, you would do better to offer for someone like my stepdaughter," she said.

"I have no desire to marry." He turned to face her. "It is something I have, indeed, been avoiding for these ten years and more."

"Then why—"

"Do not ask me why!" he snapped. "I do not know why. I know only that I would have you to wife. And I warn you, I am not a patient man."

The carriage drew up outside Farington House. Lord Stervigton dismissed the footman and assisted Cecelia to alight. "I shall call upon you tomorrow," he said, looking down at her with a frown that warned he would not be denied. Then, under the interested gaze of Blackwell and two footmen, he raised her gloved fingers to his lips. "This is no game, I play," he said. "It started as one, I will admit, and for that I once more apologize. But I am in earnest now. Remember that." Swiftly he released her hand and returned to his carriage.

Cecelia remained where he had left her, the hand he had kissed held tightly against her heart, her mind a swirling kaleidoscope of hopes, dreams, and longings she dared not voice for fear they would prove as false as they had before.

* * *

From the moment she awoke the next day, Cecelia found she could think of nothing but Lord Stervigton's promised call. One minute she was sure she should adamantly refuse him, the next, remembering his smile and the feel of his lips upon hers, that she would be a nodcock to do so. She sat for long moments staring off into space, her embroidery forgotten beside her, and did her best to enumerate Lord Stervigton's faults and the multitude of advantages to remaining a widow. Then she would pick up her needle, embroider a few stitches so clumsily they would need to be picked out again, and exonerate him of all fault.

Finally Cecelia put down her stitchery altogether. It was no use. Her heart was well and truly lost. If only she could be as sure of his feelings for her.

At half past ten, a note was delivered. Cecelia's heart plunged to the tips of her silk-shod toes. Though she had never seen his handwriting before, she was sure it must be from Lord Stervigton. He writes to tell me he has made a mistake. He is not coming. He is withdrawing his offer. Cecelia put the note down on the occasional table, staring at it with a worried frown as if it might suddenly rear up and bite her.

I suppose I must open it sometime, she told herself taking a deep breath. But just as she was screwing up her courage, Blackwell arrived with a second note carefully folded and sealed. "The chambermaid found it in Miss Farington's room. I'm afraid her bed has not been slept in and the housekeeper reports her maid is missing as well." That said, Blackwell stepped back, doing his best to become invisible. Curiosity fought with propriety and won hands down.

"Oh, dear." Cecelia tore open Euphronia's note at once. She must be all right or she could not have written it, but still— "Oh, dear," she said again looking into the invisible Blackwell's eyes.

"Milady?" The butler leaned slightly forward, agog to

255

know what had happened but doing his best to retain his dignity.

"She's gone to Gretna Green," Cecelia said. "She's run off. With . . . with your nephew."

"John?" Blackwell looked thunderstruck. "Miss Farington has gone to Gretna Green with John?" He could not have been more shocked had Cecelia told him the chambermaid had run off with the Duke of Wellington. Blackwell frowned. He did not approve of runaway matches, nor of marrying outside one's class.

"I do not know what is to be done," Cecelia began, when a commotion was heard outside the door. She rose quickly to her feet. "Perhaps they have thought better of it and returned," she said, following Blackwell into the hall.

"Says he twisted his ankle on the pavement," one of the footmen was saying, his voice high with excitement. "Says the pavement needs repair and should have been seen to."

Lord Stervigton, looking rather pleased with himself, limped past Blackwell and Cecelia and into the front parlor assisted by the footman.

"Thank you." He sat down on the sofa, smiled, and then appeared to wince as he remembered his twisted ankle. "If you would be so kind as to send for some brandy?" he asked in a weak voice. "I'm afraid I'm in considerable pain."

"Lord Stervigton."

Lord Stervigton ignored Cecelia and handed the butler his hat and cane, before reclining back upon the pillows. "It's probably broken," he informed Cecelia. "I shall have to remain at least a month."

"Lord Stervigton, you cannot remain. Euphronia has run off to Gretna Green with the footman."

"Indeed?" Lord Stervigton raised a lazy eyebrow and accepted the glass of brandy which Blackwell handed him. "My condolences to your footman, but I fail to see what that has to do with my broken ankle."

"But something must be done!"

"Why?" he inquired reasonably. "If I am not mistaken, Miss Farington is of age and in possession of a considerable fortune entirely at her disposal. There is nothing we could do even were we so inclined."

"But—"

"Thank you. That will be all." Lord Stervigton dismissed the waiting servants, much to their disappointment, and sat up. "I see you have not read my note."

"No. I—whyever did Euphronia elope? She was so set on an elaborate June wedding. The dress is all but finished, the invitations have been writ. It was to be the wedding of the season. Whatever shall I do?"

Lord Stervigton gave her a considering look. "You will simply say there has been a slight mistake. It is Lady Farington, not Miss Farington, who is to be married in June."

"But—"

Lord Stervigton rose to his feet and walked without the slightest trace of a limp to where Cecelia stood, Euphronia's note still clutched in her hand. "We will now cease to talk of Miss Farington." He put his hands upon Cecelia's upper arms and drew her close. "Would you like to know what I wrote to you?"

Quite unable to speak, Cecelia nodded.

"If you remember, I spoke last night of the vast difference between Lord Farington and myself."

Cecelia nodded again, remembering the dark sensations his touch had aroused as much as his words.

"In the note I wrote to tell you exactly what that difference was. You see, Cecelia, I would marry you because I am desperately, hopelessly in love, and find I cannot live without you."

"Are you quite sure you are not hoaxing me again, Lord Stervigton?" Cecelia asked breathlessly. "Your leg is obviously not broken and—"

"How shall I convince you that I am in earnest?" Lord

257

Stervigton asked, his crooked smile much in evidence.

Cecelia braced her hands against his chest as her heart soared. He was in love with her! Why had he simply not said so last night? Well, and so was she in love with him. But he need not know that just yet.

"How may you convince me?" she asked, her eyes wide and innocent. "I am sure I have no idea, my lord. You see, gentlemen are forever having accidents outside my door. I am quite inured to their importunities."

"Cecelia . . ."

"And, in any case, I am afraid I have fallen in love with someone else."

"What?" His hands dropped to his sides. "But you cannot . . . Not when I . . . Are you quite sure, Cecelia?" He looked down at her, his blue eyes dark with something akin to fear in their depths.

Cecelia nodded. "I am quite sure," she said. "You see, he is quite the most wonderful man I have ever met, and I love him desperately, though he is poor and the sole support of an invalid mother and five sisters and has red hair."

"In that case . . ." Lord Stervigton grinned and took her in his arms again. "I can only say that I wholeheartedly approve your choice, and shall definitely attend the ceremony."

"Even with your broken ankle?" she teased.

"Even with bootblack in my hair, if you wish," he countered. "But let us discuss the wedding details later. There are more important things to attend to now."

As, indeed, there were.

Best Man

by

Elizabeth Morgan

"Dearest Sarah, this is wonderful news!" Miss Lydia Grayson hugged her sister warmly, and the sparkle in her blue eyes was due to more than just her natural vivacity. "I know how deeply your feelings are engaged, and I hope that you and Ned will be very happy together."

The younger Miss Grayson smiled a shade tremulously as they resumed their walk in the garden of Berkeley Square, only a short distance from the house on Curzon Street where the two ladies lived with their widowed mother. As they strolled in the bright sunshine of an April morning, they made a charming pair; both were of medium height and fair, though Miss Sarah Grayson was generally accounted to be the prettier, her hair being of a truer golden hue and her features more delicate. When the two of them were side by side, it could be noted that Miss Lydia's hair was more of a light ash brown, and her eyes a shade darker blue; above all, her chin was definitely firmer, and her expression, even now, lacked the gentle sweetness that characterized her sister.

"I'll confess I was a bit afraid to tell you," Sarah admitted shyly. "You have always been so opposed to marriage, and nothing Mama or I could say has ever been of any use in persuading you to the contrary. I thought that you might be angry with me."

"Angry? Never with you, my love," Miss Grayson replied, shaking her head. "I simply fail to share your romanticized view of the world. For most women, marriage is at best a new set of constraints, and at worst a form of enslavement to a tyrannical male."

"But all men are not tyrants," Sarah objected. "Think of Ned, for instance."

"Ned is a true gem, and indeed he does not seem to share the odious qualities of the majority of his sex."

The younger girl laughed. "I am not sure that he would be much flattered by your description!"

"No, certainly not, and I beg you not to repeat a word of this to him; we do not want to put him off by revealing the eccentricities of his new sister-in-law!"

Miss Grayson's tone was light, but her self-mockery had a serious edge. It was true that the expected obedience of a female to her husband was a factor in her low opinion of the wedded state, but there was more to it than that. By the age of fourteen, she had realized that her father was making her mother's life a misery, with an endless string of mistresses and gaming debts. Mrs. Grayson's tears had been shed in secrecy, or so she believed, valiantly maintaining a happy facade before her two daughters. Sarah had been too young to know any of what was going on, and when Mr. Grayson had died of a fever the year of Lydia's coming-out, he left behind an idealized memory of a loving husband and father. But not for Lydia; she had never revealed her knowledge, in order to spare her mother's feelings, but behind her scathing quips about men and marriage lay a real sense of disillusionment.

At the time of her father's death, her bitterness toward the male sex was strong, and she had turned aside a number of offers with polite but stubborn refusal. Shortly thereafter, it was revealed that her father's self-indulgent encroachments upon his inheritance had reduced the family fortunes to a level that could barely be described as genteel, and the number of her suitors declined sharply. That was only further evidence for her opinion that most men considered a wife to be little more than a financial commodity. And those few who had been willing to overlook that vital shortcoming had been rapidly put off by her lack of gratitude for their attentions.

Now at the age of twenty-two, Lydia had found no reason to amend her views about marriage, although she did admit that not all men were as weak and irresponsible as her father. Edwin Brooks, her sister's admirer and now her betrothed, was one such exception; he was quiet, serious, and in Lydia's opinion rather dull, but there was no doubt that he loved Sarah and would strive to be a good husband.

"Have you set a date for the wedding?" Miss Grayson inquired.

"In June," Sarah replied dreamily. "It is the traditional month for brides, you know, and neither one of us wants to wait any longer than necessary. You, of course, must be my maid of honor, and Uncle Gerald can give me away."

Miss Grayson could not refrain from making a face. The prospect of actually having to participate in the wedding was distasteful enough, without having to endure the company of her mother's brother, whom she considered a prosy bore. Uncle Gerald Fortescue and his wife Augusta held strong views upon propriety in general, and during their infrequent visits from their home in Salisbury, they never failed to comment upon Lydia's unbecomingly headstrong nature.

"And Ned has asked his best friend to stand up for him," Sarah continued. "His name is Jack Worthing, and we are supposed to meet him tonight at Lady Gillingham's. Ned says that they have been friends since childhood, and that we are all sure to like him."

The phrase "Ned says" was already becoming an irritatingly frequent part of her sister's vocabulary, but Miss Grayson chose to overlook this evidence of Sarah's besotted condition. She was grateful to have had no experience of falling in love herself, because it invariably transformed sane persons into fools. In any case, it was certain that Ned's friend would be just as respectably dull as he, a fact which brought Miss Grayson some comfort, since as maid of honor and best man, they would undoubtedly have to spend considerable time in each other's company.

"I am sure that we will all like this Mister Worthing," Miss Grayson said, with the merest hint of mischief in her voice. "Just think of all the amiable qualities his name suggests!" And as the conversation degenerated into a humorous consideration of other virtuous-sounding names, the sisters strolled back in the direction of their home.

Lady Gillingham's party was well attended, so much so that she could happily describe it to her friends as "a sad crush." The evening was clear and not too chill, the musicians were skilled, and the hostess was renowned for the quality of her suppers. The Graysons were there in force, Sarah looking lovely in white muslin trimmed with blue ribbons, and Lydia in her favorite gown of pale gray sarsenet.

"You both look so charming, my dears." Mrs. Harriet Grayson sighed, modestly unconcerned that she also was a remarkably pretty woman. Only a few threads of gray in her own blond hair gave away the fact that she had just celebrated her forty-second birthday. Her only thoughts, however, were centered upon her offspring.

"Sarah, you have made me so happy," she smiled. "Ned is such a fine young man. I could only wish that your sister would have the same good fortune."

"Mama . . ." Miss Grayson responded in a playfully warning tone, recognizing a familiar theme.

"Now, Lydia, dear," she chided gently. "You know that I don't mean to argue with your behavior, but you are always so critical of the gentlemen you meet. I feel sure that if you could only be a little more, well—"

"Fawning?"

"Oh, no!" Mrs. Grayson responded, confused as usual by the sharp edge to her elder daughter's sense of humor. "I meant only that more flies are caught with honey than with vinegar."

"I don't especially like flies, Mama, and I have no intention of trying to catch one, by either means. But don't worry, I promise you I shall be the soul of cordiality to everyone I meet tonight!"

Mrs. Grayson sighed. It was true that her daughter's conduct was always scrupulously polite in company, but her complete absence of flirtatiousness stood out in contrast to the lures that most women used to attract the opposite sex.

Mrs. Grayson would never have desired her daughter to behave coquettishly, but as she could not imagine a world in which a girl would not wish to be married, Lydia's indifference to men left her utterly bemused.

For her own part, Miss Grayson was quite content to enjoy an evening of dancing and conversation, free of the pressures of being "on the catch" for a husband, and for that reason she was a popular partner. It was much later that evening when she finally paused to catch her breath, sinking into a chair as she waited for her dancing partner to procure her a glass of ratafia. Male voices approached behind her, around the corner of the wall, and as she recognized one of them as Ned's, she began to rise to greet him. But then the words she heard stopped her cold.

"I don't agree with you," Ned was saying. "I think that marriage will be wonderful."

"It will be hell." The other voice was deeper, and very male. "As your friend, I consider it my duty to remind you that women are the very devil."

"Oh, come now, Jack, that's doing it up a bit too brown. I know many fine women, and so do you."

"They're all alike under the surface, Ned. A little smile, a little flutter of the lashes, while they reach in to empty your pockets. A man is entitled to his enjoyments, but he's a fool to think that there is no price to be paid afterward."

Lydia was rigid, her temper rising as she listened. So this was the famous Mr. Worthing, mouthing such insulting rubbish!

"I'm not talking about the muslin company, Jack. But even so, I seem to recall a few females of whom you have become rather enamored."

"Even the most respectable ones are not above keeping an eye to the main chance. My mother, my sisters, even my former fiancée all threw affections out the window when a title and fortune presented themselves. I learned long ago that romantic love is a sham, and that men are fools who allow themselves to be led around by their—"

"No, Jack, I cannot agree with you. I love Sarah, and I

know that she loves me."

"Very well, then, let us say that you and she are both under the influence of the compulsion to reproduce, which you insist upon calling love. And I will even allow that she may not be after your fortune, a possibility which, if true, would make her unique among the others of her sex. I maintain that it is the very nature of women which makes it impossible to bear their company. If a woman is not a simpering ninny, as insipid as she is ignorant, then she is a termagant who will not rest until everything is done her own way."

"Sarah is not like that at all, Jack, and I insist that you meet her before you make such ridiculous statements."

"Very well, then, introduce me to your paragon, and I will endeavor to keep an open mind. But I am not so easily charmed as you by a pretty face, and if I believe that you are mistaken, I will consider it my duty as your friend to persuade you to abandon this marriage scheme."

The voices moved away, and Miss Grayson allowed herself to let out a long, fuming breath. How dare he pass such harsh judgments upon her sex! It was not that she herself was any more in favor of matrimony than he, but rather it was the absurdity of his arguments that made her blood boil. Yes, there were some women who were mercenary and shallow; in fact, she numbered several among her acquaintance. But with what callousness was he condemning all for the sins of a few! And with what self-righteous arrogance did he consider himself to be so superior as a male!

Fortunately for her composure, the music struck up once more just as her partner returned, stammering apologies for his tardiness in wending his way back through the crowd, and Lydia gratefully accepted to dance. That accounted for the redness of her cheeks for the next few moments, as her temper gradually cooled. Perhaps it was for the best that she had overheard that horrid conversation, because now she was prepared to fight back. She was not about to let that odious creature spoil Ned and Sarah's happiness; in fact, she was quite looking forward to making the acquaintance of Mr. Jack Worthing.

Lydia made her way back to where her mother and Sarah were sitting, just in time to see Ned introducing the ladies to his friend. In contrast to Ned's medium build and fair good looks, this man was taller, dark-haired, and somehow more dangerous-looking. His close-fitting coat of midnight blue superfine was cut by the hand of a master, and he carried himself with an assurance that did not soften the intimidating effect of his presence. He was bending over to kiss Sarah's hand, and when he straightened, an easy smile on his lips, he caught sight of Lydia as she approached. The smile faded for a moment, and then returned with a slight twist.

"There you are, Miss Grayson," Ned exclaimed. "I have just presented to Mrs. Grayson and Miss Grayson my friend John Worthing. Allow me to present him to you; Miss Grayson, Mister Worthing."

Mr. Worthing bowed over Lydia's hand. "I am charmed indeed, Miss Grayson."

"Oh, surely not by a pretty face?" she replied coolly.

He glanced up, startled, and she could see that his eyes were very dark, almost black in their depths. However, there was nothing for them to read in Lydia's face but faint amusement, and his first instinctive impression of hostility faded.

"I would not have used the word 'pretty,' Miss Grayson. 'Lovely' would be a better description, for both you and your sister."

Lydia's mouth firmed imperceptibly. Abominable flatterer! If he thought he could make her simper, he could think again!

Sarah, however, was a different matter. "You are too kind, Mister Worthing." She smiled at him shyly. "I am so pleased that you will be a member of our wedding party; I know that no one else would serve Ned so well as best man."

"Now, that's a phrase I have always viewed as a contradiction in terms," Lydia murmured, and this time Mr.

Worthing's head came around sharply to look at her once more.

"Lydia!" Mrs. Grayson reproved. "I beg you to recall your promise to me this evening! Mr. Worthing, you must excuse my daughter's sense of humor."

"Willingly, ma'am. That is, of course, if Miss Grayson will honor me with the next dance?"

And Lydia found herself being led out upon the dance floor, all too aware of the approving smiles of her family. She knew what they were thinking: an eligible man is showing interest in Lydia! The thought made her shudder.

"Are you cold, Miss Grayson?"

She looked up at him, seeing an ironic sparkle in his eyes that she mistrusted. "Not at all, sir."

"May I say that in addition to being lovely, you are quite accomplished as a dancer?" The polished gallantry slid from his lips with just the right touch of sincerity.

"Yes, indeed, sir, you may say it, just as you may say that you are the emperor of Cathay. In neither case am I obliged to believe it." Her tone was so calm that for a moment he wondered whether he had heard aright. Then her meaning sunk in, and he frowned slightly. Miss Grayson appeared to have taken him in instant dislike, and he was determined to find out the reason why.

"You do not appreciate compliments, Miss Grayson?"

Lydia regarded him with a touch of amusement. "I do when they are sincere, Mister Worthing. Otherwise, I should have to be a simpering ninny, would you not say?"

His grip upon her hand tightened. "I believe I did say. You were eavesdropping upon us earlier?"

"Not at all. I was simply minding my own business, when someone came up beside me and started spouting all manner of nonsensical and offensive things."

"I am sorry if you were offended, Miss Grayson, but believe me, I should never have said what I did had I known you were listening."

"Oh, do not apologize, sir. I loathe hypocrisy in all forms, and I was glad to be able to hear what you think of my sex without the encumbrance of polite fictions."

"Well, then, Miss Grayson, I will speak plainly. It seems to me, judging by your little jest earlier about a 'best man,' that your opinion of the male sex is no higher. You should not therefore mind if I tell you that I find equal contradiction in the term 'maid of honor.' "

Lydia gasped aloud, and only the years of dancing practice prevented her from missing her step. "How dare you imply that women have no honor?"

"I would amend that to say that whereas a woman's honor is a virtue much prized, it has a price attached, and that price is generally marriage to the highest bidder."

That sentiment echoed Lydia's own beliefs to an unsettling degree, but she was not about to say so. "And is that the fault of the woman, or the fault of the men who prevent her from owning property or securing an independent means of livelihood?

"And besides, you are referring to honor only in the sense of, er—"

"Chastity?"

"Yes, chastity!" Lydia attempted not to blush; after all, she was the one who had initiated this frank discussion. "But honor also means fidelity to one's vows, and in that area, I do not think much of men's so-called honor."

"A gentleman stands by his word, Miss Grayson."

"Yes, but only if that word is given to another man!"

Mr. Worthing was silent, and in that moment the musicians called for a pause. "Let us continue this interesting conversation elsewhere, if you will," he proposed. "Is it too chilly for you to step out on the terrace?"

It was not, and they seated themselves upon a carved stone bench beyond the French doors connecting the drawing room and the terrace. The light was fading gently into dusk, but the glittering candles from the drawing room cast a soft glow upon the terrace.

Looking at Mr. Worthing now, Lydia became suddenly aware that he was undoubtedly a very handsome man. Indeed, had it not been for his despicable opinions, she might have found him quite attractive.

She did not realize that in that first swift glance, he himself had made a rapid, practiced assessment of her charms in which a number of virtues were catalogued. The thoughts now passing through his mind were not unlike her own: a damned fine-looking woman, but like all women, with a head full of nonsense. Although he had to admit, a few of the things she had just said were not so very unreasonable.

"Miss Grayson, may I ask why it is that you have decided to engage me in this debate?" he asked. "I realize that my statements offended you, but as they were not addressed to you in the first place, I fail to see why they are any of your concern."

"They concern me, Mister Worthing, because anything which affects my sister concerns me. You have been asked to participate in this wedding, and by all appearances you seem to regard your role as being the one who persuades the groom to cry off.

"I am not overly fond of the idea of marriage myself, but if this is what Ned and Sarah want, then I will do all in my power to make it happen. And what is more, if your opinions are going to poison Ned's view of women, and lead him to be a bad husband for Sarah, I will do all I can to stop you from spreading those opinions."

"But if my beliefs are sincere? What then?"

"Then I must make you change your mind!"

"And how may that be accomplished, pray?"

"I don't know, but you must let me try. Help me find some way to prove to you that women can have the same positive traits as men, and be worthy of the same respect. Please, Mister Worthing, for Ned and Sarah's sake."

Worthing paused to consider this. "Very well, then. If we can think of some arena in which you can attempt to prove your so-called equality, then I must agree to reconsider my opinions of your sex, and refrain from dissuading Ned from entering into matrimony?"

"Yes, that's it." Lydia nodded.

"And we are agreed that to avoid any hypocrisy, we shall be completely frank with one another, sparing no language and hiding no sentiment, however candid?"

"Yes!"

"And if you lose your nerve, or attempt to use what I call feminine wiles instead of logic, then I may say whatever I like to Ned without your interference?"

She nodded again, but a bit more slowly.

"Very well, then, Lydia, you may start by calling me Jack."

"Why?" She gasped, taken aback by this sudden familiarity.

"Because men call each other by first names, as do women, and for us to do otherwise would defeat your purpose."

"Very well, I agree. Jack." It felt peculiar to utter his given name with such freedom. "But only when we are in private; it would be improper to use that form of address in front of others."

Worthing folded his arms, leaned back, and grinned. "Agreed. And, I have just decided on the perfect arena in which you may attempt to demonstrate your equality. It will be a boxing arena, in fact; boxing is a perfect example of a manly sport, and I am sure that you will strip to advantage, as the expression goes."

"No!" Lydia jumped to her feet, blushing furiously and all too aware of his amusement at her expense. "That idea is totally unseemly—"

"Ah, but you agreed that no such hypocrisy as social propriety would impede our experiment. And you said that you wished to prove yourself equal to a man."

Lydia paused, thinking fast. It was unthinkable for her to accept his challenge, as well he knew; but how could she beg off honorably, by a man's standards?

"If a boxing match were to be fought between a man weighing one hundred pounds and a man weighing two hundred pounds, would it be considered fair?"

Worthing shook his head. "Of course not."

"Then I reject your challenge on similar grounds. Having equal qualities does not necessarily mean being completely equal in a physical sense, and as I obviously am smaller than you, no match between us could be fair."

"You are quick, Lydia, I will grant you that," he conceded. "I will have to bow to your logic, which I find impeccable. You may expect another challenge from me tomorrow, however."

"Of course." Lydia took a step closer to where Mr. Worthing was still seated on the bench. "Oh, and Jack? Do you know what a woman may do when another woman makes a remark in her presence that is deliberately intended to discomfit and embarrass her?"

"No."

"I thought not." She then delivered a resounding slap to his face, and marched back into the drawing room.

The challenge arrived upon the very next day, as the Misses Grayson were sitting down to take tea with their mother. The billet was addressed to the elder Miss Grayson, and Lydia opened it reluctantly, all too aware of her companions' brimming curiosity. As she scanned the contents, a small frown knit her brow.

"What is it?" Sarah inquired. "And who is it from?"

"It is from Mister Worthing. He desires me to go riding with him tomorrow."

"Oh!" Sarah replied in a significant tone, exchanging a speaking look with her mother. "He must have been quite taken with you last night."

Mrs. Grayson was quick to echo that sentiment. "Indeed he must have. This is a very flattering invitation, Lydia, which I hope you will not refuse; Mister Worthing struck me as a very proper young man, whose manners were most charming."

"Ha!" replied Lydia, to the bewilderment of her family. "But rest assured, I have every intention of accepting."

"Then why do you frown so?" asked Sarah.

Lydia paused, realizing that her thoughts must have been reflected in her expression. And those thoughts had been centered upon what scheme Jack was plotting for her discomfiture! She considered herself to be a good horsewoman, but no doubt he intended some trick to demonstrate her inferiority as a female.

"I was just thinking that—that—"

"That it would be improper of you to make such an excursion with a veritable stranger," Mrs. Grayson finished for her, ever mindful of the proprieties. "Sarah and Ned can accompany you."

"Oh, yes, that would be delightful," her younger daughter responded eagerly. "I'm sure that Ned will agree, and we will make it a real outing."

Lydia was momentarily nonplussed; it was one thing to have some sort of competition take place in front of a groom, and another entirely to be under the watchful eyes of Sarah and Ned! How could she explain to them what was going on, without revealing the true reason behind it all—that the very marriage of those two dear people might be at stake?

She was still pondering that question on the following morning, as the three of them cantered together in the direction of Hyde Park. The clattering of the horses' hooves upon the pavement made it too noisy to converse until they reached the park, but when they did, Lydia determined to speak.

"Sarah and Ned, I think you should know that Mister Worthing has rather a funning sense of humor."

"I've known that for years," Ned agreed, with warmth in his kind brown eyes. "He was famous as a jokester when we were up at Oxford together, and some of the things he got up to—oh, but I should not divulge any of that to you ladies."

Lydia felt a moment's irritation at Ned's old-fashioned gallantry, as she would much have liked to hear more details, but Sarah virtually glowed. Some women apparently liked to feel protected by a man, Lydia mused, even if it meant being treated as some sort of delicate flower that would wilt at a harsh word. She herself much preferred Jack Worthing's more direct style, for all that she found him abrupt and insolent.

"What I meant was, last night he and I spoke about matching our skills in different areas. Only as a silly wager, of course. But I should not wonder if he plans to make some sort of challenge to me today."

At that moment, the object of her thoughts came riding up, greeting them all with good cheer. His eyes fell appreciatively upon Lydia's trim riding habit, which was of a flattering shade of maroon. It also showed off her figure to advantage, all of which he noted in a flash, betraying nothing in his expression except for a certain gleam in his eyes which only Lydia seemed to notice. She felt her face going slightly warm.

"Miss Grayson was speaking just now of some sort of challenge," Ned offered conversationally. "I am certain, of course, that she was being a bit fanciful."

"Not at all," Mr. Worthing contradicted. "Indeed, I would like to propose a test of horsemanship, now that I see that both of the ladies are so at ease on horseback." And in fact they were, both having been trained to the correct posture, and to hold the reins with assurance.

"I prefer to be a judge, if you please." Sarah laughed. "Lydia is far more skilled than I."

"Very well, then; if you and Ned here will serve as judges, Miss Grayson and I may settle our—"

"Wager," Lydia interrupted. "Our little wager."

Worthing nodded his comprehension. "Are you prepared to accept my challenge, Miss Grayson?"

Lydia signified her assent with just the merest toss of her head. What, after all, could he propose in the sedate confines of Hyde Park, before witnesses?

"I challenge you, Miss Grayson, to trade horses with me. If your skills are indeed equal to mine, you should be able to handle my mount, and I yours."

The other three all gasped, but Ned was the first to find

his tongue. "Surely you are jesting, Jack! Your horse is a high-spirited beast, too strong for any lady to be able to control!"

Those words, however, had an unfortunate effect upon Lydia's pride. "I beg to differ, Ned," she began, only to be interrupted by Sarah.

"Mister Worthing, surely your horse is too large for my sister!"

"Now Miss Grayson, I would never suggest it for a delicate creature such as yourself; however, the elder Miss Grayson appears to me to be unusually tall for her sex, and not in any way frail."

Lydia glared at him; he may as well have called her a great, strapping wench! And the fact that her sister was pleased by his flattery was yet another irritation.

"I accept your challenge," she declared boldly. "Let us do it immediately."

So, under the amused and slightly shocked eyes of Sarah and Ned, the two of them dismounted and changed horses. As Mr. Worthing boosted her into the saddle of his own mount, Lydia felt a certain qualm; the horse was perhaps two hands taller than her own, and there was no doubt that it would take all of her skill to handle him. As she looked down into Worthing's mocking eyes, however, she was fired with the determination to succeed.

The challenge was to ride together, at the same speed, toward a distant elm, and as they set off, Lydia was just barely able to manage her new mount. Mr. Worthing, however, was supremely at ease upon the smaller horse. She had to admit that he was a superb horseman, and that his relatively greater strength made it much simpler to control the reins. When they reached the elm, he turned to her with a look of triumph.

"Why, Miss Grayson, you have done very well," he said with the merest touch of condescension. "I did not expect you to sit my horse so well. You must now admit, however, that your skill as a female is not equal to mine."

"I admit no such thing," Lydia protested, her face aglow

from her recent efforts. Something about this was not quite fair, but she could not put her finger upon it . . . Then it came to her.

"The test is unfair because we are differently mounted. I challenge you, Jack, to ride back sidesaddle."

The look of consternation upon his face was priceless. "You don't mean—"

"Yes, I do! As long as you are seated astride, you have every advantage in keeping your balance and control. And since I am not permitted to sit in such a manner, you must therefore sit as I do. Then we will see who is superior!"

With a reluctant smile, Jack swung one long leg over the horse's neck and immediately struggled to find his balance. The raised pommel was designed to be hooked by the rider's knee, but Jack's legs were much too long, and the best he could manage was to try and wedge his thigh against the horse's neck. Meanwhile, the horse shifted uncomfortably at the lopsided extra weight and danced a few steps forward, at which point Lydia was extremely gratified to see him slide off the saddle and land upon the ground with a decided thump.

"You see, Jack, it is not such a simple matter to ride as women do; it requires considerable balance, which you must acknowledge to be a superior skill."

Jack was still brushing himself off, nothing bruised except his pride. "Once again I must bow to your logic, Lydia," he admitted. "I had not considered the art of the sidesaddle. My only regret now is that I may not in return demand that you mount astride, lest we shock the delicate sensibilities of our friends. That would be a challenge I would truly like to see!"

Lydia was forced to blush at Jack's suggestion, which clearly involved some sort of mental image of her dress hiked up to show her legs, clad only in pantaloons. "Luckily that is impossible, as you say," she said frostily, just as Ned and Sarah rode up to them, with concern written upon their faces.

"What on earth happened, Jack?" Ned exclaimed. "We

saw you take some sort of fall!"

"Merely an awkward dismount." Jack shrugged. "However, I am willing to acknowledge defeat. Miss Grayson has gotten the better of me in this round, but perhaps her luck will change the next time. Now, Miss Grayson, may I assist you in alighting, so that we may return to our own mounts?"

There was of course no choice but to accept his assistance, although as Lydia felt Jack's strong hands circle her waist, she felt a tremor pass through her, no doubt of lingering indignation. He lifted her from the saddle easily, as though she were a mere featherweight, and the sensation was admittedly pleasing. When she looked into his eyes, however, the mocking gleam had returned, and as they continued their ride, Lydia was left to wonder with some apprehension what the next challenge might be.

Meanwhile, plans for the wedding continued apace, and in the days that followed, the Grayson household bustled with activity. There were invitations to be ordered, menus to be planned, and above all, a gown to be designed for Sarah. Mrs. Grayson was a skilled needlewoman, and she had always stretched her modest income by providing her daughters with clever imitations of the latest styles. Unfortunately, Ned and Jack were present at one of the ladies' debates over the advantages of sarsenet versus satin, and the groom was prompted into a bit of levity.

"Vanity, thy name is woman, eh, Jack?" Ned teased, yet with fondness in his tone as he regarded his bride-to-be.

Jack, however, was inclined to take the criticism at face value. "You are quite right," he replied. "With all due respect to the ladies here, the fairer sex is renowned for thinking of nothing but frills and furbelows, whereas a gentleman thinks nothing of them."

Miss Grayson raised her head from the pattern card she had been studying. "Oh, indeed, Mr. Worthing?" she asked, a shade too politely. "Do you maintain that gentlemen do not have equal care for their own mode of dress? I suppose that the handsome cravat you are wearing took no more than a few seconds to arrange, and that the shine of your boots was achieved by the natural aging of the leather."

"Not at all, Miss Grayson," he replied. "I, however, am content to wear the same boots and the same coat many times, whereas ladies must always be seen in something new. No matter how much they possess, they must always be clamoring for something more."

Even the gentle Mrs. Grayson took umbrage at that. "My dear Mr. Worthing, you must not judge all women by the frailties of a few, and indeed I must wonder at the ladies you have known."

As she spoke, Lydia found herself imagining all too clearly the females — certainly not ladies! — whom Mr. Worthing had probably known. Her mother was continuing to speak, however.

"My daughters and I do not disdain to wear a frock from a former season, if it is well made and of classic style."

Jack bowed in her direction. "You are one in a thousand, ma'am. I still believe that no lady would be caught in public wearing the same gown twice in a row."

Lydia's blue eyes sparkled. "Is this another challenge, Mister Worthing? If so, I accept. And in fact, I shall offer to wear the same gown *three* days in a row, beginning tomorrow eve."

"Lydia, how can you?" Sarah asked, unsure whether her sister was speaking in jest. "Tomorrow is Thursday, and we have been asked to parties every night until Sunday. You cannot wear the same gown out in public!"

"Yes, I can, if only to prove to Mister Worthing that the thing can be done."

Mrs. Grayson, who was about to protest, caught the slight smile upon Lydia's countenance, and from long experience, comprehended that her daughter was up to some mischief. So she simply settled back more comfortably against the stiff cushions of the sofa, content to bide her time until the plan should be revealed. The rest of the visit passed amicably, and when the gentlemen had taken their leave, and Lydia unveiled her scheme, the three of them enjoyed a chuckle at Mr. Worthing's expense.

And so it was that Saturday evening, at the soirée given by the Earl and Countess of Rockford, Lydia found herself being solicited to dance by Jack Worthing. That gentleman wore an expression of self-satisfaction, bordering upon triumph.

"You look lovely tonight, Lydia," he complimented her. "In fact, you have been quite in looks these past three nights, and I must say that although you chose to abandon my challenge, I am gratified at the results."

"I'm afraid you are mistaken," Lydia replied sweetly as he led her into the movements of the dance. "I have by no means given up."

Jack looked down at her with a touch of weary resignation. "You females are all alike." He sighed. "No doubt you think to fool me because I was not present last night at the card party you attended; however, I prevailed upon a female acquaintance of mine to watch for you, and to give me a precise description of your dress. It was quite different from the gown you wore the night before, and from the gown you are wearing at present."

"Do describe all these dresses to me, I pray you."

"On Thursday, you wore light blue muslin with a low round neck and long sleeves. Then last night, you wore gray gauze, with a high neck and half sleeves."

"Over an underdress of . . . ?"

"Light blue. Surely you do not mean it was the same!"

"And why not? All that was required was a bit of quick needlework, with which my mother was more than happy to assist. We simply removed the sleeves, and pinned the fabric into the neckline; under the overlay of gauze, none of the stitching was visible. So, it was the same gown worn twice."

"Lydia, I felicitate you and your mother upon such a clever conversion, but the gown you are wearing now is red, with long sleeves. There is no way you can flummox me into believing that it is the same as the blue."

"No, you are correct. But it is not precisely a gown; it is a pelisse, and I am wearing the blue gown underneath it. You can see the blue behind the button loops in the front."

Worthing's sharp eyes dropped to her bosom, examining the details of her attire, and once again Lydia found herself blushing. Perhaps it had been an error to call his attention to her clothing, and more precisely to what was underneath!

When he raised his eyes to hers once more, his own sparkled with irritation. "I do not consider you to have played fair, Lydia," he said. "The challenge was for you to be seen in public with the exact same gown."

"Not quite. I promised to wear it, which I have. I did not promise that it should not be altered or concealed."

"You deliberately employed a ruse to trick me!"

"Yes, I did, but I nonetheless adhered to the letter of your challenge. You have no cause for indignation; rather, you should be felicitating me upon my ingenuity, which is a trait the members of my sex share in abundance."

He acknowledged the hit with a rueful smile, which had the disconcerting effect of making him even more attractive. As they continued to dance together, Lydia was very aware of his physical grace, and of the way in which the combination of that grace with strength was exerting a strange pull upon her senses. Better to remind herself of all the reasons she had for disliking Mr. Jack Worthing!

"I have met your challenges so far, Jack; are you now beginning to change your mind about the inferiority of the female sex?"

He raised one arched eyebrow. "Perhaps you have convinced me that your sex can be more clever, or rather devious, than I had supposed." He ignored her small snort of protest. "And you have used logic to your advantage, which I confess I did not expect from a female."

She forced herself not to respond to that leading statement, but rather to pursue her original intention. "So, Jack, are you willing to end your opposition to Ned and Sarah's marriage?"

"Not yet, I'm afraid. You have not yet proven to me that a woman can have the same sense of honor as a man."

Jack's mouth was set in a rather grim line, and Lydia knew that he was thinking of an unpleasant memory. She decided to draw a bow at a venture.

"Jack, are we still being frank with one another?" He nodded, and she continued on. "Then pray let us be seated at the end of this dance, and tell me what happened between you and your former fiancée."

The request clearly took him aback, but when the music ended he led her toward a vacant settee. He began to speak, and if his tone was harsh, it was not enough so as to draw the attention of anyone around them.

"About three years ago, I met a young lady who was, or so I thought, my very ideal of a woman. She was well-bred, well-spoken, and did not manage to bore me within half an hour of our acquaintance, unlike the vast majority of your sex."

"And beautiful, I presume?" Lydia added dryly.

"Of course. The most beautiful girl I may ever have seen."

That reply brought no satisfaction, but only a strange pang somewhere in the region of Lydia's heart. She dismissed it, however, as he went on.

"After several months, during which she doted upon me, casting aside numerous other suitors, I offered for her. She, and her father, accepted with prodigious gratitude and affection, and she professed her love in the most effusive terms, I assure you."

"And then?" Lydia prompted.

"And then she made the acquaintance of Lord Brompton, rich as Croesus, fat as a flawn, and possessed of the intelligence of a mole, and before I knew it she had written me an artfully tear-stained letter, declaring that 'after agonies of indecision, she had realized that we would not suit,' and the engagement was broken."

"I see. And her engagement to Lord Brompton was then announced at once?"

"After a decent interval. One week."

Lydia winced. "But surely, Jack, you cannot assume that this hard-hearted"— she paused —"well, *creature* —is representative of our sex! Why, I for one would view such behavior with utter loathing, and so would most of the women I know."

Jack shook his head ruefully. "I'm afraid I neglected to tell you that the females in my own family had behaved according to a similar pattern. My own mother, after the death of my father, married a man for his wealth, and so did my two sisters."

"How old were you at the time?"

"I was already at Cambridge. My sisters were then sixteen and seventeen."

"But do consider, Jack. A woman recently widowed, with two daughters on the verge of their come-out and a son at an expensive school! Did your father leave a substantial inheritance?"

Jack gave her an odd look. "No, in fact I had some inkling that things were not quite right after his death, but I had no right to insist upon a full disclosure of the financial affairs. That was resolved between my mother and our man of business."

"I cannot presume to judge a situation about which I know almost nothing; but could it be possible that she did what she thought was best for her children? And that your sisters, who were still at home during that time of distress, understood that they could help by reducing the burden upon the family? If you will allow me this impertinence, what is the source of your present income?"

As she had spoken, Jack's countenance had paled. Now, he paused for a moment before replying, as if to draw breath. "My stepfather and my mother died shortly after the marriage of my second sister. I do not know, in all honesty, if my income is derived from his or from hers. I had always assumed the latter."

Lydia remained silent for a moment, allowing him to digest these new ideas. There was surely no point in asking him about other females of his acquaintance, since they obviously were in the profession of exchanging intimate favors for monetary ones. But at the least, by forcing him to contemplate his family history from a different point of view, she knew that she had shaken the foundations of his opinion of her sex in general!

When she spoke again, it was in a gentle tone. "Jack, I am truly sorry for all the pain that you have been caused, and in particular for the unfortunate end of your engagement. But you see, there are reasons which may explain the behavior of some women in our society — not your fiancée, to be sure! — but reasons which may help you to understand that our motivation is not always that of greed."

His head was slightly bent, and when he turned his face toward her, his dark eyes were shining with an odd moisture, and he was smiling. "Lydia, you are an impertinent miss to be sure, but you have changed my way of seeing things tonight. I have not contacted my sisters in some time, but I am thinking that a visit is long overdue."

"That is a capital idea," she approved.

"And now you must gratify my own curiosity. You stated when we first met that you had no high opinion of the state of matrimony, and you yourself are still unwed, despite the absence of any very severe flaws."

"You are too kind," she replied sardonically.

"True, you have a sharper tongue than most women, and you employ no arts to attract, but you are comely and well behaved, and your family, if not well-to-do, nevertheless moves in the first circles. Why is it that you are still on the shelf?"

Jack's blunt assessment, though not precisely flattering, was accurate enough, Lydia had to acknowledge. "The reason is that my opinion of your sex is every bit as low as yours has been of mine. I have no desire to shackle myself to a self-important tyrant who will expect to command my faithful obedience, while in all likelihood he will consider himself free to indulge in every sort of profligate behavior."

Jack gave a soft whistle. "My, my. There's no mincing words with you, is there? Might I ask what examples have led you to such a conclusion?"

"Is it not obvious that our own prince regent has conducted himself thus, and has set a standard of behavior that is followed by some of the most respectable members of the ton?"

He shook his head. "That's not good enough. Scandal has always attached to the lives of princes. I suspect there is another example, closer to home."

"You are right. My own father, a fine, upstanding citizen, nearly ruined our family because of his addiction to the gaming table. And despite having the love and loyalty of my mother, he had to have his ladybirds as well. My mother knew, of course, and because she tried so hard to keep it from us, I never told her that I had found out. But when I learned the truth of what he was, I could never look at men in the same way afterward."

"I am sorry, Lydia." Jack frowned. "That was no doubt a very painful experience for you, and for your mother. But despite what you may think, most men are capable of behaving honorably. Some are weak, as your father was, but that is a flaw of character that may be found in either sex."

"Perhaps you are right; but what I have always failed to understand is why my mother continued to hold him in affection. Or why so many of my female acquaintances describe themselves as being happy in the married state. I can see no reason for their possible enjoyment of a condition in which everything is taken away, and nothing is given in return."

A little smile began to form upon Jack's handsome mouth. Lydia was revealing more than she knew about her lack of experience! At that moment, their conversation was brought to an abrupt halt by the end of the music, and the approach of the gentleman to whom Lydia was promised in the next set. As she took her leave of him and was led away, however, Jack began to mull over the prospect of her seduction. Not a real seduction, of course, but a subtle assault that would serve to teach her that the male sex had something to offer, after all!

Miss Grayson, blissfully ignorant of Mr. Worthing's new plan of campaign, was feeling quite cheered. It appeared that her arguments in defense of women were working upon his cynicism, and she no longer feared that he would try to sabotage Sarah's wedding. For once a female had outwitted him!

Those pleasant thoughts were occupying her mind as the two young ladies sat in the morning parlor, sewing quietly. There were a thousand things to do as the date of the wedding approached, not the least of which was the preparation of the trousseau without which no bride could consider herself properly dowered. Lydia was putting tiny stitches into the hem of a handkerchief and Sarah was mending a reticule when a knock upon the door interrupted their peace. It opened to reveal their butler, Hawkins.

"I beg your pardon," he intoned, "but there is a morning visitor. Will you receive Sir Thomas Lawley?"

"Of course. Please send him in," replied Lydia. She had known Sir Thomas for years, and although he was a widower in his midforties, and thus in strict terms a potential suitor, he had always treated her with a reassuringly distant friendliness.

Sir Thomas was ushered into the parlor, and both ladies rose to greet him. He was attired in riding dress, which was expensively made but tailored modestly, with none of the extravagant large buttons or tasseled boots favored by the dandy set. Of average height, he wore his brown hair in a neat crop, and his hazel eyes sparkled in a friendly fashion.

"How do you do, Miss Grayson? Miss Grayson?" He shook their hands enthusiastically. "I hope I am not intruding upon you at this hour."

"Not at all, Sir Thomas," Lydia replied. "Pray be seated. You find us engaged in nothing more exciting than sewing,

285

and we are glad of the interruption; it seems that we have done little else since Sarah's engagement was announced."

"That was the very reason for my call. Miss Grayson, please allow me to offer you my sincerest congratulations, and state my belief that you and Mister Brooks will be very happy in your life together. Ned is a fine fellow, and I am delighted to see him choose such a charming bride."

Sarah smiled warmly at him. "Thank you, Sir Thomas, for your kind wishes. You must not attempt to flatter me, however."

"No flattery is needed, my dear. Both of the Misses Grayson are known to be among the prettiest ladies in London. And speaking of pretty ladies, is your mother at home?"

"No, she is not," Sarah replied. "She has gone to visit Lady Waring, and expected to be gone the better part of the day."

For a brief moment, Sir Thomas's expression was crestfallen, but then his excellent manners took over. "Well, I am certainly fortunate to have found you two ladies here, so that I may catch up on all your news."

At that moment, a blinding thought had occurred to Lydia. "Sir Thomas, pray do not think this impertinent of me, but had you intended to pay a call upon our *mother?*"

The guilty look upon his face was an immediate giveaway. "I had thought — That is, I — " His voice trailed off in shy confusion.

Meanwhile, the Misses Grayson were exchanging a speaking glance. It was obvious from the gentleman's manner that he had not come to pay a simple call, but rather to pay his addresses!

"Dear Sir Thomas," Lydia said soothingly. "Pray rest assured, we think it a capital idea! It is just that we are a bit surprised."

"I do apologize, Miss Grayson; I had not intended to make my feelings known in such a way, as though I were an awkward schoolboy! But your mother has been dear to me for many years, and I suppose the thought of speaking at last has rattled my nerve."

Sarah spoke up. "Why have you not come forward before now?"

"I did once, about a year after your father passed away. But she told me that she still cherished his memory, and that she would not think of remarriage until the two of you were safely established in your own households. I have kept my word not to speak of the matter until that time.

"And now, since you, Miss Grayson, have made it known that you do not wish to marry, and you, Miss Grayson, have become engaged, I have allowed myself to hope that your mother may be willing to accept my suit."

The two ladies beamed at him. It was not difficult to imagine their mother and Sir Thomas as a couple, now that the idea had been suggested; they shared modest tastes, were of a similar gentle humor, and would no doubt live in complete domestic harmony. It was also surprising to consider that both had shown a similar staunch loyalty, Mrs. Grayson to her daughters and Sir Thomas to his affection for Mrs. Grayson.

"We will do everything we can to help your suit prosper," Sarah assured him. "The two of you would suit famously. And besides, there is nothing I would like better than to have another wedding in the family! Who knows but what even Lydia might be next?"

Lydia laughed at the teasing remark, but as the conversation continued in a lighthearted vein, she found herself thinking that if her mother had indeed accepted Sir Thomas's hand in marriage years ago, Lydia's own views about men might have been very different. His depth of feeling was a complete contrast to her father's shallowness, and the firmness of his character would have brought a sense of reassurance to the family that had been sorely lacking.

Was it possible that she was mistaken, and that it was not in the general nature of men to be dishonest and selfish? First Ned, and now Sir Thomas had come into their lives, and her knowledge of them both suggested that perhaps what Jack Worthing had said was true: that weakness of character was not a trait specific to either sex.

Even Jack Worthing himself, albeit no saint, gave the impression of having a steadfast nature, placing value in moral principles and considering his word as his bond. Thinking about such qualities made it *almost* possible to overlook some of his faults!

It was thus in an unusually receptive frame of mind that Lydia met Jack Worthing that evening at Lord and Lady Pendleton's spring ball. It was definitely the event of the Season, as evidenced by the long row of carriages at the door, and by the sounds of gaiety that made it difficult to hear an ordinary conversation.

Jack was the first to solicit Lydia to dance upon her arrival, and he seemed to be holding her more closely than usual, although the crush of guests made this unremarkable. There was a certain look in his dark eyes, however, that made Lydia's heart start beating inexplicably faster.

"You are looking even more lovely than usual, Lydia," he told her when the musicians paused, and unlike the similar words he had spoken before, it did not sound like flattery.

"This gown is a new shade of blue," Lydia replied with unaccustomed shyness. "I thought it rather becoming."

"It is not the gown, although of course I find it charming. It is you yourself, Lydia. Your smile, your charm, your lively wits — just you." And he raised her gloved hand gently to his lips.

Another dance began, and as they moved together gracefully, Lydia was aware of nothing but the feel of Jack's strong hand holding hers, and the electricity she sensed from his tall, lean body. She felt suddenly lightheaded, and could scarcely breathe: was this what was meant by falling in love? This sensation of giddiness, this pull of the senses that had nothing to do with logic or reason, could they be signs of that emotion she had so long despised?

Jack himself was meanwhile experiencing a shock of his own. When he had decided earlier to pursue Lydia Grayson, he had thought it to be no more than a diversion, to give her back some of her own medicine about the "worthlessness" of the male sex. But when he had spoken the actual words to her, he had found himself thinking how lovely she really was. Unbeknownst to him, his words had come straight from the heart. And now, as he looked into her eyes, there was no calculation in his mind, only an awesome feeling of admiration and desire.

Without pausing to consider his actions, he tugged at her hand, leading her through the crowd and into a small side parlor that was for the moment vacant. Then he put his hands upon her shoulders, forcing her to face him.

"Lydia, I have never in my life wanted anything as much as I want to kiss you now," he said, and when she made no protest, he bent his face to hers. But it was no gentle, courteous kiss; it was rough and passionate, and his arms came around to hold her in a crushing embrace that somehow did not hurt at all.

When he finally raised his head, Lydia drew a deep breath. "Jack," she said wonderingly, "I think I love you."

Before he could reply, however, the echoing approach of footsteps forced them to step apart. No one came into the room, but Jack shook his head before Lydia could speak again. "We cannot talk here, my sweet. There is too much danger of our being overheard. But you will allow me to call upon you tomorrow morning, I hope?"

She indicated her agreement with a tremulous smile.

"Then let us part for now; it will not be for long. You must leave first, and then I will follow in a few minutes, so that no one perceives we have been together here. But first—" He gave her one more kiss, this time swift and gentle. "Now go, Lydia. Until tomorrow!"

She obeyed him in a happy daze. As she rejoined the party, it seemed as though the entire world had been transformed in the short space of a few minutes. This was love! Now she could understand what made that mysterious phenomenon so compelling, and how women could disregard reason and willingly succumb to masculine charms. Why,

289

even the very thought of Jack's kiss made her breathless once more.

And tomorrow he was coming to call! He had given her heartfelt words of praise, he had kissed her, and while he had not said he loved her in return, he no doubt would have done so had they not been in such a public place. The thought of Jack feeling shy made her smile. When he asked her to marry him, she knew without a second's hesitation that her answer would be yes.

Sir Thomas Lawley's voice broke into her reverie. "Miss Grayson! May I have a word with you, if you please?"

Lydia turned to greet him, and she was not so engrossed in her own happiness that she could not perceive a look of radiance upon his smiling face. "Certainly, Sir Thomas. You look to be in excellent spirits this evening."

"It is all because of you and your sister, Miss Grayson. After I saw you this morning, and you both gave me so much encouragement, I decided to waste no further time in telling your mother that my feelings for her have remained unchanged. I thought I may as well take the chance, and end the suspense of waiting! So, I sought her out this very evening, at the early supper, and she has agreed to accept my suit!"

"Oh, Sir Thomas! This is great news indeed! How can it be that she accepted so quickly?"

"I had scarcely uttered a dozen words when she gave me the most distressed look. It gave me a severe jolt, I assure you, and of course I immediately begged her not to heed me in the slightest, and to forgive me for causing her the slightest degree of offense. But then, she interrupted me to say that to the contrary, she had been in love with me for years! It was only her stubborn pride that prevented her from telling me long ago that she had changed her mind."

"What a wondrous night this has been!" Lydia exclaimed, thinking not only of Sir Thomas's happiness, but also of her own.

And they were not alone in such thoughts. As he waited in the parlor for a prudent interval to elapse before making his own reappearance, Jack Worthing reflected upon the irony of his situation. He, who had so often scorned the word love, had fallen its victim! Never before had he encountered any woman who could make him doubt his unshakable views, much less convince him that he could not possibly live without her. And that was exactly how he felt about Lydia. He wanted to do more than make love to her; he wanted to talk with her, to engage in spirited arguments, and to hear her novel opinions. He wanted simply to be with her, and for the first time in his life, he had no difficulty whatsoever imagining himself sitting quietly by a fire, watching a woman with loving eyes as she cradled his baby in her arms. The image was so marvelous that he could scarcely believe his good fortune.

Thus it was that the shock was all the greater when he walked out of the parlor and saw Lydia across the room, holding hands with a man obviously much older than she. He was nice in his appearance, wearing a discreetly tailored coat which belied considerable wealth.

"Lydia, I have so much to thank you for," Sir Thomas was saying, though his words were inaudible to Jack. "I will be proud to be able to call you my daughter."

As Jack watched transfixed, Sir Thomas kissed Lydia's hand, and then, in a rush of affectionate gratitude, bestowed a brief kiss upon her lips. Lydia's answering smile and wave struck Jack to the heart, just as the words "goodbye, Sir Thomas" reached his ears.

It was sunny upon the following morning, and Lydia's mood was equally bright. The night before had ended with tearful congratulations between mother and daughters, as Mrs. Grayson had shared her happy news and Lydia confided her own expectations. Now she waited in anticipation, having been discreetly left alone by her mother and Sarah.

When Hawkins ushered Jack into the salon shortly after ten, Lydia stood, and had taken a joyful step toward him when she saw the hard expression in his eyes. "Jack? Is something wrong?"

"Not at all, Miss Grayson," he replied coldly, and she felt as though she had been struck by him. "I have come merely to congratulate you upon your impending engagement."

Lydia was utterly confused, as well as frightened. Something was very wrong here; was he not supposed to propose to her first? And why was he so seemingly angry? As she attempted to put her fears into words, he spoke again.

"Who is he, Lydia?" Jack's voice was suddenly impassioned. "What is the name of your rich, titled lover, the man who kissed you only moments after I did?"

Things were suddenly becoming more clear. "Do you mean Sir Thomas Lawley? He is not my lover!"

He cut off her protest. "Do not attempt to hide behind more hypocrisy. Despite your fine words about female honor, no sooner have you left my arms than you are selling your favors in exchange for a title. I should have known better than to be taken in a second time, but it shall never happen again."

"You are so wrong, Jack! That is not at all what was going on—you must let me explain!"

"I do not need to listen to your lies. I am only grateful that I made no offer to you, so that I was spared being jilted once again. I thank you for the salutary lesson about the female sex, Miss Grayson, and now I shall take my leave of you, with good riddance."

"No! Stop!" Lydia panicked as he strode toward the door. "Jack, I beg you to listen: Sir Thomas is going to be my father!"

Jack paused in midstride, and with his back still toward her, his dark brows met in a frown of bewilderment. *"What* did you say?"

"He kissed me from gratitude, because I encouraged him to offer for my mother, and he did, and she accepted. He is going to marry my mother, not me!"

"Oh, my God." Jack turned around to face her, with a look of torture upon his handsome face. "Miss Grayson, I must beg for your forgiveness. I ought to have trusted you, but when I saw that man kissing you, all I could think was that the same nightmare was happening again, only this time it was worse, because I loved you. Is there any way I can possibly atone?"

Lydia rushed forward, meeting him in a desperate embrace. "Yes, there is," she said, breathing into the shoulder of his coat. "First, you must stop calling me 'Miss Grayson.'"

"Yes, Lydia." He smiled, rubbing his cheek against the smoothness of her ash brown hair. "Darling Lydia."

"And now you must tell me again that you love me."

"I love you, Lydia."

She sighed deeply. "And now you must kiss me again as you did last night."

The Grayson house was virtually overflowing with guests at the wedding reception, as not one of their many friends had wanted to miss the once-in-a-lifetime sensation. For the first time in anyone's memory, there had been a triple ceremony on that bright June day, as Sir Thomas Lawley, Mr. Edwin Brooks, and Mr. John Worthing were officially joined to their new wives. It had been agreed that all three men would be considered to have served each other as best man, as all three ladies would be honorary attendants upon each other.

The portly, conservatively attired gentleman who had given away all three brides was the first to offer his congratulations to Mr. Worthing. "I never thought I would see this day," Mr. Gerald Fortescue intoned as he pumped Mr. Worthing's hand. "But my niece Lydia has always been so headstrong that I fear you will have your hands full keeping her in check."

"Alas, my husband is right," Mrs. Augusta Fortescue agreed, pursing her thin lips and shaking her head. "Her lack of obedience has been most unbecoming. I can only hope that you will find a way to master her spirit."

"Do not worry, Aunt Augusta." The new Mrs. Worthing smiled tolerantly at her impossible relations. "I intend to be a very dutiful wife. I have been persuaded that matrimony is indeed a desirable state, and will do all in my power to make my husband happy." Her left hand, which her husband was holding, received an affectionate squeeze.

"Besides, I fear I do not agree with you, Mrs. Fortescue," Mr. Worthing said. "I wish neither to hold Lydia in check nor to master her spirit. It is not the proper role of the husband to demand obedience from his wife, but rather to form with her a partnership of mutual respect."

Both Mr. Fortescue and his wife were aghast at such outlandish talk. "But surely you cannot think that a female is capable of comprehending any matters of true substance!" Mr. Fortescue expostulated.

"Indeed I do," Mr. Worthing affirmed. "I have that information on the very best authority." And so saying, he further shocked his new relations by kissing his wife, quite shamelessly, as the Fortescues were later to say.

A Wager for a Bride

by

Dawn Aldridge Poore

Miss Lucinda Symonds looked out the window at the sights of London as the carriage bounced and bumped over the street. It was midday of a fine spring day in April, and, because of the weather, there was more traffic in the streets than usual. "I knew we should have left earlier," Drucilla said with a frown, glancing out through the curtains at the jostling wagons and horses.

"Don't frown so, Cilla," Lucie said to her sister. "It's great fun to watch everyone from here. Look, those people on the corner seem to be having quite an argument."

Drucilla sniffed audibly. "You really should close your curtains, Lucie. There's no need to be watching such common sights. I can't imagine what Edwin would think of it."

"Edwin's a stick-in-the-mud," Lucie answered, opening the curtain as wide as possible so she could see. "I think we're moving along now." She looked back and grinned at her sister. "Now, Cilla, don't get mad about my comments on your dear betrothed. Edwin knows how I feel about him." Lucie adjusted her spectacles on her nose and peered outside again.

"Yes, he knows," Cilla agreed, "and he's worried that you're going to turn into a perfect hoyden."

"I rather hope so," Lucie said with a giggle, "if for no other reason than to shock Edwin." Before Cilla could answer, Lucie grabbed her hand. "Look, Cilla, isn't that Annie Travers? I think it is." She pushed her spectacles up on her nose and leaned forward, peering through them. "It is! I haven't seen Annie in an age, not since way before I went to Edinburgh." She banged on the front of the carriage to signal the coachman to stop.

"You're not going to *speak* to her, are you?" Cilla gasped. "Surely not! Not right here in public! You know she ruined her reputation with William Lovatt. Ruined, completely ruined."

Lucie turned on her in surprise. "Whatever are you talking about, Cilla? I know Annie was always prideful and headstrong like all the Travers, but she'd never do anything wrong."

"She did." Cilla peered around Lucie's head. "It was while you were staying with Aunt Stewart in Edinburgh, I suppose. Last fall. You know how those Lovatts are — always pushing the limits of propriety." Cilla smiled slightly. She loved nothing better than a really good bit of gossip. "You know how the story goes on all the Lovatts, too — they always fall madly in love at first sight. It happens to all of them. Anyway, William Lovatt fell in love with Annie, or so he told her. He *compromised* her, and then he went off to the Continent and left her." Cilla moved to see better. "Yes, that's Annie," she whispered conspiratorially. "Can you imagine her having the nerve to appear on the street!"

"Where else would she appear?" Lucie asked, banging on the front again as the carriage began to pull over to the side of the street, "Annie and I have been friends for years and I intend to speak to her. The Symonds never abandon a friend, especially one in need."

"You can't go out on the street and talk to her, Lucie." Cilla was scandalized. "I heard she's gotten the cut direct from everyone, and the same will happen to you if it becomes known that you're talking to her." Cilla looked at her in horror as Lucie started to open the carriage door. "No, I forbid it, Lucie. If you won't consider your own reputation, think of mine. Think of Edwin!"

"Piffle on Edwin . . . and on his mama and papa," Lucie said as the carriage stopped and the driver jumped down. "Edwin certainly wouldn't stoop to kindness."

Cilla grabbed at her hand as the driver opened the door. "Don't do this, Lucie. Do you see who Annie's talking to — that's William Lovatt's cousin and he's worse than William ever dared to be. Mad Jack Lovatt they call him."

"*That's* Mad Jack Lovatt?" Lucie paused a second, then

tossed her head. "I'm going to speak to Annie, no matter what. What could happen on the street corner, and, besides, I've heard some of those tales about Jack Lovatt. They're simply too farfetched to be true,"

"They aren't — farfetched, I mean. Edwin swears they're true. He should know because Jack Lovatt fell madly in love with Edwin's sister, Diana. Just instantly, like all the Lovatts do."

It was Lucie's turn to stare. "Diana? Good heavens, I thought Lord and Lady Caswell kept her under lock and key."

Cilla nodded. "They do and thank goodness for that. Mad Jack Lovatt would have spirited her away if they hadn't been so vigilant." Cilla reached out an imploring hand. "Don't go, Lucie."

"If Annie's in trouble, then I must. Papa says we must always stand by our friends."

"Lucie," Cilla said hollowly, "you're going to ruin yourself and take me with you."

"Cilla, don't be silly," Lucie said, getting down from the carriage. "I won't be a moment — just long enough to say hello." She turned and smiled back at Cilla. "Don't you want to come with me?" She chuckled as Cilla jerked back out of sight and pulled the curtain so she wouldn't be seen.

"Annie," she called as she drew near. "How have you been?" Annie Travers was now standing with her back to Lucie and as she turned, Lucie was shocked. Annie's face was swollen and blotchy, her hair was unwashed and stringy, and she had obviously been crying. She forced herself to stand straight and tall, displaying what she had left of the famous Travers pride. She looked at Lucie, but didn't speak.

"Whatever is wrong, Annie?" Lucie said as she drew nearer. "Surely you haven't forgotten me?"

"Lucie," Annie said, trying to be brave as tears rolled down her cheeks. Lucie went to her and hugged her, drawing her close as Annie put her head on Lucie's shoulder. Lucie tried very hard to keep the amazement from her face, but wasn't successful. Annie Travers, under her cloak, was breeding — and far along.

Lucie glanced up in surprise only to discover the man everyone called Mad Jack looking intently at her. He was dark, almost bronzed, and had very dark hair that curled around his face in the latest fashionable cut. He had obviously been in a fight or duel at some time and had taken a slash across his left eyebrow and cheek as there was a thin white line that made his eyebrow lift in the middle. The scar ended toward his ear, and must have been quite a nasty gash when it was made. He was elegantly dressed as befitting a man who ran with the best of society, and his face had a slightly mocking expression. Lucie reached up and pushed her spectacles further up on her nose to get a better look at him.

"Miss Symonds, I believe," he said, his voice as mocking as his expression. "If you have quite embarrassed Miss Travers enough, I'll see her to her lodgings." He reached out and took Annie's arm.

"Embarrassed?" Lucie felt her face flame. "Miss Travers and I are old friends—we were in school together. I daresay I've known her longer than you have. Furthermore, I do not appreciate your lack of manners, sir." She looked back down at Annie. "Annie, tell me what I can do for you. I . . ." she paused awkwardly. "I didn't know."

"There's nothing to be done," Annie said, standing tall and trying to smile. "Jack's right—this is no place for us to talk. I'll come see you soon."

Lucie shook her head. "We're going to the country to stay for a few weeks. Drucilla, as you might have heard, is engaged, and her fiancé and future family are coming to Haddonfields to get acquainted with all of us. I won't be in London."

"Then I'll see you later." Annie glanced uneasily at Jack Lovatt. "Thank you for being so good to ask about me."

Lucie reached out and touched Annie's shoulder. "We're friends, aren't we? We've always been friends. You know if I can do anything for you, all you have to do is ask or send word."

Jack Lovatt pulled Annie toward him. "Very kind of you,

300

Miss Symonds, but you don't need to worry. I'll take care of Miss Travers, I promise." He smiled at Lucie, a surprisingly warm smile, and guided Annie down the street and around the corner. The last Lucie saw of them was Annie looking over her shoulder and saying the words "thank you."

Drucilla waited until the carriage had started again before she spoke. "Well, did you get your comeuppance from Mad Jack? I saw you looking at him with that glint in your eye."

"There was no glint, there was no comeuppance." Lucie was silent for a moment. "Did you know that Annie's breeding?"

Cilla's eyes widened. "And you spoke to her on the street? Lucie, everyone will know about it! Edwin will not take kindly to this, I just know it. And his mama . . . I dread to think on it."

"Edwin, Edwin. Cilla, I don't care a tuppence for what Edwin or his mama think. Poor Annie, what have you heard about her?"

"Only what I told you—she ruined herself with William Lovatt and her family disowned her. I haven't heard anything since. That must have been six or seven months ago when you were in Edinburgh."

"Poor Annie," Lucie said, taking her spectacles off to wipe her eyes. "She always was impulsive and headstrong."

"Poor Annie, balderdash," Cilla exclaimed. "What about poor me? Here I am, going to have to entertain Edwin and his family, and you don't have a concern for me. You know they're sticklers for propriety. Edwin warned me that the slightest breath of any scandal would overset them and send his mama into a tizzy. And here you begin our trip by embracing Annie Travers on a street corner while she's consorting with someone like Mad Jack Lovatt! I think I need my vinaigrette." She rummaged in her reticule. Lucie assisted by finding the vial and opening it for her.

"If you'd get spectacles so you could see, you'd be able to find your own things," Lucie said, waving the vinaigrette in Cilla's general direction.

Cilla took a deep breath. "I can see everything I need to. If

301

you cared two pins about your appearance, you'd throw those hideous things away."

"I can't see without them," Lucie said reasonably. "At least, I can't see far away. I can read or do needlework without them, but I like to know who's across the park or be able to see across the street, and for that, I need my spectacles."

"You look like a bluestocking." Cilla glared at her. "And just look at your hair — all frizzy and falling down. It's just a red mop. Lucie, you're going to have to do something with your hair before Edwin's family gets to Haddonfields." She paused. "Do it for me, please. You know how much this means to me."

"Cilla," Lucie spoke firmly, "I do not intend to cause you embarrassment when the Caswells are at Haddonfields, but neither do I intend to be anything but myself. Please spare me your pleading."

Drucilla started to speak, then thought the better of it. No one could do very much with Lucinda when her mind was made up. It was an unfortunate trait she had inherited from their father. Cilla did what she always did when she encountered Lucie's stubborn streak: she changed the subject. The rest of the trip to Haddonfields was taken up with talk of Cilla's trousseau and wedding dress. It was to be a September wedding, and Cilla wanted it to be perfect. She had been planning it for months.

They had almost a week at Haddonfields before the Caswells descended on them. It was all too short for Lucie. Cilla was on tenterhooks, wanting everything to be just right for the Caswells, There were to be four of them: Lady Caswell, Edwin, Diana, and their cousin, Walter. The house was polished, shined, then repolished ahd reshined. Papa and Lucie took to riding out together just to get away from Drucilla's constant chatter about the Caswells. "Damned rum bunch, it seems to me," Papa said as they stood on a hill overlooking Haddonfields. "They don't farm, don't ride, don't do a damned thing as I can hear about. Just the kind Drucilla would like — drones on society." Papa had been a younger son who had been quite successful as a farmer and hunter. He had no time for city folk and society—those whose only concern was gossip, idling away time, and spending money. For Papa, society was a congenial group who could ride to hounds together, or else a dinner with all of his friends around to discuss the latest in farming techniques. He hated to go to town and was dragged there only when forced. "Just look at that, Lucie," he said, pointing to the neighboring farm. "Worrying about my farm isn't just my problem. Marston's having the devil's own time training his son. Seems the boy's been in London when he should be here helping with the farm and learning how to run it. Marston's trying some of my ideas—they're ready to plow for the spring and look, he'll have perfect crop rotation." He glanced sharply at Lucie. "You wouldn't be interested in Marston's boy, would you? He may come to his senses yet and, after all, his land does march with ours."

Lucie tried to stifle a laugh but wasn't successful. "Quit trying to marry me off, Papa," she said, giving him a quick kiss on the cheek. "I intend to stay around here for a long time, and, no, I would not wish to marry Giles Marston, not for any reason."

"It was just a thought," Papa said, getting back on his horse. "I suppose you'll have to stay around and run the farm since there are no sons." Papa seldom mentioned this, and Lucie never knew what to say to him when he did. This time, she simply mounted her horse and rode in silence beside him all the way back to Haddonfields House. To their dismay, the Caswells were there, two days early.

After four long days, Lucie decided that something she had read by the American Benjamin Franklin was appropriate: Fish and visitors smell after three days. Sadly, the Caswells were going to stay for several weeks, helping, as Lady Caswell pointed out continuously, dear Drucilla have a perfect and proper wedding.

After having Lady Caswell criticize her uneven stitches for the hundredth time and listening to Diana extolled as the epitome of female perfection, Lucie couldn't stand any more. She slipped to the stables and looked for her father to go riding with her. He had, so the groom told her, managed to escape an hour ago and said he wasn't coming back until dinner time. Evidently, Lucie decided, Papa didn't like the Caswells any better than she did.

Finding someone congenial to ride with was out of the question, as was asking Cilla or Diana. The Caswells felt it was improper for females to ride horses — carriages were the only correct mode of transportation for the weaker sex. Edwin was very outspoken on this point. His wife would certainly never ride. Every time he said this, Papa turned red in the face, but so far, under Mama's warning glance, he had managed to keep from speaking his mind.

She simply had to get away, so Lucie had her horse saddled and rode out alone. It was a perfect spring day, the first of May. The ground had been plowed in accordance with Papa's crop rotation theories, and the smells were wonderful. The air was filled with the scents of flowers, new grass, plowed earth, and the freshness of spring. Lucie closed her eyes and breathed deeply.

She reined in her horse at the top of the hill overlooking both Haddonfields and the Marston farm, dismounted, and sat down to enjoy the day. From here, she could see the workers in the fields, enjoy the smell of the fresh earth, and hear the sounds of the spring planting. She leaned back against a large oak, took off her spectacles and put them in her pocket, and closed her eyes.

When she awoke, her first groggy thought was that someone was being murdered. The yells and squalls were terrible to hear. Her heart pounding, she looked around wildly, but saw nothing except the peaceful farmland and her horse grazing tranquilly nearby. She scrambled to her feet and ran down the hill toward the Marstons, following the sounds. The noise got louder and Lucie slowed down as she thought she recognized it. It had to be a cat or an animal of some kind, perhaps one caught in a trap. Whatever it was, it was the loudest yowling she had ever heard. The sounds were loudest under a very tall, very large oak tree. Lucie looked around and didn't see anything, then there was another yowl, long and drawn out, sounding for all the world like a banshee.

Lucie looked up into the tree but couldn't see that far. She was fumbling in the pocket of her habit for her spectacles when she heard a rider coming toward her. She looked toward that sound, but things were blurred. She could make out the shape of a horse and rider as she took her spectacles from her pocket.

"Miss Symonds, I believe. This is a pleasant surprise." The voice had a familiar sound, but Lucie was still too far away to make out the features of the face. She unfolded her spectacles, the gold wires of the rims glinting in the sun, and put them on, pushing them up on her nose so they would fit perfectly. The face came into focus, and, to her surprise, the person standing in front of her, a mocking grin on his handsome face, was Mad Jack Lovatt.

"Is that yours?" he asked conversationally, dropping the reins and coming to stand beside her under the tree. His glance took in one of the most disreputable-looking cats Lucie had ever seen. It was up high and was stuck. It also had the loudest howl Lucie had ever heard, and was in full voice. "I think it wants down," she said, looking at the lowest limb, several feet above her head.

"An understatement," Lovatt said. "I don't mind rescuing damsels in distress, but I really don't care for cats. Still," he turned and grinned at her, a most pleasant grin this time, "when duty calls, we Lovatts always answer."

He removed his coat of dark superfine and started to throw it down on the ground, but Lucie took it and held it. It was rather expensive to toss down, she thought to herself. She looked back and Lovatt had already begun climbing the tree. After the first limb, it was an easy ascent. He reached the cat and tried to put his hand out to it. "Damn," Lucie heard him mutter as the cat swiped hard at his outstretched hand. "Devil ingrate." There were several more imprecations as Lovatt tried again to hold the cat as it swiped and hissed at him. Lucie had heard her father say every one of those things at one time or another — and in a much louder voice, but for some reason, now she was mortified. She turned around and concentrated on looking at Lovatt's horse. At last, she heard Lovatt descending, grunting and muttering under his breath as he did. She risked a look upward and had to force herself not to laugh. Lovatt was clutching the cat to his chest with one bleeding hand, the other was hanging on to a limb, and his face showed the signs of battle. Lucie couldn't decide if all those marks had been made by stray branches or by the cat.

The cat was decidedly unhappy. It again set up a howl, and Lovatt tried to hush it. He stood on the lowest limb, right above Lucie's head. He was breathing hard.

"Miss Symonds, if you'll try to reach up and take this animal, I'll hand it down to you." He lay down on the limb and held the cat downward. Lucie reached up, but before she could grab the cat, it hissed, howled, turned and scratched Lovatt again, then jumped to the ground, its back arched as it spat at the horse. Lucie made a grab for, it, but it backed away, still hissing and spitting.

Behind her, she heard a noise and whirled just in time to see the limb give away and Lovatt fall to the ground with a thud. She ran over to him. "Are you all right?" she asked, bending over him and pushing her spectacles up to keep them from falling off.

"No," he moaned, his eyes closed. "Perhaps. Let me take stock. I think I may be dead."

"No, I assure you that you aren't dead," she said, sitting back straight on her knees and looking at him. "Nothing seems to be broken or twisted."

"So *you* say. From my vantage point, *everything* feels broken." He sat up and shook his head groggily. "I'll be lucky to survive."

"Don't be melodramatic," Lucie said. "It was just a fall." She looked at him. "Good heavens, there's blood all over your shirt!"

"Courtesy of your dratted cat. I knew there was another reason for me to hate cats."

"It isn't my cat. I don't even own a cat."

Lovatt stood up gingerly and dusted himself off. "My God,

306

do you mean I went through all of that and it wasn't even your cat? I've mutilated my entire body for a *stray?*"

"Well, it was the kind thing to do," Lucie said as she offered him his coat. He motioned for her to keep it for a moment as he wiped blood from his hands and neck with a handkerchief. Then he took the coat, but didn't put it on. "Let me rescue my horse from this crazed feline," he said, "then I want to talk to you." He walked over to the horse and picked up the reins. The cat looked at him with large eyes, walked warily in a large circle around him, then came up and rubbed against his boots. "Go away," he said, bending down and giving it a push. "I hate cats." He led his horse over to Lucie. "Now, Miss Symonds, were you out for a walk, or has this vicious animal scared your horse away?"

"My horse is up on the hill."

Before Lucie knew what was happening, Lovatt had thrown his coat across the saddle, and was walking up the hill beside her. He talked of inconsequentials — the weather, the crops — until they reached the top of the hill and found her horse still there. Lovatt looked around. "A very nice place. Do you come here often?"

Lucie nodded. "Haddonfields is where I live, so I've always ridden up here." She started to mount her horse, but Lovatt stopped her. "Could we talk a few minutes?"

Lucie hesitated a moment, then nodded. They went to sit under the tree while their horses grazed. "I'm surprised to see you in the country," Lucie said, trying not to appear too curious.

"I'm staying with a good friend of mine, Giles Marston." He looked at her. "I wanted to talk to you about Miss Travers. First, I want to apologize for being rude to you when we met in London, but I was . . . I wasn't myself. I had just discovered Miss Travers and that . . ." He paused while he groped for words.

"That she was disowned by her family and was *enceinte?*"

He nodded. "As you know, my cousin William was madly in love with her, and I'm sure he didn't know of her condition when he left. He would never do that."

"He did." Lucie could have bitten her tongue for being so blunt.

"There are always two sides to everything, Miss Symonds." He pulled a blade of spring grass and chewed on it as he thought. "I don't know what you've heard about the Lovatts, but they're known for two traits: one, none of us can ever refuse a dare or wager, no matter how stupid or risky; and, two, we always fall madly in love at first sight with someone. It happens to all of us." He looked at her and smiled, his dark eyes lighting up. "My father, for instance, is a pattern card for the Lovatts. In his younger days, he took every dare made to him, gained a reputation as 'Devil Lovatt' and was considered to be a rakehell of the first water. Then one day he was passing by a bookstore, of all things, and saw a lovely woman. He fell instantly in love, married her, and became a model husband and father. Mother tells the story often." He paused and looked at her. "As I said, it happens to all the Lovatts."

"And what of William? I don't see that he's in the way of becoming a model husband and father."

He leaned back against the tree and stretched his legs out in front of him. Very nice legs, they were, Lucie thought to herself, then blushed. Lovatt didn't notice. "I think William would be, if he knew he was a father. Do you know the story?" Lucie shook her head and Lovatt went on. "William fell in love with Annie Travers and she with him. They were planning to marry, but there was a terrible quarrel several months ago, and she told him to get out of her sight and never come back." He glanced at Lucie. "The Travers are a prideful lot, you know." Lucie nodded and he continued. "William was devastated. She wouldn't see him, she wouldn't speak to him. He tried to write, but she returned his letters. He finally decided to go to the Continent to get over her. The last I heard from him, he was in Spain."

"Are you saying that he's innocent in all of Annie's problems?" Lucie asked. "It would seem to me . . ."

"No, no, not that at all," he said hastily, interrupting her. "None of us knew about Miss Travers's, um, problem. I had heard she had been disowned by her family and had written to her telling her I would take care of her, but she returned my letter with a note telling me that she could take perfectly good care of herself. I hadn't seen or heard of her until I saw her on the street corner when you stopped by. I was, to put it mildly, quite overset."

"And what did you do?"

Lovatt looked at her wearily. "All I could. I offered money, which she refused; I offered her a place to stay, which she refused; I begged her to let me send her to William, and she refused. Frankly, Miss Symonds, that's one of the reasons I wanted to see you. Do you have any influence on her at all?"

Lucie shook her head. "It's the Travers pride. There are times when no one can reason with it."

"I know." Lovatt paused. "I've had someone watching and trying to make things easier for her. I've been paying part of her rent and the doctor's fee, and trying to provide food without her knowing that I'm doing it. The baby was born two weeks ago — a girl."

Lucie looked at him in surprise. "What is it, Miss Symonds?" he asked, a touch of mockery in his voice again. "You seem surprised that I should look after my own. Don't tell me you believe all the stories about me?" He laughed. "No matter," he added bitterly, "everyone believes them." He paused a second, then continued. "Back to Miss Travers, I've sent my man to Spain to get William and bring him back. I'm sure once William knows what's happened, he'll be able to reason with her, but it may be a while before he's found and returns."

"What do you want me to do? I seldom see Annie, even though we are friends. There's no possibility of my getting away from Haddonfields for several weeks since my sister's fiancé and future family are visiting us."

"Oh, yes, the Caswells. Giles told me." He stood and extended a hand to help her. "I don't know what you can do right now, Miss Symonds, but I do wish you'd think about it, and perhaps the next time we meet, you might have a suggestion for me." He looked around casually. "Do you ride every day?"

"Almost." Lucie looked uneasy. "It really wouldn't be

proper for us to meet here, though." She started to invite him to Haddonfields, but realized that Lady Caswell and Edwin, those sticklers for propriety, would hardly welcome the sight of Mad Jack Lovatt strolling into the house on a social visit.

He smiled at her and helped her onto her horse. "I ride every day. If I see you, perhaps you'll have time to talk." He tossed his coat over the pommel and mounted easily. "Thank you for listening to me, Miss Symonds. Even that has been a help."

"You're welcome . . ." She stopped abruptly, realizing that she didn't know his address. All she had ever heard him called was Mad Jack Lovatt. She certainly couldn't say *that*.

Lovatt threw back his head and laughed, realizing why she had stopped. "Technically, I'm Lord Lovatt, but I think I would prefer it if you could call me John or Jack. I really don't relish being styled Mad Jack."

She blushed furiously. "Good day, Lord Lovatt," she said stiffly as she kicked her horse. The horse, enjoying the fresh spring grass, chose to ignore her and started back toward Haddonfields at a leisurely walk.

"Good day to you, Miss Symonds," she heard him say cheerfully.

In a moment, she risked a look backward to see if he was still there. He was headed for the Marston house, oblivious to the fact that the cat was following along behind him, its tail straight up in the air, twitching at the end. Lucie laughed all the way to Haddonfields as she thought what his reaction would be when he realized he had acquired a cat — and a thoroughly disreputable one at that.

Back at Haddonfields, Lucie got involved in dressing for dinner and then playing cards with Walter, so she didn't think of telling Cilla about her meeting with Lovatt. Lucie suspected that the main reason Walter was with the Caswells was to be thrown directly at her head, and to that end, Lady Caswell was always planning things for Walter, Lucie, Cilla, and Edwin to do. Walter was much like Edwin, although where Edwin was blond, Walter had dark brown hair. He had

the pale Caswell complexion, and the same rather protuber-
ant, pale blue eyes. Lucie found him congenial, but dull and
unexceptional. Unfortunately, he was every bit as straitlaced
as Edwin, and Lucie constantly had to watch her tongue to
keep from shocking him. Walter, like all the Caswells,
shocked easily.

The next day, Lucie was thinking of riding again to the big
oak tree in hopes of seeing Lovatt. She had thought much
about Annie Travers and remembered that Lovatt knew
where Annie was, even though Annie had refused his help.
Even if it was impossible for Lucie to visit her right now, at
least she could send Annie a letter of friendship and support.
Lovatt would have her direction.

She was just getting her habit out of the clothespress when
Cilla burst into her room. *"He's here!* I couldn't let Lady
Caswell or Edwin see him, so I hid him in the front room. *Do
something!"*

"Whatever are you talking about, Cilla? You look as if
you've seen a ghost."

Cilla collapsed into a chair. "I wish I had. A ghost would be
preferable to Mad Jack Lovatt. He's actually here, Lucie, in
this house! The nerve of the man. You know why he's come
here, of course." Cilla pushed her hair out of her eyes. In her
agitation and mad scramble up the stairs, it had come unpinned. "And do you know what else, Lucie? The strangest
thing – he's carrying the most horrible, most wretched-look-
ing cat I've ever seen. Why on earth would he bring something
like that to Diana?"

Lucie stared at her, trying to sort out what she was saying.
"Cilla, calm yourself. First, Lord Lovatt is here . . ."

"Mad Jack." Cilla nodded. "And you know why."

"To bring a cat?"

Cilla glared at her. "Don't be silly, Lucie. I told you about
the quirk all the Lovatts have – they fall in love at first sight
and don't give up until they've captured their quarry."

Lucie felt her heart lurch. "And he's here. With a cat?" In
spite of herself, she smiled.

"Yes, he's here, and I know he's after Diana. I told you how he chased her all over London and made her life a misery. She couldn't go anywhere. Lord and Lady Caswell were frantic that he would ruin her reputation." Cilla stood and wrung her hands. "He's discovered she's here and has come to carry her away. He thinks we won't be so vigilant here in the country." She turned, her eyes wide. "If he insults Diana, Edwin will be forced to call him out. Edwin detests the man anyway. Lucie, *do something!*"

Lucie tossed her habit across the bed. "All right, I'll see if I can talk to him. Do Mama and Papa know he's here?"

Cilla shook her head. "No, you know how they are. Any company must be greeted, wined, and dined as if they were all old friends. I didn't dare tell them, especially Papa. He'd have Mad Jack sitting down at cards with Edwin and Diana. Papa's just isn't socially perceptive."

"An understatement." She sighed and frowned at Cilla. "I'll go down and talk to him, but I'm of the same mind as Papa. Frankly, I'd rather have Lord Lovatt in the house than that giggling, insipid, silly Diana Caswell. She's the only person I know who's more of a fribble than Edwin."

"Lucie! They're our guests, and Edwin is . . ."

"Right now, Lovatt's a guest, too." Lucie pointed out, going out and slamming the door behind her.

The small front drawing-room door was closed and Lucie paused a moment, her hand on the lever. She could hear noises inside and put her ear to the panel. It seemed Lord Lovatt was having an altercation with the cat. From where Lucie was listening, the cat seemed to have the upper hand. She opened the door and went inside, pulling the door shut behind her.

Lord Lovatt was on the sofa, his handkerchief wrapped around the cat's head, rather like a falcon's mask. He had a long scratch on his cheek, right under his scar. Together, scratch and scar made a line all the way from forehead to neck.

"I've brought this damned cat back to you," he said without preamble. The cat was struggling to get away and he was holding it with both hands and arms. "The thing sat outside my window and howled all night." He let the cat go and tried to get the handkerchief from its face, but it leaped out of his grasp. It ran into the wall with a thump as both Lucie and Lovatt chased it around the room. Lovatt finally grabbed it by its tail. The cat screeched, splayed its legs, and jumped backward onto Lovatt. He held it fast and removed the handkerchief from its face. The cat glared at Lucie as though she were responsible, jumped from Lovatt's grasp to the floor, and proceeded to sit and groom its paws.

Lovatt sat back down on the sofa, brushing cat hairs from his coat. "That creature knows I detest cats," he said with distaste. "I certainly hope you can succeed in at least giving it a bath. I don't think you'll be able to teach it any manners."

"Probably not," Lucie said, sitting down across from him and trying not to smile, "especially since it isn't my cat. I told you yesterday that it didn't belong to me, so I'm afraid you'll have to take it back."

Lovatt shook his head. "Absolutely not. I'm finished with the thing." He leaned back and glanced around. "Was that your sister I met as I came in? Giles mentioned that there were two of you. He also suggested I become acquainted with your father since I'm trying to learn something about farming methods."

"You? *Farming methods?*" Lucie could have bitten her tongue. "Surely not! That is . . . I didn't . . ."

"You didn't think I would care about farming methods," he supplied helpfully. "Actually, it's something of a new interest." He grinned at her. "My father dared me to become the best estate owner in the country. I intend to show him I can do it."

"Oh, so you have, as you said the Lovatts do, settled down and become exemplary."

He nodded and smiled at her, not the rather mocking grin she had seen before, but still a smile full of mischief. "Not settled yet, but, yes, I'm afraid the Lovatt curse has struck. I suppose it was time. In truth, I was getting more than tired of life in London."

Lucie closed her eyes and tried to formulate what she

should say. "Lord Lovatt, I really do not believe your, um, pursuit will be at all successful. Perhaps you should look elsewhere for another object of your affections."

He leaned forward. "Is that the final word, Miss Symonds?"

"Yes." She looked at him levelly, noting what very fine eyes he had. Other than his rakehell reputation, the rather insipid Diana would do well to catch Mad Jack Lovatt. Lucie couldn't imagine what he saw in Diana, a rather mousy blonde who was as prim and priggish as her brother.

Lovatt looked slightly over Lucie's head, as though thinking of something. "Thank you for your candor, Miss Symonds, but I refuse to give up all hope." He smiled at her. "We Lovatts are known for perseverance as well. Perhaps my luck will change."

"Perhaps," Lucie said, standing to show him to the door. The sooner he left, the better. As she moved between the chair and sofa, she tromped on the cat's tail, and the cat screamed and spat at her, raking the hem of her gown with its claws.

"Your cat seems displeased with you, Miss Symonds," Lovatt said with a chuckle. "Perhaps it needs attention." He paused, looking down at the scruffy cat. "And, as I mentioned, a bath as well." He turned and looked right into Lucie's eyes. "You have very fine eyes, Miss Symonds. But then, I noticed that even when you were wearing your spectacles."

"Thank you, Lord Lovatt," Lucie said, moving again toward the door. His compliment disconcerted her, and she felt the beginnings of a blush. She reminded herself he was here because of Diana.

"Why do you wear them?" he asked, pausing by the door.

"What? My spectacles? I wear them, Lord Lovatt, so I can see. Isn't that the usual reason?"

"Oh," he said in obvious relief, "I thought you might not need them. Some females wear the things so they can appear intelligent."

"And some of us don't appear that way?" Lucie couldn't keep the sarcasm from her voice.

"My town bronze seems to have fled here in the country,"

314

he said with a grin. "May I come back to visit again and try to impress you? Perhaps I could show off my manners, my literary bent, my expertise of farming."

Hearing voices at the back of the house, Lucie glanced over her shoulder. If Diana and Lady Caswell should come now . . . "I'm sorry, Lord Lovatt," she said hastily, "I'm not really sure of our social arrangements. Perhaps later." She almost shoved him out the door.

He looked curiously toward the back of the house. "In that case, I shall look forward to later, Miss Symonds." With that, he was down the steps and Lucie sagged back against the door just as Lady Caswell came into view, Walter and Diana in tow.

"Good heavens!" Lady Caswell said, recoiling in horror, "whatever is that thing?" She pointed to the corner.

Lucie followed her gaze and discovered the cat there, standing in the corner, its back arched, ready to pounce right onto Lady Caswell. Dashing across the hall, she snatched up the cat which did not appreciate her efforts at all, and quickly tossed it onto the porch. "I'm so glad you saw that creature, Lady Caswell," Lucie said quickly. "It came in when the door was opened, and we hadn't been able to find it to get it back out." She glanced out the front window and couldn't stifle a smile: Lovatt was riding down the drive, not looking back, and the cat was following at a discreet distance behind him, its tail straight up.

"Good," Lady Caswell said. "My dear, I've planned an outing for all of you children, and we'll leave within the hour. I had hoped we could visit an old acquaintance, but I find she's not at home, so I thought perhaps just a carriage ride would familiarize me with the country. You and Drucilla will act as guides, of course." As she usually did, Lady Caswell sailed off, neither knowing nor caring if anyone opposed her plans. Walter and Diana followed her, but not before Walter gave Lucie a particularly beaming smile.

Drucilla came up and put her hand on Lucie's arm. "I know you and what you're thinking, Lucie, and don't say anything. Just go with us. You'll have a good time, I promise." She peered around the hall and glanced at the closed drawing-room door. "Is *he* gone?" she asked in a whisper. Lucie nodded and Drucilla took a deep breath. "I'm glad. That man is dangerous."

"Don't be silly. Lovatt's not dangerous to anyone. He seems quite exemplary, in fact. I don't know how all these stories about him came about. He's very well mannered."

Cilla looked at her in surprise. "Lucie, how can you say that! Everyone in London knows what he's like. Edwin says the man is so bad that he's socially beyond the pale. Many more escapades and he'll be cut just as Byron was."

"Oh, Edwin says! Cilla, how you can bear that . . . that *person* is beyond me. Both he and Diana — and, yes, Walter and Lady Caswell too — are insipid prigs. I just hope you don't expect me to stay with you once you're married. I'd be insane after a day!" Lucie stalked across the floor and started up the steps, then turned and glared at Cilla. "Dangerous, indeed! That milk-and-water Diana should fall to her knees in thanks that Lovatt cares for her. Heaven only knows why he would." She turned and stomped up the stairs as Cilla stared after her in amazement.

No matter what Cilla had promised — Lucie did not have a good time. In fact, the afternoon was interminable. Lady Caswell insisted on driving all about and seeing every house in the neighborhood. Lucie was forced to prevaricate and tell her there was illness at Marston House to keep her from stopping by there. The story wasn't too far from the truth: at that point, Drucilla looked as if she were really going to be ill.

In the meantime, Walter, with Lady Caswell's obvious encouragement, was being more than attentive to Lucie. By the time they returned to Haddonfields, Lucie felt her smile was frozen onto her face for eternity. She simply couldn't face the Caswells anymore until she had to at supper, so she slipped outside and went down to the stables. Lady Caswell sent Walter to fetch her.

The next few days were uneventful, although miserable for Lucie. Lady Caswell kept throwing Walter at her head, arranging trips and card games and other events. For her part, Lucie kept trying to think up ways to dodge being with him.

Unfortunately, Lady Caswell was better at throwing than Lucie was at dodging. By the end of the week, Lucie was more than overset. "If I have to spend another hour with Walter or Edwin," she protested to her mother, "I think I shall scream."

"One must be hospitable," Mama said. "Do you think Drucilla is as tired of Edwin as the rest of us are?"

Lucie grinned at her mother. "I think his attractions are beginning to pale. I never knew what she saw in him."

Mama nodded. "I think Drucilla's in love with the idea of being married, and Edwin happened to offer for her. That's why I wanted to have the Caswells here for a while — I thought Drucilla might become — how shall I say it? — disenchanted."

"Mama," Lucie said with a laugh, "you're a schemer. I wondered why you invited those people here for such a stay. One thing — how did you arrange for Papa to be so tolerant?"

"I threatened him if he wasn't," Mama said. "By the by, have you seen him this afternoon? He was going over to Marstons to talk to Giles about something — a grain drill, I believe he said. I had hoped he'd return in time to accompany all of us to the village."

"If I know Papa, he'll make it a point to stay at the Marstons until after we've gone. I know I would."

Mama nodded. "I'm sure you would. But then, Lucie, you're exactly like your father. That's why I always ask you what he would do, because you think the way he does."

"I could do worse, Mama. I could think as Drucilla does."

Mama laughed and reached for her mending. "Drucilla seldom thinks, dear."

The trip to the village was accomplished without Papa. It was almost suppertime before the family and guests all gathered together. "We'll need to wait a few minutes. I've invited guests, and they might be late," Papa said, relaxing in his favorite chair. "Do you know Marston's boy, Giles? I'd thought he was going to London and turn into nothing more than a social fribble, but he's come back to the country and has the promise to become a real farmer. I do believe he has a good feel for the land."

"I certainly don't know why anyone would want to become

a farmer," Edwin said, sitting down next to Lucie. He crossed his arms and his fingers slid surreptitiously across her bare arm. Lucie stared at him in horror, but he was smiling pleasantly at Papa. Lucie thought perhaps she had imagined Edwin's intentions, but in just a moment, he slid his hand down between them, the back of his hand resting against her thigh. "Farming," he said to Papa in a normal tone of voice, "is not exactly a desired calling."

"What?" Papa was turning red in the face, and Lucie was trying desperately to move farther away. Papa was ready to give full voice to his sentiments, when Lucie felt Edwin stiffen beside her. She followed his gaze, and there was Giles Marston and Mad Jack Lovatt standing in the doorway. "Sorry we're late," Giles said, nodding first at Papa, then Mama. There were audible gasps from all the Caswells, as well as a squeak from Diana.

"Think nothing of it," Papa said, standing and glaring down at Edwin. "I was just talking to Caswell here about farming."

"Splendid," Lovatt said, walking into the room. "One can't ask for a better life than tilling the soil. Getting into nature, as it were." He smiled down at Edwin. "A pleasure to see you again, Caswell, as well as your charming family." He smiled and nodded all around. "Lady Caswell, Diana." Lady Caswell made a strangled noise as Lovatt smiled familiarly, then said hello to Walter.

Edwin stood. "Mr. Symonds, may I speak to you privately?"

"Why not later, after supper?" Papa said, completely oblivious to the undercurrents in the room. "Everyone knows Giles Marston, and Lovatt here tells me that you've all met in London. He's here to learn about farming."

"A likely story," Lady Caswell said, rushing to Diana's side. Lucie looked at Diana, expecting to see her fainting, but instead, she was smiling archly at Lovatt and batting her eyes. To his credit, Lovatt was not looking at her. At least, Lucie thought, he has better sense than to be obvious about his attachment to her.

"And what better place to learn," Lovatt said. "Giles and I have decided to implement some of Mr. Symonds's new techniques. He tells me that crop rotation is the key."

"It is that," Papa said with certainty. "That, and careful manuring." He glanced around. "Since everyone knows everyone, shall we go in? I'm damnably hungry."

Dinner was more than a disaster. Lovatt managed to insinuate himself between Lucie and Diana, while poor Drucilla was forced to sit between Edwin and Giles. To her credit, she conversed a great deal of the time with Giles, denying Edwin the opportunity to say much of anything. Lovatt, for his part, talked across Lucie to Papa, conversing mostly about grains, cows, fields, and grain drills. Actually, Papa did most of the talking. The Caswells all sat rather silently in their seats, glowering at Lovatt.

The conversation after dinner was just as bad. Giles and Lovatt finally took their leave, saying they had to be up early to see about the farm. No sooner than they had gone, Edwin stood and glared around the room. "Sir," he said to Papa, who was sitting comfortably in his favorite chair, "I simply cannot countenance you inviting such people to a family gathering. Perhaps you don't know very much about Lord Lovatt's character."

"Nonsense," Papa said, stretching. "I've always been an excellent judge of character and Lovatt seems a right sort to me. He's planning quite a renovation of his farm. It's been double-cropped, you know. Actually, he's invited me down to see it and give him some advice about what to do to build up some of the soil." Papa stood up as the clock chimed. "I don't want to spoil the fun for you children, but I need to get up early tomorrow. I promised I'd go to John Marston's and demonstrate a new idea I had — thought I'd make a slurry of manure and water and spread it. Ought to be easier that way." He smiled at everyone. "You children stay up as long as you wish and have a good time." He glanced at Mama. "Good night, my dear." With that, Papa was out the door, leaving Edwin standing there, fuming.

"Anyone for cards?" Mama asked brightly.

* * *

The next morning Lucie was downstairs eating breakfast when Walter came in. "Wonderful morning," he said, sitting down beside her. "Last night was something of a social disaster, but I'm sure our family is generous enough to let bygones be bygones." He paused. "I'm sure your father will see reason after he realizes what a complete rogue Lovatt is."

Lucie wasn't at all sure that Papa would be dictated to in his choice of guests, but let that pass. "Breakfast?" she asked.

Walter sat rather close to her, and spent his time on small talk about his tailor, his clothing, and his social life. Lucie made all the polite noises, and was looking for an avenue of escape when Mama came in.

"I want to commend you on your daughters, Mrs. Symonds," Walter said, smiling broadly. "You have two lovely, well-mannered daughters who are certainly a credit to you." Mama nodded as Lucie started to get up. "Of course," Walter continued, "it's a pleasure to see such biddable girls in this day and age." He smiled at Lucie. She glared at him and sat back down.

"What do you mean — biddable?" Lucie shoved her spectacles up on her nose and frowned as she peered at him.

Walter kept smiling. "A most formidable compliment, I realize, but altogether true in this case. I mean, Miss Symonds, that you and your sister are every man's feminine ideal: meek, malleable, yielding. I, for one, am delighted to see it. These are very rare qualities in these modern times."

"I want you to know . . ." Lucie began, but Mama interrupted her. "Lucie, my dear, what a wonderful compliment for you and Drucilla. However, my dear Walter, I'm afraid I really can't agree." She smiled at Walter. "They both seem headstrong to me, but perhaps I know my daughters all too well."

"I'm certainly not meek and malleable, and Drucilla isn't either," Lucie said with heat. She stood up. "I'm going down to the stables, Mama. I thought I saw Papa ride in a few minutes ago and I wanted to talk to him." With that, she flounced out, fuming.

320

She was still muttering when she reached the stables. Papa was there, currying his horse. "Went to John Marston's and got almost everyone working on the slurry. Put Giles and Lovatt to overseeing the grain drill, then I came back for a while." He smiled at her. "I thought I'd leave those two alone for a while to see what they could do. Didn't want to get too technical with them. They're just learning about farming."

"Papa, am I meek and malleable?"

He took one look at her, threw back his head, and laughed. "Damme, but no. Who told you that?" He paused. "Don't bother to tell me—it had to be one of those damned priggish Caswells."

"Walter." Lucie sat down where she could watch him work.

Papa gave a snort of disgust as he ran his hand down his horse's side. "Look at those flanks, will you? Now that's a handsome, healthy animal. Lovatt said he envied me this horse." He applied the currycomb again. "Walter thinks you malleable, my . . . my eye! I wish Drucilla would come to her senses and see what those people are really like."

Lucie stood and walked around the horse, admiring it. "Mama says Cilla's not in love with Edwin." Lucie paused and sat down on the mounting block, thinking. "Do you believe in love, Papa?" she asked, surprising even herself. She blushed. "I know you must, because you and Mama . . . That is, I suppose what I'm asking is how does one know if one is in love? Drucilla thinks she is, but Mama says she isn't. Lovatt's madly in love with Diana, but that's probably because of how all the Lovatts are."

Papa laughed. "One at a time, my pet." He moved his horse around so he could look at Lucie as they talked. "First, do I believe in love? Yes, I'd have to say I do. I know that in these modern days love isn't considered a fashionable emotion, and I do know of many marriages that are successful when the people involved don't love each other. Those couples, however, are agreeable and extremely fond of one another. I've even known of couples who didn't marry for love, but later fell in love."

Lucie pondered this. "So you would say that it's better to be in love than out of it."

He laughed and nodded. "I think, my pet, that love is very nice to have." Papa grinned at her and began combing the horse's mane. "I must admit I've always been in love with your mother."

"I know that," Lucie said, "but how did you know? How can Mama be sure that Drucilla isn't in love when Cilla thinks she is?"

"That I wouldn't know, pet. Your mother always knows these things. As for how I knew I was in love with your mama, I knew it immediately. I took one look at her — I was standing at the doorway with John Marston — and I told him, 'There's the girl I'm going to marry.' John laughed at me, but, Lucie, I don't know how or why, but I *knew.*"

Lucie smiled fondly at him. "You sound as if you had Lovatt's experience. Everyone says the Lovatts fall madly in love at first glance. I didn't really believe such a thing was possible."

Papa came and sat down near her, perching on a hitching post. "I'd heard that about the Lovatts, as well. It happened that way to Lovatt's father, as I recall. Yes, I know it's possible — it's something that's happened not only to me, but to others in this family as well."

"Well," Lucie said firmly, "it certainly isn't going to happen to me." She pushed her spectacles up on her nose and looked out toward the fields. "Do you ever wish either Cilla or I had been a boy, Papa? It would give you someone to help you with the farm."

He laughed and grabbed her in a huge hug. "Don't ever think that, poppet. I like you just the way you are." He sat her on her feet. "I think I'm going to have to see that you get proper instruction in crop rotation and double cropping, however. I don't believe Edwin will ever try his hand at farming."

Lucie laughed along with him at the thought and the two of them walked back toward the house together.

Later in the morning, Lucie was in her room, writing a letter to Annie Travers that she hoped Lovatt would deliver for her, when Drucilla came in, shutting the door behind her. Lucie glanced up. "I thought Lady Caswell was planning to help you with your embroidery this morning," Lucie said, surprised. "She doesn't think any more highly of your stitches than she does of mine."

"I told her I had a headache," Cilla said. "It wasn't the truth, but I simply couldn't bear another minute of sitting there listening to her tell me how I should behave." She pulled a small chair up next to Lucie's desk. "Lady Caswell keeps ranting and raving about Lord Lovatt. One would think he plans to abduct Diana as soon as he can get his hands on her." Cilla leaned back and rubbed her temples. "I knew if I didn't get away, I really would have a headache." She opened her eyes and glanced at the desk. "What are you doing?"

Lucie sanded her letter and put it down to dry. "Writing to Annie Travers. I thought I'd go over to the Marstons to ask Lovatt to deliver it. He knows where she is."

"You're not! Lucie, I beg you to reconsider. Annie is completely beyond the pale." There was a short pause. "Do you mind if I go with you?"

Lucie looked at her in surprise. "Make up your mind, Cilla. One minute you're saying that Lovatt is the devil the Caswells think him to be, and the next minute you're ready to risk Edwin's wrath to go with me. Are you sure you want to go?"

"Piffle on Edwin," Cilla said petulantly, not meeting Lucie's eyes. "Yes, I want to go."

"Mama's going as well. She wanted to call on Mrs. Marston."

Drucilla got a dogged expression on her face. "All the better. Lady Caswell can't very well complain if I accompany you and Mama." She paused. "Do you think we could manage to get away without any of the Caswells knowing where we're going?"

That was impossible. Lady Caswell was duly scandalized, and pointed out to Mama that no self-respecting mother would take her unsullied daughters into a den that harbored Mad Jack Lovatt. Mama smiled and went right on, inviting

Lady Caswell and Diana to accompany her unsullied daughters. The offer was refused.

"I fear you may have shown your future in-laws your independent streak," Mama said to Cilla as they drove off in the carriage. "I rather fancy Edwin will want to take you to task when we return."

"Piffle," Cilla said with a toss of her head. Mama was then obliged to take her to task about using such slang.

The Marston farm wasn't quite as well kept as the Symonds's farm, but there seemed to be quite a bit of activity in the fields. As they drove along the edge of a big field near Marston House, they saw the disreputable cat sitting on a rock beneath a tree, washing its paws very carefully while it kept a watchful eye on its adopted master. Lord Lovatt and Giles Marston were out in the field, along with Papa, following along beside a piece of machinery. "Papa's new grain drill," Lucie explained to Cilla. "He's showing them how to use it. They both," she paused for emphasis, "want to learn about farming."

"A very noble calling," Cilla said, turning her head almost backward to see what was going on. "Papa has often said so himself."

The call on Mrs. Marston was uneventful. They were treated to tea and some of Mrs. Marston's famous biscuits, covered in blackberry jam. The usual pleasantries were exchanged, Lucie left her letter for Annie Travers with a request for Lord Lovatt to see that it reached its destination, and Mama invited everyone over to supper on Friday night. Mrs. Marston accepted, saying that she hoped Lord Lovatt wasn't bored out here in the country, and that she also hoped that Giles became better acquainted with his neighbors. On that note, the Symonds left.

They went around by the village and then started across the bridge toward Haddonfields. In the sharp curve just beyond the bridge, they met a driver in a curricle who was going so fast around the curve that he took up almost the whole road. John, the coachman, was an expert with the ribbons, or they would have crashed for certain. As it was, all the Symonds landed topsy-turvy in the ditch as the other driver rushed on past them, never even slowing down. When the dust finally settled, the carriage was at an angle in the ditch, and Mama, Lucie, and Cilla were in a pile against the side of the carriage. "Is anyone hurt?" Mama asked in a muffled voice, trying to untangle herself.

"I don't think so," Lucie said. "We're just overset."

John had come around and was peering into the carriage. "Are ye all right?" he asked anxiously. "Wasn't no call for such, I tell you, that man ought to be drawn and quartered, runnin' over folk in such a way."

"I know," Lucie said, crawling out the door as John helped her. "Who could that have been? It had to have been the rudest person alive. He didn't even stop to see if we were harmed. I know he saw the carriage go into the ditch."

"I could have sworn it was Edwin," Cilla gasped, tottering onto the roadway and touching her forehead. "I just got a glimpse of the driver, but I could swear it was him." She looked at her fingers. "Mama, I'm bleeding!"

"You really shouldn't swear, dear." Mama looked at her calmly, and ran her fingers over Cilla's head. "It's only a bad bump and a break in the skin. I don't think it's serious, but we do need to get you back to Haddonfields."

"We're closer to Marston House than Haddonfields," John said, eyeing the damage. "I'll unhitch the horses and get the master. It won't take a minute to cut across to where he's working. I'll get a carriage from the Marstons." He looked at them anxiously. "The master 'ud have my head if anything happened. Will you be all right until I get him?"

"Of course, John," Mama said. "We're not hurt. Be sure to tell him that. I don't want him trying to rush over here and killing himself on the way."

It seemed quite a long time until Papa came into view, but they heard his horse before they saw him. "Here he comes," Mama said with a sigh. "I knew he'd come at a gallop. Your papa is such an impulsive man."

Papa came dashing around the curve in a cloud of dust and pulled his horse up short right in front of the carriage. In a moment he was off and holding Mama to make sure she was all right, then turned his attention to Lucie and Drucilla. About then, Lovatt and Giles Marston came around the curve, almost as fast as Papa had been. They dismounted and surveyed the damage. Giles came over to Drucilla and looked at her head. The wound seemed to be bothering Drucilla more than it had – she swayed slightly and sagged against the side of the carriage.

"My dear Miss Symonds," Giles said, putting an arm around her to prop her up. "I have a carriage right behind us. Are you all right?"

Cilla managed a tear and made a rather inarticulate sound as a carriage came rumbling around the curve. In a trice, the men had all three ladies inside. Papa took one quick look around, then asked Giles to accompany them to Marston House. He and Lovatt would stay there and see to getting the Symonds's carriage back on the road and to Haddonfields. Giles was glad to oblige.

"Do you know who ran you off the road?" he asked as they went toward Marston House. "I can't imagine anyone taking that curve at that much speed."

Cilla moaned theatrically. "I got only a glimpse of the man, but I could have . . . I thought it might have been Edwin."

"Nonsense," Lucie said. "Edwin would never have the grit to go at a good gallop, much less take a curve with enough speed to run someone off."

Cilla shook her head. "Sometimes I think I . . . we may not know Edwin very well." She looked at Giles and smiled wanly. "Thank you so much for coming to our rescue."

To Lucie's amazement, Giles smiled tenderly back at Cilla, patted her hand, and looked altogether like a love-struck calf. Lucie looked at Mama and was again amazed – Mama was looking at Cilla and Giles with a very satisfied smile.

They waited at Marston House for a while until Papa and Lovatt returned. Cilla was quite improved by the time they were ready to return to Haddonfields. As they left, Lucie paused by Lovatt. "I left a letter for Annie," she said softly, "in the hopes you would see that it gets to her."

"I shall," he answered. "There have been some changes—may I meet you soon to talk about her?"

Lucie hesitated. Did he truly want to talk, or was this simply a ploy? She didn't want him at Haddonfields dangling after Diana.

"If you recall, I go for a ride every morning," Lovatt said noncommittally. "I usually go by the tree overlooking Haddonfields and Marston House."

"Where we first met?" Lucie said with a smile.

He looked at her strangely. "No, I remember the first time distinctly—we met first on the street corner. When we met at the tree, it was the second time." He paused. "I ride early."

On the way to Haddonfields, everyone was silent. Cilla was staring moodily out the window, Mama was glancing from Cilla to Lucie and then frowning, and Lucie was occupied with thoughts of her own. What, she wondered, was going on between Cilla and Giles? Worse, and even more perplexing to her, why did she herself seem to be attracted to a man like Mad Jack Lovatt, a man who was an acknowledged rake, a roué, and who was in mad pursuit of Diana Caswell? He was handsome; he was, despite his reputation, kind and considerate; and she found herself thinking of him more and more.

It would, Lucie thought wearily, be much better when everyone returned to London and left the Symonds in the country, settled back into their usual quiet lives.

Back at Haddonfields, Edwin came into the hall as they entered the house. "Drucilla, my dear, whatever has happened to you!" He rushed to her and looked at the cut and large, purple bruise on her head. In a few words, Cilla told him of their accident, and then paused. "I got only a glimpse of the man who ran us off the road, Edwin, but he looked remarkably like you."

Edwin raised an eyebrow. "Really? I would hate to think, my dear, that you were unable to recognize me immediately and think I resemble some ill-born coachman. I thought you esteemed me more highly." He looked at her reproachfully. "I'd say that the culprit was probably some quasi-outlaw like

Lovatt. If you thought it was me, you must have been slightly addled by the blow to your head."

"That must be it," Cilla said mechanically. "Now, if you'll excuse me, I have a raging headache." She went up the stairs.

"Poor child," Edwin murmured as Cilla disappeared around the corner. "She certainly needs the stability of marriage."

Mama smiled and put a hand on Lucie's arm to keep her from saying anything. "Yes, of course. Tell me, Edwin, is your mother busy? She and Diana asked me to help with some embroidery and I'm afraid I'm late. Of course, an accident is sufficient grounds for being late, but I'd like for you to join me in explaining to them." Mama took Edwin's arm and led him down the hall toward the drawing room favored by Lady Caswell, chattering all the while.

Lucie shook her head slightly. How did Mama manage to be civil to those people? With an expression that was a cross between a grimace and a smile, she went upstairs. The time had come, she decided, to quiz Drucilla.

Lucie went up to change clothes before going to talk to Cilla. In her room, she discovered that she was badly bruised along her leg, possibly where she had landed against the carriage door. It hadn't hurt at all, although the second she discovered it, it began to throb. She called for a bath and soaked her leg until the water was tepid. By the time she felt better and had dressed, it was almost time for supper. She went to Cilla's room, only to find Cilla in bed, sound asleep. Lucie looked down at her sister, two years older than she, but in many ways younger. The bruise on Cilla's forehead looked large and livid against her fair skin, and the cut had a thin edge of blood on it. Cilla herself was restless, tossing and moaning in her sleep. Lucie left quietly and went to find Mama. They looked in on Cilla and decided to let her sleep as long as she wished. Mama didn't think the bruise and cut were serious, but allowed that Cilla's restlessness might be because of her headache. "We'll send for the doctor if she isn't feeling better by morning," Mama said, closing Cilla's door behind them and pausing to think. "Right now, she may have something on her mind besides the cut on her head."

"Her heart?" Lucie asked, a worried expression on her face. "Mama, I don't think Cilla really loves Edwin."

"I'm sure she doesn't, dear, and I believe I've said so before. Now all we have to do is make Drucilla aware of that fact." She hushed and smiled broadly as they approached the Caswells. "Diana, what a lovely dress!" She included the entire Caswell family in her smile. "I'm always amazed by your exquisite taste."

Lucie glanced at Diana and was amazed as well. Diana looked wretched in a sea-green that made her complexion look dull and muddy. Lucie sighed as she took Walter's arm and went in to supper. She would never have Mama's knack for being social—she simply couldn't say the correct thing unless it was really so.

Her night was restless. She had determined not to speak to Lovatt again, but all Lucie could think of during the night was Lovatt reminding her that he went riding early every day. By the time morning came, she had decided that she owed it to Annie Travers to ride out and talk to him. She was out shortly after daylight but, even that early, just caught sight of Lovatt riding back toward Marston House. Quickly she urged on her horse and called out his name. She thought at first that he hadn't heard her, but then he stopped and glanced over his shoulder. He turned his horse and came back to where she was waiting under the tree.

"I'm delighted to see you, Miss Symonds," he said, smiling and dismounting. He helped her from her horse and glanced around for a place to sit. "Over here." He motioned to a large rock. "We can sit in the dry here." Lucie sat down beside him and wondered what to say next. There was a long pause.

"This must be quite a popular spot to meet and chat," Lovatt said absently, picking a blade of grass and nibbling on its end. "I've seen Giles and your sister up here two or three times."

"Cilla?" Lucie was aghast. "You must be wrong—Cilla

doesn't care for riding and seldom gets out of the house. And as for meeting a man anywhere, I simply can't imagine Cilla . . ." Suddenly she had a flash of the look on Giles Marston's face as he looked at Drucilla in the carriage. "Not Cilla!" she finally managed.

"Oh, I'm sure it was nothing improper," Lovatt said absently, ignoring Lucie's scandalized tone. "Perfectly normal to see neighbors from time to time." He turned to look at her and smiled. "I'd like to talk to you about Miss Travers if you have time."

"That's why I came," Lucie said, refusing to look into his eyes. "Did Mrs. Marston give you my letter to her?"

He nodded. "And Miss Travers already has it." He laughed at Lucie's stare. "Miss Travers has accepted — finally — my offer of help and she and the baby are staying in the village where I can watch after them with a miminum of gossip. Mrs. Marston has been a great help with that — she looks in every day on them. I was afraid of gossip if I did it myself, although I do stop by as often as possible." He laughed and looked at Lucie. "You should see the baby. It's William made over and is the most amazing thing. Every time I speak to her, she smiles at me."

Lucie was surprised at his reaction to the baby. "Females learn that trick early on, milord." She laughed. "I can just see you tickling her under her chin and making baby noises. Just what would the ton think of that side of Mad Jack Lovatt?"

He laughed with her. "I assure you that it would be the *on-dit* of the day." He paused. "Actually, I had no idea babies could be so fascinating. I can't wait until William sees her."

"Is he on his way back?"

Lovatt nodded. "My man located him in northern Italy and he's on his way home. He should be here within the week or shortly thereafter, depending on the weather." Lovatt chuckled. "It seems that William is both amazed and delighted to discover he's now a father."

"Do you think he'll marry Annie when he arrives?"

Lovatt nodded. "No doubt about it. Actually, that was never the problem — as you recall, Miss Travers and the famous Travers pride were the obstacles, or part of them anyway. I'm not absolving William since I know he can be just as intractable. I must say, though, that it took all my powers of persuasion to convince Miss Travers that William loved her and wanted to marry her. She had written to him about the baby, and hadn't received an answer. I finally found the letter, unopened, in William's things. It had reached his house after he had left. When I showed it to Miss Travers, she believed me. She's already received a letter from William." He glanced at Lucie and smiled. "I don't know the contents, but Miss Travers was a changed person after she read it."

Lucie breathed a sigh of relief. "I'm so glad. There's no problem to Annie being a June bride then."

"No, they'll be married by mid-June, I'd say." There was a moment's hesitation and Lucie glanced sharply at Lovatt. He was frowning, hesitating over whether or not to say something. "What is it?" she asked quietly. "Is there some other problem?"

"Yes. One problem, or potential problem," he said slowly. "William may have to call out" — he paused for a long moment — "someone who's been annoying Miss Travers with unwanted attentions." There was another pause. "Or I may have to do it before William returns."

"Are you going to tell me who's had the temerity to bother Annie, or do I have to visit her and find out for myself?"

Lovatt considered as he shredded some blades of grass. "Edwin Caswell," he said finally. "It's a very delicate situation and I don't want to cause any ill feeling between myself and your family. Nor do I want to embarrass your sister."

"*Edwin?* You must be mistaken. Edwin is such a milksop that he wouldn't dare force his attentions on someone. It would offend his exalted sense of propriety. Besides, his mother would kill him."

"There are, Miss Symonds, people in this world who enjoy preying on those who are more unfortunate than they, for one reason or another. Many times, like Edwin, these vultures mask their baseness behind a mask of propriety."

Lucie interrupted him. "Don't give me any sermons, Lovatt. I fully realize that Edwin is shallow and insincere, but he does have a full appreciation of his place in society and he certainly wouldn't let a breath of scandal tarnish that."

Lovatt frowned. "That's true to a point. I don't mean to sound like some evangelical, but some people are simply mean-spirited. Edwin, I think, may be one of those. He wants to present a well-mannered front, and he does follow all the rules of society. Unfortunately, Edwin's sense of propriety doesn't extend to Miss Travers. He saw her the day after she came to the village, and he seems to believe she's fair game." He glanced at Lucie. "He seems to feel that because she's borne William's child that she . . ."

"I understand," Lucie said quickly. "Annie's not like that at all—she's warm, loving, and impulsive, but never depraved."

"That's all true," Lovatt said quietly. "My immediate problem, though, is your sister. I really can't expose Edwin Caswell without causing agony for Drucilla, and I'm reluctant to do that."

"You'd probably be doing all of us a favor." Lucie grimaced. "I can't abide those people, and I know Mama and Papa aren't overly enamored of them either."

Lovatt laughed. "I thought as much. Your father doesn't think Edwin shows the proper interest in farming."

"All the Caswells . . ." Lucie began, then stopped abruptly. The real reason Lovatt didn't want to say anything to Edwin had just occurred to her. It was Diana. Lovatt couldn't very well pursue Diana if there was a feud between him and Edwin.

"All the Caswells what?" Lovatt prompted, smiling at her.

She forced a smile as she got up. "All the Caswells are city folk." She walked toward her horse. "Since it's no secret she's here, I'm going to visit Annie. Where is she staying?"

Lovatt walked easily over to where she was standing and took her arm. "She's at the vicar's guest house. Aside from Annie and the Caswells, what's bothering you? You seem distant this morning."

"Nothing." She took a step backward and something brushed against her leg. She jumped in surprise, right into

Lovatt. He held both her arms to keep the two of them from falling as Lucie pressed against him. For her, the contact was a shock along her whole body. She stepped back, catching her breath, breathless from being next to him, rather than from shock. Lovatt, still holding her arms, looked down. There was the disreputable cat, rubbing against his boots. "At last you've proven good for something," he said with a grin at the cat. "Are you all right, Miss Symonds?"

"Yes." Lucie's voice was a little shaky. "I was merely . . . surprised."

Lovatt glanced at his hands still holding her and eased the pressure on her arms. He did not let her go. "As was I," he said, a strange note in his voice. "Lord Lovatt," she began, then caught a glimpse of movement in the far woods. "Who's that?"

Lovatt immediately released her and turned in the direction of her gaze. "I do believe, Miss Symonds, that your sister is also out for an early ride." His scarred eyebrow lifted in surprise.

Lucie peered through her spectacles. "Impossible. Cilla would *never* ride alone, early or late. Furthermore, she seldom gets up before eight." She stared at the distant figure, now disappearing into the woods. "That *is* Drucilla. What on earth can she be doing out at this time of the morning, and on a *horse?*"

"Meeting someone?" Lovatt suggested.

"Impossible. Cilla would never do that. First, she's very conscious of Edwin's sensibilities, and second, who on earth would she be meeting? The only people one meets out in the woods are rogues and cutthroats and . . ." She stopped, blushing.

"And the likes of Mad Jack Lovatt?" He was amused. "I assure you, Miss Symonds, I'm entirely innocent and on my best behavior."

"I know you are," Lucie said, embarrassed. There was a pause as they looked at the place where Cilla had gone into the woods. "Should we follow her and make sure she's all right? Cilla really isn't very good with horses."

Lovatt helped Lucie to mount. "I think perhaps not. I'm going that way, so I'll make sure Cilla gets back home. There might be a great deal of explaining to do if the two of us rode up together." He looked up at her and Lucie was surprised to note that he seemed nervous and slightly unsure of himself. "May I come see you tonight and talk to you? Alone? There's something I must tell you."

"I don't think the Caswells would welcome your presence." She hesitated. "However, if you feel it's absolutely necessary to talk to me privately, I'll be taking a walk in the garden after supper."

"I prefer to come crashing in the front door, Caswells be damned." He grinned. "However, if you're worried about their extreme sensibilities, I'll see you in the garden." He swung easily onto his horse and smiled at her, the cat scratch and the scar giving him a rakish look. "Until then, Miss Symonds."

Lucie had been home for over an hour—and on tenterhooks—before Cilla came in. She met Lucie in the hall and nodded absently before going on into her room. Lucie started to follow her, but decided to wait a few minutes. Something was bothering Cilla and though Lucie wanted to discover what, she didn't want to overset her in any way. It would be best to approach her when there was time to talk. In the meantime, she went to hunt up Mama to help her get together some things to take to Annie.

Mama was in the dining room, issuing orders to the staff. "Lucie, we've just received word from your Aunt Sybil that she's dying and your father and I are going to have to go to London."

"Again?" Lucie asked before she could stop herself.

Mama sighed. "Yes, again. Your father says it's just another example of Sybil crying wolf, but I'm afraid not to go. I suggested he should go alone, but he won't hear of it. You know he doesn't get along with Sybil at all."

"An understatement," Lucie agreed. "Mama, does this

mean the Caswells will be leaving as well?" She couldn't keep the hope from her voice.

Mama shook her head. "I'm afraid not. Actually, Lady Caswell has offered to stay here and chaperone you and Cilla while your father and I are gone."

"Oh, heaven help us," Lucie moaned.

"It shouldn't be too bad," Mama said briskly. "Besides, if you and Cilla are here, it should give your father and me an excuse to leave London rather quickly. I imagine if it's true that Sybil is crying wolf, we'll be returning in a day or two."

Mama and Papa were packed and gone by noontime. Lucie had planned to go to Cilla's room and talk to her as soon as it was quiet, but Lady Caswell, never one to let a social opportunity pass, had arranged a visit to the church to examine gravestones. Lady Caswell sat in the church and waited while Edwin, Drucilla, Walter, and Lucie made rubbings of some of the older stones. It was definitely not the way Lucie had planned to spend the afternoon.

When they finally returned to Haddonfields, Lucie again didn't have the opportunity to talk to Cilla, but she did find the time to dash off a note to Annie, asking if she could visit the next day.

Supper was a dull affair. Lucie hadn't realized how much Mama had kept everything going along. Without her, conversation was almost at a standstill. Lucie made a few attempts, but Walter was the only one who wished to talk. Cilla sat and toyed with her food, paying little attention to anyone around her. Edwin, too, seemed preoccupied. After supper, Lady Caswell suggested cards, but no one was interested. Lucie, aware all evening of Lovatt's s impending visit, needed to slip away to go to the garden alone, but Walter tagged at her heels the entire evening.

"I do believe I have a headache coming on," she finally said. It was halfway true by that point. "If you'll excuse me . . ."

"I feel the same," Cilla said, standing up and joining her. "I fear I haven't recovered from our accident yet. I've had a headache since then, and it seems to be getting worse and worse." She touched the purple bruise that was beginning to turn green around the edges. It *was* unsightly and had to hurt her, Lucie thought.

They left the Caswells and went up the steps together. It was the perfect opportunity to talk to Cilla, but there was no time. She had promised Lovatt, and she had to be there. She would have to slip around back and get to the garden unobserved to meet Lovatt. She smiled as she wondered what Lady Caswell would make of her meeting a man in the garden. Perhaps, she thought to herself suddenly, he was really coming by to glimpse Diana, sitting prim and proper beside the drawing-room window. It was a lowering thought.

Still, she needed to talk to Cilla, and the sooner the better. Something was wrong with her. "Cilla," she said impulsively, putting a hand on Cilla's arm, "I need to talk to you. Would it be all right if I came to see you in an hour or so?"

Was it Lucie's imagination or did Cilla pale visibly? "I simply can't, Lucie," Cilla mumbled, not meeting her eyes. "My head hurts abominably, and I plan to go straight to bed."

Lucie gave her a quick hug. "I understand."

To Lucie's surprise, Cilla threw her arms around her neck. "Oh, Lucie, no matter what, I want you to know I love you!" She made a sound like a sob, ran up the rest of the stairs, and into her room.

Lucie paused before her door, torn. A promise was a promise, and she had promised Lovatt she'd be in the garden. Regretfully she went to her room and got her dark shawl, then slipped down the back stairs and went around the corner of the house into the garden. As she had halfway expected, no one was there.

She made a turn or two around the garden, avoiding the lighted patch in front of the drawing-room window, and avoiding looking at Diana sitting there like a wax statue. She could hear Lady Caswell playing the pianoforte and singing, and the sound made her glad she was in the garden instead of the drawing room.

She stopped by the hedge and listened intently; she thought she had heard a twig snap, but there was no other sound.

With a sigh, she sat on a bench in front of a large bush and looked up at the moon. It was a lovely night, warm, full of the lingering scent of early June flowers. She felt something brush against her leg and jumped, stifling a scream. It was the cat.

"All right, Lovatt," she whispered, furious, "I know you're here. Where are you?"

There was a chuckle behind her and Lovatt emerged from the bush, stepped across the bench, and sat beside her. "Merely admiring your loveliness in the moonlight, Miss Symonds," he said with a smile. "I must say the combination of the night, the moon, the flowers, and your beauty was quite heady."

"Is that why you hid in a bush?" Lucie's tone was acid.

He chuckled again. "No, I was there to make sure no one else was around. Your reputation, you know, might suffer if it were generally bruited about that you had an assignation with Mad Jack Lovatt in a garden in the moonlight."

"I would hardly call this an assignation, milord." Lucie kicked at the cat as it clawed at the hem of her gown. "How do you bear this creature?"

"I detest the thing, but I have discovered that it and I have much in common: both social outcasts, both unwanted, both . . ."

"Stop, stop!" Lucie tried not to laugh out loud. "Please don't malign the poor cat with such a comparison." They looked at each other and smiled. Good Lord, Lucie thought to herself, no wonder he's broken hearts all over England. In the moonlight, the man was devilishly handsome, with a touch of the dangerous about him. She took off her spectacles and forced herself to look back at the blur of the house. "What was it you wished to discuss, milord?"

"Will you stop calling me 'milord' and start calling me Jack?" He moved a trifle closer to her and shoved the cat out of the way with his boot. "I thought we were going to be friends." There was a pause. "Lucie . . ." he began but stopped as the cat arched its back and spat into the darkness.

"Miss Symonds? Miss Symonds? Are you here?" It was

Walter, calling her from around the corner.

"If I don't answer, maybe he'll go away," Lucie whispered, putting her spectacles back on and shrinking back into the darkness of the bush.

"Those damned Caswells never go away. I'll disappear until you can get rid of him." Lovatt stepped back over the bench and hid in the lush foliage of the bush. "Hurry," he whispered. "These dam . . . these spring flowers make me want to sneeze."

"Don't you dare," she mumbled as she smiled at Walter. "Walter, what a pleasant surprise."

"I thought you had gone to bed with a headache, and I was surprised to see you when I looked out the window. I wasn't sure it was you until now. I thought there were two people out here." He came to the bench and sat beside her. Lucie heard a muffled growl from inside the bush.

"Just me sitting here alone," Lucie said brightly. "I do have a terrible headache, Walter, and felt I needed a bit of fresh air. The house is so stuffy this time of year."

Walter glanced at the house. "All the windows are open, except the drawing room."

Lucie smiled. "Yes, Lady Caswell has quite an aversion to fresh air. I assure you, Walter, that I'll be fine. I'll just sit here for a few moments and then go on to bed."

"All right." Walter did not move. "Miss Symonds — Lucie — there's something I need to say to you."

There was another rustle inside the bush and Lucie looked around in alarm. "Could it possibly wait, Walter? I'm really not feeling like a serious discussion right now. My headache, you remember."

"I should wait, I suppose, but I feel I cannot." Walter grabbed both her hands in his, swung in one movement from the bench to the ground, and fell to his knees right in front of Lucie. "Miss Symonds — Lucie — my dear, my love, I cannot tell you what is in my heart. Surely you know how you have tormented me in my dreams and feelings all these weeks. Miss Symonds, you are the goddess of my dreams, the woman who fulfills all my expectations." He squeezed her hands and looked soulfully into her eyes. In the background, Lucie could hear Lovatt making inarticulate noises inside the bush.

Lucie tugged at her hands, but Walter wouldn't let go. "Walter, please, this is hardly the time or the place." She glanced behind her at the bush which was rustling and moving.

"Any time or place is the right time for love," Walter said, first clasping her hands to his chest then kissing her palms. There was an audible snort from inside the bush and Walter looked up at Lucie in surprise. She coughed to cover Lovatt's noise.

"I'm flattered, Walter, I truly am, but right now . . ."

"I understand, my dear. You need time to consider my proposal." He grimaced and shifted slightly. Lucie realized he must be kneeling on a sharp rock. "I know I was hasty, my darling, but my heart was overflowing."

Lucie tugged her hands loose. "Walter, I couldn't really . . . I think of you as a wonderful friend, but I could never marry you."

Walter stood suddenly, a petulant look on his face. "Why not? Edwin told me there would be no problem."

"Oh." Lucie thought a moment, moving around to cover the sound of Lovatt's chuckle. "Did Edwin put you up to this, Walter?"

"Not really. That is, I wanted to ask you, so he told me what to say. He said it worked on your sister, so he was sure it would persuade you." He glanced at the end of the bench where the cat had leaped up and sat, staring at him. "What's that?"

"A cat," Lucie answered briefly. "As to your proposal, it was a wonderful proposal, and would persuade any female, I'm sure."

"Then you'll marry me? You're persuaded?" He reached for her hands again.

Lucie leaned back into the bush. "I cannot, Walter. Your declaration would persuade any female except me," she said, trying to save his feelings. "I'm sure it would, except . . . except." She paused and crossed her fingers behind her back, then jumped as Lovatt grabbed them. "Except my affections

339

belong to another." It sounded terrible. Besides, Lovatt was tickling her back now. "Stop," she hissed between clenched teeth.

Walter looked offended. "Certainly I'll stop, Miss Symonds, and I do apologize for my declaration. I had no idea you had formed an attachment for another."

"I didn't mean for you to stop, Walter. That is, yes, I could not allow you to go on when I cannot accept, but I do want us to be friends." Lucie jerked her fingers from Lovatt's grasp and folded her hands in her lap. "Can we be friends, Walter?" She jumped as Lovatt poked her in the back with a twig.

Walter dropped to his knees again. "Always," he said dramatically, throwing his hands wide and knocking the cat for a tumbling loop. The cat immediately set up a howl and fastened itself on Walter's back, holding on with all four paws. Walter jumped up and began to run. The last Lucie saw of him was when he rounded the corner of the house, yelling for help while the cat clung for dear life, its yowling almost drowning out Walter's cries.

Lovatt came out of the bush brushing leaves from his hair. "So that's how it's done," he said, sitting down beside Lucie. "No wonder I've never gotten it right."

"Oh, and you've offered for dozens of females, I suppose."

"Never one, but I've thought about it dozens of times. At least now I know how." Lovatt shook with suppressed laughter. "The Caswells will be out here in a minute, en masse, to make sure you're all right, so we have only a moment." He chuckled aloud. "I'll always remember Walter as he looked running around the corner."

"Poor Walter. You shouldn't make fun, milord."

Lovatt glanced at her, a strange look. "I certainly would never do that. As a matter of fact, Walter and I also have some things in common." He paused. "I'd better leave before Edwin and the rest of the Caswells come running out to save you, so I can't say everything I had planned." He stood. "One of the things I did want to tell you was that I've decided to have a talk with Edwin about his unwanted attentions to Miss Travers. I think that's best."

Lucie stood to look into his eyes. "That might ruin your chances with Diana. I've heard of your attachment for her."

Lovatt turned, then took her arm, and looked steadily into her eyes. "Miss Symonds, I have no attachment for Diana Caswell, I promise you that. I know the word of a supposed rakehell isn't accounted for much, but I can say that I've never broken mine, and I give you my word on this."

Lucie frowned and searched his face for expression. "You yourself told me about the Lovatts falling in love at once, and I've heard several people talk about your pursuit of Diana all winter. The *on-dit* was that you were madly in love with her."

He bit his lip as he considered what to say. He sat down on the bench, glanced toward the house, and pulled her down beside him. "I'm ashamed to tell you the tale, but it must be done." He took a deep breath. "It was a wager. Giles and I were standing around the fringes of a dull party at Almack's one evening, and the Caswells came in, all of them in a phalanx surrounding Diana. Lady Caswell began disclaiming to the housetops that her daughter was protected, virtuous, and all those other things insipid girls are supposed to be. Naturally, I couldn't refrain from commenting on it, and Giles bet me a hundred pounds that I couldn't have ten minutes alone with Diana. I took the bet." He grinned at her. "There's no excuse except the famous Lovatt propensity for taking a dare." He looked back at the ground in front of them where the cat was leisurely making its way across the grass to sit under the bench. "True, I pursued Diana all winter, but my only object was to win the wager with Giles. There was never any attachment — nor will there ever be. I'm going to pay Giles the hundred pounds and be done with it."

The cat began rubbing itself against Lucie's ankles and she reached down absently to scratch its head. Before she could answer Lovatt, they heard Edwin calling her from the steps. "I must go now," Lovatt said, rising and pulling her to her feet. "Don't think too harshly of me for wagering on a lady's virtue. I'm reformed now." With that, he bent down and kissed her lightly on the lips. "Almost reformed, anyway," he whispered, disappearing into the darkness as Edwin and

Walter came around the corner. The cat gave them a disdainful glare, and then padded off into the darkness.

"Are you all right?" Walter asked. He looked worse for the wear.

"Fine," Lucie said shakily. "I believe I do need to go to bed now, though." She fled into the house and up the stairs before anyone could say anything else to her. She didn't dare breathe until she was in her own room with the door shut behind her. Then she walked to the mirror and touched her lips with her fingers. To her surprise, she looked the same as always.

Lucie had trouble sleeping, and kept waking up. Shortly after midnight, she thought she heard a noise and sat up in bed. It sounded like a carriage arriving, and she looked out the window, but could see nothing. She lay back down, and in just a few minutes, heard the sound again. She got up, but, again, saw only the darkness. She went to the big window at the end of the hall and thought she saw the dark shape of a carriage just going out of sight. Puzzled, she went back to her room, but couldn't sleep. Restless, she got back up, prowling around her room, trying not to think of Lovatt. Finally, completely disgusted with herself, she decided to see if Cilla felt any better. If she'd been sleeping since supper, she might want to talk now, and, to tell the truth, Lucie needed someone to talk to. Her own emotions were in a turmoil.

Lucie knocked softly on the door, then opened it. The room was dark and Cilla was sleeping quietly. Lucie started to close the door when she noticed clothes strewn all around. Something was wrong, this wasn't like Cilla at all. Quickly she went in but the moonlight wasn't bright enough for her to see, so she went to the bedside and lit a candle, trying not to wake Cilla.

She needn't have bothered. Cilla wasn't in the bed. In her place was a bundle of clothes covered with a quilt. Lucie looked around in alarm and saw a note propped against the mirror. It was addressed to her and quickly she opened it. *My dearest Lucie,* Cilla had written, *I know this will come as a shock to you and to Mama and Papa, but I felt I had to do something and do it now. There was no use to wait. If you ever fall in love as I have, you'll want to marry immediately, as I do. I've eloped with the only man I'll ever love. Lucie, wish me well. Your loving sister, Cilla.*

"She's eloped with Edwin," Lucie gasped. "I can't believe it." She sat down hard in a chair. "Not Cilla and Edwin. I can't believe she'd do this. I can't believe *Edwin* would." She got up and went into the hall, absently slamming the door behind her. She sagged against the door, the candle in her hand, the full implication of Cilla's elopement hitting her. Whatever would Mama and Papa say?

"What's going on here?"

Lucie whirled, almost dropping the candle. Edwin came out into the hall, wearing his dressing gown. He had curl papers in his hair. *"Edwin!"*

"Of course it's me," he said irritably. "What's the matter? You look as if you've seen a ghost." He reached up and touched the curl papers in his hair. "Oh these," he said with an embarrassed laugh, pulling them from his hair, bringing quite a bit of hair with them. Lucie noticed absently that his hair was thinning. She searched for something to say.

"Ghost? Yes, that must have been it. I was reading Mrs. Radcliffe and couldn't sleep. I thought I heard something outside."

"Mrs. Radcliffe!" There was disapproval written all over his face. "What trivialities. You should be reading Mrs. More or something equally uplifting. I assure you that ghosts exist only in Mrs. Radcliffe's mind." He turned and went back toward his room. "This family," Lucie heard him mutter as he closed the door.

At least Cilla hadn't run away with Edwin, but then, who? With a flash of inspiration, Lucie remembered the expression on Giles Marston's face. Giles, it had to be Giles, she realized, but what would the families say? How could she find out if Giles had gone with Cilla? There was only one person who could help her find the answer.

She had to see Lovatt, and she had to see him now.

Lucie went back to her room to wait until morning to see

343

Lovatt, but it was no use. About two o'clock, she gave up and put on her dark dress and cloak, then went down to the stables. She tiptoed in and saddled her horse, terrified at any moment that one of the stablehands would come in and ask what she was doing. She walked the horse a distance from the house before she mounted it, then stopped and tied it before she got to Marston House, walking the last quarter mile. At the house, she had no idea what to do. Which one of the rooms was Lovatt's and how did she get inside to see him? She walked around the house, trying the doors. Here in the country, people seldom locked their doors.

Sure enough, the kitchen door was unlocked and she opened it, slipping inside. A furry streak brushed by her legs and she had to stifle a shriek. It was only the cat which had adopted Lovatt. The cat started up the stairs as though it knew its destination, so Lucie followed it, terrified that one of the Marstons would grab her at any moment. Upstairs, the cat stopped in front of a door and began purring. Satisfied, Lucie cautiously opened the door and walked inside. The room was empty, and hadn't been used for a while. "Why couldn't you," she whispered to the cat, "have found Lovatt for me?" The cat stared at her without blinking.

Back in the hall, Lucie looked at the row of closed doors. It was too risky to try them, and she didn't know what to do next. The cat sat in the middle of the hall and watched her as she tried the closest one. There was someone inside in bed and she tiptoed in. It was Mr. Marston, as best as she could see. Hastily, she turned and went back into the hall, pulling the door gently closed. The cat stared at her, its eyes gleaming in the light from the single sconce burning in the hall. Lucie decided Mrs. Marston would have the next room, so she took a deep breath and tried the fourth door on the hall. As she opened it, someone spoke, and she almost fainted. The cat leaped in front of her and landed on the bed with all four paws planted. "Get off me, you damned wretch!" Lovatt came bounding out of the bed, holding the cat. He had on only his nightshirt.

Lucie stepped into the room and closed the door behind

her. "Lord Lovatt . . . Jack . . ." She could go no further. She put both hands over her spectacles so she couldn't see.

"Lucie? My God, what are . . . Just a minute." Lucie heard him toss the cat on the bed and fumble around for his clothes. Then there was the sound of the flint as he lit the candle. "Now."

She turned around. He was more or less dressed and was staring at her, not with his usual expression, but with a hard look on his face. "You'd better have a good explanation."

"Please, I need your help. I need to know if Giles has eloped with Drucilla. I didn't know who else could help me." She said it all in one breath.

"Giles and Drucilla? Good Heavens, Lucie, what a foolish thought. People like Giles and Drucilla don't elope."

"Cilla has. She left me a note, and I thought she and Edwin had gone away, but then he came out into the hall with curl papers in his hair and so it has to be Giles." She knew she wasn't making any sense, but, right now, she couldn't think straight. There was something about Lovatt's *dishabille* that was most disturbing.

"I'll prove to you that you're wrong. I'll go get Giles."

"Just be quiet. Please."

He looked at her. "Lucie, do you really think I want the Marstons to find you in my room in the middle of the night? Give me some credit."

He was back in only a few moments. In his hand was an envelope that he handed to her. "There's no need to read it since I assume it says the same thing Drucilla's note says. I apologize to you — it does seem they've eloped."

"What can we do?"

Lovatt sat on the edge of the bed and the cat curled up against him, purring loudly. He glanced down at it in irritation. "I hate cats." He frowned. "Why should we do anything? I think both families would be quite happy to have them married."

"Yes, but in a church, and Drucilla in a proper dress."

"Ah, a June bride? Does it mean that much to you?"

Lucie nodded. "Not to me, but to Mama and Papa. And to

the Marstons." She held out her hands to Lovatt. "We could probably catch them and persuade them to come back before anyone knows. They've probably started for Gretna Green and they left only about an hour ago. I heard the noise."

Lovatt raised his scarred eyebrow. "Horse or carriage?"

"Carriage, I think. We could catch them on horseback."

Lovatt sighed. "Not *we. I. Y*ou're going back home if we can get you out of here without anyone knowing about it. Your reputation will be in shreds." He stood up and reached for his coat and boots, pulling them on. "Come on, and be quiet."

"You can take my horse — it's already saddled and waiting."

"Let's just get outside first."

They tiptoed out into the hall, stopping every time a board creaked, then went down and through the kitchen to the outside. Just as they got outside, they heard the cat begin to whine to get out. "Oh, damme, that cat!" Lovatt said. "If it wouldn't make so much noise, I think I'd shoot the thing. Wait over here." Lucie waited in the shadow of a bush until Lovatt came creeping back out, the cat in his hands. He set it down and walked away, the cat following him. Lucie caught up with him and took him to her horse. Together they rode to Haddonfields, and there Lovatt left her, promising to stop back by as soon as he could.

By daylight, Lucie had almost worn a path in her carpet. At eight, she heard the Caswells get up and start downstairs for breakfast. She dashed down the stairs to try to keep them from looking in on Cilla. At the foot of the stairs, Edwin, Walter, and Lady Caswell were standing transfixed as Giles and Lovatt walked in with Drucilla. "Ah, there you are, Miss Symonds," Lovatt said, glancing at Lucie. "However did you make it back before we did? I told Giles and your sister that as much as I hated to be bested in a wager, you have proven yourself a better rider than I." He reached in his pocket and extracted a pound note. "Here's my payment, and I hope tomorrow we might ride early again. Perhaps then I might regain my wager." He turned to Cilla. "Thank you for acting as

346

a chaperone, Miss Symonds. Shall we go, Giles?" With that, the men were out the door.

Edwin turned on Cilla, furious. "You deliberately went riding out with the likes of Lovatt? I can hardly credit that, Drucilla. Think of your reputation — of *my* reputation."

"I think of little else, I assure you, Edwin. Shall we go upstairs, Lucie?" She stalked by the Caswells and took Lucie's arm. "I need to talk to you." Lucie hurried with her, hoping the Caswells wouldn't notice that neither sister was in riding clothes.

"What a sad lack of breeding," Lady Caswell remarked as the sisters rounded the corner of the stairs. They heard no more.

Lucie slammed the door behind them. "What happened?" she asked shortly. "Lovatt's pulled us from the fire, but how?"

Cilla put her hands over her face. "He caught up with us and convinced us that it would devastate our families if we didn't get married properly in a church. He's going to take us to London so we can get a special license and be married while Mama and Papa are there. He promised we wouldn't have to wait." She raised her tear-stained face to Lucie. "Oh, Lucie, I love him so! I had no idea that love could happen so fast, or be so sure."

"Giles, you mean?" Lucie asked warily.

Cilla nodded. "Of course I mean Giles. I could never marry Edwin, never. Not now, not when I know really what love is. I'm going to tell Edwin this morning that I simply cannot marry him."

Lucie took a deep breath. "Well, that's a blessing, at least. You can't do it until later, though. You look like something the cat dragged in." She had a mental image of the disreputable cat dragging Cilla in and giggled. "Why don't you have a bath first, then tell him. I, for one, shall be delighted to see the last of the Caswells." She yawned. "I could use a nap myself." A sudden thought hit her. "Oh, Lord, I wrote Annie Travers and promised to visit her this morning. Don't tell Edwin until I get back."

"I won't," Cilla said wearily. "I won't leave my room. Lu-

347

cie," she said impulsively, turning at the door to look at her sister. "I wish you could fall in love. It's a wonderful feeling."

"So I've been told," Lucie said dryly.

Cilla left and Lucie frowned as she dressed to visit Annie. She took several things, among them a dress she had embroidered for the baby. When she got downstairs, the Caswells had finished their breakfast, and Edwin had gone out on business. At least, Lucie thought with a sigh of relief, there would be no scenes until she returned.

She decided to walk to the village so she could enjoy the early June day. The air was soft, filled with the scent of spring flowers and a hint of freshly plowed ground. It was wonderful.

At the vicar's house, she knocked to leave a jar of jelly for the vicar, but no one was home. She wedged the jelly beside a flowerpot by the door and went around back to the guest house. As she got near, she heard Annie screaming. Dropping her basket and presents, she ran to the door and flung it open. There was Edwin, a fistful of Annie's dress in his hand, shoving her against the wall. "So you think you're better than I am, you slut," Edwin snarled, hitting Annie across the face. Lucie sprang from the door and started hitting Edwin on the back, yelling at him to let Annie go. In the background, the baby began to cry. Edwin, more powerful than he appeared, turned and grabbed Lucie's wrist with his other hand. "You're no better than she is," he said hoarsely. "I've seen how you've led Walter on. Well, I know what you want." He jerked as Annie kicked him on the leg.

"Do you enjoy beating women, Caswell, or is the weaker sex all you dare to challenge?" The voice was deadly and icy. Lovatt stood in the doorway, pale with the effort of controlling himself. "Out of respect for the vicar's furnishings, I have to ask you to come outside." His hands were curled into fists.

Edwin loosened his hold on the women. "By God, Lovatt, I've wanted to teach you a lesson. It's time one of your betters taught you some manners." He sprang for the door as Lovatt sidestepped, then caught Edwin with a blow to the side of his head. Edwin grabbed for Lovatt, and they rolled out of sight.

Lucie started to go outside, but Annie grabbed her. "Lucie, help me save the baby!" She ran for the cradle and picked up the baby. "Whatever happens, Lucie, promise you'll see that William gets the baby." There was the sound outside of a horse coming up rapidly. "Walter," Lucie guessed. "If it's Walter, they'll hurt Jack." She started toward the door, but Annie handed her the baby. Annie was staring straight out the open door.

"William," she cried, walking toward him, everything else forgotten. He held out his arms to her. "Sweetheart," he said, giving her a kiss. Then he lifted his head and glanced over his shoulder out the door. "What's Jack doing?" he asked, trying to see as the two men rolled and tumbled in the dirt. "Looks as if he's giving someone a thrashing."

"Defending my honor," Lucie said, shoving the baby between William and Annie. There was no need to tell William what had happened. She and Annie looked at each other and smiled. Then Annie turned her attention to William and the baby. There was no need for Lucie to stay longer. She went outside and shut the door behind her.

Lovatt was just getting up, a dirty, bloody mess. Edwin was out cold on the ground, looking, if possible, worse than Lovatt. The cat came up, rubbed against Lovatt's legs, then went over to sit beside Edwin and proceeded to start washing its paws. Lovatt glanced toward the cottage with its closed door.

"Another June bride?" he asked with a lopsided grin that looked more like a grimace. Evidently it hurt him to smile.

"Yes, and I want to thank you. Everywhere I go today, you seem to have done exactly the right thing. First, thank you for bringing Cilla back and then for helping Annie and me."

"No thanks needed." He gingerly wiped blood and dirt from his face with his handkerchief.

"Here, let me." Lucie took the handkerchief and adjusted her spectacles so she could see better. "There. Do you know something I've discovered, Jack Lovatt? You're a complete sham."

He looked startled. "What do you mean?"

She rubbed at a particularly stubborn streak of dirt mingled with blood and he winced. "I mean that you've carefully cultivated this image of yourself as a complete wastrel and rakehell, but you're not like that at all. You're one of the kindest, most caring men I've ever seen. You remind me of Papa — all gruff front and tender heart."

"You're completely wrong, as usual," Lovatt said, "however, I do want to ask you something." He paused as she stood back and looked at him. "You're going to look terrible in a few days," she said. "Now what do you want to ask me?"

"If I'm going to look terrible, I can't," he said with a grin, then touched his split lip. "I was going to ask you to marry me, but then I know how much being a June bride means to you and you certainly wouldn't want to marry a man in my condition. That means June a year from now, and I don't think I can wait that long. You know how the Lovatts are." He rolled his eyes and sighed. "I suppose I'll just have to go off to the Indies and get over you. But then, the Lovatts never get over a true love." He looked at her, laughter dancing in his eyes. "I'm doomed."

Lucie laughed. "You certainly are, Mad Jack Lovatt. You're doomed to spend the rest of your life with me." He tried to kiss her but winced — it hurt too much. "Do you think," she asked impishly, "that you could manage to get two special licenses? Mama and Papa could get rid of both Cilla and me at one time."

He held her at arm's length and looked at her seriously. "Are you sure, Lucie? I know I love you — I have since you walked onto that street corner to talk to Annie, right in the face of all those hypocrites in London. It was one of the bravest things I've ever seen." He put his finger over her lips as she started to speak. "I love you and I always will. I came to see Giles just so I could be near you, and I've grown to love you more and more. I don't want you to marry me if you don't love me as I love you." He paused. "I should say that I want you any way at all, but . . ." He stopped, searching for the right words. "I want you to care for me in the same way I care for you. I don't know how to say it — I can't find the right thing to say, but I want you to know that I love you, Lucie."

"That's the right thing to say, Jack." She put her arms around his neck. "I love you, too. I really do." She reached up and kissed him, softly at first. "I don't want to hurt you, Jack."

"I'll let you know when to stop," he said.

After a while, she heard Edwin begin to moan, but they ignored him. The cat came over to stand at Lovatt's feet, purring. "I think we're going to have to take this cat along on our honeymoon," she said, laughing. "And as for June brides, I'd marry you at any time, but I don't want to wait a day longer than we have to. Do you really think we can get two special licenses?"

Lovatt glanced at the door, then reached up and removed her spectacles, folding them and putting them in his pocket. "Perhaps we'd better go for three. We may set a record." He pulled her close to him and kissed her again.

"Jack," she said dreamily when he finally stopped kissing her, "licenses aside, I'm sure we will."

THE ROMANCES OF LORDS AND LADIES
IN JANIS LADEN'S REGENCIES

BEWITCHING MINX (2532, $3.95)

From her first encounter with the Marquis of Penderleigh when he had mistaken her for a common trollop,
Penelope had been incensed with the darkly handsome
lord. Miss Penelope Larchmont was undoubtedly the most
outspoken young lady Penderleigh had ever known, and
the most tempting.

A NOBLE MISTRESS (2169, $3.95)

Moriah Landon had always been a singularly practical
young lady. So when her father lost the family estate over a
game of picquet, she paid the winner, the notorious Viscount Roane, a visit. And when he suggested the means of
payment—that she become Roane's mistress—she agreed
without a blink of her eyes.

SAPPHIRE TEMPTATION (3054, $3.95)

Lady Serena was commonly held to be an unusual young
girl—outspoken when she should have been reticent, lively
when she should have been demure. But there was one tra-
dition she had not been allowed to break: a Wexley must
marry a Gower. Richard Gower intended to teach his wife
her duties—in every way.

SCOTTISH ROSE (2750, $3.95)

The Duke of Milburne returned to Milburne Hall trusting that the new governess, Miss Rose Beacham, had in-
stilled the fear of God into his harum-scarum brood of
siblings. But she romped with the children, refused to be
cowed by his stern admonitions, and was so pretty that he
had the devil of a time keeping his hands off her.